KORIAN

ISBN: 978-1-9990209-1-0

Cover by: Rebecacovers

Editor: Mary Metcalfe

Book Formatting by Indie Publishing Group

KORIAN

GIORGIO GAROFALO

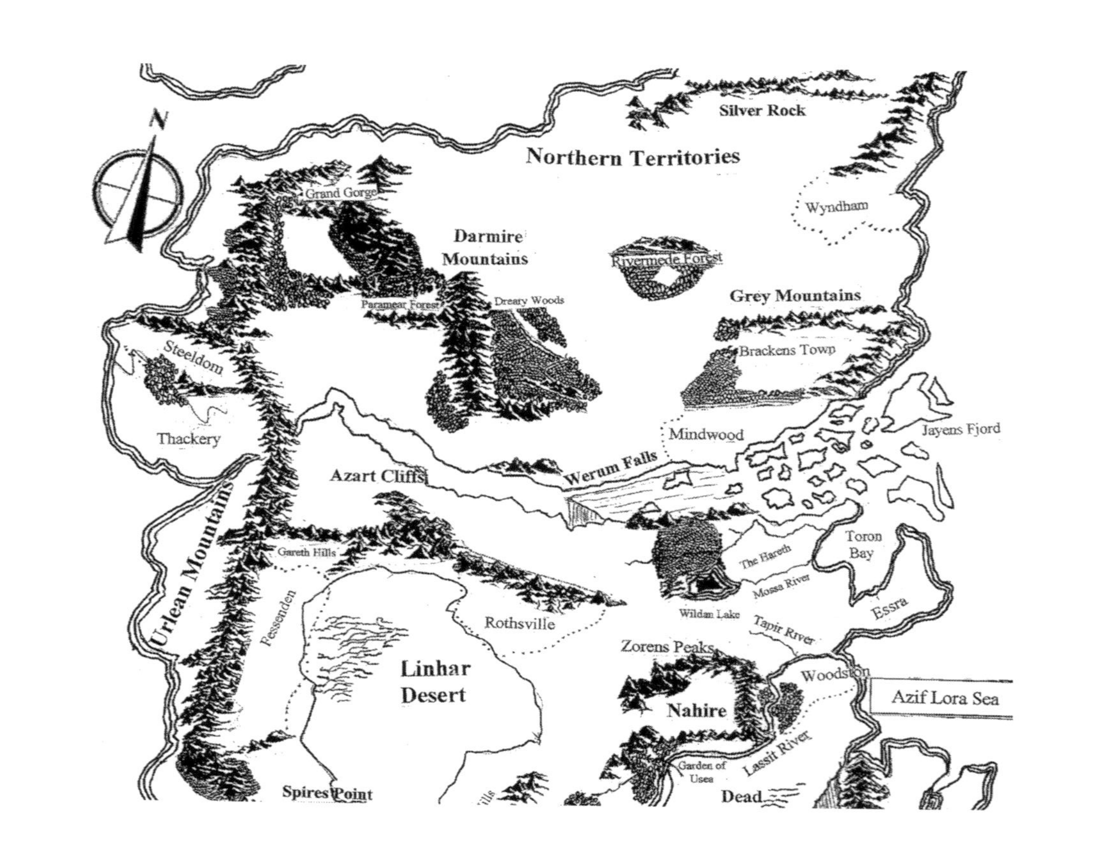
N
Silver Rock
Northern Territories
Grand Gorge
Wyndham
Darmire
Mountains
Rivermede Forest
Grey Mountains
Paramear Forest
Dreary Woods
Brackens Town
Steeldom
Thackery
Mindwood
Jayens Fjord
Werum Falls
Azart Cliffs
Urlean Mountains
Gareth Hills
Toron
Bay
The Hareth
Mossa River
Wildan Lake
Essra
Pessenden
Rothsville
Tapir River
Zorens Peaks
Linhar
Desert
Woodston
Azif Lora Sea
Nahire
Lassit River
Garden of
Usea
Spires Point
Dead

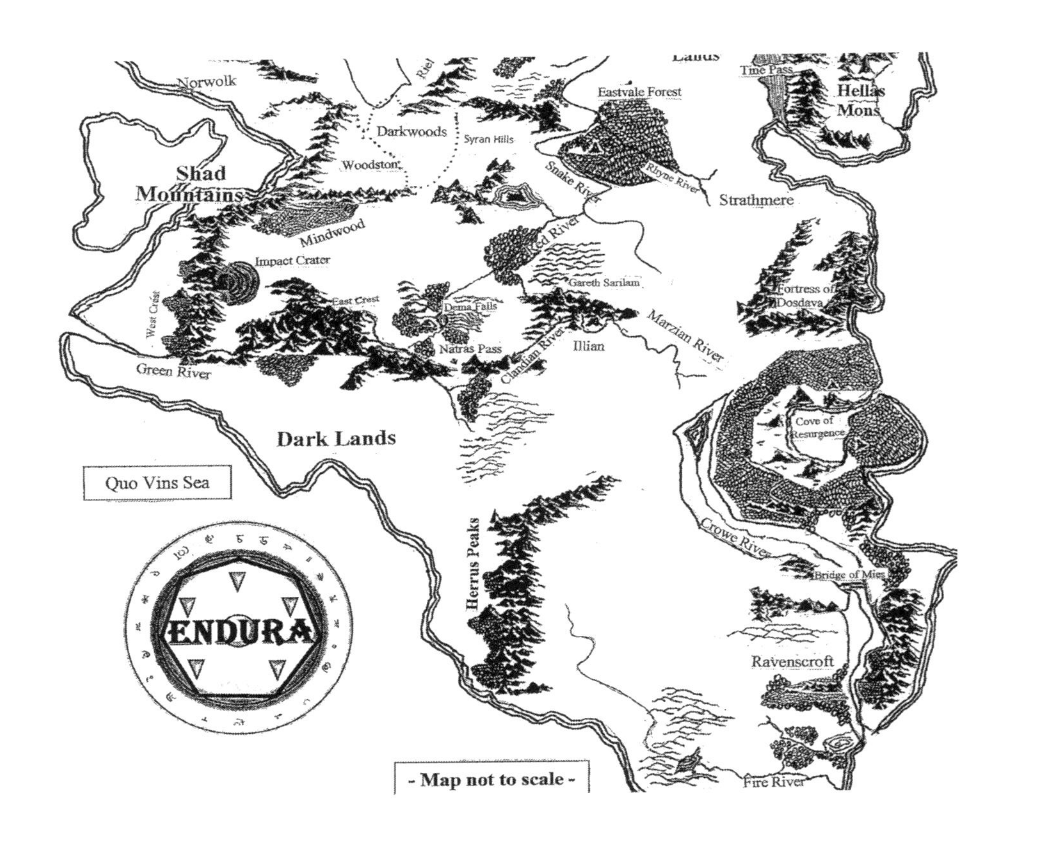
Norwolk
Riel
Darkwoods
Syran Hills
Eastvale Forest
Time Pass
Hellas
Mons
Woodston
Shad
Mountains
Snake River
Rhyne River
Strathmere
Mindwood
Red River
Impact Crater
Gareth Sarilam
Fortress of
Dosdava
East Crest
Dema Falls
West Crest
Marzian River
Natras Pass
Clandian River
Illian
Green River
Cove of
Resurgence
Dark Lands
Quo Vins Sea
Herrus Peaks
Crowe River
Bridge of Mies
ENDURA
Ravenscroft
- Map not to scale -
Fire River

BOOK 1

THE MANIAN'S SPEAR

CONTENTS

PROLOGUE

SOMEWHERE BEYOND THE stars, in one of the estimated billions of galaxies in the observable universe, you'll find Endura, a wondrous world every bit as vibrant and alive as Earth. It is where this tale unfolds.

Before recorded history, in the age known as the Late Antiquity—tens of thousands of years before this tale begins—an indigenous humanoid race of beings called Ruids ruled Endura. In those vanished times, preserved now only in myth, legend and other dark and musty places, the virtuous Ruids went about their tranquil lives with a genuine innocence. Besides a relaxed and passive temperament, ancient Ruids shared one trait unique to their race and crucial to this story: they had no propensity for hatred, wrath or jealousy. It was not a matter of choice or morality for Ruids; it was their nature.

Although slightly taller in stature than humans, their physical characteristics, skin texture and cognitive capacity were essentially identical except for one thing: Ruid hands were typically wider and their fingers were thicker than those of their human counterparts. Between the forefinger and smallest digit, Ruids had one thicker appendage that curved inward like a claw.

During the Late Antiquity, days were filled with the kind of contentment that comes without the boundaries of expectations. All life subsisted in a perfect balance with nature until the day a giant fireball fell from the sky and plunged Endura into a lingering dark period. A strange enduring sickness fell over the land. The age that followed, spanning thousands of years, seemed to have been intentionally left untold and forgotten.

It was towards the end of this dark period when the appearance of humans was first recorded and Endura's destiny, and that of its races, would be forever changed...

1
THE MEETING

Let he who bears fault for its cause bear also the burden to restore righteousness or prepare to forever endure in suffering wretchedness.

—Cerulean Book of Scribes

THE ECHO OF cracking wood bounced off the tall trees. Were the branches groaning, splintering, and falling? Was this the sound of nature recycling or was it something else?

Six-year-old Doric froze and listened. His legs were taut like springs. The sound dissolved quickly, swallowed up by the cool air that had suddenly descended over the thick woods of Rivermead Forest. He looked back into the clearing, hoping foolishly to find his father leaning against one of those large trunks, smiling back at him, but instead, he found only shadows growing in the dimness.

There was an unsettling stillness. Even the critters that were usually out and about at this time of dusk were nowhere to be seen.

"Listen to me!" His father shouted.

It was one of Doric's earliest memories. Sitting on damp grass, Doric looked through tear-filled eyes up at his firstling father. Out for a walk near the southernmost part of Brackens Town, the daring and precocious boy had wandered into a row of hedges and stepped out the other side.

"Don't you ever go there! You see this row of bushes?" his father asked, pointing to the line of shrubs all the way up the hill, ending where the tree line began. "There is danger in there. You must never go past this line. That is the forbidden zone. Do you understand?"

"Ranger. Doric not go there. Ranger," Doric repeated with childlike enunciation.

That was a long four years ago. On this evening, Doric was alone in the forbidden zone, far beyond that row of hedges.

Leaves rustled, brush stirred, followed by silence. The wood and foliage were far too thick to have been moved by the wind.

Pay it no attention, he told himself and resolutely started towards the sound.

"It has to be tonight." The words from the other night reverberated in his mind.

Two nights ago, while all the townsfolk had gathered on the main boulevard to partake in the Sammas Day feast, those words, whispered loudly into Doric's ear, had startled him out of his preoccupation. Sitting quietly picking at his food, Doric had been watching the goings-on, captivated by the alcohol-influenced conversations and crazy antics of people he knew well and who, not two hours earlier, seemed...normal. Watching others was something Doric did for amusement. He liked picking up subtle signs, movement or quirks to predict their actions and then watching them if he was right. On that night, there was plenty to observe.

Six rows over, boys and girls his age, and slightly older, filled two tables to capacity. Their laughter and delight were apparent but just not quite audible on account of the volume of the more boisterous parents. His father bellowed loudly with laughter and struck the table raucously with his hand. He seemed happy. That made Doric feel good.

No one had noticed Thane, Doric's best friend, walking up behind Doric.

"It has to be tonight," Thane whispered.

"What has to be tonight?"

"Just listen!" Thane said, resting his hands atop Doric's shoulders.

Thane and Doric were the same age and shared an uncanny resemblance. In fact, Thane could have easily passed for Doric's brother.

Thane leaned forward and whispered, "Later, when your father sleeps, head to Rivermead Forest. I'll be waiting for you there. Tonight, I'm going to show you something great." He tapped Doric's shoulders and ran off behind the row of nearby houses.

Back in the thick brush of Rivermead Forest, Doric pressed through thick bushes along the tree line, evading the many branches that hung down like long tentacles and stepped into the forest. He paused and listened. *Guess it was the wind*, he thought.

Thane and Doric were inseparable. There was a strange bond between them Doric could not explain. Thane seemed to tolerate Doric's quirks and always said things Doric wanted to hear. Others, especially children his age, avoided Doric, often mistreating him and making him the butt of their jokes. They had each other, it seemed, and no one else.

I'm going to show you something great. Doric knew leaving Brackens Town was a bad idea. In fact, being here was contrary to everything he'd been taught, but he couldn't help himself. For as long as he could remember, he had craved to venture into the forbidden zone.

Where are you? Doric thought, growing impatient. Darkness was beginning to fall over the forest, and there was no sign of Thane.

Doric took two steps, paused and listened. *Good,* he thought. *Calm down. There's nothing there.* He bit his lip and chuckled nervously.

Alone, in the midst of the tall trees, with daylight dwindling and an eerie stillness in the growing shadows, it wasn't the forest and its veiled inhabitants that frightened him, but rather his father and the thought of facing him when he returned.

Finding this place seemed unnaturally easy for Doric. The excitement of breaking the rules and exploring where others in Brackens Town had not ventured was exhilarating—even at his young age. The darkness posed no obstacle. He had travelled through the night and all the next day without stopping to rest. While Doric knew he should be tired, hungry, and thirsty, he felt strong and alert.

A sound to his right startled him. Thane lumbered out from among some thick bushes, grunting his discomfort at the spiny branches that scraped against his skin.

"What took you so long?" said Thane coolly, while brushing debris off his clothes. He seemed restless and was acting strangely.

"What?" Doric asked, shaking his head incredulously. "I've been here for—"

"Wait," Thane interrupted. "It's around here somewhere," he said, looking into the woods.

"What is? What are we looking for, Thane?"

"Not sure. I've seen this place before. Dreamt about it."

Doric's expression suddenly changed. He cocked his head to the side. "A doorway? Is that what you're looking for?"

Thane froze. "A doorway in the thick of the woods," he added. "You've seen it too?"

Doric began to pace. "I think I've had the same dream." He stomped his foot excitedly. "Seek the door," he said, recalling something from memory. Then together they said, "And find the truth beyond the threshold."

Behind Thane, on the opposite side of a clearing, surrounded by tall trees, a strange noise began to compete for Doric's attention.

A thought suddenly entered Doric's head. He ignored the threatening noise for the moment. He had a moment of clarity in his young mind.

He turned to Thane, but before he could utter a word, a powerful gust of wind almost toppled him. Fallen leaves began to swirl around them like a cyclone. In the thickening cloud of churning leaves and debris, Thane managed a wry smile. The swirling mass moved toward Thane and began to cover him like a swarm of bees until only his right eye remained exposed. It gazed deeply at Doric without blinking and then it too was covered.

"Doric," came a muffled voice from inside the mass. "It's time. Face the truth."

Leaves exploded outward. The wind abruptly stopped. Thousands of leaves began to rain down gently, but Thane was gone.

Doric's brows arched. His lips pursed. The thought entered

his mind like a voice of wisdom preaching a truth he'd always known but had chosen to deny.

It wasn't Thane or anybody else that directed you to come here. You've seen this place in your dreams hundreds of times. You knew you had to be here tonight.

"Face the truth," he said out loud, repeating Thane's last words. *Thane was never your friend. He was real only to you. You're a fool, Doric. Loneliness...has played with your head.* In his mind, children were pointing at him and laughing hysterically.

A low, guttural sound started from somewhere behind a row of trees. Branches snapped loudly. A deep rumble spread through the forest.

The sound startled Doric and snapped him back to the present. He slid behind the nearest tree. A moment later, the deep rumble stopped. Doric slowly peered around the trunk.

The temperature had cooled. His breathing quickened. Doric could see his breath, though beads of sweat appeared on his brow.

A shadow, large, and dark, with wide shoulders stood in the clearing. Doric gripped the branch tightly, ignoring the pain caused by the many prickly needles that pressed into his palms and fingers. The creature's size was alarming, and its clicking stutter sound made Doric gasp. The beast raised its large head and sniffed exaggeratedly, jerking its thick leathery head from right to left.

"Skine," Doric whispered as he jumped back behind the trunk. He had never seen one, but knew what it was.

"Fierce predators and kings of the sky," his father had told him. They travelled in packs, but this one appeared to be alone.

It doesn't know I'm here. It better not know that I'm here, he hoped.

He peered around the thick trunk again. The large animal,

erect on its hind legs, scowled at him with scarlet eyes. The broad shoulders made its abnormally long arms hang out to the side. It clenched its sharp, deadly claws and rested on them menacingly.

"If you should come across one, close your eyes and pray to Samjees," his father had said.

The clicking from the opposite side of the clearing grew louder. It turned to a low, throaty growl, so deep Doric could feel it in his chest. The skine lowered its head without moving its sunken red eyes from Doric's direction. The eyes, set deep in the skull, opened wide. Grimacing, the beast exposed four long, sharp tines. Suddenly, large wings sprouted from its back and it sprang. With a vicious swoosh, it disappeared over the tall trees.

Almost a minute passed. Doric exhaled a long, slow, drawn-out breath. Unknowingly, he had been holding it all this time. As the tightness in his chest gradually subsided, the eerie silence returned.

Stop wasting time, Doric. Move on already and get out of here. It's gone.

He managed three steps. A shadow appeared above, and something large crashed through the trees, sending branches and leaves over him. Wings began to beat, vicious and deafening. The skine was on him before Doric could raise his arms. Powerful talons gripped Doric's shoulders, and claws dug into the boy's flesh. Doric's bones snapped under the intense pressure. The skine lifted Doric off the ground, carrying the screaming boy further into the dense woods where it tossed him against a tree. Doric's right arm bent awkwardly, and his forearm splintered. Pain rushed into his shoulder and neck. His vision blurred. A gristly bone fragment stuck out of the skin as blood squirted in sync with his pulse.

The creature used its long, lizard-like tail and talons to push off an adjacent tree. It fanned its wings above the boy and descended. Retracting its wings, the skine stooped, and with its large, clawed talon, hoisted Doric up by the crop of his unkempt hair. Doric peered into the creature's primal red eyes, cold and without pity.

The skine tilted its head and pulled back its flat, creased ears. Even in terror, Doric noted part of the beast's left ear was gone. It emitted a furious roar and raised its arms. Its claws came down on Doric's shoulders. The bones in his shoulders shattered, and the downward pressure sent shards into his lungs. The intense force snapped the boy's vertebrae. Doric dropped to the ground. His lungs emptied of air. He wanted to roll away and disappear, but he couldn't move. There wasn't any pain. In fact, he didn't have any feeling in his body at all.

The forest began to sway, and a dark veil covered Doric's world. The creature's breath was hot against his face. He anticipated the pain that should come once your neck is ripped open.

He closed his eyes as three words formed in his foggy mind. A thin stream of blood began to flow from his nose. Doric packed the words tightly into a ball, and with all the remaining strength he had in his small trembling body, he sent them out into the darkness, hoping his father would somehow hear them. His words did not reach his father.

That day, alone on the muddy ground of Rivermead Forest, with his arm shattered, vertebrae snapped, Doric became aware of his gift for the first time. Suddenly, in the cold, sweeping darkness, he saw his father's face.

A man riding a partekii, a far distance away, suddenly experienced a surge of blood from his nostril. Drops fell onto his gray beard and a strange ringing started in his ears. A sharp pain above the nape of his neck, at the base of the skull, struck him sharply.

He felt a jolt as if struck by a club, knocking him off his partekii. Thoughts entered his mind and formed words.

Forgive me, Father! The words were loud and clear.

The man stumbled to his feet, smiling.

"Thank you!" he said, looking up to the sky. "There is another. Thank you," he whispered again, climbing onto his partekii. "There is another," he repeated again and rode off hastily.

Doric opened his eyes to find himself lying on the root of a tree. He wasn't quite sure how long he had been out. There was no sign of the skine.

The nightmare of the skine's attack flashed vividly in his mind: deep punctures on his upper chest and back, shoulders, bloodied and crushed and the gruesome bone fragment sticking out of his forearm. Slowly, he brought himself to look at his arm. Except for streaks of dirt and blood, there was no sign of trauma. Doric shook his arms and neck and sat up. He had no wounds anywhere on his body.

"So, this is it? This is supposed to be the truth I'm supposed to find beyond the threshold?" he shouted into the night. *No surprise there*, he thought. He knew he had the power to heal. Ever since he was a child, he had found his wounds would mysteriously heal themselves. What he didn't expect was what came next. A voice, not his own, entered his head and spoke to him.

Twelve long months had passed since Doric had ventured into the forbidden zone. Outside the open window, bright stars in the clear night sky looked down on the quiet, deserted streets. Dawn threatened to creep over the horizon and splash its radiance and warmth over the sleeping town.

Brackens was a bustling town. Born from a time long forgotten, it had been a sanctuary for the townsfolk, separating them from the rest of the world; a place that provided warmth and safety for the quiet, passionate people who called it home. Brackens was part of the expansive world beyond its boundaries, but in many ways, it was a self-contained universe that had adopted the personality of its people. To outside eyes, it projected warmth and newness, though fresh eyes had not looked upon Brackens Town for centuries.

Young Doric stirred in his bed. The sweat-dampened sheets were tight around his small body. Tossing and turning, he struggled against a nightmare. He dreamt of barren lands and a giant crater, some sort of an enormous chasm with a bottom hidden by a pool of gray mist. In the mist were rows upon rows of decaying animal carcasses. A dark shadow crept towards him from the opposite side of the giant chasm.

In his bed, the sheets squeezed tighter around his small frame. Between muffled moans, the child reached out with his hands to protect himself from something that was not there. His father, in the next room, lay aware but helpless to do anything to ease the torment raging in his son's mind. He sensed his boy's fear through his faint whimpers.

In his nightmare, Doric heard the familiar voice that still came to him from time to time. Over the last year, the child had learned to trust the voice. When Doric needed support, the voice filled the void with words of comfort and understanding. When he needed guidance, the voice offered words of wisdom. Tonight, it had an urgency that had never been there before. This time, the voice warned of terrible times and a great suffering.

Doric sat up sharply, wide-eyed and still breathing heavily. In the dimness, his face held an expression of terror. He rubbed his eyes and wiped his brow with the sheets. The beating of his heart slowed with each familiar object he saw. Shadows of branches and leaves danced on the wall, and the familiar scent of damp field grass hung in the air. As he laid back down, Doric wondered how he could possibly fall asleep again, for he needed his rest. Tomorrow was going to be a long day. It took well over an hour but he managed. Only this time, his sleep was deep and undisturbed.

The next morning, a bright fire was on the hearth, though the sun was warm and the wind was in the north, rustling the leaves at the tips of trees. It was autumn, and outside, everything looked fresh. Seth Devinrese, Doric's father, sat by the open window of the kitchen, his gaze fixed on something that held his attention outside. His right arm rested on the table next to him, and his four thick fingers tapped the table rhythmically. The view over the rooftop of the nearby houses was of the breathtaking mountain peaks in the distance.

Doric awoke and joined his father. Over breakfast, they discussed the day's chores. It was just the two of them. Doric's mother had died before he had even learned to walk.

"Your sleep was disturbed last night." His father spoke the words as a statement, though they were meant as a question. They had moved around to the shop at the front of their home after finishing their breakfast. Most of the homes in the town contained a small room at the front that was used as a shop or for some other trade purpose, and the Devinrese home was no different. Seth Devinrese had mastered and continued to carry out the art of making tools and utensils from iron. He was the town's blacksmith, as was his father and his father before him.

"Was I that loud?"

"If it were my guess, I'd say the Puckles heard you from next door," Seth retorted.

"He spoke to me last night," Doric said.

Since the last Sammas Day celebration, Doric had spoken often of a new imaginary friend named Crogan. Seth had become increasingly concerned about his son's vivid imagination and well-being. First there was Thane. He had not heard about him for about a year, and now there was Crogan. He humored his son when he spoke of Crogan. Still, Seth often marveled at the details Doric provided of the outside world that Doric had not actually seen firsthand. What was most disturbing to Seth was that this new friend was human.

"Who? Crogan?"

Doric stared ahead blankly. "His words scared me. He sounded worried. I've never heard it like that before."

"I'll tell you what, Doric," Seth said as he unlatched an iron lock and gave three loud raps on the wooden door with his four-fingered hand. He waited a few seconds and pushed the wooden wall out and up, forming a large canopy over the interior of his place of business.

"Don't worry yourself over this matter until Crogan makes an appearance," he said, believing wholeheartedly that day would never come.

Seth placed something in a cloth sack, handed it to Doric and told his son what he wanted him to do.

Even at this early hour, the street was bustling with activity. Doric welcomed the crisp, autumn morning breeze. He felt alive. A few houses down, two young girls jumped back from a large wooden door when three loud raps were given on the other side.

When the door opened, he was blasted with the aroma of scented oils and soaps from the shop within. Doric walked by this house every morning and had come to anticipate the sweet scents as a fresh start to each new day.

"Hi, Doric!" Little Tana caught him by surprise and kissed him on the cheek. "Do you want to play with me?"

Doric beamed. His cheeks and ears, visible between strands of hair, turned deep red. "No. I...I can't."

He lowered his head and resumed walking, but his pace had hastened. Tana watched him for a while. She shrugged and turned back to her friends.

Doric turned onto the town's largest and busiest boulevard. Around the circular gathering place, long tables were set in long rows. An area off to the side was left empty to provide a place for dancing.

I can't believe a year has passed, he thought.

Today was the morning of this year's Sammas celebration, a harvest celebration named after Samjees, the supreme god of all the gods. It occurred annually on the first full moon of the ninth month. Shortly, they would hear the ringing of bells from the town hall announcing this special day and the start of the festivities.

A partekii-drawn cart, filled with wheat from the fresh harvest, made its way down the street. Doric often marveled at the mystery and beauty of the partekii. Instead of fur, their skin was smooth and scaly, like that of an amphibian. They could change the color of their skin as a defense mechanism to evade skines, and as a result, could not be identified by a single or unique color.

A man's voice, animated and loud, directing where to place this and that, took Doric's attention from the partekii. The mood was cheerful, but for Doric, disheartening thoughts flooded his mind, leaving him with a haunting feeling that something was terribly wrong.

Things had changed in the last few months—more than he could ever remember. His people, descendants of Ruids, were pleasant and tranquil, yet trust had disappeared. Anger had become openly displayed. His father had put a lock to the latch on his doors a few months back because theft had become a common occurrence. Unlikely events of mischief had begun happening routinely in the tiny and historically peaceful community, and some incidents leaned towards the bizarre. Crop yields were abnormally low despite conditions better than they'd been in years. Farm animals had become sick; some simply stopped eating and died. Over the last several months, when the storms came, beginning with the sandstorms from the south, it seemed to Doric the gods had turned their attention elsewhere.

A hand fell on Doric's shoulder, stealing his attention away from his disheartened thoughts. The sun's position was directly behind a man's head, covering his face in shadow. Stout, with wide rounded shoulders, his face seemed a dark shadow engulfed by a bright, white halo.

"Good morning, boy."

Doric moved sideways to gain a better view. A warm smile spread across the leathery skin of the husky man's face. Doric recognized him. It was Thom Meggs. "I plan to make tonight's celebration especially memorable, son." He turned to walk away, then stopped.

"Have you seen Wade Maggis?" he asked.

Doric shook his head.

"What about Troy Fletcher?"

"No, sorry," answered Doric.

Thom nodded and ruffled Doric's hair. "I'm sure they'll turn up," he said.

Strangely, over the last several weeks, people had disappeared from the peaceful town, causing unease in the townsfolk. Yet they all held a foolish optimism that they'd eventually just turn up. After all, things like this just didn't happen in Brackens Town.

Thom Meggs was the town's Raif. The Raif, or leadership role, was originally held by Caleb Meggs 350 years earlier, around the time families first established settlements in these parts. It had remained a hereditary position in the village ever since. Though a vice regal position, the Raif never really wielded political authority. Brackens remained a loosely organized society and never faced threats from outside. As such, the Raif's role was now merely symbolic.

As Doric neared his destination on Blackburn Street, footsteps closed behind him. When Doric turned, he found Lorne Maggis, Wade Maggis's son, standing there wearing a sinister grin. His eyes fell on Doric as heavy as an axe. He stood steadfast, holding a small stick in his hand, which he struck on the palm of his other hand methodically with a one-two-three-thud, one-two-thud pattern.

Doric stepped back. Lorne followed, step for step. The older boy's eyes were dark and piercing. His gaze frightened Doric more this time than it had any other time. There was a brief pause when both boys stared directly into each other's eyes, the way prey locks eyes with its predator just before the predator pounces.

Lorne leaped, but Doric shifted to his right. The sudden movement surprised Lorne. He lost his footing and fell into the spiny bushes that lined the street behind Doric. Lorne leaped to his feet and bellowed. Red-faced, he brushed twigs and thorns from his arms and clothes. He grew angrier when he saw the scratches and blood on his arms.

Doric had already darted off past Blackburn and between the houses towards the wheat field outside of town. Behind him, Lorne closed the gap.

"You can't run forever!" Lorne screamed.

There was a path up ahead, which Doric veered onto in an effort to get home faster. He slid to a stop when he was startled at what he saw on the path ahead. At that same moment, the familiar sound of the large bell atop the town hall rang out.

A man on a partekii stormed down a quiet, deserted path. He gave the reins a firm tug and the partekii came to a stop. He followed the path ahead with his eyes. It curved around the wheat field, disappeared behind a row of small trees and reappeared towards the top of a distant hill. It coiled like a giant venomous snake.

He was nearing the end of his journey and was looking forward to the pleasantries of a warm meal and a soft, comfortable bed—at least that's what he hoped. This comforting thought did not last long as the emptiness of his mind was again filled with the anxiety he felt about the forthcoming celebration. The child he had come to meet would follow in the footsteps of countless others before him. He wondered if the child had the resolve and fortune to succeed where all others had failed.

The man had ridden alone as he had for as long as he could remember. This event he was attending, the Sammas, was one he did not intend to miss since his motives went far beyond participating in the extravagant celebration. He had a duty to enlighten the child and his father to the child's true identity and predestination. The time had come where it was absolutely necessary to make his presence known to the child. While the child was far too young to accept the burden he had been destined for, there was no longer the luxury of time. He needed the child now.

The man travelled exceptionally light, bringing only small rations of food and water, along with a long wooden staff slung diagonally across his back. There wasn't anything extraordinary about the staff. Although one end was skillfully and decoratively carved, the rest of it resembled a long, relatively straight branch that had been hastily snapped off a tree.

As he entered the town, he thought of how long his nomadic life had continued and felt weary. Days had become weeks, weeks had turned to months, months to years. He had lost track of the time long ago.

He had no home to speak of and no people that he could refer to as family. The only contact he had with others—any contact with substance—were contacts forged telepathically. The communication always began with a sudden jolt, like a quick rap to the back of the head, usually preceded by an influx of shapes and images that formed thoughts. The thoughts were always those of wanderers seeking help: calls for answers and guidance. The senders often attempted to come to terms with new realities and direction. Although invasive, he had learned to welcome the thoughts, for they had proven to be his only source of true companionship. All those who held the ability to trespass into his thoughts shared a common bond.

The communications acted as a beacon, directing him towards the source. The latest beacon had come from the child within the village he was approaching.

As the man neared the top of the hill, he began to sense semblances of life. Up ahead, he could hear the distinct laughter of children playing. Among the children's laughter he felt safe. Firstling men, women and children stirred amongst the wheat. Stocks of wheat were piled up against each other and placed in separate areas of the field.

A woman noticed him first. She stopped what she was doing, stood upright and stared. He raised his arm to wave, but she dropped the scythe, turned and disappeared back into the sea of gold. A few seconds passed and numerous heads began popping up. One by one, they began to venture out towards the gravel path he had just passed and followed up the hill behind him.

He saw a child streak onto the middle of the path and stop suddenly. There was yelling coming from an older kid who ran up behind him. It wasn't clear what was being said, though it was obvious from the tone he was quite agitated and angry. The older kid ran into the smaller boy, shoving him to the ground and then, upon seeing him approaching, darted back into the field. The younger child came to his feet, dusted himself off and stood steadfast, holding his position.

The boy had hair like dried-up yellow grass and bold, piercing brown eyes. He stared in defiance as if to say, "What do you want?" He clutched a cloth sack in one hand, and the thumb of his other hand was hooked onto his belt.

As the stranger neared, he maneuvered his partekii around the boy. The child did not move. He returned the gaze unwaveringly, even though he could not see the man's eyes, concealed as they were by shadow beneath his hood.

You have too great a nerve for your own good, little one, the stranger thought as he rode by. He glanced back once more, but the child was gone.

At the top of the hill, the town on the other side came into view. The gravel path ended on the crown of the hill. Up ahead, the path widened and branched off into several smaller paths.

Rows of elaborate houses made of roughcast limestone, washed white with half-timbered fronts, lined the streets. The homes were generally long and narrow, with steep tiled roofs. Many of the houses had large wooden doors, open at the moment, revealing stocked stores of varying goods within. All in all, the homes appeared carefully designed and skillfully built and gave the effect of comfort and warmth.

It was apparent to him the people of the town took pride in their community. Flowers were abundant in gardens in front of their homes, softening the harshness of the ancient walls of the houses. People were preparing the area for the forthcoming celebration. Long tables, almost as wide as the street itself, were set in perfect rows across the boulevard.

In the center of a circular area where tables were being assembled stood the tree named the Tree of Life, with its distinctive bark and heart-shaped leaves. He'd seen this same tree in almost every town he'd visited.

The man pulled on the reins and came to a stop in front of the town hall. He dismounted. Countless eyes in open windows on the second floor of surrounding homes looked on with a mix of excitement and apprehension. Not only was he the first visitor to come to their town in many, many years, but he was also not of their own kind.

From somewhere within the mob of people, he heard the animated voice of a child. A young boy squeezed through and sprinted towards him, burying his grinning face into the man's robe. The boy wrapped his arms around the man's waist and squeezed.

"Now there, hello to you too," the man said, speaking for the first time. His voice was surprisingly soft for his large frame. He couldn't conceal his delight at the emotion the child displayed, and a beaming smile crossed his lips.

I knew you would come! The words were not spoken, but the man could hear them. He realized he had found the child he was seeking. The boy pulled away.

"I knew you would come, Crogan!" the boy repeated, this time speaking it out loud while staring directly into Crogan's eyes.

Crogan dropped to one knee to get a look at him. He recognized the boy. It was the same child he had passed moments earlier. He studied the boy's features for a moment and caught sight of an unnatural birthmark on the right side of the boy's neck.

The birthmark was not discolored in any way, though the skin there was raised into a distinct pattern. There was an outline of a circle the size of a man's thumbprint. Outside the circle, from the top center, around the left side down to the bottom center, were five evenly spaced, small triangular peaks. Directly in the middle of the circle was a small, round, black mark.

Crogan stared admiringly at the boy and thought, *I have heard you calling for some time now. Enjoy today, little one. We have much work to do and too little time.*

Doric nodded.

"Doric!" The call came from somewhere among the throngs of people who had gathered around Crogan. The stranger took his dark, contemplative eyes off the boy and turned to find the owner of the voice. Seth stopped several feet away, looking at the visitor as if he was staring at a ghost.

"Crogan?" he asked apprehensively.

Crogan studied this rather portly, tall fellow for a moment. He had the type of face one could easily warm to. Crogan pulled the hood off his head, revealing long locks of gray hair that fell just below his shoulders. His features were weathered and forlorn, but prominent. He ruffled the boy's hair and took a step towards Seth.

"I am," Crogan responded, sounding less than proud.

Seth unknowingly took a step back. He glanced down at his beaming son. In his eyes, Seth could feel his son saying, *I told you he would come.*

At that moment, Seth was overcome by a huge sense of relief. He felt his concern for his son's well-being had been for naught, and his son had not been imagining things at all. Then a blanket of fear smothered him.

Lorne Maggis stared at the events unfolding before him with unsparing eyes. He tapped his hand methodically with a small stick. He scowled, turned and stormed away.

Crogan added, "You must be Seth, father of our newest member of the Fraternity of Huntsmen."

2

THE CELEBRATION

SETH CLOSED THE shop early. His head ached with the realization of just how much he didn't know. His son on the other hand, seemed different. Although normally precocious, today he fidgeted uncharacteristically like a typical, excited seven-year-old boy. Doric was beaming; his face was flushed with joy. The sack Seth had given him earlier was still in his hand. Seth watched Doric and Crogan, seemingly in conversation, though no words were spoken out loud. Strangely, he felt something foreign: a hint of jealousy.

"Father?" Doric asked excitedly. Seth shook his head and smiled, feeling a little guilty.

"I'll get some tea," he said and left the room.

Crogan and Doric were seated by the fire. Muffled voices and sounds of merriment spilled in through the open window. Doric's eyes remained glued on Crogan, a grin etched on his face. Crogan smiled. No words were spoken. Crogan wondered if his attempt at a smile appeared genuine. He felt uneasy about what he was about to say, but he relaxed when Doric's smile broadened and he repeated, "I knew you would come," shaking his head, wide-eyed.

When Seth returned, he set down the tea and let out a long breath. "How is this possible?" he asked, breaking the silence. "This silent communication of yours?"

Seth glanced at Doric; whose eyes remained fixed on Crogan.

"That, my friend, is complicated," Crogan replied remaining focused on the boy. "Consider it a gift, many generations old."

"You must forgive my directness," Seth pressed. "But, why are you here?" he continued, his tone stern but not adversarial.

Doric turned towards his father, his smile disappearing.

"It's all right, my boy. I understand the need for answers," Crogan said.

A few times, Crogan attempted to start, unsure of the right words. Finally, he managed, "Doric is a rare child."

The boy tilted his head inquisitively. He placed the sack on the ground, never taking his eyes off Crogan. He then raised his knees, squeezed them together with folded arms and rocked excitedly.

"Normally, this happens much later," added Crogan, looking directly at Doric.

"What happens?" asked Doric with a candid eagerness.

Crogan turned to Seth. "I have heard Doric's thoughts for some time. I know his dreams, sense his emotions and feel his fear. Space and distance have no effect. The connection is always clear."

Turning back to Doric, Crogan added, "Your thoughts are powerful, my boy. So strong, they ravage my mind." As he said it, he tapped his temple with his finger. "Yours burn a hole in here." Crogan smiled, ruffling Doric's hair. "You can imagine my surprise when I learned you were just a child."

"Earlier, you said Doric is the newest member of a fraternity. There are others?" Seth's voice cracked.

Crogan leaned forward and looked deeply into the boy's eyes.

"You're not alone, Doric. There were many like you once, many who shared your gifts. As I sit here today talking to you, there is one other out there." He leaned back in his chair and turned towards Seth. "Doric may not yet have the resolve but he will. I can help him."

"With what?" Seth asked.

"Doric has special…" Crogan paused and searched for the words, "Unique qualities."

Seth and Doric watched him with blank stares.

"I know you know what I mean," Crogan said. "Doric has an amazing ability to heal. Where most would die from such an injury or wound, Doric's body regenerates, each time getting stronger. He does not need food or water." The expressions on both father and son conveyed understanding.

"When has Doric ever said, 'I'm hungry'?"

Seth nodded silently.

"But you eat, don't you, my boy? You eat because it's what we do," he said, pointing to Seth and himself. "Living things need to eat to live. You eat to fit in, but you can do without, can't you?" It was a rhetorical question.

"You're a tracker, a pursuer. Call it having an internal compass. You will never lose your sense of direction. You were born a seeker."

"A seeker of what, Crogan? He's just a child!"

"A child he is, yes. A huntsman's predestination was established long ago. You have no choice, my boy. It is a part of you. Soon you will yearn to venture out if you haven't already. It is where you belong, where you will feel free."

Seth glared at his son. He knew all too well what Crogan spoke of.

"I wish more than you know for more time to help the boy harness his gift," Crogan said. "But you, and I, and all the people of Endura need him more now than ever before."

"We are just a simple people. And he's still just a boy!"

Crogan sighed. "Out there is an inspiration. It is as beautiful as it is deadly," he said, pointing out the window to the great landscape as dusk moved in.

"We all go about our lives, and a series of coincidences, decisions, chance meetings or events shape us. Doric's fate is different. It was set in motion long ago, or at least a part of it was. If he hasn't yet, soon he will feel it, a powerful calling, towards a sacred place where it is said a treasure or some great power is hidden. It is what Endura desperately seeks. He and all huntsmen do not know where or what it is they seek, but it has been prophesied that awareness will come when the time is right. It is said what is sought has the power to unite us all."

The fire popped and let out a sigh. Crogan's face turned somber.

"A lingering darkness surrounds us. You know of what I speak. It suffocates. It lures. You have felt it. It has already touched your community. Some of your people have disappeared."

"How do you know this?" Seth interjected.

"Do you know why things are the way they are?" Crogan said. "Why firstlings and humans have come to be the way we are?"

Seth shook his head. "We have lived on this land for generations. No one ventures outside our boundaries." He paused then looked at Doric again. "We're so disconnected from the outside we've lost touch. The elders sometimes tell stories of the olden days, but I don't know of what you speak."

"I have lived a long, long time," Crogan began. "There was a time when both races existed in peace."

It seemed like a good time to pause and present his offerings. Crogan reached into a large sack that lay at his feet.

"I have something for you," he said to Doric, pulling out two small, black, shiny irregularly shaped stones. He passed them to the boy, and once they touched Doric's hand, they began to radiate a brilliant white light.

"Only a huntsman can wield the power of these stones. These, my boy, are tools to help you see in dark places. Consider these my Sammas Day gift." Crogan said.

While Doric excitedly examined the stones, Crogan heaved a large leather-bound book out of the sack. Dust floated into the air. The book was ancient and frail. On the cover was a heptagon shape. At each point of the heptagon, embedded in tiny recesses, were seven small metal shapes resembling little tears.

"Over two thousand years ago, in the city of Nahire, firstlings and humans lived together in peace."

"Nahire was real?" asked Doric wide-eyed.

"Oh yes, real indeed."

"This, my friends, is the *Cerulean Book of Scribes.* Much of Nahire's history is in these pages. Many of the entries were made by King Zoren Ro himself."

Crogan handled the book delicately as if it would crumble. It was clear he regarded it with reverence.

Placing his hand on the book he said, "Over seven hundred years after King Zoren disappeared, an event happened in Nahire, one so terrible, it separated the races. Humans have held firstlings responsible ever since. Many have simply forgotten why humans and firstlings have come to be the way they are. Firstlings live now in isolation, as far away from humans and their influence as possible. Time has created a curtain against all that once was. For centuries, Endura and its people have adapted to the new world.

Many who were born well after that time now hear about the great city only as myth. Many humans have never seen a firstling but have still learned to despise them."

"What was Nahire like, Crogan?" asked Doric, still rocking back and forth in his chair.

Doric's eyes—wide and attentive— expressed an interest far beyond what Crogan had anticipated. Crogan had hoped to skip this part, choosing instead to focus on Doric, but one look into Doric's eyes convinced him otherwise. Crogan sighed, leaned forward and obliged.

"In the New Age, Nahire was a grand city. Its wondrous stone streets weaved through seas of majestic, white flagstone buildings. It was as if the city radiated on overcast days, creating its own warmth. In the four corners of the city and by the main gates, were King Zoren's giant symbols of unity and freedom. They were six giant statues of kings that guarded the city. The two main statues looked outward towards the magnificent landscape, visible from a great distance. Intimidating yet welcoming, they inspired and beckoned everyone from all over to Nahire. The remaining four stood at the corners of the city jutting into the sky, their large round eyes fixed down, always watching and giving the citizens a sense of safety."

Crogan paused there. Doric was leaning forward. He had stopped rocking, but his eyes were still open and fixed on Crogan. Crogan smiled and added, "But that was then, Doric. Nahire is in ruins. Its history, like its buildings, has turned to dust and faded into obscurity. Nahire is referred to now in myth and in legends. It is however, the place where the lineage of the Kings began."

"Crogan. I mean you no disrespect," Seth said firmly, "Your story is interesting, but I am still trying to understand why you are here."

Crogan nodded in understanding. He opened the book and

found the page he was looking for. Just as he was about to read from the ancient book, a loud knock startled them. A moment later, Raif Thom burst into the room.

"Well, what are you waiting for? The celebration has started. The last partekii-drawn cart from the field has arrived."

"We'll continue this later," said Crogan as he placed the book down on the table.

"What's going on?" asked Thom after seeing the worried look on Seth's face.

The men quietly walked past him and stepped out into the cool night.

The entire town had gathered. The evening was clear and cool, perfect for a party.

"Spare no expense," Raif Thom had preached. It had been an interesting year. Besides, they had many things to thank Samjees for; today they had received a visitor for the first time anyone could remember.

In the large, open area on Root Street, great iron cauldrons brimming with boiled meat hung on hooks and chains over fires. Large tables set around the cooking area and along the main street were filled to capacity.

Food was in abundance. Crogan enjoyed the ale from barley, wheat and oats and ramen, a duck-like bird, boiled with beards of fennel, nuts and spices.

For a year now, the stranger sitting across from Doric had been part of his life. When he'd seen the stranger approaching on the path, he'd no idea who he was until he'd heard, *you have too great a nerve for your own good, little one,* reverberate in his mind. The words had sent his heart racing with excitement.

Seth nudged his son, stealing him from his thoughts.

"Eat up."

The boy was far too excited. He had no interest in food on this night.

In the background, music signaled the end of dinner. Three firstlings assumed the responsibility of entertaining the masses with instruments akin to a lute, a pipe and tabor, and a stringed contraption with a flexible neck, which generated a sound that felt like the brilliance of a shaft of sunlight in the growing shadows of dusk.

Merriment was widespread. Young ladies kicked off their shoes and skipped around the dance area. Young boys stood to the side watching the girls, too shy to ask them to dance.

Ama, a spirited young lady, wearing a taupe dress and a beaming smile, took Crogan by the wrists and whisked him off to dance.

The evening turned cool, but no one noticed. The chilly air carried melodies and screams of delight into the night.

Ama left Crogan and snatched up Doric. On her way to the dance area, Tana stepped out in front of her. The little girl stood steadfast with hands on her hips. They understood each other. Ama winked and released Doric's wrist, she curtsied and left to find another.

Tana grabbed a surprised Doric's hand. "Come!" She took him to the open area, skipping the entire way.

Crogan spotted Seth and maneuvered towards him.

Taking Seth by the elbow, Crogan leaned in close and said, "It's time."

They left an ambience of cheer and radiance and stepped into darkened stillness. The sound of their footsteps grew louder the farther away they moved from the celebration. When the sound of the celebration faded to distant mumbling, Crogan stopped and leaned on a fence that bordered the street.

"Seth, what I'm about to tell you borders on bizarre. As I said earlier, you have to trust me."

"After today, there isn't anything that can surprise me."

"I think you may just reconsider after I'm done."

"Try me."

"As I said earlier, the world beyond Brackens Town is wondrous," began Crogan. "Many like you go about their quiet lives oblivious to what fate has brought to their neighbors. Beyond the mountains to the north and south, in the vast expanse, and even in obscure parts of Endura, no one is immune. There is a sickness among us, a dark plague. People disappear. The wills of men, women and even children are stolen. But the sickness doesn't bring death; it is far worse. Decomposing shells of people remain, hideous versions of what they once were, now consumed by a dark, vengeful force."

Seth's brows rose inquisitively. In the distance, muffled laughter erupted from merry revelers.

"Not long ago, I came upon a quaint little town," Crogan started. "A man stumbled onto the path in front of me. He was trembling and muttering incoherent things. He was so close I could see the sweat on his brow, his vacant eyes, his flaccid expression and pale countenance. He did not acknowledge me. He seemed to be in a trance, as though he were walking in his sleep."

Crogan turned to face Seth. "I followed and watched him walk blindly for days. He did not stop to rest or sleep. On the evening of the ninth day, he reached Werun Falls. I thought for sure he would plunge to his death. Instead, he began to cross the old bridge over the falls. He never made it to the other side. A giant skine swooped down, scooped him up and carried him away. I tracked him to a place where black smoke hovered above a range of mountains that dwarfed the rock formation known as the Tine Pass. He had been dropped there to settle in among many other wanderers. They all converged aimlessly onto a narrow pass towards the opening of a cavernous hole. The bottom of the deep chasm on either side of the path was obscured by a thick sheet of darkness."

Crogan's eyes squinted as if he was watching the events in front of him.

"I heard the pounding of chains," he continued. "I crouched behind a rock among the mob of wanderers, close enough to feel the suffocating evil that emanated from this place, but far enough that I felt I could turn and run at the first sign of trouble. Then from the darkness, near the opening of the cave, I saw it: a large, black silhouette in the shadow moving opposite the mob. The stream of wanderers parted to let the large specter through until it stepped out of the darkness. It stood as still as a statue. Its eyes, two bright orange flickering orbs, looked directly at me. In that moment, a feeling of panic and dread smothered me unlike anything I have ever felt. Before I turned to run, I caught a glimpse of the side of the mountain. It was alive and seemed to move as if covered by a mass of insects…but they weren't insects, they were people clad in armor. I ran, and I did not stop for a fortnight until I reached a path on the other side of that ridge earlier this morning," said Crogan, pointing to the path he had ridden in from.

"Seth, that town was Brackens Town. I arrived weeks ago. The man I followed came from your town."

Seth stood up from the fence he was leaning on. "Wade Maggis?" he said, without hesitation, then added, "What are you saying?"

"I'm saying this plague has touched your town as it has many others. I have borne witness to unspeakable things. Towns are being destroyed and stripped ruthlessly of everything. Murder is rampant and brutality towards men and firstlings is spreading. Seth, that thing out there is building an army."

Laughter and song filled the night from the celebration underway.

"And this is just the beginning." Crogan took Seth's arm and squeezed it tightly. "I need Doric. We all need him."

"He's just a child, Crogan," pleaded Seth.

"A special child."

Seth shook his arm loose and started pacing. "I don't even know who you are. Do you realize what you're asking?"

"I realize if Doric doesn't help, it won't matter. Nothing will. There won't be anyone left to save. An assault on Endura is looming. I am sure of it. Celebrate with your people tonight. In the morning, gather your belongings and leave. Find the sanctuary. It is a place called the Den. Head south. Don't worry about knowing where to find it. It will find you. Your people will be safe there."

"This is lunacy."

"Listen," Crogan urged. "On my travels, I came upon a mysterious creature, gentle in nature, with powers revered as one who could see the unseen and put substance to that which has not yet occurred."

"A fortune teller?" Seth blurted out jeeringly.

"Far beyond a fortune teller. The moniker given was Harwill, the Ruid word for prophet. The Harwill told me things about myself I did not know, things that had not yet happened that have now come to pass. But there was one thing it said that I remember above everything else; I memorized it long ago: a prediction about a resurgence of the Azura, the Ruid word for gatekeeper."

Seth scowled. He was growing impatient.

"It will all become clear in time. I believe this dark shadow with the fiery eyes is aware of this prediction. Huntsmen have been sought, found and murdered. The absence of huntsmen means that sacred place that mirrors the mark on their neck will never be found."

Crogan closed his eyes and began reciting:

"Before two thousand years from the first King's birth,

There will come a child, a surge from beneath still waters.

A shadow amongst races in this dark, doomed world.

He will bear likeness to his kind but not from woman born will he be.

Through fate he will find a passion like no other.

A tormented soul, it shall lead to find truest peace.

But, when tears of his beloved fall and mingle with those from his own eyes

And fall upon a sea of red atop his family's name, the purest pain and sorrow shall follow.

For it will be at that moment of sorrow, when the world seems damned and hope is lost,

That the gods will open the gate and invite him in.

Passion will drive blind vengeance, and his legend shall grow, and people will proclaim his name.

He shall strike fear in those doomed to darkness.

It can only be he alone that restores the union of a forgotten time."

Crogan opened his eyes. Seth stared at him blankly.

"What is that supposed to mean?"

"I'm not sure, but two thousand years since King Zoren's birth is just months away, seven to be exact."

"A child," Seth said mockingly.

Crogan sighed and lowered his head. "It's all we have. I have never shared that passage with anyone. I have simply preached the Azura will help us. I believe in it, Seth. Hope is all we have."

Crogan exhaled. "This darkness has always been," he continued, lifting his head again to meet Seth's gaze. "It's not new. It is an ancient malice that has waited. Ruids of old, you see, were immune. It is in your nature to resist temptation, but something has changed you. Regardless, long ago, this evil stumbled upon a conduit and has slowly seeped into our world. Only now, the trickle has become a deluge."

"What is this conduit you speak of?"

"Not what, who."

There was a long pause. "What dread have you brought to our peaceful town?" Seth's expression changed to worry. "Who is the conduit?"

"His name was Adam Hades."

It was as if the sheer mention of his name served as a calling. Suddenly, back in the center of the town, the music that had filled the night abruptly stopped.

In the dead of night, they heard a terrifying scream.

At the same time Crogan and Seth had walked away from the party to talk, somewhere far away, a young man and his mentor were making their way through a dense forest. The older of the two knew the forest could bite when least expected and even kill if one was not prepared. He knew they had to make haste, as they did not want to get stuck in the thick of the forest in the night.

Although dusk was fading quickly outside the forest, it had little to no effect on the environment within this dense wood.

Very little sunlight could penetrate through the leaves. Day or night, it was always the same; darkness completely consumed it.

The two had travelled for some time. The younger of the two, a huntsman, carried a small stone in his outstretched hand. It emitted a vibrant, bright light. The trunks of the trees recoiled as if being exposed to something alien.

When the trees ended abruptly, both sighed in relief. The elder dismounted from his partekii and began preparing to settle for the evening.

"We camp here tonight," he said.

There was no argument from the other. He was far too weary to carry on.

"Hurry and shut that light, Will," the elder said.

The young man put the stone back in the sack. As he released it, the surroundings immediately turned black. It wasn't long before the two men slept, unaware of the horror that had befallen the little community of Brackens Town somewhere far away.

Back in Brackens Town, the wind suddenly picked up. Fallen leaves scurried across the cobblestone streets. Flames from torches surrounding the gathering place blew out. Those that remained, flickered wildly in the rapidly cooling breeze, casting sinister shadows on the houses bordering the streets. The hair on exposed skin began to rise. Some firstlings stopped dancing and looked at one another, wondering if others shared the same eerie feeling.

From the shadows, evil emerged, bringing with it the stench of thousands of years' worth of pain, anguish, death and decay. It came in an unnaturally large human form, adorned from head to foot in menacing black garb. The form covered ground at an astounding pace, waltzing into the town from above the hill as if expected as a guest. It made no attempt to hide its presence.

It had a designed scheme that it planned to fulfill, regardless of the cost.

Its haunting shadow danced behind it. The sharp iron spikes of its spurs clanged against the jointed plates of the metal covering its feet. Its heels struck the ground with hard jerks, sending echoes off the surrounding houses.

A young woman seated at the first row of tables emitted the initial scream of horror at the chilling apparition. She squeezed her child tightly and backed away. Heads turned towards the disturbance to behold the approaching menacing entity.

In the background, the music stopped.

The uninvited guest came to a stop as it neared the first row of tables. Even though a black hood covered the crown of the daunting skull shield, its glowing orange embers for eyes peered at them from behind two narrow slits.

"The boy. Give me the boy!" it screeched. The sound of its voice, deep from within its black breastplate, molded and forged from unholy plate armor, permeated the air. It was a loud, unworldly, gravelly whisper. The firstlings flinched at the sickening sound.

Raif Thom emerged from the frightened crowd. He was the first to address the terrifying figure. He stepped forward slowly, hands out as if to calm an angry dog. He stopped abruptly when the figure turned towards him. Its eyes glowed.

"Doric Devinrese. *GIVE HIM TO ME!*" the figure shrieked with clenched fists.

"Wait. Who are you and what do you want with Doric?" The Raif's voice quivered, despite his effort to remain steadfast.

The cloaked figure replied, "I will leave with the boy. You decide the cost."

Alarmed, the Raif replied, “You will leave with no one.” He sounded unconvincing with shaking hands and a wavering voice.

The cloaked presence stood as still as a statue, pausing as if giving the Raif a chance to comply, but there was never any doubt about its purpose. It relished the terror.

It raised its arm and pointed into the crowd of firstlings. A rumbling came from beneath the breastplate. It pulled its arm in with palm exposed to the Raif. The rumble grew to an inhuman roar. It thrust its arm forward. Although the creature didn’t make contact, the Raif’s chest collapsed, crushing his sternum and ribs, killing him instantly. An invisible force drove the Raif through the air and over the heads of terrified firstlings. Blood spewed out of his mouth, showering firstlings beneath him who watched in horror as he crashed down heavily atop the tables.

Doric stopped dancing. He grabbed Tana’s hand and squeezed tightly. A foreign feeling of absolute dread washed over him. The music suddenly stopped. Tana stared inquiringly at Doric as blood suddenly splattered on her face from above.

Raif Thom sailed over their heads. For a very brief moment Doric caught a glimpse of his eyes: lifeless and forever frozen in a terrified grimace. Tana’s scream was drowned out by the terrified shrieks from adults who started scampering away in horror.

Crogan and Seth stormed out from between houses, yelling Doric’s name. Their shouting attracted the cloaked visitor’s attention.

Doric gripped Tana tightly. He heard Seth shouting above the panic that had engulfed the people of Brackens Town. The tall, dark figure turned towards Seth and spotted Doric.

A firstling nearest the dark figure reacted instinctively to constrain the unwelcomed visitor when it took its first step towards Doric. Fear was inconsequential; protecting their own mattered even though they had no means of fighting back. The tall specter did not falter. Instead, it reached under its cloak, unsheathed a large sword and swung with implausible power and precision, striking the firstling below the chin. The blade continued unimpeded. The firstling's headless torso took a step before crumbling to the ground.

Another firstling charged from the opposite side; a chair raised over his head. The creature whirled and struck the chair with its fist, shattering the chair and snaring the firstling by the throat. The firstling writhed until his face turned blue, and the flailing stopped. The creature flung the lifeless body into the crowd. Cries of pain and terror exploded into the night.

The figure then arched his back and emitted a gruesome howl so powerful those rushing away from the scene covered their ears.

Death had visited their peaceful community. The atrocity continued; the murderous rampage reached an incredible pitch. The creature fed off the carnage. Rather than grow tired, it struck and lunged more viciously. The air swarmed with the thick odor of warm entrails. Bodies littered the ground. The firstlings had no weapons to protect themselves since none had been needed before this hellish night. The cloaked intruder moved effortlessly from one side of the street to the other with incredible swiftness, never losing sight of Doric.

And then something strange happened when the figure came upon Lorne. The figure's sword was raised to strike. Instead, he hoisted Lorne up off the ground and peered into his eyes.

"I have use for you," it sneered, flinging Lorne Maggis aside.

Crogan and Seth finally reached Doric.

Crogan felt drawn to the figure. Something about him

seemed strangely familiar. He realized it was the same dark shadow that had glared at him weeks earlier in the Tine Pass.

The dark specter stopped its campaign momentarily. It stood erect and turned towards Crogan. Its eyes blazed—bright and smoldering—in the cool evening. It spread both arms, extended its chest and raised its head to the sky. The air began to swirl. Tables lining the streets, between the dark specter and Doric, began moving without being touched to clear a path for it. They started to vibrate. The movement then turned into a violent shaking. Suddenly, tables and chairs were launched, with absurd force, into the air and out of the creature's way.

Tana turned to run. Doric lunged to restrain her. A piece of her dress ripped off in his hand. The sudden jerk knocked her off balance, and she fell just as a table passed by where her head had been.

Others weren't as fortunate. Hundreds of lifeless bodies began littering the streets and the once vibrant gardens.

Crogan fell to one knee. He grabbed hold of Tana and Doric. "Run, and don't look back!" he shouted, and then he shoved the children forward.

"Get them out of here, Seth!"

The dark figure reached under its cloak, removed a thick black leather whip and cast it underhand. The crack pierced through the night. The leather whip's tip suddenly peeled back, exposing a sharp, pointed metal spike. The peeled ends were two strands of ribbed leather that flailed about like flagella.

Before the metal tip of the whip reached him, Crogan found a chair lying on the street nearby. He hurled it in the creature's direction and sprinted behind the nearby Tree of Life.

My staff. Where's my staff? Crogan thought. His heart raced.

The flagellum-like arms ensnared the chair. The leather tentacles squeezed until the chair exploded into pieces.

The dark figure lashed a second time. The thick, ribbed

leather whip whistled through the air. The metal tip struck the trunk, and the tree trembled from its roots. The loose ends of the creature's weapon whipped around the trunk and swiped at Crogan, thrashing and scratching at his legs.

With effort, Crogan managed to wriggle away. Then, just as suddenly as it had begun, the assault ended.

Doric and Tana raced down the deserted street. Seth struggled to keep up.

The dark figure extended its right arm towards a large tree off to the side of the street. The monster made a fist and jerked its arm to the left as if tugging an invisible chain connecting its hand to the tree. The base cracked and splintered, and the giant tree toppled.

The firstlings hastened their pace and passed the tree as it crashed onto the ground. Another tree up ahead began to sway. Seth panicked and shoved the children forward. They fell and rolled onto the street away from the limbs of the tree. Seth wasn't as lucky. A large branch caught him beneath the waist and pinned him to the ground.

Snap! The sound was crisp and clear, even above Seth's pained shrieks. The children looked back in horror, but the creature was gone—at least that's what Doric had hoped, until he saw two small, bright orbs, hovering in the air above the fallen tree. The creature's shape—draped in shadow—had melted into the night, and only its eyes, blazing incessantly, were visible in the darkness. Slowly, it descended. When its feet touched the ground, it resumed its long, sinewy strides with an eerie grace. In one hand, the whip cracked repeatedly against the cold stones, in the other, its sword swayed menacingly with each stride.

"Run, Tana!" Doric pleaded.

Snap! The sound of the whip grew louder, as the figure neared. Tana sobbed and held Seth's hand.

"Please, Tana, run!" Doric screamed again.

Snap! Snap! Still she didn't move.

Then the stench of the decrepit creature hit them. Tana looked up and glimpsed the true essence of wickedness. She let out a gasp. The dark figure recoiled and hissed. It returned the whip to its belt, took another step forward and hovered over the fallen firstlings.

Doric stepped up and positioned himself between them. The glowing orange embers of its eyes seemed to smile at the child's defiance. It tilted its head back and emitted another guttural roar.

The snapping of branches stifled the creature's howl. Twisted fragments of the fallen tree rose up and cleared a path on the street. One man, holding a staff, marched towards the dark figure, a determined and intense expression was on his face.

"Your power has grown stronger," the dark specter shrieked. It stooped, snatched Doric up by his shirt, and it coiled its arm around his waist. It stepped towards Seth and Tana, looked again at Crogan mockingly, raised its sword and brought it down towards Seth's head.

Crogan thrust his staff forward so his arm was fully extended. His lips moved, uttering words of conjuring, and he jerked his wrist upwards. The sword was torn out of the creature's grasp and flew end over end towards Crogan. Before it reached him, it crumbled to dust and dissipated into the night.

The daunting, dark figure grasped Doric's frail neck in its powerful hand and glared at Crogan with blazing eyes.

"Don't come any closer," the creature screeched. "Your admiration for these creatures will destroy you, Crogan. They're nothing but fertilizer."

How does it know my name?

A sudden feeling of nausea swept over Crogan.

"Put the boy down, Aaron," Crogan ordered.

It was like running into a brick wall while in an all-out sprint: the jolt was sudden and numbing. The realization was shocking.

There were no features, just menacing dark garb concealing any shred of humanity. In the creature's smoldering eyes though, he sensed it: Aaron's spirit; the essence of evil, even more potent after all these years. Somewhere in the deep, guttural uttering, Crogan heard jeering.

"You were a coward then and an even bigger coward now," Crogan shouted. "Still hiding behind a mask."

The creature made a fist and extended a forefinger. "I should have killed you long ago," he wailed.

"Like you murdered your father?" Crogan was shouting.

Aaron hissed. His eyes glowed as if infused by a blast of fresh air.

"Still blind. King Edric was not my father," Aaron roared. "Adam Hades, the one true god, is my father. His spirit is more potent than you can imagine."

Crogan crept closer. Aaron squeezed Doric's neck. The boy gasped.

"Stop!" Aaron shrieked. "Now there will be only one left. He will not see the next day's noon." Aaron took a few steps back.

"Wait!" Crogan's shout was an appeal this time.

The expressionless, menacing face shield glared at Crogan. The exchange lasted only a moment, and then Aaron, with Doric in his grasp, leaped over the fallen tree.

"Doric!" Tana screamed. A hopeless look of terror was fixed in Doric's eyes as he disappeared behind the fallen limbs of the tree.

In a rage, Crogan cast his staff at the fallen tree. It rose up and sailed off to the side as if it was a twig. Seth lay spent and gasped for air.

Tana fell to her knees, sobbing inconsolably. Through watery eyes, she stared blankly into the night as leaves scurried across the dark, deserted street. There was no sign of Aaron or Doric.

Crogan bent to help Seth, but Seth swiped his arm angrily aside.

"Get away from me!" he shouted. His eyes, bloodshot and cold, glared at Crogan.

"You brought death."

Crogan stepped back and staggered. He was spent and horrified with what had just happened and with himself for his inability to stop it.

"What have I done?" he cried under his breath.

3

THE COVE

SIXTEEN-YEAR-OLD WILL SHYLER woke suddenly and sat up sharply from the uncomfortable surface that had served as the previous night's bed. The firstling's eyes were closed, and his four-fingered hands were pressed firmly against his temples. Pain stabbed at the back of his head.

It's never hurt like this before.

He rolled onto his knees and rested his head on the ground. The rapid beating of his heart slowed as the pain subsided. He exhaled and fell sideways onto his back, and a stream of thoughts and images entered his mind.

It was early morning and the sun was not yet visible on the horizon. The sky was overcast, and the thickness of the forest surrounding him shielded most of the available light. There was just enough for him to see his surroundings, though he was not yet attentive to them. One particular word entered his mind that stood out amongst the others. The word stirred unease and anxiety.

"Danger!"

He sat up again, staring blankly ahead. The thoughts were rapid and sharp.

"I found him…the boy called Doric, but I failed to protect him. He's been taken."

Crogan began to relate the horrible events that had just transpired.

"That dark phantom I told you about, he's called Aaron. He has the boy. Now he's coming for you. You don't have much time."

Will turned towards his old friend and guide, Padron. He rested peacefully, snoring and stirring beneath the heavy blanket, oblivious to the ill thoughts and warnings flooding Will's mind.

"He knows where you are. Beware the noon hour. Find a sanctuary. Contact me only then. Keep your wits. May Samjees be with you."

Will waited a moment. The communication ended. He sat, absorbing all that Crogan had said as he stared blankly at the calm water. His heart beat faster. He blinked repeatedly and started to become aware of his surroundings.

The morning was crisp. Nearby, the partekiis shifted their weight and bobbed their heavy heads as they moved about in restless circles. Their color had recently changed to blend with the ground. They appeared more like bronze effigies than living creatures. Two holes on each side of their head—serving for ears—rapidly opened and closed, producing soft fluttering noises. They were attempting to interpret new sounds from this peculiar environment, where the air seemed unusually heavy.

Will wiped his eyes with his firstling digit and gazed out across the almost perfectly circular inlet and into the dense forest on the other side. The trees were on hills sloping down to where

Will sat. It was as if he sat on a stage, and the trees were the audience in a large theater. Behind a less dense section of trees, set in what appeared a perfect line around the cove, were several sharp mountainous peaks. Their surfaces seemed flat and smooth, resembling a wall more than they did the sides of a mountain. Hovering above the sea in the distance, thick fog billowed. He found it strange there was no fog floating above the unnaturally circular body of water where he stood. The sight of the narrow opening out to the sea gave him the impression the land was being pinched shut by an invisible hand trying to shield this area from the rest of the world. He felt an icy shiver.

Faint sounds came from the old man lying beside him, a small mound covered in a large brown blanket rising with every breath, one end a mop of gray-white fur and the other end two large feet. Beneath the gray-white mop of disheveled hair, a mouth appeared to move from somewhere within the long-spotted beard.

Padron, or Pads as Will liked to call him, was far more than a mentor. He was his best friend. Both were from Essra on the eastern part of Endura, just south of Toron Bay. Like other huntsmen of the fraternity, Will's was a lonely childhood, and Padron, although much older, had suffered his own personal loss and shared in his own type of isolation. They found companionship and a special kind of contentment in each other.

The first time they met, Will was nine years of age. Padron had heard of Will before he had met him. In fact, everyone in Essra had. The odd boy who kept to himself. The boy whose wounds would spontaneously heal. He was different than the other children, but sometimes a lack of understanding breeds fear. How could anyone have understood Will's abilities? He was an easy target for the other children.

One fall day, seven years ago, Padron responded to a series of sounds from the barn behind his home. They sounded like strange, pained yelps from an animal. The old barn had been abandoned months earlier. It was supposed to be empty but inside, Padron found Will lying in partekii dung and covered in blood. Padron rushed toward him just as Will retreated into a strange catatonic state. On Will's cheek, blood poured from a gash just below his right eye to below the tip of his nose. As Padron watched with disbelief, the gash sealed shut before his eyes.

Later that day, Padron learned Will had been ambushed by three boys wielding sticks with thorns. They had lured Will into Padron's barn and into an empty partekii stall. The fact that firstlings would reach a point of displaying this kind of behavior and violence was a concern in itself.

Padron had cleaned Will up and taken him home, never forgetting the reaction of Will's parents, surprisingly calm; they dismissed it as a common occurrence.

Will had never told him who the boys were. He'd answered the question the same way each time with, "It's not important." Ever since that day in the barn, Padron had not been able to get rid of the boy. Truth was, Padron welcomed the friendship. He'd lost his wife and daughter two years before meeting Will, in a freak accident, when a giant tree had been struck by lightning, and a large branch had fallen onto his house. The ensuing fire had taken his home and his family.

When Crogan came calling one spring afternoon four years ago, Padron had not been about to send Will out on his own. Will was also a bit of an oddity in another sense. He would often claim others would purposely place objects in his path or trick him into hurting himself. Padron called it being clumsy. After four years together in the wilderness, Will had matured and so had his confidence. He had become quite the prankster, poking fun at Padron any chance he got. Padron welcomed it despite his outward display of displeasure.

A beam of sunlight pierced through the clouds, passed between limbs of trees and settled on the surface of the pool. A small area towards the middle was illuminated. Will followed the beam, admiring the directness and brilliance of the ray as he walked slowly towards the old man. For a fleeting moment, Will could swear he saw movement in the water. He stumbled over his friend and lost the image.

"Ouch!" Padron threw his blanket off and bolted to his feet, surprisingly agile for one who constantly complained of aches and pains.

"What's your problem, boy?" Padron inquired. His eyes were hot and bright and his lips, a sharp line beneath a disheveled beard.

Will ignored him and peered at the bright spot, unwavering and still on the surface of the water. It was only for an instant, but he was certain of what he saw: long, flowing, black hair falling over an attractive face with an intense brooding look.

Padron shook his head. He moved the hair from his face and patted down his beard. He called out to his young friend again. This time he got his attention.

"Gather your things. We have to leave now," Will urged.

Padron stared blankly. His face was the color and texture of old paper.

Will briefed his friend about Crogan's warning. While

Padron gathered his things, something odd began to happen. Will grasped his chest; a sudden wave of faintness came over him.

"What's happening?"

His chest heaved as if he had just completed a lengthy run. He turned his head from side to side to free himself from an invisible noose tightening around his neck. Gasping for air, he felt the world spin sideways and placed an arm on Padron's shoulder. Suddenly, Will's eyes opened wide and his breath escaped him. It was only for a moment, and then his grip slackened, his facial muscles relaxed and he inhaled slowly. He was overtaken by a peaceful calm. He moved away from his friend and walked towards the edge of the water. Once again, he looked, this time not as a firstling but as a huntsman.

Padron was about to speak when Will placed his finger to his lips. "Shhhhh. Listen."

Ahead, the cove lay motionless. On the other side of the water, all he could see were the trunks of the trees in the foreground and impenetrable darkness beyond. There was so much to support life all around them, yet something was eerily absent.

When they had approached the area the previous night, they had not been able to assess their surroundings in the dark before settling down for much-needed rest. There had been times in the past when they had abandoned their trek to evade danger. On this day, escape was not an option. This place was special. Will could feel it.

Will realized he may have just stumbled upon that which had been sought for generations but eluded many before him. *Could this be the place?*

Will stared directly into the blackness of the water in the center of the cove; words began to take shape in his mind, words he had never heard before. Padron's concern turned to amazement when Will spoke. The young man's face tensed as he spoke in a mature, confident tone normally uncharacteristic of Will. Then he began to recite the passage of the Cove of Resurgence.

"There is a place where nature has been deceived. This place should be teeming with life, but is absent of it. The air and water have been occupied with a more important task. The sound cuts through the air like a dull blade and trees shield this place from the outside world, and light from the heavens, but for a series of narrow beams centered on the surface of a small, circular body of water. It is here, beneath the surface, where it shall find its final resting place."

The passage ended. When he came out of his trance, the tips of Will's fingers were pressed against his neck, feeling the raised edges of his birthmark. His eyes were fixed on the center of the cove.

Padron grasped Will's arm. They moved towards the bank and peered into the water. Will grabbed a hold of Padron's wrist and leaned out further. His reflection was absent. In fact, there was no reflection of the trees on the surface. The water resembled a shiny, black marble floor. Will extended his foot out expecting to tap it on the surface and hear a sharp rap back. Instead, he slipped and tumbled in.

The surface returned to its motionless black slab state as Will's head disappeared beneath the surface. Padron fell to his knees screaming out his friend's name, but the pool remained calm. Suddenly, a hand crashed through the surface. Padron grasped it, heaved Will out and dropped him onto the ground.

The boy coughed and spat out water. The mysterious pool remained still.

"Are you all right?"

Will nodded, his lips were quivering.

"What do we do now?" asked Padron, relieved.

"How am I supposed to know?" replied Will with a grunt.

He got to his feet and paced. His eyes moved between the banks, the trees, the water, and the vast mountains beyond the distant trees. Still dripping, the strange feeling returned. This time, he was prepared and gave in to it. Near the base of the mountain stood a cavernous opening he had missed earlier.

"There!" Will cried out, pointing with his elongated digit.

"Where? What do you see?"

"That middle peak, that's where we have to go."

Will started immediately. He made no attempt to pack his supplies. He merely jumped on his partekii and looked down at his older friend.

"Well?" he said. "Are you coming?"

"Will, I don't see anything. What opening?" Padron grumbled as he mounted his partekii. The two raced off towards the cavernous opening, which to Will greatly resembled the gaping mouth of a hungry beast.

Will reached the base of a hill. The mountains loomed a short distance ahead. The ground here was too jagged and unsafe for the partekiis, so they'd dismounted. Will reached into a sack and pulled out a small black stone. Padron was still far behind.

Will looked back to the cove. It seemed too perfect, too untouched. His heart raced with excitement and nervousness at the thought of Crogan's warning. Time was of the essence. He glanced up at the sky. *Several hours still till noon.*

"Let's go. Get a move on!" Will yelled back at Padron, motioning with both hands.

"Stop! Where are you going? Have you lost your mind?" Padron ranted between pants.

He caught up to his young friend, who was standing still, staring at the cave directly in front of him.

"It's about time, old man."

Will looked down at the rock in his hand. It was aglow but dimmed by the daylight. He turned to Padron.

"Are you ready?"

"Ready for what?" Padron said, turning to look at the solid rock face.

Will grabbed Padron by the wrist, and without warning, pulled him towards the wall. Padron's footing gave, and he screamed in anticipation of an impact. He raised his free arm to brace himself. Instead, he melted into the wall and found himself inside a dark chamber. It was instantaneous, as if stepping through a curtain of air. Once through, cool damp air blasted his senses. He scolded Will, who had already abandoned him to survey the surroundings. When Padron turned towards his friend, he was amazed at what he saw.

Just enough light from outside filtered in. They were in a large room, floored with limestone that sloped down steeply. It was a breathtaking gallery of stalagmites, pillars and other rock formations. Halfway into the room, there was a large, thick flowstone column twenty feet high and more than a foot wide. The deeper they moved into the darkness, the more prominent the brilliant light from the mystical stone Will held in his hand became. At the bottom of this room, they heard a great volume of rushing water. From the bottom of the room, they travelled down a passage for what seemed an hour. Along the walls, beneath their feet and all around, the passage was overrun with insects. They looked like crickets but with longer bodies, varying from black with white spots to completely white.

"What are you staring at?" Will asked, feeling thousands of pairs of tiny eyes watching him and his partner. "Don't worry, we're just passing through." His words echoed back eerily.

Farther down, the number of insects dwindled, and the light now shone on sections of rock that possessed a beauty no sculptor could possibly reproduce. A faint sound came from somewhere even farther down the dark passage, until eventually, a stream came into view. The water was clear as glass with the exception of isolated patches of foam floating on the surface. After a while, the stream veered and plunged down sharply.

As they continued, they came to another large chamber. At the rear of the chamber, six passages led out from it.

"So, which one?"

"That one," Will said, pointing to the third from the left.

The passage he chose was long and narrow, approximately twenty feet high, but only two feet wide. The base of the passage tapered in such a way that walking or even standing, was becoming impossible. At one point, the two had to scale the walls to keep from getting stuck. They followed this section to what appeared at first to be a dead end, but upon closer scrutiny, ended up being a gathering of fallen rocks. Up the fallen rocks they scrambled.

At the top, they found a narrow opening that led to what appeared to be a passage, beyond which they were forced to crawl. One at a time, they squeezed through a long, twisting tunnel two feet in height and width. Will's only concern, beyond getting stuck and dying, was time. Nearly two hours had passed since they first entered the cave.

Will approached the end of the tunnel ahead of Padron. The passage here narrowed and turned into a tight squeeze. After a bit of a struggle, Will pressed through.

A powerful sensation of victory overcame Will. It was as if he was nearing the end of a long, grueling race and the finish line stood mere feet away. The impatience of youth took over.

"Just a little further, old man. You'll be all right. Take your time. I have to see what's beyond the opening. I can't wait. Be back in a few minutes."

"Will, wait!" Padron shouted. "Crazy kid," he whispered when he heard Will rustling about. He shook his head and hurried forward, grunting and mumbling to himself.

Will was in a cooler place, surrounded by suffocating darkness. Stale air blasted his senses. Strangely, the stone in his hand gave off little radiance in the surroundings. Behind him, Padron kept calling.

"Will. It's dark in here. I can see your light. I'm almost there. Wait for me."

"It's darker in here!"

Will's heart was beating rapidly. His excitement heightened his senses.

"Hurry up, old man!"

There was no response other than an echo. He sensed the room was large. Beneath his feet, the surface felt hard as stone, yet at the same time, pliable. He knelt and shone the light on the ground to see what it was that he was walking on, but there did not appear to be anything out of the ordinary.

Will started to move about.

"You out yet?" he yelled back.

Strangely, for the first time in his life, he had lost his sense of direction. He continued with his left hand extended, feeling his way. Occasionally, he would encounter an object in his path and he'd change direction.

He came upon a light about two hundred feet directly ahead and about twenty feet down from where he stood. The light resembled a round orb with no apparent source: a bright, round sphere that did not appear to radiate outwards or cast any light on its surroundings.

"What's going on, Pads? Hurry, old man!"

"About two feet to go. Don't do anything stupid, Will!"

Will couldn't stand the wait. He began to walk in the direction of the orb, slowly at first and then faster as his excitement grew. He was running in the darkness when his foot struck something, and he tumbled, sliding on the cold, rough surface until the ground disappeared beneath him. Extending his arm blindly, he managed to grasp the ledge. He could not tell how steep the drop was, nor did he intend to find out. He released the stone instinctively to free both hands. With fingers and hands raw from rubbing against the rough surface, he pulled himself up with great effort.

When he came to his feet, breathing heavily, he shook off his fear and turned to find the mysterious light again. It had changed. A black spot had appeared in its center. It was growing larger quickly. There was no time to ponder what it was.

As he heard Padron yell, "I'm out!" Will felt a sudden jolt in his chest. Something sharp, long and narrow pierced his chest above the sternum and exited his upper back. He fell, and a wave of faintness swept over him. He felt trapped in a huge vise that was squeezing the life out of him.

Focus, Will. It will pass, he told himself. Struggling frantically to breathe, he brought his hand to his chest and felt the warmth of his blood. He lay still, staring into the darkness.

Padron heard a pain-filled moan. He couldn't tell where it was coming from. There was a heavy thud against the wall of the cave to his left. The ground shivered with the blow.

"Will! Where are you?" he yelled. "Knock it off!" Padron called into the darkness. He was annoyed now.

There was no sign of Will, or the light from his magical stone. Padron fell to his knees, thinking he could cover more ground by crawling in the dark. He called Will's name repeatedly, but still there was no answer. His knees and hands ached from the rough ground and the sharp edges on the rocks. In desperation, he pressed on.

A faint light grew out of the ground, in the spot where Will had seen the orb earlier. Its brilliance intensified. Gazing into it sent sharp pains into Padron's eyes, causing them to tear. Padron rose to his feet, shielding his eyes, but the light source vanished as suddenly as it had appeared.

The darkness was brief because a flame spontaneously ignited from a torch above him. The sudden burst startled him. A second flame burst from a torch adjacent to the first, then another and another until a multitude of torches blazed around the room. The room lit up, but there was no sign of Will.

Padron surveyed his surroundings and saw a narrow stone staircase across the abyss that connected the surface he was on to a small ledge on the other side of the chamber. Obstructing a clear view of the large, domed ceiling were two, thick, ancient timbered logs that spanned the length of the room. They were set about three feet apart, one end resting on a ledge recessed into the wall of the cave where a large round boulder sat, its diameter wider than Padron was tall. The other end rested on a heavy slab of rock atop a vertical stone pillar that rose out from the floor on the small ledge. Three mysterious objects sat on a table at the base of the stone pillar.

A pained moan came from behind a rock. Padron found Will lying on his back. He was covered in blood.

"Will!" he screamed. "Hold on. Breathe. It'll pass."

A gruesome hole in Will's chest was seeping blood. Strangely, the ground around him was clean and dry. He watched with disbelief as some of Will's blood trickled onto the ground and disappeared into the surface.

Will began gurgling and the act of breathing became a struggle. He gasped and fought for air. His eyes rolled back, and he started to convulse; slowly at first, and then the convulsions became violent. After about half a minute, the shaking lessened, and Will's eyes began to blink rapidly. When the convulsions stopped, slowly, Will began to focus on his surroundings while the damaged tissue began to regenerate before Padron's eyes.

"Come on. That's it, come back."

The open wound on Will's chest sealed shut, and then, with his friend's assistance, Will slowly sat up.

"What's the matter, old man? Are those tears?" Padron smirked and wiped the tears from his face.

"Even though I know the outcome, I'll never get used to that." Padron smiled, and they both came to their feet.

Will found the steel object embedded in the wall of the cave. It was covered with his blood. Some dripped and pooled on the ground beneath it. The object looked to be a long, slender metal spike. A portion of it, about the length of his forearm, was sticking out of the wall. He grabbed it with both hands and tugged. It didn't move. He pulled it a second time. Again, it didn't budge.

"What is that?" Will said, hoping Pads had an inkling and could shed light on it as he was apt to do from time to time. He looked to Pads as a wise old man who seemed to always have some insight into just about everything. Padron just shrugged.

"That thing came right at me…as if it knew where I was standing," Will said as he wiped blood from his hands onto his pants.

A peculiar soft tapping started from somewhere within the chamber. It stopped, but seconds later, it started up again. This time, taps came in quick succession. More of the same sounds began to fill the chamber and the noise grew in volume. It seemed to permeate from the walls around them.

A strange, ten-legged, peculiar, arachnid-looking creature, slightly larger than a tarantula, crawled out of a hole in the wall. A second, slightly smaller one followed from the same opening. The tapping in the chamber grew louder. Other arthropods of varying sizes, began to emerge from other holes in the walls and from the floor. Hundreds began to come up from the passage they had emerged, and more came up from the edge of the steep drop. Many descended from the ceiling at the end of thick webs.

In the flickering light from the torches, Padron observed their mouths: abnormally larger and wider than they should have been for the size of these frightening creatures. They were opening and snapping shut repeatedly. Very quickly, the walls, floors and even the ceiling of the chamber, was filled.

A number of them scurried over to the ground beneath the spike and using their two appendages, longer than their legs, resembling arms with pincers, scooped Will's blood from the ground into their mouth.

"Great! They want blood!" Padron shrieked. He grabbed Will's arm and pulled him towards the narrow stairway a short distance away.

Padron tripped. The arthropods pounced and swarmed his leg. Will pounced too, batting the creatures from his friend's leg. The arthropod's pincers grabbed and tore at Padron and Will and their bites, from two fangs in their remarkably powerful tiny jaws, were incredibly painful. Padron's bled; Will's began healing immediately. The repulsive creatures swarmed them. The firstlings pressed forward blindly, ignoring the detestable crunching beneath their feet.

Will reached the stone staircase first. He brushed the last of the bothersome creatures off his clothes and started across. He looked back once just as Padron started his own trek across.

"Hurry! Don't look down!" Will shouted.

The staircase was longer than Will expected. His legs throbbed from the effort, and he worried about how Padron was making out. The strange arthropods were unrelenting.

Will leaped onto the ledge, avoiding the last few steps. He looked back. His friend was painstakingly inching his way across. As Will shouted encouragement and urged his friend on, he made note of the ledge he was on. It was solid rock, twenty feet long by twenty feet the other way.

The ancient logs sat on the large rectangular slab that rested horizontally atop a large rock column more than twenty feet tall. Immediately in front of the pillar was a waist-high stone table. Three objects rested on it: a spear, a brown sack and a palm-sized metal talisman positioned between the two.

"There you are," Will said. "I found you."

He touched the talisman's cool finish and wiped away layers of dust. He did not move it, at least not yet. His heart was beating rapidly with excitement.

The spear was an oddity. It lay across the table and extended slightly beyond the edge. The other half was embedded into the stone pillar.

Padron let out a sigh as he too finally reached the small ledge. The stone staircase was completely covered now with those horrid crawling creatures. They did not cross the threshold onto the ledge. They stopped at the last step. Many fell into the bottomless pit below.

"What do you make of those?" Padron asked between breaths.

"Strange. Look at the spear."

Will gently lifted the sack and passed it gingerly to Padron as if expecting it to crumble. He touched the spear, believing it firmly lodged in the solid rock. Surprisingly, it started to move. Will gave it a tug, and the spear emerged in its entirety. He held it up admiringly and marveled at how light it was.

A dry, scratching sound echoed in the chamber. The huge column behind the table began to descend into the ledge. Overhead, the ancient timbers descended along with the column, creating a growing incline.

The ground of the chamber suddenly began to shake. Will grabbed the talisman from the marble table. Behind them, a crack appeared on the staircase. It broke apart and plunged into the darkness below.

"We're not going back that way!" yelled Padron.

Cracks appeared in the ceiling and on the walls around them. Rocks and rubble began falling, and dust filled the room.

A portion of the ledge beneath Will's feet cracked and began to separate into two large pieces. The marble table cracked and shattered. Will chose one side and leaped. Padron remained on the other. By now, the vertical column had sunk to just above the marble slab. The timbered logs were steeply sloped.

The boulder in the recessed wall on the opposite side of the room swayed with the violent tremor. It leaned forward and slowly toppled onto the ancient wooden beams. The boulder swayed, the logs creaking under the weight until the boulder settled and began to roll. The steep incline of the logs propelled the giant boulder towards the cracked ledge where the two firstlings were trapped.

The room was dark now. The rumble grew louder.

"Pads, get down. *Now!*"

Padron fell to his stomach. The boulder reached the ledge in seconds. It bolted past them and crashed into the wall. The trembling stopped, and a blast of musty air entered the room.

4

THE BRIDGE OF MIES

WILL BRUSHED OFF the thick layer of dust, rubble and rock that covered his head. He breathed some in and gagged.

"Pads! Are you all right?" he managed.

"Over here," Padron moaned.

Many torches had been smothered with debris and extinguished, but two still burned. Behind them, the boulder sat tranquil, half of it fixed into the wall of the cave. Beside the boulder was a large crack and an opening wide enough for the two to fit through.

"Hurry up!" Will shouted.

Padron gathered himself, and the two felt their way in the dark with the items they had just found clasped firmly in their hands. They crawled through the narrow gap between the boulder and the wall of the cave into another unknown.

They were in a long, narrow corridor with a high ceiling and damp, rutted walls. Dim light from the chamber they had come from filtered into the area. Ahead, the path twisted and turned and curved into uninviting darkness. *Three stones safely stored away with my partekii; a fine place for them*, thought Will.

Their eyes had grown slightly more accustomed to the dark. Will pressed forward and Padron reluctantly followed. The ground was soft, and the walls of the cave were cracked throughout. Water seeped through, running down in a slow, steady stream, disappearing into the ground beneath their feet. The further they travelled down the tunnel, the darker it became until they were completely wrapped in darkness. Their every muscle was tensed. Padron grabbed a hold of Will's cloak. It gave him a false sense of security. To make things worse, their feet repeatedly sank into the soft ground, hampering their movement.

"What now?" Padron whispered.

"We look for a way out."

"How do you suppose we do that?"

"I'm just following my instincts."

No sooner had he uttered this last word when the two suddenly sank to their knees. The ground beneath them gave way and down they plunged.

They were free falling in a dark narrow shaft swallowed up completely by darkness. Cool musty air blasted their faces as they bounced off what seemed a moist, spongy surface. Will let go of the spear and surrendered to the darkness. About to relax his grip on the talisman, the shaft curved suddenly. His rear struck the surface, and he began to slide on his back. The shaft had turned into a long tunnel with a downward slope. They were helpless, in complete darkness, tossed up, down and from side to side. Until this moment, Will had not realized just how loud he was screaming. Mud and sludge slammed into his face and into his mouth. He gagged.

Up ahead, Will saw a glimmer of light. The passage ended abruptly, and he exited the cave. He arced at the apex and came down on the rough yet welcomed surface. He looked back and spotted a hole on the lower side of the cave concealed by shrubs.

He heard screaming. Padron rocketed out of the small opening, narrowly missing Will. He, too, found the welcoming ground with a thud. The cloth relic from the cave was still clutched firmly in both hands.

A whistling followed from inside the dark passage. The sound turned into a high pitch. The spear jetted out and sailed over their heads, struck a tree, passed through, and impaled itself in the next.

Padron grunted as he stumbled to his feet. Will looked around—no sign of their partekiis. Down the rocky slope, through the branches of trees, the dark surface of the cove was just as still as he had left it. He surveyed his surroundings to get his bearings and found that gaping mouth of a beast, as he referred to it, where they had entered the cave hours ago. They were a good thousand yards east of it now.

He retrieved the spear, grabbed Padron by the arm, and looked around again for their partekiis. There was no sign of them anywhere.

"Let's go!" shouted Will.

The two darted off towards the cove on foot.

They burst into the clearing blindly. Ahead stood the still

blackness of the water. Padron bent at the waist, breathing hoarsely. He rested on his knee with one hand and held the cloth relic with the other. Will stuck the spear into the soft ground and placed one hand on his exhausted companion's shoulder.

"Are you all right?"

Padron nodded.

Will looked down at the object in his other hand. In the weak light of the cloudy sky, the talisman still maintained a vivid sheen, even after all its time in the cave. It was a circular metal object, a narrow outside ring surrounding a geometric seven-sided shape. In its center was an all too familiar mark, a circle surrounded by five evenly spaced inverted peaks. The narrow, circular part of the talisman was scored with extravagant markings. Not understanding how, Will found meaning in these strange shapes and designs etched into the cool metal.

Words from a forgotten tongue, Will thought. "It's Raffa Diem," he said, as he followed the markings around the object.

"*Ra dorun keif Ruid na dumon lyr szara na'orel,*" Will said. He paused and added, "*Aur en non.*"

"What does it mean?" Padron asked from his slouched position.

"A message," Will said, tracing the etchings with his finger.

"Of what?"

"The union of Ruids, humans and Endura is in your hands," Will answered, surprised with how clear the meaning was for him.

Outside the boundaries of the cove, the mist had not dissipated. Thick, impermeable walls of white fog remained, surrounding the cove and shielding the two from the rest of the world. He couldn't help feeling a sense of awe at the object he held in his hand. Firstlings before him had spent their lives searching for this place and this object.

"What are you waiting for?" Padron asked. "At the bottom of the cove, it shall find its final resting place." He motioned with both arms towards the water.

Will knew what he had to do. He took one last look at the object. *You've waited long enough,* he thought, then he raised his arm over his head. Padron stepped back. The talisman flew out of Will's hand out towards the middle of the cove. It skipped once and disappeared beneath the surface.

Padron felt a chill spread through his body, as the talisman made its way to its final resting place.

The air took on a different disposition. There was an unnerving stillness. A small ripple, like the dent a tiny raindrop would make in a puddle, spread outward. Magically, strange colors and contours appeared on the surface of the water. Figures began to take shape and mirror the trees surrounding the pool. Reflections danced on the multitude of ripples. The ripples turned into waves. The leaves on the tips of the trees rustled, as the wind kicked up. Fallen leaves swirled, and the thick branches of the towering trees began to bend precariously with the wind.

Towards the center of the pool, the water effervesced. It lasted for just a moment, and then the firstling's attention was drawn upwards to the sky. The clouds churned in the intensifying wind.

A narrow column of water suddenly sliced through the surface of the water. The column climbed until it pierced the sky. The harsh wind picked up droplets of water and tossed them about. The firstlings shielded their faces against the force of the intensifying wind and fought to stand upright.

Four narrow finger-like sections of cloud cleaved from the rest of the swirling gray mass in the darkened sky. They folded and coiled over each other and began to descend slowly, dwarfing the two awestruck firstlings in a threatening shadow.

The column of water rose even higher and began to spread. The steady stream suddenly moved outwards like a giant, expanding circular wall from the middle of the cove. It looked like an enormous upside-down waterfall with its apex hidden by the dark clouds.

Will and Padron fought their way to the woods and hid under the root of a large tree. The coiled cloud disappeared into the rising wall of water. Almost immediately, the wall of water returned to the center until only a thin column remained. The whole ordeal took less than a minute. The wind began to subside until it became a subtle breeze, and then the thin column collapsed. Water splashed and sprayed, the force of which sent large waves crashing onto the banks of the cove.

Minutes passed. The firstlings emerged from their hiding place. The cove returned to a dead calm. Something about the area, however, had changed.

"Something is not right," Will said.

The two fixed their gaze on the cove. Will's heart was beating rapidly. Padron placed a hand on Will's arm. His pulse, too, had quickened. The water within the cove remained as still and clear as glass.

Something sliced through the surface of the water. It was only for a second, and then it quickly submerged.

"There. Did you see that?" Padron yelled.

Two hands suddenly pierced the surface in the middle of the cove. A head covered with long, black hair surfaced and bobbed. Arms flailed, and water splashed as it disappeared beneath the surface. It emerged again, but this time there was no mistaking the sound of a long, pained gasp for air.

It was a woman. The two rushed into the water.

A shivering, frightened human woman sat on a log on the embankment of the cove. Her face was battered. The wounds looked fresh. She had bruises on her neck and arms. Her lip was swollen, she had a cut on her cheek, and her left eye was bloodshot.

Will and Padron hovered over her with blank stares. They were exhausted. Yet just as sure as the strange artifacts they held in their hands, there was no mistaking this was a frightened young woman sitting in front of them. She was undoubtedly beautiful. The soft contours of her face, the delicate lines and expressive eyes, were clear beyond the bruises. But there was something else. It wasn't quite apparent on the surface, but she had a kind of energy in her eyes, a hidden strength and resilience. Will was drawn to her. She had a regal flair about her despite her present condition.

Padron gestured with his hands to get Will's attention. The look on his face expressed confusion. They were looking for a child. At least that's what was prophesied.

"Are you all right?" Will asked.

The woman coughed. The gold-colored nightdress she wore, spotted with blood, was pasted snuggly to her body. She appeared out of place and out of time, as if plucked from her bed. So many questions surfaced in the firstlings' minds.

Slowly, her shivering calmed. She relaxed the tension in her hands. One was clenched into a fist. In it she held something: a piece of cloth rolled into a ball. She unraveled it slowly to expose a handsomely detailed, white silk fabric, heavily quilted and adorned with an embroidered "K.R." in golden stitching in the center. The patience and care exhibited by its maker was plain to see.

The woman raised her head and managed her first good look at the two. Both had queer expressions on their faces that she likened to one of having seen a ghost. Red stains, that looked like blood, covered their clothes. The younger one had wiry hair, and his skin seemed to be pulled back from the nose. He was a good-looking young man, not conspicuously handsome, but he had a light about him. His shirt was completely soiled on the front. There was a hole about an inch wide in the upper chest area, and his shirt and pants had numerous small ones throughout. When he turned around there was an even larger hole on the back. The older was disheveled. His shirt and pants were also covered with tiny holes, but he had cuts over his body; some still bled. Then she noticed their hands and smiled.

"Firstlings?" she managed.

Why is she smiling? Will thought.

"What year is it?"

"It's 2031," replied Padron.

"Lucius?" She spoke softly, her eyes down.

"Who?" asked Padron.

"Lucius Murough."

"The Manian?" asked Will.

Manian, or Ishtan Mar, the Ruid word for one who wields the power of magic and conjuring and the gift of foresight was an art shared by few; Lucius was the most powerful Manian of record.

"We haven't heard that name for many years," said Will. "But I know someone who can help you."

The woman looked like she was beginning to relax.

"Please," Will said, "we need to get away from this place."

The woman dismissed the comment. Her attention was drawn to the linen in her hand. Her face took on a dispirited look.

"He saved my life," she said softly, "and then threw me into a world of solitude and grief. Now it's 2031. So many years… everyone I loved is dead and gone. I never got to tell him." She looked up. A tear streamed down her cheek. "He'll never get to know him."

Padron knelt beside the woman. "I'm sorry," he said and gently placed a hand on her arm.

"I made this," she said, pointing to the linen. "It's beautiful isn't it?" She traced the letters with her finger and then clenched it tightly again.

She looked up with sad eyes. "I should be dead. Into the hands of Samjees he offered me." Her features changed, becoming more uncertain. "But I'm alive, right?" she asked. "I must be," she added. "Why else do I hurt all over?"

"Who are you?" asked Will.

"The truth is, it wasn't me he was protecting. I'm just the chalice: the chest. He was protecting something far more precious than me. He was protecting—"

She was cut short when loud knocks and snapping wood burst from somewhere within the forest. The strange sounds came from two distinct locations.

They listened for a sign, a clue of what approached. There was a distinct, foul odor in the air. Trees swayed, branches and bushes bowed and scratched at whatever moved past them. Will had an unbearable pain in the pit of his stomach, a palpable fear unlike any he'd ever felt before.

"What was that?" the woman whispered.

"We need to get away from this place." Will repeated, his voice cracked. He stood, holding the spear. There was a roar from somewhere behind them and to their left.

Whatever approached from the right was even closer. Twigs snapped on the other side of the thick bush. Will caught a glimpse of a swift-moving shadow. Whatever it was, it was big. Heavy steps approached.

Will's partekii crashed through the brush and leaped over a

fallen log out into the clearing. He sensed Will's excitement and began trotting towards him smugly. Padron's partekii followed, changing color as it emerged from the forest into the clearing. Behind them, the sounds grew louder, filling them with terror.

Will climbed onto the saddle and hoisted the woman up behind him. Padron also climbed onto his animal, and the two partekiis with their frightened and spent riders dashed around the cove towards the thick wood on the other side and into the darkness beyond.

Will's partekii raced ahead and swerved in and out of the trees, beneath low branches and over fallen tree limbs. Padron's partekii followed closely behind. When the trees finally ended, all that lay beyond was a thick, white blanket of fog. The partekiis came to a stop, and the three listened attentively. There was no sound beyond their breathing.

"We have to get out of this mess. We head southeast and find the canyon," Will said, motioning in the direction of the fog. "Once there, we need to cross the Bridge of Mies. The town of Ravenscroft lays a short distance from there." He thought of Crogan's message. He meant to find a sanctuary and contact him.

The three approached the fog and it engulfed them.

"Stay close."

"Don't worry about me," Padron responded. "I'm right behind you."

The trek was tedious and slow. It was difficult to see more than a few feet ahead. They started their trek, moving initially downwards into the valley, but after travelling on level ground for some time, they started on a steady incline. Two hours later, the gorge came into view on the right. They turned southeast, moving parallel with the edge of the cliff.

They came to a dilapidated wooden bridge suspended between the narrowest sections of the canyon. Hundreds of feet below, the Crowe River, completely concealed by thick fog, should be flowing peacefully, as the mist swept over it. The opposite side of the bridge was hidden from view, blanketed in the murkiness of the sweeping fog. On both sides of the bridge, rotting rails leaned awkwardly, daring the three travelers to test the feebleness.

The woman tightened her grasp around Will's waist. The old timbers creaked and bent under their weight. Will's partekii took the lead; its shoes knocked heavily on the ancient wood. The sound filled the riders with angst.

Which step will be the last before the bridge gives? Will couldn't help but think.

The fog rushed by as they crept across the bridge and brought with it a strange and horrible smell. With a rattle of chains, the familiar and unwelcomed clatter started again.

"We're not alone," Padron whispered. He continued forward reluctantly to stay close to Will.

From somewhere behind them came chilling scratching sounds.

"Come on!" Will cried out as he quickened his pace across the old planked bridge.

An object whisked by, close to his head. Another passed by his ear, closer this time. Arrows came at them from out of the mist. The woman squeezed tighter. Will pulled on the reins, and the partekii came to a stop.

"We're trapped!" Will shouted.

The next arrow struck Will's partekii in the chest. The creature shrieked, and its legs buckled. A second arrow struck its head, bringing the animal down onto its side.

Will and the woman fell heavily onto the bridge. The impact

jarred the linen from the woman's grasp. Frantic, she ignored the arrows that whizzed by and darted after it. Near the edge, the linen found a hole in a rotted plank and fell through. She fell to her knees and extended an arm, but she was too late.

Her scream was piercing. The linen was swallowed by the thick, flowing fog. The "K.R." embroidered on the white silk handkerchief was the last thing she saw before it disappeared into the mist.

Will leapt after her, grabbed her waist as she knelt, pounding the planks with her fists, and he carried her back, screaming, behind the dead partekii.

"You can't worry about that now," Will shouted.

Padron dismounted and ran to Will's side. Behind them, Padron's partekii let out a cry. Two arrows found their mark, and it too fell.

"The canteen. Give me the canteen!" Padron cried.

The canteen was an oversized bota bag made of leather, typically used to carry water or wine. This particular canteen carried something far more potent.

"No," Will said defiantly.

"There's no other way. I don't have time to argue with you."

"There's got to be something else we can do."

Padron grabbed Will by the shoulders. A roar erupted from somewhere nearby as a whistling sound passed overhead.

"Listen to me. We're going to die here if we don't do something. You were picked for a purpose. You're not going to fail, you hear me? I believe in you, Will...believe in yourself. Protect the woman, and get out of here."

The woman sat with her head down, sobbing. Reluctantly, Will handed the canteen to his friend. Padron slung it over his head. He started to rise, but Will squeezed his arm.

There was a terrified and doleful expression on Will's face. He just stared at his older friend without saying a word. No words came to mind that could express what he felt at that moment.

Padron smiled. "I'm so proud of you," he said. He handed Will the sack they found in the cave.

"Act quickly. Don't hesitate." Padron smiled ruefully. "May Samjees always guide you," he said, and with that he was off.

Padron started tentatively at first, but then started to run towards the unseen end of the bridge opposite the side they had come from. He gripped the canteen tightly. His strides were long as he glided smoothly over the ancient planks. An arrow passed, narrowly missing him, but he kept on. Strange shapes became discernible up ahead as he neared the end of the bridge. Padron knew what this meant and understood clearly what was about to happen. Anxiety and apprehension engulfed him, though he refused to give in to fear.

An arrow struck him in the abdomen. He slowed but did not fall. Conscious of his beating heart, labored gasps for air, and the unbearable pain that spread throughout his body, he removed himself from the pain and picked up his pace.

He managed a few steps when another arrow struck him in the shoulder, followed immediately by another in his chest. Their impact stopped him dead in his tracks. Struggling to breathe, faintness overcame him, and he fell to his knees. Blood poured freely, but he paid it no attention. He had one last thing to do, and there was no way he was going to let the boy down.

Padron gasped. The bridge swayed ahead of him, and he struggled not to lose sight of his task. Another arrow ended its flight in Padron's upper chest, and he fell onto his back. He lay staring up into the gray of the overcast sky. *Can't even take one last look at the blue sky,* he thought.

He brought the canteen up to his chest. His breathing slowed. Clumsily, he gripped the cap of the canteen with his other bloodied hand.

With the last of his remaining strength, he turned the cap and heard the welcome hiss of sparks as they travelled down a short wick. Large, indiscernible dark shapes approached and surrounded him. Padron shut his eyes.

Will had an idea. He placed the ancient sack Padron had given him down gently. On all fours, he crawled over to his dead partekii and grabbed a heavy wound-up bundle of thick rope from the saddle. With both hands, he carried it to where the woman sat sobbing and dropped it in a heap. He rushed back once more and retrieved the spear that lay beside his dead partekii. Arrows continued to whiz by.

"Stay with me," he said to the woman while he took one end of the rope and tied it securely around the grip of the spear. Her head was still down. She bobbed it once in acknowledgment.

Behind him, Padron's screams faded into the fog.

Come on, Will. Focus.

The fog was still thick. It obscured the canyon wall and the surrounding area. Will peered into it hoping for a view of something, anything that would serve his need. He thought he spotted a large object growing out of the wall of the gorge, a little above them and within his reach, or so he thought. He guessed it was a large trunk of a tree.

He turned to the woman, "I'm only going to have one shot at this. I'm going to try and hit that tree over there," he said pointing into the fog. "When it hits its mark," he said trying to sound confident, "Grab on and hold tight. We're going to jump, okay?"

The woman, with tears still streaming down her battered face, nodded silently. Will did not know if what he said registered, but he didn't care. There was no time.

Padron's cries stopped abruptly. Will gave the rotted rails in front of him a firm kick. They broke away easily and fell, giving him an unobstructed path off the edge. He took a breath, stood and raised the spear.

A threatening snarl and sharp hiss from behind him startled him. The gruesome sound was chilling and unlike anything Will had ever heard before. A large form, covered in armor, stormed out from the curtain of fog. Its putrid smell reached Will before the daunting figure did. Most of the figure was concealed by armor except for the sallow skin of certain exposed parts on its arms and hands. It stood taller than Will, and it had broad shoulders. Its cold, lifeless eyes peered at him through narrow gaps in the elongated eye slits of the half metal crown. Half its nose was gone, as was its lower jaw. It was a shell of decaying flesh and emaciated muscle holding a sword in its grotesque hand. Loose, rotting flesh hung off the bones like tattered rags. It leaped towards Will in an all-out dash.

Will hurled the spear with adrenaline-infused strength towards the advancing creature. The spear struck the creature in the chest and the force drove it against the rails on the opposite side of the bridge. It shattered the decayed wood on its way off the edge with the spear lodged firmly in its chest. The creature's weight took the end of the rope, still attached to the spear, down with it. At Will's feet, the rope began unravelling.

Will grabbed the sack Padron had given him, slung it over his head and found the other end of the rope among the rapidly uncoiling cable. He tied it around his waist. The woman wrapped her arms around him from behind and squeezed.

"Are you ready?" he yelled.

Will never got an answer. Heat from an incredible explosion

engulfed the bridge. The force of the blast drove Will and the woman off the edge. They fell as a sheet of fire spread above them and engulfed everything it touched. The rope was now draped over the rotted planks, one end still attached to the spear impaled in the creature's chest, the other around Will's waist.

When the rope uncoiled completely, it went taut. The sudden jolt sent pain shooting through Will's back and gut. The shock squeezed the breath out of him. On the other side of the bridge, the creature's descent also stopped. Its corpse—face up, arms and legs spread—jerked, but the spear remained intact. Their combined weight, greater than the creature's, began to draw it back up toward the bridge while Will and the woman descended on the opposite side.

The spear then came out of the creature's chest and Will and the woman began to free fall. When the spear reached the bridge, it became lodged across rails. The sudden jolt, more intense this time, paralyzed Will momentarily and emptied his lungs.

The woman lost her grip. Her screams echoed off the nearby canyon walls as her hand brushed Will's leg on her way down. She managed to clasp his foot. They swayed suspended beneath the burning bridge. Above, the rope—tied to the spear wedged across planks—started to burn. Around them, burning pieces of the bridge rained down, narrowly missing them.

Will managed to suck in air and shouted, "Are you all right?" His heart thumped. "I'm going to reach down. Don't you let go!"

The woman held on, but her grip was slipping. She reached with her free hand to connect with Will's. Their fingers had just lightly brushed when a large plank from the bridge struck the woman on the back of the head.

Her eyes opened wide. They fixed on Will, but they were vacant. Then, as if time had slowed to a crawl, Will watched helplessly, as she let go. Her long hair and dress flailed in the wind until she disappeared into the mist.

Will's shrieks echoed throughout the gorge. He shook wildly and began to sway. His arc grew, and with a final kick of his feet, reached the side of the cliff. Seconds later, the remainder of the bridge collapsed.

Spent, beaten and alone, Will held onto the shoots jetting out of the side of the cliff. No more unsettling sounds came from above. No one was left to hear his screams.

Burning bridge debris fell onto a ledge far below the spot where Will still clung to the wall. Covering this ledge was a thick blanket of compacted straw. The falling debris ignited the straw. As the flames intensified, a woman's body fell heavily onto the ledge. The straw absorbed the impact. She lay motionless, facing the sky as if she was sleeping. Flames encircled her.

From a crevasse by the ledge leading into a cave came movement in the dark. A giant hand, wide and dense, with long, thick fingers and grimy blackened nails, reached out from the darkness. The giant hand almost covered her entire body.

Ignoring the heat from the flames, the hand cradled the woman and raised her up slowly. Suddenly, the woman opened her eyes and moaned softly. The giant carried her into the darkness, unbeknownst to Will, who had himself reached a ledge two hundred feet up.

5
THE PLIGHT OF THE LOST

THE EXQUISITE LINEN, held moments ago in the delicate hand of the mysterious woman, settled gently onto the surface of the river. It continued its journey, riding the current on its fated plight that had begun long ago.

A violent explosion destroyed the weathered bridge above. Burning fragments and scorched remains of grotesque beasts crashed into the river, spraying volumes of water onto the banks. The linen drifted through the chaos peacefully, as if guided.

Days turned to weeks, weeks to months. The explosion on the Bridge of Mies became a distant memory, but the spilling of blood became commonplace throughout Endura. The same dark creatures that attacked Padron and Will stormed into settled regions, leaving ghost towns. In some regions, creatures would sweep in to find abandoned and vacant villages. Those better prepared abandoned their lives and journeyed into the wilderness to evade, or at least delay, certain death.

Word spread of a place called the Den: a sanctuary said to offer safety. Thousands searched for it, few found it. Some said it didn't exist, others said, "The Den finds you." It was hidden under the surface of Endura and said to be an extravagant and complex multi-levelled city. It might as well have been a dark cave crawling with mangy creatures—any protection from the horror that Endura had become would be eagerly embraced.

The mysterious handkerchief pressed on, navigating its way down the Crowe River into other bodies of water. After nearly six months, the linen floated into a bog where it became tangled in a thicket of weeds. Weeks later, a violent storm jarred it loose, and it pressed on into a swiftly flowing brook. Bounced about by violent rapids, it plunged over a steep waterfall to the rocks below.

It drifted into the Fire River where it wedged between rocks. Summer turned to fall, then fall to a biting winter that smothered the land. Winds blew angrily, lamenting the course Endura had taken. Beneath the icy surface, the linen rested.

When spring arrived, a cascade of melted ice and snow from the nearby mountain jarred the linen loose, and off it went once more. It drifted by the remains of a charred and broken wagon. The cargo—torn clothes, pieces of once-treasured furniture, books and fragments of children's toys—were strewn across the ruddy ground like relics of a forgotten time. There was no sign of life. Occasionally, unmanned wagons pulled by spooked partekiis would dash by on deserted paths. The linen continued onward. Objects once dear to someone faded into the darkness of the forthcoming night.

For months, the linen navigated through weedy water. One day, it drifted past a man, or at least what remained of him. Face down in the water, his head and outstretched arms bobbed and moved as if beckoning the linen towards him. A spear, lodged in his back, had passed so far through, it secured him to the bank. The bloated fingers of his dead hand snared the linen as it drifted near.

On higher ground, not two hundred feet from the dead man, a figure stooped over something in front of a run-down cabin. The strange man raised a corpse to a vertical position and labored to remove an article of clothing from it. He had no attachment to the dead, no concern for the life each represented: someone's child, mother, father, friend. Each was no longer a memory since none were around to remember them. Homes had been destroyed. Bodies littered the ground, and the air buzzed with insects.

The ragged man was short and lean and square in the shoulders; his face was dark and weathered from the sun. A thick scar ran above and around the brow of his left eye, beneath his socket and down over his cheek. The eye was covered with a black leather patch. His good eye was large, deep and dark. His skin had stretched taut against his skull, making his nose seem sharp and the scar wide.

The linen caught his eye. He reached the bank and admired the linen for a moment. He reached towards it, but it was not ready to be caught. The current swept up the linen and off it went again. The one-eyed man stood and watched it for a while and then returned to disturbing the dead.

Days later, the linen found a lake, and there it remained for several weeks. Another violent storm rolled in. Rain fell for days. The water rose and flooded the land. Then, on the ground of a forest, with the Herrus Peaks looming nearby, the linen found a cozy spot, and there it remained for the next two years.

Thick trees and wild vegetation offered the linen protection until the evening a tiny neap stumbled onto it. The odd little rodent with ears inside its head went about its business as usual. At the base of a tree, it brushed by something soft and partially submerged in the ground. It tugged with its tiny teeth and unearthed the silky white fabric. Taking its new treasure into the water, the neap carried the fabric through the weeds, using its long, scaled tail, towards its nest chamber up the stream.

Preoccupied, the creature was unaware of a nearby predator lurking, waiting for an opportunity. A large orp swooped low, snaring the neap and the linen in its powerful talons, and carried them deep into the night.

In the distance, an orange glow flickered in the darkness. The large bird creature swept over Natras Pass and over the source of the light: a series of sporadic fires that burned fiercely on the ground below. A second orp swooped in and startled the first large, owl-type creature. The newcomer swiped with its talons to steal the neap from the other's grasp, and the other predator lost its grip for a moment, just long enough for the linen to fall free. It floated towards the flames while the fight over the tiny neap continued above the nearby peaks. Soon, the loud orps' shrieks faded into the night.

The linen settled on the surface of a seething pool of bubbling water located within a hollow at the foot of a small round hill.

The water was warm, its taste rancid, yet somehow refreshing. The reflection on the surface of the water grinned at the man with one eye. The man peered down at his disfigured face in the mirror of the water. He rolled his tongue over his rotting teeth, rubbed his wet fingers across his scar beneath the patch and winked at the image that stared back. He tossed a rock into the water, making his image warp and break into pieces.

Reminded of how long it had been since he had last bathed, he thought of his skin as if it were a thing he could cast off, an accessory that he could shed. Scrubbing the grime from his skin was not an option. It would make him feel vulnerable and weak.

The man with the scar and eye patch glanced up at the sky. He knew he was close. Buzzard-like creatures circled, plunged and rose again to hover over carnage. He had followed the smoke for days and was nearing Natras Pass. *What priceless treasures have these fools who thought there was hope of survival left for me?*

He owed his survival to his decision to reject others of his kind. In return, he had been treated to the same absence of kindness his entire life. He felt invisible.

Directly ahead, the mountains loomed. He was only a few minutes' walk away when he felt a presence emanating from the pass ahead. He heard nothing, but was acutely aware of the dead waiting for him. He could not, would not, turn back.

Almost at the entrance to the narrow pass, he passed charred remains of dead humans piled one on top of each other in a ditch. Their belongings were scattered. The stench of decay hung in the air, but this time, the smell bothered him. Unusual after all these years, he did not know why, but felt he needed to get away from this place.

He walked by several pools filled with bubbling water. Steam rose out of them. He was drenched in sweat. His attention was drawn to a rustling sound from the path behind where he had just walked. Turning, he saw the leaves and branches off to the side, behind a pool and a row of trees, swaying gently.

"Who's there?" His voice was deep, and his words were slurred.

He thought he heard heavy footsteps moving through the thick wood. He walked back towards the sound with great trepidation. Then he noticed a coarse canvas sack, woven from a hemp-type fiber, set on the ground next to the pool of bubbling water. He was certain it had not been there upon his arrival.

Something caught his eye. It was a beautiful, embroidered piece of linen floating on the surface of the pool beside the burlap sack. He recognized it instantly, even if it had been two years since he'd seen it. This time it didn't get away. It was bright white without a blemish on it and cool to the touch. The letters "K" and "R" were stitched in gold into the fabric. He had no way of knowing anything about its origins, no way of knowing it was enchanted and tied to a great purpose. He simply eyed his newest prize admiringly, when movement from inside the sack startled him.

He loosened the knot gingerly and looked inside. A young human boy lay curled up inside. For a moment, the man considered turning and walking away, but the sound of the child's voice lured him. Against his better judgment, he raised the naked and grimy child out of the sack. He looked to be around two years old.

Curiously, the man with the scar examined the child closely. He was sure someone had left the boy for him to find. The child opened his big gray eyes. There was something captivating in the child's eyes. The man fixated on them. He saw his reflection in them, a mirror of himself, almost like a glimpse into his own soul. He watched what he had become, his cruelty and anger and the pain he had caused. With every callous act he observed, the harder it became to breathe. His skin tightened and turned a sickly shade of gray. His facial muscles tightened. He felt light-headed as his eyesight faded. Then the child smiled, and the feeling passed. As he set the child down, he noticed the edge of something odd sticking out from the folds of the sack: a note with crude handwriting.

Your journey has brought you to this place and this child. It is time to fulfill your part of the plan. Raise him to be a good man. Be his teacher. Share your wisdom. Most importantly, teach the child what the seven intended. You will receive a sign when your obligation is to end. On the day you find peace, his journey commences.

Almost three years has passed since Will's ordeal at the Bridge of Mies. Will barely recognizes what's become of the Endura he once knew. Towns, roads and places once frequented by people are deserted. Apart from the melancholy sound of the wind, the land is deathly silent. Fresh in his mind is the devastation he passed in the town a few hours back. Buildings had been ravaged and burned. Smoke and the buzz of insects had long since disappeared, and only scattered bones, exposed or half buried, remained of the dead.

This is all my fault, he thought. His failure tormented him every day.

Will was walking on a dirt path with eight other men. Crogan was among them leading the way. They had two omara with them, longer and leaner than oxen, with substantially larger and more elongated skulls and deep, black fur with a white eel stripe across their spine. Their powerful, athletic bodies were perfectly built for the task. They pulled an empty uncovered wooden wagon. The wagon's bed had been reinforced with several layers of wood, and the wheels were larger than normal.

"Let's stop up there," Crogan said, pointing to a grove off the path.

It was a cool night, the kind Will enjoyed most. On cool

nights, he felt more invisible. After that day on the bridge, Will went into hiding. For two years, he had hidden in the mountains, quite content to lead a reclusive existence. Surely, the ill fate of the mysterious woman should have spelled disaster. But the day of reckoning, as prophesied, two thousand years from the first king's birth, came and went, and darkness had not consumed Endura.

Will's appearance had changed. Physically, he had become thin. He walked with a slouch, thinking it would make him appear more obscure. His once bright, rich brown eyes, honest and caring, had become sunken and dark. Scars covered his body, evidence of his labored and troubled existence over the last few years. More importantly, his body no longer spontaneously healed. He retained all his gifts with the exception of two: the ability to regenerate and heal and to communicate telepathically. Both gifts had left him that horrible day on the Bridge of Mies, when Padron had died, and the mysterious woman had fallen into the mist.

The men journeyed to search for giant slabs of rocks: monoliths that could be fashioned by craftsmen into just the right shape and size. Their aim was to secure the materials and replicate an ancient stone gateway. For two years, Crogan and a team of the strongest men from the Den had searched the banks of the Lassit River. Although abundant in the mountains and hills nearby, these stones had to come from the banks of the Lassit River. At least that's what Crogan had said. The work was both tedious and dangerous as Aaron's spies were always lurking. To avoid sinister eyes, the group travelled at night.

Now that they'd stopped to rest, Will sat with his back against a tree. He gripped the sleeves of his shirt in his palms so the sleeves would not rise to expose his hands. He had become accustomed to doing whatever was necessary to hide his firstling trait and his identity. He did not feel safe among his kind, and even worse, he felt ashamed.

"I need you, Will. I can't do this without you. They need you too, even if they don't know it yet." Will recalled Crogan's repeated attempts for his help. He'd found Will's secluded dwelling and frequented it often, using kindness, bribery and even trickery to entice Will to help. Will could not recall why he'd given in to Crogan; perhaps it was an escape from complete isolation, perhaps he'd wanted to believe Crogan that there was still hope. Regardless, nearly a year ago, he'd agreed to help.

The symphony of snorts, snuffles and wheezes suggested, for Will, that all of the men in his company, including Crogan, had fallen asleep. He took a swig of water and rested his canteen on the ground. When the canteen's wooden exterior struck something, at first, Will mistook it for a root, but when he examined it closer, he was pleasantly surprised. A large rock of just the right size was buried beneath the surface.

He called out to Crogan. The Manian awoke with a heavy sigh and sat up. A *What now?* expression was all over his annoyed face.

"What about this one?" asked Will. He held a stone in his hand, and the light radiating from it lit up the area.

Crogan carefully examined Will's find. He turned to Will. "I think you have something here."

Crogan woke the others and they spent the rest of the night digging and chipping away. During the day, they hid in the nearby forest and rested. They resumed the next evening, and near dawn, spent and weary, the men had succeeded in extracting it. They labored tirelessly, sculpting it to size, and then, on the morning of the third day, they finished. When darkness came, they secured it to the wagon and rested.

"Crogan?" Will whispered.

The Manian grunted and opened one eye.

"Do you think this is going to work?" Will continued.

The slow, rhythmic snoring of the others confirmed the two alone were awake.

"I do," Crogan replied, lying on his back and staring up at the trees. "The gateway we are constructing is not the first, though I suspect it'll be the last. It is not for us to decide. The gods have a plan.

"For what it's worth, Will, I don't believe you failed that day on the bridge. I'm not sure what part the woman had to play in it, but you were meant to find her," said Crogan with certainty. "Do not underestimate the forces at play, Will," added Crogan.

"While circumstances continue to get worse, for reasons I cannot explain, all is not lost. The date of reckoning from the prophecy has long since passed, yet we're still here. For this reason, I believe in some way you did succeed. This gives me faith that one day we will find him, the Azura, the Gatekeeper. Either that, or he will find us."

Crogan sighed. "Yes," he said confidently. "This is what I believe, Will. We have to believe, otherwise we will destroy ourselves." Crogan lay down on the ground and stared up at the green canopy of leaves above them.

"One more thing, Will. I believe there will come a day when all of Endura will know for all of history that you were responsible for finding the path to salvation."

A short while later, the two slept deeply. It was the first time in years that Will did not dream of the Bridge of Mies.

A few days later, the eight men, led by Crogan, entered the Den. Will was not among them. He had departed hours earlier to return to the mountains, content to resume his secluded existence.

The omara, exhausted with the effort, hauled the heavy load down a long, sloping passage with a low ceiling inside the underground city.

The Den spanned a great distance beneath the surface: from south of the Garden of Usea, to just north of Natras Pass. The city was a marvel. It was a self-sufficient world, made up of eleven levels. The city was equipped with hydraulic underground waterways and sections containing wine and oil presses, cellars, depots for cereals and storage rooms. Each level was accessible through ramps or staircases. Some openings served as water wells spanning the eleven levels.

There were endless tunnels. Each was identified by a distinct number. Crude doors on both sides of the many tunnels opened to hundreds of chambers of various sizes where families dwelled. The rooms were just high enough for most people to walk upright without banging their heads.

Some tunnels were connected by large doors that only opened from one side. Gatekeepers would tend to these doors. They were added for security to protect the inhabitants. Only the correct words would make the Gatekeepers open the doors.

Several larger open areas, usually near the end of tunnels, were common areas that served as kitchens. These rooms had narrow openings to the surface that acted as ventilation chimneys to exhaust smoke. Animals were kept in the topmost level to minimize odor.

For hours they had pressed on through one tunnel after another. Finally, Crogan and his crew exited the passage from an exceptionally long winding tunnel into the largest chamber of the subterranean city. They were deep beneath the Syran Hills at a place called Navalline.

It was early in the morning, though people had already begun gathering. Crogan had chosen this place because it was the largest single room in the Den. It was a central hall, with a high, domed ceiling. A series of dwellings carved into the walls bordered the open space. The cells were accessible by paths which snaked up the sides. Cells higher up were more recessed than those below. Many had balconies that were occupied by curious onlookers.

A strange light emanated from the surface of the outer walls of the cells around them. Even the stone floor and doors seemed aglow. Light seemed to radiate from the stone itself. The surface appeared to have been crudely brushed with a kind of substance that made the stone come alive and glow brightly. Uneven brush strokes that spanned the walls, up and down and sideways and crisscross, illuminated the area until it took on a kind of festive overtone; illuminated cells coiled up the sides of this large chamber creating a cheerful atmosphere. There were no torches. All the light in this large room came from that strange substance smeared on the walls and floor.

The omara finally reached the bottom. Excitement was in the air. People watched as scores of men labored to remove the large stone from the wagon. Vertical monoliths, carefully crafted to resemble two identical, twelve-foot rectangular columns, four feet apart, already stood in place. Finally, the slab they had just brought was hoisted across the top of the two vertical stones to complete the gateway.

Crogan took up the ancient sack Will had found in the cave three years earlier. He held the spear in his other hand and stepped in front of the stone structure. Thousands of ashen faces looked on. Many had not seen the sun in years. They were tattered, tired and hungry, but together they still held on to something powerful.

"How did it come to this?" Crogan whispered. *That so many would look to me for hope?*

The buzzing slowly subsided to murmuring and then a deafening silence.

"I stand before you this day humbled," Crogan called out to the crowd and paused. "Humbled because of what we have become. I do not look upon you as strangers but instead as brothers and sisters. Often, when I feel the gods have abandoned us, I take a moment to consider all of you." Another pause. His voice was surprisingly clear to everyone.

"Look around," he said. "In all this chaos, in all this misery, we are still here. We have each other, and today I give you a gift from the gods," he continued, pointing to the stone structure.

"What stands before me is the truth. It is a gateway to freedom from this chaos. For there will come a day when one of you will walk through this gateway and prove that the gods have not forsaken us."

Crogan plunged the spear into the ground and released it, letting it sway. Then he untied the ancient sack from the cave.

"May the gods be with us," he mumbled.

He took the open sack and emptied it by throwing it towards the threshold of the Portal. Black dust flew towards the opening, but then, as if striking a flat surface, it spread to cover the opening. It increased in density and darkened further, drinking up the moisture in the air until eventually it turned to a thick, black, still pool of fluid. The crowd gasped.

Crogan took the spear from the ground, held it in front of him, and then over his head for all to see. He turned towards the Portal and tossed the spear into the black pool. The spear was swallowed up. It didn't come out the other side. Crogan then followed the spear into the Portal. But he passed straight through, dry and without a mark on him.

"Today is a day of reckoning. A plan, more than two thousand years in the making, has come to this," he continued. "Perhaps you or the one standing beside you, or perhaps even someone on the surface not yet among us, has been chosen, one who is righteous and pure of heart, to walk through this Portal and emerge with the spear. The chosen will be the guardian and gatekeeper, the Azura, touched by the gods, and with their grace, will strike fear in those doomed to darkness. That name will be proclaimed for generations to come as the one foretold to destroy the gateway that's letting this evil into our world."

The silence was replaced with a low, collective murmur.

"All of you here and in every part of Endura, who by the grace of the gods have not yet fallen slaves to Aaron, must come to this place and walk through this gate. Find the spear and find your destiny. Spread word to others to come to this place. I will follow to the ends of Endura the one touched by the gods, and if it be the will of the gods, will lay my life down. For the finder of the spear, my brothers and sisters, is the last hope for us all."

Excitement grew. Boys, girls, men and women walked through the Portal. Each one emerged empty handed.

6

HELLAS MONS

The matchra tree grew near Nahire in the Garden of Usea, a multi-stump sapling with heart-shaped leaves. Seventy-four years after King Zoren's birth, a fierce storm uprooted the tree and tore it to pieces, save for a single stump, which found its way into the Snake River. Elliot Reese, founder of the northern settlement, found it lodged against a bank, took it from the river and planted it in Strathmere, where the tree grew stout. Years passed, and its appearance changed. It is said the tree became infested with vermin and snakes that inhabited its base and roots, yet within the bark and leaves, it was believed many therapeutic and healing properties were harbored.

There it prospered for many generations until the quake of the year 720, when ruptures under the surface spewed hot molten rock, ash and gases, resulting in the formation of a large mountain. The matchra tree was swallowed up by the mountain, and inside the crag, found a home.

The entrance to the crag, where the tree grew strong and tall, was guarded by a series of rocks referred to as the Tine Pass because of an eerie likeness to the gaping mouth of a predator. Beyond the Tine Pass and in the labyrinth of the cave, the matchra grew rich in the darkness.

—*Cerulean Book of Scribes*

FAR FROM NATRAS Pass, on the easternmost point of the land, Hellas Mons looms over the city of Strathmere. At less than thirteen hundred years old, it was a young volcano formed in the aftermath of the great quake of AZ 720. The land looked very different before and after that event. Violent tremors triggered large fissures that allowed molten magma beneath the surface to escape and decompress aboveground. Year after year, the accumulation of layers of its own eruptive lava and magma helped form the towering mountain. At its apex, Hellas Mons eventually reached a height of over ten thousand feet.

Snow-covered peaks, once concealed by clouds, have since become completely covered by a veil of dark smoke. Several vents connecting reservoirs of molten rock underground to the surface have for centuries sent pulsating dark smoke up into the sky.

The land surrounding the mountain has been obscured by a dark shroud of smoke for so long, no vegetation has survived.

The area around the mountain is dead, fitting for the unspeakable things that go on inside the mountain.

In front of the mountain, guarding the path leading to the opening of the cave, is the Tine Pass: a natural phenomenon made of rock that is as menacing as it is extraordinary. The opening bears a likeness to the skeletal jaws of an angry beast. Two large, giant columns of rock, symmetrically angled on both sides, point upwards and taper to a tip while two, angled in the opposite direction, give the eerie appearance of large fangs.

Behind the large gaping jaw, dizzying crevasses on either side of the path expand downwards into darkness. The chasms are endless pits with bases concealed by shadow. The path itself is narrow, about twenty feet at its widest and about two hundred feet from the fangs to the opening at the base of the mountain.

Near the opening of the cave, hot blasts of air incessantly assault the path. Once inside, narrow streams of lava flow steadily through numerous rivers, snaking through the floor of the cave. A steady hiss from the molten rivers echo off the cold walls and mix with the clang of blacksmith's hammers. Cries of anguish and torture from hundreds of enslaved craftsmen continuously reverberate through the stale air. There is no place for compassion in this place.

At the rear of the chamber, mining carts sat stationary. In each were piles of well-crafted swords, daggers, axes, spears, shields, skull shields and other weaponry. Armor-clad drones, shells of their once-living forms, pushed the loaded carts to other sections of the mountain where they would be assigned.

Stragoy serve as masters. They are completely clad in armor except for their faces. The exhausted blacksmiths, immune to the gruesomeness of their captors, no longer pay them any attention. Stragoy have a common expression in their black eyes, vacant and lifeless, but their likeness ends there. Some have grotesque, bulging foreheads, others sharp, protruding cheekbones, with no lips and dark, charcoal, rotting skin. Some Stragoy bear sunken cheeks, deep hollows spotted with patches of decaying flesh. Others have parts of their skulls or jawbones exposed. The Stragoy are walking corpses in various stages of decomposition, mere shadows of their former selves. They have no identities or ability to think or communicate; each has a single purpose: to serve their master.

Outside Hellas Mons, beneath the heavy cloud of dark smoke, and beyond the Tine formation, skines swooped and dropped new arrivals continuously. Each wanderer shuffled into the cave and descended into a labyrinth of tunnels, as if they had travelled this path thousands of times.

From the tunnels into an enormous chamber filled with a sea of others like themselves, new arrivals entered. Although already bursting with other wanderers, the chamber was surprisingly quiet.

In the center of this underground room, the ancient matchra tree loomed. It looked ethereal in the dimness. Surrounding the tree were seething pools of water that fed several streams travelling out of the chamber. Seeds, in the form of tiny frizzy fibers, fell into the pools and disappeared beneath the surface. Carried by streams, the fallen seeds settled deep into fractures within the rock. Periodically, fountains with powerful, eruptive power sprayed the seedlings thousands of feet into the air where they dotted the sky and were carried on the wind to all parts of Endura. When they eventually settled, trees with the distinctive heart-shaped leaves, which have come to be called the Tree of Life, would grow.

The original Tree of Life, or its trunk, as wide as ten men, was buried in the solid ground. The floor around its base was cracked and frayed. Thick roots around the base twisted and disappeared into the ground. The trunk was gray with deep wrinkles and scars as if from years of torture. In parts, the bark was rotted and dark, thick, black liquid ran down it. Its branches were twisted with ghastly claw shapes. At the base of the tree were shreds of blood-stained clothing.

Suddenly, a light leaf-like rustling began, followed by the sound of a large door creaking, only amplified a thousand times. The deep rumble shook the ground and the matchra tree shuddered. Above, where the ceiling spiraled into the darkness, the sound grew louder, looping its echo over and over. It was feeding time.

The walls of the mountain quivered. All those crowded in the area near the tree stood idle, lost in catatonia, without so much as a flinch when they heard the rumble…all except one.

There was no specific reason why this random new arrival turned and walked toward the tree. Perhaps it was his proximity to the tree, or perhaps it was some bizarre telepathic response, but with a blank stare, he spread his arms wide and grabbed hold of the trunk.

His arms and face began to take on an odd, sunken look. The black, oily substance on the trunk of the tree stuck to his exposed skin and began to tug it between cracks in the bark. Parts of the man's face and arms stretched grotesquely as the thick black slime—alive and pulsing—began to spread over his skin. The poor soul's one visible eye, blank and expressionless, turned upwards into the darkness. Color faded from his skin. Blood pulsed from pores in his arms to run down the bark in thick strands.

Bones snapped. Flesh and muscle began to tear and rip apart, but the terrifying sounds of his demise fell on deaf ears. The exposed skin of his body was completely covered by the black fluid. The torso bulged. Blood burst from the intense pressure and digestive power of the fluid. The black liquid consumed the upper torso and moved to the lower half of the man's body. Black liquid surged, sucking and digesting, as blood sprayed onto the coiled roots.

Several hours after the feeding began, the last of what once resembled a man disappeared. His stained and tattered clothes lay piled at the base of the tree. Leaves rustled, expressing their satisfaction.

New arrivals stirred again and ambled towards the pools in steady lines. They dropped to their knees and lowered their faces into the water and drank. When they raised their heads, the transformation was complete. From that moment on, their brain, tissue and organs ceased functioning in the conventional sense. Only an outer shell remained. The process of rotting and the transitioning to Stragoy had begun.

Armor-clad Stragoy organized new recruits into groups and armed them with weapons. Appropriately prepared, they ventured through the endless tunnels of Hellas Mons and exited onto the sides of the mountain where they stood and waited. The throng of lost souls now numbered in the thousands.

This evening, the moon looked exceptionally bright through the thick smoke above Hellas Mons. The wall, cold and hard behind his back, served as his safe place. Doric tapped the back of his head rhythmically against the stone wall while focusing on the waxy sphere in the sky.

Pale moonlight splashed into his cell through an opening in the ceiling and illuminated sections of the room. Doric closed his eyes to avoid looking at it. He had plenty of time to look on his surroundings with disgust during the day. Night was his peaceful time. When the moon passed by the orifice in the ceiling and disappeared from sight, Doric was once again plunged into thick, impenetrable darkness.

For almost three years, he'd been imprisoned deep within the labyrinth of Hellas Mons. A heavy iron door separated him from the horrors outside his room. It rarely opened, but when it did, a wave of terror would wash over him and he'd retch.

Beyond the heavy door, the steady knock of hammers and cries of torture persisted around the clock. Doric had faced his own share of intolerable torture over the years, but it was the loneliness that was destroying him. Still worse, he did not know why he was being punished.

The room was dark again. A scurrying sound came from somewhere nearby. Quietly, he moved towards the sound. Something warm brushed up against his arm. He snared it, and in the dark, whispered to it, a small furry rodent as if it were a long-lost friend.

Hours later, he awoke, and the early morning light sprayed against the wall of his prison chamber, which was exposed to the sky by a narrow orifice forty feet above. It was a long rectangular room, about twenty feet long and twelve feet wide. A wooden crate in the corner overflowed with feces. The walls were smooth with tiny ledges, though too small to serve as sills.

In almost three years, Doric had tried hundreds of times to scale them, always to face a rapid and painful descent to the ground. The steady scraping and rubbing of his firstling trait, the large digit on his hand, into the crevices and cracks in the stone surface had resulted in hardened callouses. His digit was now abnormally long and sharp at the end. It repulsed him, though he was repulsed by what he had become even more.

Doric stood and stretched. His naked feet ached from exposure to the cold, rough surface. They were scarred to the point where they no longer looked like his feet, but rather two strange appendages attached to his legs. Gingerly, he staggered to the wall, contemplating another fruitless attempt to escape, but he dispelled the idea and sat back down. He felt far too weary.

Leaning against the wall, he pulled out a soiled piece of fabric from his tattered shirt and brushed it against his cheek. He let his mind wander to fonder things, of Brackens Town, of his father and of Tana. All that was left of Doric's past were his memories and a piece of Tana's dress. He kept it close always. Thoughts of her gave comfort but also brought nightmarish pain. As much as he tried to escape into his fond memories, they were often replaced by the night Aaron took him into the shadows.

On the night of that last Sammas Day celebration in Brackens Town, Aaron had leapt with Doric still in his clutches over the fallen tree, and Doric had felt a sudden weightlessness as if submerged in a pool of darkness. The pressure in his head had become unbearable, tightening against his temples. Breathing had become difficult. A loud whistling in his ears had drowned out all sound except his pained gasps.

He had emerged from the pool of darkness quite suddenly. He'd felt his breath being sucked out of his lungs and realized the air around him was being drawn out of the chamber. Aaron's daunting figure had stepped back and crossed the threshold into the dark hall outside. As the room swarmed with dust and debris, a vortex had surrounded Aaron. Before the door slammed shut, Doric had caught a glimpse of Aaron dissolving into the vortex until it had swallowed him up. Aaron had vanished.

Shortly afterwards, the terrified boy had heard from Crogan for the last time. "Doric, I have failed you."

Doric was ten years old now, so much older than the seven he was when he was first brought here. Where most seven-year-old children experience fear as a normal rite of passage, Doric's fear was all too real. Where fear manifests itself in ordinary children as they explore the world around them or confront new realities, Doric was plunged into a nightmare worse than any night terror he could have imagined. The monster in another child's closet would quiver with fear from the evil he has had to face. He had no one to hold, no one to soothe him or to talk to him when he trembled or cried; Doric was truly alone. Where fear waxes and wanes in most children as they grow, Doric's instead intensified day after day. His fear made his heart pound so loud it beat out of his chest, especially each time the scary stranger, clad in dark leather, entered his dungeon.

Three days after he was brought to his prison, the stranger came to him for the first time. He was covered from head to foot in dark armor. He wasn't a Stragoy. Doric knew that much. The stranger did not reek of death. His grin was wicked as he strode into the chamber with an eerie confidence. The armed stranger hovered over Doric, squeezing the handle of his dagger tauntingly.

Doric watched him closely. Even though the stranger paled in size to Aaron, he was still threatening. What was even more unsettling than the intimidating appearance was that he seemed to be reveling in Doric's fear.

The visitor stared at Doric with callous eyes. Suddenly, and without provocation, he grabbed Doric's wrist forcefully, pulling his arm taut. He unsheathed the dagger with his other hand and sliced a gash in Doric's forearm from his elbow to just above the wrist. Doric screamed in pain. The man waited until blood began to seep out before he released him. He stood and walked out.

Behind the door, Doric thought he heard laughter. To Doric's horror, his wound did not mend.

Several weeks later, he was visited again by the same cruel stranger. This time, the stranger lingered by the door glaring at him before strolling into the chamber. Although Doric pleaded for mercy, his visitor drew his sword again, this time carving a mark on Doric's other arm from the tip of his shoulder across his bicep. He stood and watched Doric as blood oozed from his fresh wound.

"Look at you," he said coolly.

"What do you want with me?" Doric asked, pleading for compassion.

"It was only a matter of time," the visitor answered, tapping the palm of his hand with the dagger. "You have fooled all of them, but not me," he jeered.

The tapping seemed eerily familiar to Doric. It was rhythmic.

"How does it feel to be insignificant?"

"Why are you doing this? I've done nothing to you," Doric cried. Suddenly, he remembered this same rhythmic tapping from his past.

"Here, I have power. More importantly, I have you."

"Why are you doing this, Lorne?"

"Ah! I underestimated you, freak." The visitor removed his face shield. Lorne Maggis stood in front of him. His eyes had become even darker: sunken and expressionless below a flat, wide forehead. Lorne pressed the edge of his sword against Doric's neck, reveling in his anguish.

"Nobody is here to protect you." He chuckled sinisterly. "I have been ordered to watch you. Bad news for you, good for me."

He pulled the sword away.

"What's happened to you?" asked Doric. Tears streamed down his face.

"I've become part of something special." Lorne sheathed his sword and removed a dagger. "You're just like the others, a faceless ghost who serves only one purpose."

Lorne leaned in on Doric's chest and pressed Doric heavily against the wall with his elbow. Doric hacked and coughed. Lorne placed the blade on Doric's cheek, just under his left eye, and he sliced down to his chin.

"Let's see if that heals," he said while walking out of the room, closing the door behind him.

These visits and acts of violence became routine. Doric's body became Lorne's sculpture, pieces of him being carved away night after night. The more grotesque he became, the more Lorne reveled in his work. This continued for months, until one morning, Lorne returned with two Stragoy at his side.

"Good morning, Doric," he said mockingly. "It appears we have something in common."

Dawn eased into the room. The shadows on the faces of the Stragoy made them even more menacing.

"Do you believe in coincidences?" Lorne asked. "I didn't until today," he said with a sly smile. "I came across a slave that looked like someone I once knew. Would you like to meet him?" asked Lorne not expecting a response. He bobbed his head once quickly without taking his eyes off Doric. The Stragoy immediately raised Doric to his feet.

"I found my father," Lorne added as he turned pretending like he was about to walk away. He stopped, and with his back to Doric said, "Oh, and I found your father too."

Doric tensed and lunged reflexively at Lorne, but the Stragoy held him back. "Yet, in their own way," Lorne continued, "they're both already dead."

The frail boy was escorted from his prison chamber, up and then down several sets of dark passages. The blows of hammers on anvils grew louder. After a time, they arrived at a large room where rows of enslaved blacksmiths, kept alive simply because of their craft, worked tirelessly.

Doric took a quick glance at the Stragoy behind him. He recognized him. His skin had cracked and grayed in parts and the left side of the face had decomposed, but there was no mistaking him. It was Lorne's father. He shoved Doric forward forcefully.

"There," Lorne said, pointing towards a wretch sitting against the wall. "It's time you said hello."

Doric stepped forward. Sunken cheeks and hundreds of scars from Stragoy scourging littered his father's body. One of his eyes was glazed over in a muddy hue. It was fixed open. The other was closed.

"Father?" he said tearfully. "What have they done to you?" A sharp pain swelled in his chest.

Slowly and with effort, Seth opened his good eye and looked upon his son. He managed a smile. "Doric, my brave boy," he managed. His frail body shook. "I prayed for this moment, to look upon you once more."

Quietly, and with visible effort, Seth whispered, "Don't cry for me."

Doric took his father's hand.

"Don't lose hope," Seth managed. "There's a reason they brought you to me. Turn away…don't look back."

Doric turned and glared at Lorne. A strange feeling grew in his heart, something he had never felt before. The thought of begging for mercy quickly dissipated when he saw the grin on Lorne's face.

"Survive, Doric. Survive and do what you were born to do. Don't forget who you are."

"Take him," ordered Lorne.

"Wait!"

The Stragoy carried Seth to the side of the river of molten lava, and without regard or hesitation, tossed his frail body in.

"*No!*" Doric screamed. His cries echoed throughout the large room.

Once Seth's body touched the surface, it burst into flames. Without emitting a sound, his face turned up to the ceiling. His eyes slowly closed. Gradually and unhurriedly, with a kind of peacefulness that was absent in the large chamber, Seth's body, engulfed in flames, melted into the molten river and was gone.

Doric was crushed. When the coolness of the leather lash pulled tight around his neck, he paid it no attention. Lorne jerked the lash, driving Doric onto his back.

Then Lorne clutched a heavy mallet and stood above Doric, who lay sobbing on the cold surface. Lorne raised the hammer, and with both hands, brought it down with all his weight on Doric's knee.

On the day Seth died, another significant event was taking place in a remote region of Endura. In a cabin, nestled in the mountains and concealed by Eastvale Forest, on the banks of the Rhyne River, lived a man, his wife, their two children and the wife's mother. They had survived peacefully there for almost four years while unspeakable horrors took place a thousand feet below. The remote location had served them well, providing separation from the atrocities beyond their walls. The only winding path up the mountain to the cabin had been skillfully concealed by thick shrubs and branches. But the once fresh, crisp air in these parts had now turned rancid, as had the mood inside the old wooden home.

The warmth of the crackling fire gave a false sense of welcome and warmth, as the days here in comfort and safety were numbered. Inside, the family hurriedly prepared for an escape.

Yesterday, a gathering of Stragoy was spotted marching towards them just two days away. In the smallest bedroom of the cabin, a tiny human girl sat quietly beside an old woman's bed, gently holding on to her frail hand while the woman slept. The old woman had fallen sick a few months back. It began as a fever and then her breathing had become shallow and labored. A subtle wheeze accompanied each breath. She had steadily worsened until she had become bedridden a few weeks ago.

Although the girl remained naïvely hopeful, she was aware they would be leaving her grandmother behind; too frail to travel, her grandmother was knocking on death's door. The girl watched the steady rise of her grandmother's chest, wishing for her to draw her last breath and find eternal peace. The wish, so painful, was still better than having to live with the guilt of leaving her behind.

Up until now, her father had shielded her and her brother from the reality of death. Their father had brought his family here when the girl was just under a year old. Then Thackery, their prior town, north of the mountains, was destroyed by Stragoy just two years ago.

Old and frail, the old woman's body showed the effects of the sickness. What remained of a once great woman was a shrunken shell covered with loose, spotted skin.

Suddenly, the old woman opened her bloodshot eyes and turned her head, "I'm so glad you're here, my little sunshine," she whispered, forcing a smile.

A radiant smile spread across the young girl's face as she held her grandmother's hand tenderly.

"Are we alone?" asked the aged woman.

"Yes," replied the girl.

"Will you grant an old woman one last wish?" she asked. "And listen to what I am going to tell you, and promise me you'll obey?"

The young girl nodded. The old woman mumbled softly. She paused for a moment to gather strength before continuing.

"I've lived my entire life regretting my past and fearing the future so much that I have not taken the time to live in the present. I've been searching, you see, forever searching for completeness, something that would fill an emptiness I've always felt. I loved your grandfather dearly. He was a good man, but I have always felt something was absent.

"My little sunshine, the world has changed. Yet, in this horror there is still goodness. There's you, there's your family, and I'm sure there must be others out there hiding, like us. In that chaos there is hope and there is still love. Something out there is waiting for you…something beyond sorrow. In that chaos, someone is also searching for you. He just doesn't realize it yet." She coughed.

"Promise me that you will do whatever's necessary to be happy. Survive and find happiness. But I know that even if you don't find it, those around you will still profit. I am certain because of this." The woman raised her hand and tenderly placed it on the girl's chest. "Your heart." The girl took her grandmother's hand.

"Promise me that in that special little heart of yours you will seek out your own happiness. Do not be like most people who live half-lives, never knowing true unity and the potential of what could be. Find a love that few are fortunate to discover. It is the kind of love that will fulfill all your days. You must promise me you will never stop searching, no matter how horrible the world becomes. Stay alive and do not wait, as I did, for it to come to you. A treasure such as this must be sought."

Faint voices could be heard on the other side of the door.

The girl rose and was about to leave and call her mother, but the woman squeezed her hand surprisingly tightly.

"I pity those who brush past each other, exchange a glance, and choose to ignore something special," the old woman continued. "Sometimes that's all it takes to pass up a chance at true happiness." The woman stopped speaking and took in a few deep and pained breaths.

"There is something I have to give to you," she said, motioning with her eyes, too weak to move her head. She was directing her granddaughter towards a tiny wooden box that lay on a table by the door.

The girl removed a gold necklace from the box. Hanging from the gold chain was a small brass ring with a pear-shaped, violet object that resembled a tiny tear. Holding the chain and pendant, she returned to her grandmother's side.

"That was my mother's and her mother's before her. It has been passed down for more years than I can remember."

The old woman spoke softly, taking frequent breaths.

"It was given to a young woman long ago. She was told to use the ring and to pass it down when it no longer served its purpose. It is said it shall one day find its way onto the hand of he that is betrothed from birth to the owner of this ring. The union forged shall be beyond anything that human, Ruid, or Samjees could destroy. It has not served me, nor any before me."

A smile crossed her lips. "For me, it was your entrance into this world that completed my existence."

Just then, the bedroom door opened, and a young boy entered the room. He was slightly older than the girl. The girl's father and mother walked in behind him.

"What's that?" the boy asked, grabbing the ring from his sister's hand.

"It's all right," the old woman whispered to the girl when she moved to stop him. "He will return it shortly."

As soon as the boy touched the ring, it began to glow in the palm of his hand. It burned his flesh, and he dropped it, wincing in pain. His father, curious, examined it and placed it in his palm. He too winced and dropped the ring to the floor.

"This ring can have only one owner," the old woman whispered. She raised her head from the pillow, trembling with the effort and looked directly into the girl's eyes. "Find him!" she managed.

"How will I know?" the girl asked.

"Don't you fret, my little sunshine, when the time comes, you'll know."

The old woman rested her head again on her pillow. Her eyelids fluttered, and her hand tightened around the girl's hand. The girl sat with her grandmother and did not leave her side. A few hours later, the old woman's grip slackened, and she passed away peacefully.

The next morning, the young family left their haven of four years in search of another: a secret place called the Den.

7

WORLDS APART

UNSPEAKABLE THINGS HAPPENING within Hellas Mons had become commonplace. For Doric, life was reduced to existing for the amusement of Lorne Maggis. Unrelenting torture, abuse and the deplorable conditions of his chamber had taken their toll.

Lorne continued to visit without routine, slicing a part of Doric each time until no part remained untouched. As the weeks went by, Lorne's visits began to decrease in frequency. Sometimes he would disappear for months. Doric, on the other hand, slipped further into hopelessness.

One evening, a year after his father's death, Doric received a new visitor. Doric sat in the corner of the chamber, sobbing into the darkness as he did every night. A scraping sound came from the wall above. After a lengthy pause, something scurried directly in front of him. Doric could hear heavy breathing. A moment later, he heard a tapping sound on the wall. In the glow of the moon against the wall, he saw the shadow of a creature, small and humanoid, crawl up the wall like a spider and climb out of his chamber. *I must be dreaming*, Doric thought. That night he barely slept.

When Doric awoke at the first sign of light, he found a small piece of stale bread by his feet. It was just the right size for him to put it entirely in his mouth. Bread reminded him of normalcy; of home. He ate it without hesitation. His teeth were weak, and his gums were rotting, but it was the most delightful thing he had ever tasted.

His visitor returned the next night. In the morning, he awoke to find two small, similar-sized pieces of bread. It happened several nights in a row, and Doric welcomed the offerings.

After a week, Doric wanted to express his gratitude. The next night, when the scurrying started, Doric whispered. "Hello?" There was no response.

He tried several more times. Again, the next morning, Doric ate the offerings.

As the weeks passed, Doric's spirits improved. He began to associate the tapping sounds in the dark with comfort. For the first time in four years he didn't feel alone. To his relief, he had not seen Lorne for months. His wounds no longer bled.

One especially dismal night, when the wind raged outside the opening in the ceiling of his cell, and rain streamed in to puddle on the ground, he heard a strange voice in the dark.

"Hello, Doric." It startled him. It was a strange voice, like a man's voice with child-like undertones. He had not heard the visitor enter.

"Who's there?"

Again, there was no response. Instead, he heard the pitter-patter of something moving about in the dark. A cold, solid object touched his exposed calf. Doric reached for it and found a smooth, mostly oval shaped, fist sized stone on the ground. As soon as he touched it, the stone started to glow and the chamber lit up.

A small, odd looking creature, stood by Doric's feet. Doric shrieked. The creature recoiled and brought its hands up to his eyes. Doric dropped the stone.

Seconds passed. Once Doric realized his screams held no purpose, he reached for the stone, and light filled the room again. The odd little creature was gone.

"Hello?" said Doric. "I'm sorry I frightened you. Please come back. Thank you for the food."

There was only silence.

"Who are you?"

Seconds passed, and then he heard that strange voice again. "Oren."

Doric looked up to where the voice had come from. The creature was crawling up the wall on all fours.

"Please don't shine the light at me; it hurts my eyes."

Doric placed the stone on the ground. He tried touching it with just one finger. When the stone radiated again, it wasn't as bright.

The creature made his way down to the floor, shielding his eyes with his hand. He was a wiry-looking humanoid being, slimy and bald, almost skeletal, with skin a shade of pale green. His mouth was wide with a full set of omnivorous teeth and slight fangs. His nose, cat-like and keen, moved when he spoke.

"My name is, Oren," he repeated. "I'm at your service."

He stood three feet tall. He was sopping wet, wearing a tattered pair of pants, which came down below the knees and a ragged shirt. Around his waist was a makeshift belt made of a hemp-type material. He had it wrapped around a couple of times and knotted on one side. Tied onto it, was a sling.

Oren licked his lips with a long, slimy tongue. It appeared to be a nervous habit because he licked them often. He reached down with long, thin arms and dropped two small pieces of dried meat in Doric's lap.

"I see that still works," he said.

The look of astonishment was still on Doric's face. "What works?"

"Stone from the King's tomb in a huntsman's hand shall illuminate the way. Seems you managed to retain some of your gifts."

"How do you know about that?"

Oren had watched Doric for some time—years in fact. He knew Doric's disfigurements well; the scars were all over his frail body. His hair once thick, golden and lush was filthy, thin and unkempt. On his cheeks, among the many scars, were lines from steady tears. He could no longer walk; one leg was broken and bent permanently in an unnatural position.

How much pain have you endured? Oren thought.

On Doric's hands was an exceptionally large digit, the one part of Doric's ravaged body that appeared to not only have been unaffected but also to have improved.

"There is much I know, young Doric. You see? I even know your name. I thought you could use some company," the creature said, sitting down cross-legged. After a moment, he added, "Well, maybe that's not entirely true. Maybe it is I who needs company."

Doric smiled, "Welcome, I think." Something about Oren was safe and comforting. Doric had not had a normal conversation in years so he welcomed it.

"What a fine pair we make," said Oren, then squealed and snorted.

Doric spoke and spoke some more. A switch had been turned on, as he made up for years of solitude. Oren listened. The dialogue almost always reverted to Lorne's inevitable return and how afraid Doric was of him.

"I'm immune to the scars and the cuts. It's the hours of cutting and slicing of another kind, the taunting that hurts more."

Oren reassured Doric that Lorne would not be returning anytime soon.

"How do you know this?"

"Stealth is one of my many talents," answered Oren and then licked his lips. "I know he's been sent far away."

"Are there more like you?" Doric asked.

Oren bowed. "Just me…the one and only."

Doric had long since extinguished the light. They spoke for hours in darkness, and then just before dawn, Oren stood to leave. His right hand, however, was stuck to the ground. He snickered.

"When I am excited or nervous, my palms sweat." He looked down and tugged at his right foot. It, too, was fixed to the ground. "So do my feet. It's a nuisance yes, but it has its uses." He tugged his hand free.

Oren reached into his pockets and pulled a small piece of bread from each one and placed them on Doric's lap. Then he tugged first one foot and then the other from the ground and hopped towards the wall as if walking on hot coals. He leapt, sticking to the surface on all fours.

"See?"

He climbed up the wall and disappeared. For the first time in over four years, Doric's sleep was deep and free of nightmares.

Months passed. Doric became dependent on the company of his new friend. No topics were taboo. Doric reminisced about Brackens Town, about how he missed his father. He told Oren of Tana and how thoughts of her reminded him of warmth.

One night, Oren's demeanor changed.

"He is coming, Doric."

With a look of dread, Doric's face drained of color. His breathing quickened. "You have to help me, Oren," he pleaded.

"I'm so sorry, my boy. I cannot interfere. You have to trust me. One day, you'll understand."

"Please, get me out of here!" pleaded Doric, but Oren quickly scaled the wall, climbed out the opening and was gone.

Footsteps approached from outside. The door opened. Lorne stood in the doorway. The light from the torch behind him cast an eerie shadow on his face, exaggerating his nose and giving him a vile, snake-like appearance. Lorne crossed the threshold into the moonlight. He held a dagger in his right hand. With vacant eyes he asked, "Did you miss me?" and sneered.

Doric sobbed in anticipation of what was about to come.

Oren returned next evening. He found Doric with blood seeping from a gruesome cut on his upper chest. Doric didn't acknowledge Oren at all. He remained catatonic in the dark, ignoring the huntsman's stone that lay by his side. Oren gently laid his hand on Doric's wound. The thick substance oozing from his palm, soothed, but Doric stayed disengaged. They sat silent in the darkness.

"I'm ready," Doric said, breaking the silence. "I can't do what my father asked. I exist for a sick man's amusement." Tears streamed down his face. "Please, can you help me end this suffering?"

Oren knelt beside Doric.

"Of course, I can help you. But not in the way you want. I can teach you things, about the past, about who you are and to open your eyes to the truth. I can prepare you for what is to come, but only if you let me."

Doric stared blankly ahead. "There isn't anything to come. This is it," managed Doric.

"You are wrong. After all," Oren added, "it could be much worse. You could be like me."

Oren licked his lips and exhaled slowly. "I have lived a long time. If I told you just how long, you wouldn't believe me. My existence has been that of a wretched outcast. I have been forced to live in caves away from the living. I have been terrorized and beaten by humans and Ruids. I have watched life happen from a distance and outlived those I loved. And so, I do understand your pain. All seems hopeless now, but I promise, someday, it will get better.

"I must go get something important that will help shed light on things. No, it's not another of those stones," he said snickering and pointing to the huntsman's stone. "It's time you learn a little about the past."

Oren knelt in front of Doric. "Everything will be a little clearer when I get back. Promise you will wait for me."

The friendly creature took hold of the stone and placed it in Doric's hand. Light bathed the room, but Doric continued staring directly ahead, expressionless. Ignoring the stinging in his eyes from the fierce light, Oren clasped the boy's wrists and squeezed them tightly.

"Look at me," Oren ordered. His voice turned stern.

Doric's eyes focused in on Oren.

"Promise me."

There was a long pause, but eventually, Doric nodded. Oren sprung to the wall and in an instant, was gone.

Oren returned the next night. He heaved a weighted sack and dropped it down into the chamber.

"So?" Doric asked.

"You remind me of someone I once knew," started Oren. "I think you'll find his story intriguing. Like you, he was ten years old when I first met him. I wasn't always like this. I was handsome once—at least, I thought so. I suppose I'm a victim of circumstance, but that's for another time. Turns out this boy was deeply tormented. He was not imprisoned by physical walls like you, but he was a prisoner nonetheless.

"It all started on his tenth birthday when he said he heard a voice in his head, a garbled whisper, sharp and piercing."

"Like Crogan?" asked Doric.

"Not like that. It was as if it was whimpering. The voice came sporadically at first, sometimes weeks apart. He said he could never make out what it was saying. It was muffled, as if a hand had been placed over the mouth. After a couple of months, the single voice turned to two, then three and so on, until in less than six months, the hundreds of voices in his head competed for his attention. The garbled mass of voices became a steady hiss, causing him intense pain. The boy's eyes became bloodshot, his face swollen, and the intense pain made him howl. Many, except for his friends, thought he had gone mad."

"Were you a friend?"

"A good friend, yes, but not his closest," answered Oren. "There were seven. Eight with me. I was the only outsider. They were friends long before I entered their circle.

"Then one night, months after the voices began, the boy fell into a deep sleep. He slept for four days. His eyes were closed, but clearly a battle raged in his mind. He'd grind his teeth and moan, sweat profusely, and on occasion, jerk violently. We'd take turns, his friends and I, sitting by his bed, watching him and protecting him from himself. I must admit…I thought he was going to die."

Doric listened unwaveringly. He was intrigued. Occasionally, he would look up into the sky, willing the night to linger so Oren would stay. *Several hours still to go before sunrise. Good.*

"On the evening of the fourth day, the boy awoke suddenly. He startled all of us when he blurted out, 'I've got to go to the Linhar,' in a slurred voice. 'There's something waiting for me in the sand.'

"It was a crazy request. Now, we all thought he really had gone mad. I can't explain why we agreed to it, just that we did. As soon as we agreed, miraculously, he began to feel better." Oren licked his lips.

"The next dawn, this resilient boy, and the eight of us, set out on a quest to answer the calling. We had heard of the Linhar Desert; it was one of the most inhospitable places on Endura. Had we known what lay ahead for us, we probably still would have gone. Foolish child courage, I guess.

"On the seventh day, tired and lost in the midst of a golden sea of sand—beautiful but deadly—we stumbled upon a violent desert storm—a strihali. The wind drowned out the world. That's how it seemed. Huge fists of dust reached out from the thick, giant curtain of sand. We were picked up and swept away. We became separated."

He paused.

"I never saw five of them again," said Oren with down-cast eyes.

"What happened?"

"Only Lucius and Edric survived."

"And you," Doric interjected.

"Yes, me and the boy. We four play a part in my tale. As for the others," Oren's small, rounded shoulders drooped. "I hope whatever happened to them or wherever they may be, Samjees watched over them."

"What happened to you?"

Oren shuddered. "I woke up on a sand dune looking like this: hideous and alone. I had no idea why the transformation had taken place or what I was supposed to do."

Oren reached into the sack he had brought and removed a large book almost as big as his torso.

"*Cerulean Book of Scribes?*" Doric exclaimed.

"That's right," Oren said.

It looked different. The corners were charred and some of the pages blackened. The heptagon on the cover with seven metal shapes resembling tears was gone. Three small holes in a triangular shape, likely used to secure the emblems, remained.

"I found it under the rubble of what remains of your home. Brackens Town is a mere shadow of itself. I'm so sorry." Oren sighed.

"This book is written in his hand. The resilient boy I spoke of was Zoren Ro."

"King Zoren?" Doric said, intrigued.

Oren placed his hand on the book and tapped the cover. "In here, Zoren describes how, when he was separated from his friends in the desert, he was tormented for days by a giant beast that moved beneath the desert sand: a kind of serpent with arms, he said. Zoren believes the beast did not intend to hurt him but instead guided him towards a metal object that sat waiting for him on the sand. After he found the metal object, Zoren said the beast disappeared beneath the surface and did not return.

"Zoren described the object as a big, capsule-shaped box crafted out of metal. It was smooth to the touch, surprisingly cool in the desert sun and long enough for a man to fit inside. It was a wonder unlike anything Zoren had ever seen. Even with all of his strength, Zoren could not budge the object. He found a small hollow at one end that he grabbed for leverage. At that point, Zoren claimed the object bit him. Almost immediately, he wrote, the object began to hum as if it had woken up from a long sleep. Frustrated, Zoren left the object in the sand, hoping to return with others to help him move it. Zoren would never again set eyes on that object.

"A year later, Zoren met up with two of his friends, Lucius and Edric. They too had each encountered their own life-changing experience on this journey."

"What about the headaches?" asked Doric.

"Gone. And so, too, were the voices in his head."

"And you?"

"I could no longer walk among my kind. I was cursed with an exceptionally long life of solitude.

"There is not much in the book about Zoren for another twenty-two years, the quiet years after the discovery of the object in the Linhar. Zoren's story picks back up when he arrives in Nahire. But I think that's enough for tonight."

Oren bid him farewell. He left more food, took the book with him and departed.

Oren returned the next night to resume his story.

"On the banks of the Lassit River, the Portal stood as it had since before all recorded time. It was a natural wonder."

"Portal?"

"It is the most magical of the gods' creations, a gateway made of three large, rectangular-shaped stones, two vertical and one imposing slab resting on top. It stood twelve feet tall. Staring into the large opening would reveal a deep, black pool. If you placed your hand into the blackness, it would pass unscathed to the other side, making it look as though someone was extending a hand out of a black, still pool of water. It is written the Portal was placed there in ancient times to serve as the gateway to the gods.

"Two years after Zoren and his surviving friends returned from the Linhar, word spread of a prophecy claiming that a man would enter the Portal, retrieve the Eilasor and emerge a King."

"What is an Eilasor?" asked Doric.

Oren found the page he was looking for. "The year that has become known as AZ 32."

"Why do you say AZ before the year?"

"The day of Zoren Ro's year of birth became the day of reckoning, and all references to AZ mean 'After Zoren,'" answered Oren.

"This ancient book describes the finding of the Guardian, the Blue Crystal." Oren flipped through the book.

He found the page and read Zoren's own words.

I stepped into the Portal, and I emerged from a narrow tunnel, dark and seemingly endless, into a small clearing enclosed by steep, slate walls. Here, the mountains merged to form a quiet space. But there wasn't anything ordinary about this place. The walls had not an edge or crack, ledge or bulge on their surface. They climbed to great heights, converging at their crest. Beyond the crest was sky filled with orange, red, and yellow colors, a bright fiery flame, resembling an auburn cloud.

The ground was flat and smooth, absent of any blemish or footprint. Directly ahead of me, flowing down the wall and spanning its width, was a thin sheet of water. It started, not from a crack or fissure, but appeared to come from nowhere. It flowed into an invisible crack between the sand and the wall. The water against the dark slate created a natural mirror. From where I stood, my reflection was one of absolute clarity. Upon a stone pedestal directly in front of me, as smooth as the walls were tall, sat a shallow silver basin. I felt compelled to remove my shoes out of respect for the sanctity and wonder of this place.

The basin was dry and dull. It was then I heard a voice. The sheet of water cleared, and a child stared back at me.

"Hello," he said in a soft voice.

I was both astonished and afraid.

"Don't be afraid," said the child, reassuring me.

He looked familiar. I wanted to approach the image, but almost reading my mind, he said, "Do not come any closer," and snickered with his hand over his mouth.

Suddenly, I recognized the child. It was me when I was four years old.

"What is this place?" I asked.

There was laughter. "It's a place of dreams," and more laughter, then "a place of hope and of wonder."

"Are you a god?" I heard myself say.

The child giggled.

"No, not gods. We're guardians."

"Of what?" I asked.

"Why, of misery of course. Oh, and despair, wretchedness and malice too." He paused and looked at me as if I should know these things.

"Evil!" he blurted out with a blank expression, then paused in thought.

"I'm supposed to tell you of the gift we are going to give you," he said.

"My name is Bree, agent of beneficence." He put his hands up to his eyes and pressed against them.

"To protect you from the evil of insatiable desire or discontent towards another, and to protect all from the malicious desire to

deprive men of theirs, I give you my eyes," said the child. When he removed his hands, his eyes were sewn shut.

As disturbing as this was, a single tear rolled down my face. It pooled at my chin and then dropped into the basin. But it wasn't a tear that struck the surface of the bowl. It was a stone shaped in the form of a tear that clanged and rolled in the basin.

The mirror clouded over, then cleared to reveal a second image of an older boy.

"Hello, Zoren," said the reflection. "I am Evaris, agent of contentment."

I recognized him too. It was me when I was about thirteen years old.

My younger self placed his hands behind his back.

"To protect you from violence and trickery inspired by greed, and the insatiable want for power, I give you my hands." He exposed his arms, stumps severed below the elbows remained.

Another tear rolled down my face. When it fell, it, too, turned into a second tear-shaped stone, which rolled to the basin. Again, the sheet of water clouded. When it cleared, I was staring at a third image of myself.

"I'm Orgo, agent of humility." The third apparition stooped over. Large stone slabs were strapped onto his back. His legs strained and nearly buckled under the weight. With a grimace, he said, "To protect you from jealousy and the perverted love of self that drives hatred and contempt of others, I'll carry this burden for you, so you will have the strength to resist."

A tear fell and turned to stone.

A fourth, slightly older, version of myself appeared next.

"I'm Ira, agent of restraint. To protect you from evil wrought from hate and violent impulses," he paused. Behind him a wall of fire appeared. He turned and walked towards it. Before stepping into

it, he said, "I give you my body to purge you of these impulses." The flames swallowed him whole.

Another tear fell, turning to stone.

A fifth, even older, image of myself appeared next. He was wearing a long cloak. "I'm Groll, agent of compassion." He covered his face with both hands. When he pulled them away, a grotesque face minus eyes and nose stared back. Only the mouth moved.

"To protect from the desire of the wicked to inflict harm and suffering from spite or deeply rooted evil, I give you my identity." He placed a hood over his head, shrouding his featureless face in shadow.

Still another tear fell. It, too, turned to stone.

The sheet of water, like a glass, frosted over, and when it cleared, a sixth, middle-aged apparition of myself appeared.

"I am Thia, agent of reverence. To protect from intense feelings of animosity and hostility—hate in all its manifestations—I give you my heart." He exposed his chest, and with his right arm, extracted his heart, held it for a moment and hurled it towards me. The organ turned to water, splashing against my face and into the basin. When the water struck the basin, it turned to more of those small tear-shaped stones.

Another stone tear fell into the basin.

A seventh and final apparition appeared. This one was of a very old man. Although decrepit and frail, he had vigor in his eyes.

"I am Samjees, the supreme god. Do not be afraid," he said.

I was beside myself with profound reverence. Gripping the basin, a tear for each I had shed before fell into the basin.

"What's happening to me?" I asked.

The basin began to vibrate, and the air grew thick. I could not breathe. Stones began to rise out of the basin. They arranged themselves, coming together like a puzzle to form a larger stone. Suddenly, a roaring boom exploded from the sky and lightning struck the side of the mountain, cascading down the slate wall. Large sections of the cave wall broke off, changing shape as they fell. A large crack appeared, spanning the entire height of the wall. It broke free and began to fall. It resembled a massive spire. Before it struck the surface, it contracted and turned to a palm-sized stone. It struck the basin, bounced off the surface and fell near the entrance.

Lightning struck the mass of tiny tear-shaped stones hovering above the basin. A great force knocked me off my feet. I was driven back and landed on top of the rock near the entrance. The fire in the sky was sucked into a vortex, taking with it the magical stone that hovered above the basin. After a time, a pungent smoke dissipated into the sky. The sheet of water, along with the image, disappeared. Through the dissolving smoke, I saw a crystal, radiating a cobalt blue, hovering above the remains of the basin. I grasped it in my hand. It was warm and smooth to the touch. My life appeared before my eyes. I witnessed virtue and righteousness and was completely overtaken with incredible comfort and peace.

I heard Samjees' voice again, but I could no longer see him.

"Behold the Eilasor," said the stately voice. "Bound are you to he who will heed temptation. As long as the Eilasor endures, jealousy, greed, selfishness, malice, wrath and hatred will remain confined to darkness. It has the power to destroy and restore life. Take it, our sacrifice for you and all your brothers and sisters. Go now, build me a great city, and rule over it in peace."

When I turned to leave, I heard his voice for the final time.

"Zoren, that rock at your feet, it is from the realm of the gods. Keep it safe, as you will the crystal. Trust in it when all else fails in the face of the purest evil. It shall be a beacon of hope and serve to that end when all else fails."

I took the stone in my hands and committed my life to protecting it.

Oren stopped reading and looked up at Doric. Even with Doric's permanent facial disfigurements, the boy's eyes appeared bright and animated and expressed just how enthralled he was with the story.

Oren reached into his pocket, and he removed a perfectly symmetrical stone.

"Zoren gave this to me years later. He told me one day I would find use for it. Magnificent isn't it? It was forged by the gods."

"That's the actual stone?"

It was charcoal colored, unusually smooth and covered with bright specks. Doric was overcome by a visceral sensation of looking into the sky on a clear night: boundless and full of wonder. He sensed an incredible power trapped within it.

Doric reached for it, but before his fingers could touch it, Oren jerked the stone away.

"No human other than Zoren is to touch this sacred stone," Oren said, and he returned it to his pocket.

"When Zoren emerged from the Portal," Oren continued, "the Portal shattered and crumbled to dust. Zoren fulfilled the prophecy and assumed his place as the first true ruler of Endura, beginning the Reign of the Kings. It was a reign that saw the finest years Endura had ever seen. For over seven hundred years, the city known as Nahire prospered."

Oren stopped telling his tale as the first sign of light became visible in the sky. Before he departed, he left some bread.

Oren returned as promised and resumed the story where he had left off.

"A couple of years before the finding of the Eilasor, a stranger had arrived in Nahire. A human who spoke a new language and possessed exceptional creativity and wisdom. He had an uncanny resemblance to King Zoren. In fact, at first sight, many took him to be Zoren's brother.

"This man shared much of what he knew with both humans and Ruids. What he preached, humans and Ruids absorbed. The races found it increasingly difficult to quench their hunger for his knowledge, and he reveled in the attention and glory his reputation garnered. His name was Adam Hades."

Doric searched his memory, but he did not recall hearing that name before.

"Adam appeared to have no past and refrained from speaking of it. It was Adam who coined Endura. In fact, we owe the language you speak, read and write to him.

"Not long before Zoren had walked through the Portal, Adam, too, had sought to change his own destiny by entering it. Unfortunately for Adam, he emerged the Portal empty handed. I think the disappointment of not finding the spear, changed him. As it turned out, Nahire proved too small for both Adam and Zoren. Adam wanted the crown and its power, but Zoren stood in his way. As time passed, Adam became dark and deceitful. People began to fear him. I knew there was something different about Adam," Oren said. "It was not his wisdom that set him apart; it was something deeper. It was his heart, cold and callous. Adam displayed, in one way or another, all the elements of jealousy, greed, selfishness, malice, wrath and hatred. He was so unlike Ruids; so unlike other humans for that matter.

"It all came to a head one night in the Garden of Usea. Adam put his and Zoren's fate into his own hands, and he ambushed Zoren. It was the first real battle for supremacy over Endura. In the end, Zoren prevailed. Adam lay dying at the base of the only matchra tree that grew in the garden. His blood seeped onto its roots and into the ground. As his breathing slowed and his life ebbed, so did what remained of his humanity. His features darkened grotesquely and transformed. He shrieked a most hateful cry and cursed Zoren.

"What happened next," Oren said, "haunted Zoren the rest of his days. Forces of evil were not prepared to let Adam die. From the shadows, dark, featureless shapes emerged moaning gruesome, pained cries. A number of them, too many to count, swarmed Adam and dragged his dying body into the shadows. There, his spirit has endured, trapped in some deep chasm away from light. For more than two thousand years he's been imprisoned in the darkness, and from the darkness he's been seeping his malice into our world."

There was a long pause. Doric stared at Oren through bloodshot eyes. His expression was fixed. He could not change it because of the scarring that covered his face.

"So, you see, Doric, ten-year-old Zoren, imprisoned in his own way, found his destiny, as will you. Your father is gone, but you are not alone, though you may feel you are. As Zoren faced evil and triumphed, so too shall you. There are far greater forces alive on Endura than you could possibly imagine. They are not all evil. You only need to know where to look and who to trust."

Doric was enthralled. Still, there were so many questions. "What happened to Zoren and the Eilasor?"

"Zoren disappeared not long after he drove Adam into the darkness."

Oren flipped to the last page in the book. He recited the last few words from memory. "It has begun. The world has changed. I am afraid of what is to come and fear more that I will bear witness to it all. There is a heavy weight on my heart. I am no longer the man the gods expect me to be. People pass me in the streets and turn away. I am changing...It ends there. He was never seen again."

"Doesn't that go against what you just told me?"

"What do you mean?"

"You said Zoren prevailed, but then you said he disappeared, never to be seen again."

"Perhaps, but he did prevail and we can't presume he's dead. Faith must always accompany hope," replied Oren.

"The last thing Zoren did before he vanished was give his crown and vision of Nahire to a trusted friend, Edric. It was Edric and his descendants that fulfilled Zoren's vision.

"Now, about Lucius. After the quest into the Linhar, he acquired a strange power. He came to be called Ishtan Mar, the Ruid word for a person who wields the power of magic. He was the first and most powerful Manian, with power infused by the gods. There was no other explanation for his abilities.

"Lucius built a monument on the east side of Nahire. The inspiring tribute emitted a sense of mystery and power. It was a narrow, four-sided, tapering obelisk structure that pierced the sky as high as Zoren's statues of the Kings. The structure had an impervious mirror-like surface, and inside, Zoren had placed the Eilasor. At night, the entire structure radiated a blue light; its brilliance visible from everywhere in Nahire. He made it so only the true king could penetrate the impervious wall with his hand to touch this marvel.

"Later, after Zoren disappeared, none of Nahire's Kings ever laid eyes on it or felt the cool touch of the Eilasor. In the tower it remained for centuries."

"So, why has this happened?" asked Doric. "Why has Samjees let this happen to us even after giving us the Eilasor?"

"I believe Samjees saw it coming; a world where the natural

resistance of Ruid and men alone would not serve to keep darkness in the shadow—"

"What does that even mean, Oren?"

"Doric. Think about this for a moment. Things in nature exist in a kind of balance. I'm sure you have heard this all before. One cannot exist without the other. For example, where there is dark, there is light and so on.

"One thing has swayed far from balance. We owe this to the righteousness of our ancestors. They knew not of jealousy, greed, selfishness, malice, wrath or hatred. Ancient firstlings and humans were wired to resist temptation. In fact, their fortitude helped them avoid it entirely. What I am speaking of is evil. The contrast between good and evil has swayed so far from the center that evil has grown powerful. It's become a malevolent force, more powerful than you could ever imagine.

"Back to Adam Hades. The gods knew his was a fragile will, and if tested, would fail. Hades was not equipped to resist the lure of temptation: a calling from the darkness. It was too great a power yearning to be set free. Hades' very existence threatened nature's balance. The Eilasor served as the guardian—consider it the lock that would keep Hades' spirit and his wicked intentions enslaved in darkness. The question was not if, but when, he would succumb to this, and as we now know, he gave in to it entirely. The tower, home of the crystal, was simply a symbol. It gave citizens a sense of security. As long as the crystal endured, Endura was safe."

"I don't understand, Oren. If the gods are protecting us, what changed? Why is Aaron alive, and why are all these bad things happening?"

"Evil has found another way to reach out into our world. I believe it is linked to the matchra growing in this mountain. After all, the origin of this old, cursed tree is mired in treachery and hatred. If you recall, a limb from the tree that grew in the Garden of Usea, the same tree Hades bled upon and took his last breath in this world, is the same tree that grows in this mountain. It's the foundation of all matchra trees, or Trees of Life, as they're called. They're assumed to have magical healing properties. Instead, I believe our people have been deceived. They've been poisoned slowly. Instead of healing, it has chipped away their wills and weakened their fortitude until all that is left is a shell of their former selves, vessels for evil, the living dead, the Stragoy that dwell in this mountain. Have you ever wondered why towns and villages are built around regions where these trees grow? Coincidence? No. Found another way, it has."

Oren looked up and saw the early signs of dawn wash into the sky.

"Almost time, my young friend. One last thing before I leave tonight. The Eilasor's power has depleted. It has maintained some of its potency, but it no longer serves as the Guardian, or Azura, in the Ruid tongue. Don't ask me how I know, but it is no longer in its crystal form. Yet, Hades remains in the shadow. Something else is therefore acting as the Azura."

"What do you think that is?"

Oren shrugged. "I have to believe the Azura, is somewhere out there as prophesied."

"Oh, I thought of another question. What is Aaron's part in all of this?"

"He is the manifestation of Hades' power, his voice…but there is more to this; it has something to do with the events surrounding Aaron's birth in our world. We will discuss this tomorrow."

Oren stood to leave. Dawn's light began to enter the room, and along with it, a strange-looking winged creature. It flew in and hovered above Doric. It had a chestnut head and crown with a green stripe across its breast.

"Skifter!" said Oren excitedly.

Doric looked into its eyes as they changed into a variety of colors.

When they turned black, they remained that way. It flew left, then right, and in an instant, was gone.

"It is a harbinger of change. Prepare yourself, Doric. Change is coming."

"What kind of change?"

"Don't know. Only privileged souls have ever laid eyes on a skifter. Creatures of legend they are. It is said they forewarn of changes but only to the charmed souls protected by the gods."

"Don't you see, Doric? The gods are looking out for you. No matter how forsaken you feel, you will never be alone."

"Great," said Doric, a despondent look on his face. "You call this charmed?"

"If this is what the gods have destined for you, so be it."

"Why won't Aaron just kill me?"

"He needs you."

"I don't understand."

"He still believes you can communicate with Crogan. He is looking to learn the Den's whereabouts and believes you can help him find it."

Doric considered this for a moment. "First, I don't know or have any way of knowing where it is, and second, why then hasn't Lorne asked me, not even once, where it is?"

Oren stood with a grunt. "I must leave now. Dawn approaches."

"Wait. Why has Lorne not asked me?"

"You already know why." With that, Oren left bread and dried meat, climbed out of the cave and was gone.

Doric thought only for a moment. *He does not care. His allegiance is to himself and the pleasure he is getting from the pain he has been inflicting on me. If Lorne learns the truth, there would no longer be a need to keep me alive. He could get this satisfaction from anyone, but I am the symbol of his oppression from a past life.*

The next day Doric's spirits were high. He took out the tattered cloth from Tana's dress and held it to his cheek. It was darker now, almost black and stained many times over with his blood.

Several hours later, and quite unexpectedly, heavy footsteps came down the corridor and stopped outside the iron door. Doric's heart began to beat rapidly. The heavy latch turned. As the door creaked wider, light from torches in the corridor spilled into the chamber along with an offensive stench. Aaron stood in the threshold. His eyes scorched Doric, forcing him to look away.

Aaron marched over to Doric, grabbed him by the neck and lifted him until his feet dangled.

"All these years," Aaron said. His voice was a sharp whisper. "You've given me nothing." Aaron examined every inch of the boy. He traced his grotesque scars with his fiery eyes. "It seems this torture isn't working. Perhaps a new approach?"

Suddenly, something caught Aaron's eye. He released the boy abruptly. He stooped and picked up an opaque black stone from the floor and examined it closely. Aaron reached for Doric's hand, and he placed the stone in it. The room lit up instantly. Aaron wailed, snatched it from the boy's hand and hurled it against the wall.

"Where did you get this?" he shrieked.

"I…I found it," Doric whispered, pointing to the floor. "It must have fallen from above."

"You know better than to lie to me."

Aaron examined the wall. Remnants of small feet and handprints were visible all over it. Some appeared fresh.

"So, you've been here. I underestimated you," Aaron screeched.

Aaron moved toward the door. It swung open. He looked back and glared at Doric. His eyes blazed. He stood there for what seemed an eternity. Two Stragoy that Aaron had summoned telepathically charged into the room and rushed towards Doric. They picked him up from under his arms. Doric moaned. He hadn't stood in a long time. All his weight, the little there was, was pretty much supported by the Stragoy.

The Stragoy stood upright, vacant, like drones awaiting orders, when another set of footsteps from the corridor grew louder. Lorne burst into the room, panting. He looked slightly uncomfortable and not his usual confident self when he saw Aaron.

"When the creature returns, kill him," Aaron said, ignoring Lorne. "As for this filth, get him out of here."

Doric was escorted through the tunnels in the labyrinth of Hellas Mons for hours until they came to a chamber high up on the mountain. This room had a low ceiling and a large opening on the side, but it was inaccessible from the valley below. A heavy chain collar was placed around his neck.

When the door closed behind him, and he was alone again, he crawled to the gap in the wall. The chain stopped him just a few feet from the edge. At this altitude, the wind was cold and blew more fiercely. Above him, the black cloud of smoke was even thicker. Below was a forest of dead, leafless trees with dried branches and evergreens.

Doric couldn't believe it was possible, but it was. His new home was even more isolated than the hole they had moved him from. Nearing twelve years of age, young Doric began another descent deeper into obscurity. Days turned to months, and months turned to years. Doric was not heard from again for another sixteen years.

8

A CHANCE ENCOUNTER

THE PULSE OF time swept through Endura. Eight years had passed since Finch—the man with the eye-patch—had come across the linen and the abandoned child in Natras Pass. Doric, now eighteen years of age, had been imprisoned in Hellas Mons for eleven years, the last six in seclusion. The Portal had been sitting quiescently in the subterranean city of Navalline for eight years: many had walked through, but none had emerged with the Manian's spear. Survivors continued to remain hopeful of the coming of the Azura, but faith was beginning to wane. In the Den, the number of people seeking refuge had grown to a number in the thousands. Above, the surface had become desolate and devoid of people of both races. Animals roamed, animals and maledhens, Aaron's spies: black bird-like creatures slightly larger than crows that scour the land searching tirelessly for those living and in hiding.

In an ancient forest in the northern part of Thackery—a city on the east coast of Endura and hidden from watchful sinister eyes—ten-year-old Korian crouched behind lush shrubs, eyeing the prey he'd been tracking for hours. He knew the crunch of his feet on dry leaves would give him away. After years of trying, Korian had learned exactly what it takes to be a successful hunter the hard way: succeed and eat, fail and starve.

On a stretch of grass in a small clearing, behind a row of trees, Korian silently watched an unsuspecting maret: a hare-like animal, but smaller, with stubby ears and longer hind legs. *Careful,* he advised himself. *Right distance, right conditions, easy my little friend.*

Korian placed the forefinger of his right hand in his mouth and then held it out into the open air. He picked up a small stone, slid his other hand into a leather glove he kept linked to his belt, and he grabbed hold of the Lubics V from the sheath on his back.

The Lubics V was a fascinating weapon. He had come across it a few years back. It was made of metal, flat with sharp edges, and shaped like a wing about the size of his ten-year-old arm bent at the elbow. When thrown, the weapon would spin on its axis, travelling in an elliptical path and return to its origin.

Slowly and stealthily, he assumed the throwing position. He tilted the weapon slightly, adjusted the throw angle into the wind, and he let the Lubics V fly with just the right force. The maret's stubby ears perked, and it lifted its head. It froze. Initially, the V curved around a row of trees, climbed gently and levelled out in mid-flight. Korian transferred the rock to his right hand and waited.

Stay with me. Almost there.

The weapon arced and descended. At that perfect moment, Korian threw the stone. The rock skipped in front and slightly to the left of the animal. Startled, the maret did just as expected. It dashed to the right and hopped into the flight path of his weapon.

It was overcast. Dew lingered late into morning. Finch felt it in his bones, and he could tell even before stepping outside. It took a while, but eventually he managed to get the fire started.

The past eight years had not been kind. He had become frail. He had hurt his leg several years back protecting his young companion, and it had not healed properly, resulting in a permanent limp and ineptitude. It was late fall. The hut that had served as their home for the last three years was run down. It was built on higher ground as an extension to the large trunk of a very old tree. They had built a door that opened to the hollow, dark trunk. The inside of the trunk served as access to a higher perch used for looking out over the barren wilderness and a three-hundred-and-sixty-degree view.

In anticipation of Korian's return, Finch prepared the dwelling for what he hoped was to be a hearty meal. It had been four days since they had eaten meat, and he hoped their fortunes were to change in their favor today. "Good luck, Korian," he whispered, looking towards the forest.

When he had come upon the child that day in Natras Pass, assuming responsibility for him was the last thing he expected to do. One look into the child's eyes, though, had cured the loneliness that had plagued him for as long as he could remember. Korian had given him a reason to live. Korian had taught him selflessness, compassion, patience and love. The boy had a will and a gift he did not understand.

When Finch looked upon the child and peered into his eyes that day in Natras Pass, the child's eyes served as mirrors into his own soul. He did not like what he saw, nor the pain he experienced from the effect. In fact, he had not dared to look directly into Korian's eyes since.

The middle of the hut was empty save for a small wooden table and two chairs. At the back of the hut stood two cots. On the smaller lay a collection of worn gloves.

He grabbed an empty bucket and limped past the empty garden down the hill towards a nearby stream. He knelt on the bank of the stream to gather water. When he stood, something peculiar on a boulder nearby drew his attention. Finch staggered and dropped the pail of water in surprise. On the rock was a crudely drawn symbol. He knew what it meant.

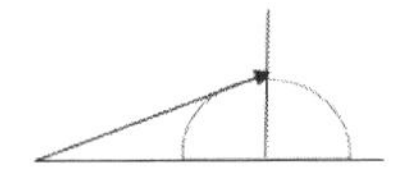

Falling to his knees, his shoulders drooped, and he exhaled as if letting out his last breath. Once he regained his composure, he stood and hobbled back to the hut. High on a shelf, behind some plates, he retrieved a wooden chest. The folded piece of paper he had found in the sack that day at Natras Pass was still inside.

Finch sat down heavily on the chair he had just set out. He recalled the many times they had felt a strange sensation of being watched. There were several occasions when they had travelled through terrain unfit for a man, let alone a child, but there had never been a reason for concern. It was as if something or someone was always looking out for the child. No living thing, or the Stragoy, had threatened them over the last eight years. Finch unconsciously tapped his bum leg with his trembling hand. He was wrong. There was one time they had been abandoned.

He knew what was coming. He should be feeling relief. After

all, this is what he had been yearning for. Years of solitude, a wretched outcast with not a soul to call friend, had taken a toll. Yet, he was not ready for what was about to happen. The end of his obligation would begin on the morning of the next sunrise.

He struck the table with his fist.

"I'm not ready!" he cried out. "Not now!"

The child was his purpose, or so he thought. The thought of not being a part of Korian's life brought him great sadness. He'd grown very fond of the boy.

"Are you all right, Finch?" Korian stood in the doorway holding today's breakfast, lunch and dinner.

Finch stared admiringly at the boy, tall for his ten years, with strong, square shoulders. His visage was thin, and his complexion was tawny from exposure to the sun. Even with a puzzled expression, he looked like he had been put together with care.

"Are those tears?"

"Nonsense," Finch answered quickly. He noticed the maret in Korian's hand. "Well done, my boy." He wiped his eyes adding, "Let's eat."

Korian savored every bite. It could be days, weeks even, before he would enjoy anything so delicious. He scraped the bone clean and threw what remained of it into the fire. Not a word had been spoken since they sat down to eat. Finch stared wide-eyed at the flame the entire meal. His mind was elsewhere. One memory after another danced in the flames. There was one memory in particular his mind kept turning over, as it had every day since he had injured his leg. The day the "so-called" protector had abandoned them.

Korian was seven years old when they had stumbled upon

an abandoned town near the base of the Syran Hills. They were nomads wandering a barren landscape, travelling from town to town through foreboding forests and terrain, avoiding people of either race. At the base of the hill, they had found a tunnel. His mind gave in completely to the memory. Suddenly, he was there, the memory so vivid he smelled the stale air inside the dark tunnel.

Wooden beams lined the walls and ceiling.

"Did you hear that? Sounded like voices?" Korian whispered.

They stopped and pressed their ears against the wooden beams.

"Den?" Korian asked.

"Trust me. The Den wouldn't want us," Finch said. He knocked on the wall. The echo of his raps filled the tunnel. There were no whispers. No voices.

They emerged the tunnel into daylight and came upon a small, abandoned town in the middle of the forest. The dirt path through the tunnel continued between rows of old, timbered buildings. It was an abandoned temporary post for settlers and travelers. At the other end of the rows of buildings, the path disappeared into the forest.

A loud knock came from their left. A wooden sign above the half-opened door of a building hung loosely and swayed back and forth, striking the frame rhythmically. Besides the wind and the rustling leaves, it was the only sound audible in the otherwise isolated ghost town.

The two split up and went through buildings looking for anything useful they could find. Korian emerged from one such structure holding a flat V-shaped, glistening, metal object. The sides of the "V" were as sharp as double-edged swords. Finch examined the object. He slid his hand along the edge and recoiled. After a few seconds, blood seeped out of his palm and began to trickle down his fingers. He threw the object away angrily. It flew end over end until it ran out of room and impaled itself into the sign that had been swaying in the wind. The sign crashed to the ground with Korian's new weapon still attached.

"Wow!" Korian shouted running excitedly to retrieve it.

Finch had taken a white handkerchief out of his pocket and wiped his hand. The mysterious linen helped quench his blood. Yet, as blood continued to seep, surprisingly no red mark remained on the fabric. Finch held it up and stared at it admiringly. There was the curious "K.R." stitched on it as clear as it's always been. It was as mysterious a relic as it was special. Regardless of what it touched, it would never soil, burn or tear. It was truly enchanted.

Korian was thrilled. He threw the new object repeatedly until he started to get the hang of it. With each toss, the weapon began to return closer to where he stood.

"Look, it comes back!" he repeated. Finch ignored the boy's excited rants and focused instead on the irritating cut on his palm.

When Korian returned, Finch was muttering to himself, angry with his own carelessness. Korian laughed mockingly, and staying true to his mischievous nature, he snatched the linen from Finch's hand and ran off.

"Bring it back! I should have left you where I found you!"

Korian examined his new toy admiringly. He spat on the glistening metal and wiped it earnestly with the linen until it shone like a mirror.

A rumble came from the path in the forest leading into the town. Dust rose above the tops of the trees. Finch grabbed the boy's hand and hurried towards the forest on the other side of the derelict settlement.

They ran down a hill and found another path at its base. Finch took a moment, bent over, and he put his hand on his knees.

"I'm not about to find out who or what that was," Finch whispered between breaths.

He had not the time to regain his composure when the ground moved. A loud thud, and then another, came from behind them. Large, thick branches swayed and snapped.

"What's that?" Korian asked.

The sound was different from the one they'd heard on higher ground. It was louder and more terrifying.

"Don't know."

There was a gruesome roar, and seconds later, a large, enraged animal burst out from the woods. It was about the size of a small house. The enormous muscles on its large body tensed, making it look round and the muscles in the shoulders more prominent. The head was abnormally large, about a third of its entire size with two horns on its snout, and on either side—two long tusk-like horns curved to a point. The square jaw was powerful, and the mouth was alarmingly large, filled with razor sharp teeth. Behind its skull was a curved, bony plate.

Its momentum carried it across the path. Despite its alarming size, it was surprisingly agile. It crashed into the wide trunk of an old tree. Leaves scattered, bark splintered, the base uprooted, and the tree folded and collapsed. The animal roared and turned to evaluate Finch and Korian. It took a few steps forward and stopped.

"Don't move," Finch whispered, barely moving his lips. "It's a hybrin. Do everything I say."

The hybrin growled, deep and threatening. Saliva spewed onto the ground from its gaping mouth. Finch squeezed Korian's hand tightly, putting himself instinctively between the animal and the boy.

The beast bobbed its head and snorted. It raised its snout to the sky and roared angrily, exposing a powerful chest with muscles, bulging and taut. Then it lowered its front legs and head and charged. The ground shook beneath his feet.

"Run!" yelled Finch.

Korian, darted off. Finch maneuvered his way around trees, running in the opposite direction. Behind him, the beast's heavy snorts and snarls were getting louder. Finch's chest tightened. Ahead, he saw long, thick roots, sticking out of the base of a massive trunk. They bulged and curled downward into the ground, forming, what appeared to be a natural cage of tubers. Thin strands of yellow moss-like vines hung like beards from the many shoots, hiding the space within the natural enclosure.

Finch squeezed between two of the larger roots without breaking stride. A moment later, the tree shuddered as the beast slammed its oversized head into the roots. They held that time.

The enraged beast tugged and tore. Its horns crashed through gaps between the roots, striking and tearing thick chunks of flesh from Finch's legs. The creature became more enraged when it saw blood. Its breath was warm and foul as its jaws snapped repeatedly. It was relentless, and the ancient tubers began to fail.

The hybrin paused. It snorted—spewing saliva— and let out another roar before it charged. Finch bolted through a small gap the creature had carved on the left. He managed two steps when the hybrin crashed through, destroying what remained of the ancient shoots. Its horn caught Finch above his knee, catapulting him deep into the brush. The sound of his muscles tearing, amplified his dread. Lying on his back, pain surged in waves, sweeping through his pelvis and into his gut. He felt for his leg: still there, but it was bent in an unnatural angle. Numb, and with adrenaline coursing through his depleted body, the beast's head appeared over the tall bushes. It snorted and hissed as it approached until its massive head loomed above him.

"Over here!" Korian shouted as the hybrin's drool fell onto Finch's face. It paid no attention to Korian's rants. In desperation, Korian hurled his weapon. It struck the hybrin's snout and bounced off. The hybrin turned its head and glared at Korian. It roared so loud, Korian had to cover his ears.

"Korian! Run!"

The hybrin and Korian locked eyes; neither moved.

A bush to Korian's left suddenly stirred, startling him and drawing his gaze. Someone, slightly taller than him, emerged from the forest. It looked like a young girl, but the head and face were covered by the hood of a red cloak. The cloak covered the body to below the knees. Brown, muddy boots covered her feet.

The hybrin snorted louder, but Korian's eyes remained fixed on the unexpected visitor. Small hands removed the hood, exposing long red locks and a soft, pale face. It was a human girl.

Finch recalled the look on Korian's face. He was captivated. She was the first living person Korian had ever seen other than Finch. The exchange between the two lasted only seconds when the growl of the enraged beast snapped Korian back.

Bobbing its head from side to side, the hybrin charged. Only it did not charge Korian. Maybe it was the red color of her cloak, or perhaps it just smelled fear, but the animal suddenly turned towards the girl. Korian darted, reaching her seconds before the hybrin. They both fell into the damp soil as the hybrin swept by. The hybrin turned for another charge. Korian bolted to his feet.

"Stay here!" he shouted and then turned and ran down the path shouting and waving his arms wildly.

Finch, still squirming on the ground, his leg numb, remained helpless as he watched Korian sprint past. Korian gasped when he stopped abruptly in front of a steep stone wall. He had trapped himself. The enraged beast was bearing down on him.

Korian's shoulders drooped. He scoffed and readied himself for the hybrin's assault and prepared for the inevitable. The hybrin was in an all-out charge. Its giant head was low, and its horns swayed with each stride. Korian leaned his back against the wall. He opened his eyes wide and stared directly at the primal animal.

The hybrin snorted. Suddenly it dug its hooves into the soft earth and slid to a stop. Its horns were inches from Korian's face. It bared its teeth and hissed, locking its enraged ruby eyes with Korian's.

Gradually the heaving of the beast's bulk began to slow until it became a rhythmic calm. Korian raised his hand and gently touched the beast on the side of its jaw. The hybrin remained still. Its sides pulsed with each breath. It seemed an eternity, but after a time, the beast raised its head, stepped back a few paces, turned and majestically trotted into the woods.

Korian stood still, watching the creature as it disappeared into the forest, and then he turned his attention back to the young girl. She was lying on the forest floor where he had left her, looking at him with a kind of awed expression.

Korian gently helped her to her feet. The young girl could not take her eyes off him. She looked deep into his eyes, and Korian smiled. She had streaks of mud on her cheek. In his hand was the linen he had taken from Finch. With it, he gently wiped her cheek. She pulled back initially, but then she let him. A smile crossed her lips, and Korian looked down bashfully.

He noticed something shiny on the ground. He placed the linen in her hand, and he knelt to pick up a brass ring hanging from a gold chain. There was a small, pear-shaped violet object embedded in the ring, which resembled a tiny tear. The girl held her breath. Korian gently lowered the ring onto his palm, staring at it admiringly.

"I think you dropped this," he said with a smile. She stared at him excitedly. "I—"

"Sara!" a man's voice cried from inside the forest. He repeated the name several times.

"It's you!" she whispered.

Korian's puzzled look lasted but a moment, and then a rather rotund man burst from the forest. His eyes, piercing and concerned, turned immediately to relief when he saw the girl. Korian eyed him nervously as the man snatched up the girl without taking his eyes off Korian.

"No, wait, Father! He—" she shouted.

The man ignored her and carried her away into the woods. Finch's linen was still in Sara's hand.

A loud pop from the fire snapped Finch back to the present.

"We were abandoned because that is how it was meant to happen," Finch said.

"What are you talking about?"

"Three years ago, the protector abandoned us. Do you think about her?"

It took a moment to register who Finch was talking about, then Korian took the ring that hung on the chain resting against his chest. "Every day," he said and closed his hand around it.

"I'm sorry for being a burden for the last few years," Finch added.

"What? You have never been a burden. I followed her that day, you know. You were writhing in agony, and I followed her instead. Sorry," he said with a smirk.

"I watched their partekii pull their wagon into the tunnel. I heard what sounded like a door slamming, and then a minute later, saw the partekii and the wagon emerge from the other side of the tunnel absent riders. The tunnel just swallowed them up. One day I will find her."

"I'm sure you will, but I need to tell you something."

Korian turned to Finch. He wasn't used to this serious side of the man. Finch's good eye was piercing and direct.

"I'm tired. I've grown old…I have many regrets. But there is one thing…one thing I'm proud of." He was going to say more but stopped. Instead, he said, "I need you to realize I'm not going to be around forever. When the day comes, you will need to carry on."

"Why are you telling me this?"

Finch ignored the question, "What have you learned from me?"

Korian thought this was an odd question. Finch was the only living person Korian had ever really known. For as long as he could remember, the man had been his friend, teacher, brother and father. Everything he knew, he owed to Finch.

"I don't know."

"Answer the question, Korian!"

"I have learned how to hunt, to survive in the wilderness. You taught me to read, write and think."

"Yes, but I'm referring to the less obvious things."

Korian looked puzzled.

"You have taught me compassion," Finch said. "In return, I hope I have managed to teach you to understand the power of evil and what it takes to resist temptation, to understand constraint and hatred, how to control anger and respect power. In time, you will learn you have the capacity to change the wills of men. Your destiny is out there. Men and firstlings will follow you."

"Do I look like a leader?" Korian said, chuckling.

"Lead them," Finch answered. He had never looked more serious. His good eye was opened wide. The urgency in his gaze caught Korian by surprise.

❖

They retired early. Finch woke Korian several hours later. He took Korian up the steps inside the old tree, up to the perch.

"I need to see the sunrise," said Finch, repeating it over and over.

They said little as they looked towards the horizon. Below them came a chorus of sounds from forest critters who brought in each morning with the same melody.

The upper limb of the sun appeared just above the horizon. The forest at the top of the valley appeared to the right; the hills gradually became mountains. High above, clouds spanned over the tops of the mountains like a heavy, magenta quilt. Finch soaked in the beauty.

He asked Korian to look at him. Many years ago, Finch had looked into the boy's eyes, and what he saw of himself almost consumed him. Today, he desired to look into those eyes one more time. Finch drew the boy close, and he gazed into his eyes. This time, he felt swaddled in absolute peace.

"Thank you," he said. "Don't forget me."

He let go of Korian tenderly. He removed the patch from his eye, exposing a deep, empty socket. Turning towards the sunrise, its warmth fell across his face. There was an odor of charred skin.

Korian was puzzled at first. He sat quietly beside Finch and stared openmouthed at the man he had grown to love, who was acting rather strangely.

Finch's skin began to crack. First his face, then his hands. In just seconds, his hair grayed, his cheeks hollowed, and his skin flaked off and starting falling away. Bit by bit, he was slowly being carried away by the wind.

Korian's puzzlement turned to horror. He moved away, recoiling at the sight.

"Don't be afraid," Finch managed through cracked lips.

What remained of his hair fell out entirely. He turned to Korian. His remaining eyeball had disintegrated. The few remaining patches of skin fell away from his jaws and his skull. Beginning at the jaw, the bone began to crack and crumble.

Just before his skull crumbled entirely to ash, what remained of Finch managed to speak one last time, "Find the Manian."

Finch disintegrated and scattered into the dawn. A gust of wind swept up the clothes that had bunched up on the surface of the perch and carried them away.

It was all too sudden, too abrupt. Korian was unprepared and in shock from what he had observed. He realized that for the first time in his life, he was alone.

Never before had Korian experienced such a loss. The world that he knew had abruptly crumbled. The twins…first pain—sharp and numbing—and then fear—constricting and paralyzing—swept through him, like waves, taking turns crashing perpetually onto the frigid sand. He felt anxious and weighted down. The only living person he had known, his friend, mentor and father, had abandoned him in the most nightmarish manner.

That morning was the most difficult of Korian's life. He spent the first part of that day moping around the hut. He barely ate. By afternoon, he worked his way up to the perch. He sat looking over the landscape for the remainder of the day. Tears streamed down his face. He thought of Sara and knew to see her again, he would need to seek her out in the wilderness. He gripped the ring around his neck, squeezed tightly and held on to it for hours. When darkness fell, he slept seated on the perch until morning.

When he awoke, he saw smoke in the distance and black bird-like creatures soaring above it: spies. *Stragoy closing in. It's time to leave*, he thought.

Korian went through the hut. He gathered the map of Endura from the wooden chest Finch had left. He packed lightly, took one last look around their home for the last three years and started down the hill into the wilderness.

The Northern Territories were his first destination. *I'll head north, through Steeldom, and use the Urlean Mountains to the east to shield me from those creatures to the south. I'll put distance between them and me and work my way around*, he thought. His trek took him both literally and figuratively into desolation. Plant growth became sparse and stunted. The deeper he went, the more skeletal the trees became. Soon, only rotten stumps littered the ground.

On the second week of his journey, he stumbled into a precarious situation. Alone with his fears, the deafening howls of wild wolfen brought a terror so palpable and intense, for a moment, he lost his focus and bearings.

Countless eyes—red and hungry—watched him from between trees and hollows. The wolfen drew nearer and their fearsome howls and barks became unbearable. From somewhere deep in the darkness, he heard a heavy thud. It was followed almost immediately by a pained yelp. A second, louder thud brought louder growls, the rustling of branches and leaves and then welcomed silence.

Korian stayed beneath the root of a large tree until dawn. He stood, shook the kinks out of his knees, stretched, took a deep breath, and then he left. He stumbled across the carcasses of two dead wolfen. Their skulls had been bashed in; brains littered the ground. There were no tracks around the animals or any indication of who or what had done this. Regardless, he was grateful.

"Thank you!" he called into the forest. He vowed never to put himself in a situation like this again.

A few months later, he reached an abandoned town reminiscent of the many places he had come across with Finch. A sign that read "Library" caught his attention. The splintered doors beneath it hung wearily. A gust of wind swung the door shut, silencing the creaking. A deafening silence surrounded him. A minute later, the silence was disturbed by strange noises coming from down the path. He darted towards the nearest door, unaware of what approached. But the door was locked.

"Here," a man beckoned from behind a door on the opposite side of the path. Korian joined the wiry man on the other side. From the crack in the door held slightly ajar, they watched six Stragoy, adorned with full armor, march by. They passed without taking their gaze from the path, the first of Aaron's slaves Korian had ever seen this close.

"Seekers looking for settlements in the north," whispered the man as he shut the door.

Finch had told Korian about these creatures and the despicable things they had done, but Korian had never come face to face with any.

"Stragoy," the man said. "They were once like you and me. Now they linger between death and the afterlife."

The man stood and addressed Korian. He was two feet taller than the ten-year-old boy.

"I am Zohar. Zohar Peat. I've been here about a month. I wasn't sure of you at first when I saw that weapon of yours," referring to the "V" on Korian's back. "There's something about you, though. You're not going to prove me wrong, are you?" His voice was as wiry as his appearance.

Korian smiled and shook his head. "No, and thank you. I'm Korian."

His good Samaritan was in his thirties. He had an ashen complexion, but looked resolute with a firm mouth. Although his clothes were soiled and ripped in places, he was reasonably well dressed. He held a heavy sack in his hands. It was then Korian realized, by the rows and stores of spices, comfits and preserves, they were in an apothecary.

"Follow me, Korian," Zohar said.

Zohar opened the door, peered outside and quietly strolled across the street. Zohar pressed his shoulder into the battered door of the library and entered. The large area of the second floor looked lived in. The windows were boarded, and the building felt separated from the rest of the world.

Zohar placed the sack down on a desk and removed some spices and a canteen with water. From the back of the room, they heard the cooing of a child. A young woman emerged from behind a tall bookshelf. She had long, unkempt, black hair and was thin except for her belly, still slightly round and protruding after recently giving birth.

"It's all right, Nora. This is Korian. I invited him to stay, if he wants to of course."

Zohar was an alchemist and teacher and knew a thing or two about medicine. He and his young wife and child had managed to evade the Stragoy for months until they stumbled upon this library a month ago. Nora had given birth to her child here.

"In the spring, we're going to head east to the coast," said Zohar. "My brother lives there. We hope to take his boat and sail off to wherever the tide takes us. We need to get away from this place." He paused. "We do have a spot for one more," he added.

Nora sat on a chair, feeding her newborn child, a blanket was draped over her breast.

"There's nothing here," she said sullenly. "They've taken everything from us." She looked at her husband and reconsidered, "Almost everything."

"Thank you. I have my own path," replied Korian.

"We have plenty of supplies," said Zohar, motioning to the books. "When the cold arrives, we'll build fires at night to avoid drawing attention to the smoke."

Months passed, and they developed a great friendship. Korian also felt a special connection with the child. She was named Mai. When Nora would ask him to hold Mai, he would lean in close, take a long, deep breath and hold the scent of the child for as long as he could. In return, Mai would stare at him unwaveringly. Every time she would cry, they would give her to Korian to soothe her.

The winter brought harsh winds and biting cold. Occasionally, Stragoy would pass during the day, but as time passed, the frequency lessened. On those occasions, the three feared the baby's cries would draw attention. During those times, again, they would hand her to Korian.

Korian helped scavenge for food and supplies. Occasionally, he would venture out and return with a wild maret, and they would cook it at night. He expressed an interest in science, and Zohar was willing to share. With access to hundreds of books, Korian read all he could. After months of seclusion though, large sections of the library disappeared. Books served as an excellent source to keep the fire burning. Soon, only a handful of books remained sitting on a high shelf.

"When the last of them is gone, we'll use the shelves," said Zohar.

One day, Korian scaled the shelves to reach those books up top. A section of shelving below his feet suddenly moved. He examined the shelf closely and pressed against it. The wall behind the bookcase pressed inwards. It was a trap door. He pushed it open and found a dark room. Inside, he found a multitude of ancient scrolls and books dating back to before the birth of King

Zoren. This room became Korian's haven. He'd stay in there, sometimes for days, quenching his thirst for knowledge.

Among the ancient texts, he found information about primitive Endura. He read about a period known as the Dark Ages and the strange sickness that had spread.

When spring finally arrived, the three exchanged a meaningful embrace and bid each other farewell. "I hope Samjees guides you to find your Sara," said Nora.

"And guides you and your family," Korian answered, taking Mai out of Zohar's hands. He kissed her tenderly on the forehead. "Goodbye. If Samjees wills it, our paths will cross again."

They parted ways, and Korian, just over eleven years of age, departed once again into the wilderness.

9

THE LINHAR

THE YEARS BECAME a garbled mass of enlightening and perilous experiences mixed with incredible solitude. Ten years had passed since Korian had last seen Finch, yet Finch was never far from Korian's mind—he was just as influential in death as he was in life. Each day, Korian would talk to him as if he was there, walking by his side. The truth was, solitude had become his only companion.

Isolation had heightened his powers of observation. Details he once ignored he now noticed with new clarity and perspective, like the beauty, and at the same time, the brutality of nature. At its best, he appreciated the play of sunlight on damp grass in the morning as it swayed in the wind, and the song the wind made through the leaves in a secluded forest: a symphony of both melancholy and enchanted melodies. At its extreme, he could still appreciate the brutality of a predator killing for food: brutal but necessary to maintain balance; the cycle of life in its natural, uninfluenced condition.

On this day, a range of gray clouds suddenly took possession of the sky: huge domes and peaks separated by deep gray canyons. The day suddenly turned dark. Lightning zigzagged, followed by loud bursts of thunder, shattering the sky with every stroke.

Korian reached the crest of a hill. He looked up to the sky and knew the downpour would soon follow. It was still two days' walk to the next town. Below, a narrow valley spread before him. The trees that lined both sides bent precariously with the wind. The woods to the right looked thicker, so he headed towards them.

A brilliant bolt of white lightning ripped across the darkening sky, seeming to cleave it into parts. Moments later came the booming crack of thunder and then, as if right on cue, heavy rain began to pound the ground just as Korian entered the woods. He found a spot beneath the trunk of an uprooted tree and sat. He knew the darkness in forests such as these could swallow you whole. His mind absorbed the sounds of the forest as the velvety darkness engulfed him. He clasped the ring that hung around his neck and thanked the gods for surviving another day.

Korian had wandered over hillsides, trekked through one abandoned town after another, journeyed through hundreds of forests, rivers and mountain ranges all in search of an elusive place in the southern part of Endura. Each night, before shutting his eyes, he would clasp Sara's ring and pray to the gods to help guide him.

He had become a wanderer, searching not only for the Manian or for Sara but also for who he was. Korian couldn't rely on others to be his mirror. Outside of his search, his only objective was survival, to feed off the land and to draw from his will to carry him forward when exhaustion and hunger threatened to consume him. He carried on without obligation, since no one knew he existed.

There was once a time in Korian's life when he felt happy. Finch saw to that. As the years faded away, so did some of his memories. Korian, now at twenty years of age, only knew abandonment and suffering. Still, he felt an incredible longing to find the girl he had met only once and for mere moments at that. Secondary to that was a task to find the Manian to fulfill Finch's last words.

When Korian had parted ways with Zohar and his family that spring many years back, he had journeyed southwest, searching for a path over the Urlean Mountains. To avoid the extreme cold the high altitude offered, Korian instead found a path, quite by accident, through a dark cavern of sensory deprivation within the mountains. It was on that journey that he came upon wondrous and inspiring cave art. He was so enthralled, he spent weeks exploring them all, absorbing every line and contour. With his intuitive nature, he interpreted much about the stories. They told of ancient Ruid life and their beliefs. Some drawings perplexed him. In these drawings, faces of firstlings appeared exaggerated in torture, pain and suffering. There was a period of darkness and then a series of drawings depicting humans and Ruids together. In one particular drawing, there was a black imprint of a hand in the corner: the ancient symbol of a bad omen.

Weeks later, when he emerged from the mountain, he came to a canyon separating him from the southern regions. He searched for a way across and eventually found it by way of an obscure path down through the Grand Gorge. The trek had been harrowing, and more than a couple of times he'd almost fallen to his death. It was times like these, and there were many, when he'd wonder with genuine bewilderment why he was made to face these challenges and to face them alone. Something primal kept pressing him forward; something he could not understand.

When he awoke the next morning in the forest, the rain had stopped, and the mist hung in the humid morning air above the forest canopy. The resonating songs of birds marked the dawn. It was midsummer, and soon the heat would become uncomfortable.

Over the years, Korian had undergone a significant transformation. After years of wandering, he had grown lean, dark and tall, proportioned and athletic. Long, disheveled hair fell in waves along his shoulders, adorning an olive and weathered complexion. His skill with the Lubics V now bordered on expert.

He filled his canteen with water that had pooled on the large leaves of some of the more ancient trees. The mist had cleared by then, and beads of sweat formed on his forehead.

"Thank you," he said to the forest and left to resume his trek towards the next town.

Late in the afternoon on the second day, after having left the cool cover of the trees, he arrived at another abandoned town and rested for two days. He gathered up what he could carry that was of any use, packed it in a sack and headed south.

A day later, he stumbled onto the red cliffs of Azart. He was awed by their grandeur. The reddish iron ore rocks that covered the surface gave the cliffs their characteristic red color. The view stretched far to the left and right, beyond his field of vision. On the valley floor, hundreds of feet below, a river flowed through the vivid, red-colored strata. Except for the Urlean Mountains in the far west, the cliffs were so vast they separated the northern part of Endura from the south. He stood on the edge and felt unnerved at the abruptness of the drop.

Travelling east, parallel with the edge, eventually he found a winding path down to the river below. He worked his way down and then up the other side, where he paused and glanced back across the gap. He drew inspiration from the view, took a breath and moved on.

Navigating his way westwards, parallel to the edge of the cliff, he came upon an extraordinary sight. He was northeast of the Gareth Hills, where he found, on the edge of the cliff, extending onto an outgrowth over the crag, a tree. Its bark was white and wrinkled, majestic in its solitude and peculiarity. It was completely out of place and time. The tree stood fifty feet high and had a swollen trunk. Full, large, veiny red leaves on long coiling branches spread out over the branches and out over the edge of the Azart cliffs. At the base of the tree was a massive bulb. Piled on the ground around it were skeletal human and Ruid remains.

This must be the flagon tree, named for its shape, he thought. He'd never seen one, but Finch had spoken often of them.

"The flagon is a magic tree," Finch explained. Korian reached out his hand to touch the flagon when large insects, ant-like but larger, stormed out of cracks in the bark and rushed toward the spot he was about to touch. He recoiled at the sight.

"Nature protects its own," Finch had said. "If you find one leafless and dead, it's most likely lived out its purpose. You would not find a round, jade-colored fruit in its branches. Some have said the tree grants wishes, not several, but a single wish. According to legend, if a charmed person should come to lay their hands on the fruit, a single wish will be granted, but at a terrible price.

"Many have tried to extract the fruit but almost all have failed." The bones laying at the base of the tree were clear evidence of that. "The fruit, you see, is not easily extracted. First, if the tree ever relinquishes the fruit, then just as the honeybee dies after it stings, so does the flagon tree. To get to the fruit, one must endure great pain and suffering and, in the end, be rewarded a single wish. The price…their life, sometimes gladly given for the reward the wish may afford to those left behind."

Korian stepped back and searched the tree for its fruit. He looked at the bones. He wondered what kind of pain and torture those brave, or perhaps foolish, souls must have endured. He pondered what must have brought them here, to have given their lives. He shook his head in wonder.

"Finch would be pretty impressed with you," said Korian to the tree. Then, in between a series of coiled branches, he found a single, round, jade-colored fruit. *Just sitting there free for the taking,* he thought. "If I could only—"

A woman's scream stole his attention. Cautiously, he crept towards the edge of the cliff and peered down.

At the bottom of the cliff, on a path running parallel to the river, closer to the opposite side of the cliff, stood a caravan of five wagons. He had not noticed them earlier and thought they must have only recently arrived.

Surrounding the wagons was a hulking man on a partekii and twenty others on foot. Those on foot wore armor and had swords drawn. Six bloodied bodies lay on the ground. The bull-necked man dismounted and circled to the back of one of the wagons. He was shouting something as he disappeared inside. The wagon swayed and groaned under his weight. He emerged from the wagon dragging a woman out by her hair. Her screams were so shrill they nearly drowned out the sound of the river. He threw the woman up against the wagon and held a dagger across her neck, taunting her. He then moved it down to her thighs and slid it under her dress. The woman stopped screaming and froze in her terror.

Others, women, children and a few men, were dragged out of

the wagons and gathered on the other side beyond Korian's view. The thickset man was positioned between Korian and the woman, making it impossible to know exactly what he was doing. When the man stepped away momentarily, the woman's clothes had been torn. He then struck her in the face with his fist. Two soldiers were summoned to hold her up, but she was determined and resilient. Her arm struck one soldier in the head and knocked off his skull shield. She screamed at the sight and looked away.

The man hit her again. This time, her head was pressed up against the side of the wagon. Blood splattered from her nose and mouth. He tore off the rest of her clothes. Standing over her, still as a post, he watched as she writhed. A moment later, he bent over and she let out a pained shriek, full of fear and anguish.

Korian turned away and crouched behind a rock. Up to this point, Korian had always been witness to the aftermath of carnage. He had never seen it in progress, nor had he given any thought to the kind of wickedness needed to carry it out.

When the screaming stopped, Korian looked again. The woman—naked, battered and exposed—lay lifeless on the ground. Her limp body was dragged behind the stationary wagons. Moments later, the unmanned wagons set off down the path exposing more dead men, women and children. The woman, who had just been tortured, lay among them.

Four men were spared. They knelt with their heads down while the hulking man repeatedly taunted them. Overcome with fear, each man shivered uncontrollably as if they had been drenched with ice-water.

Korian felt helpless. *What can I do?* The image was too much. He turned away again, sharply. The sudden movement jarred loose a rock the size of his fist. It fell over the edge and dropped to the rocky surface below.

Korian held his breath. A moment later, he heard rock hit

the bottom. With his heart thumping, slowly, he brought himself to look over the edge. Below, heads were turned upwards. He reeled back.

A reek of rotting corpses overwhelmed him as if he'd been caught in a powerful undertow, disoriented in the murk and dragged out to sea. The crunch of heavy feet, startled him. A powerful gloved hand grabbed hold of the back of his neck and shoved his head down. The pressure was so intense, his head ached and his vision blurred. He was lifted off of the ground and slammed onto his back.

He feared he would never draw breath again. Gasping for air, he rolled onto his stomach and struggled forward on his elbows. Looking back over his shoulder, he caught a brief glimpse of a living corpse with a vacant expression. The face was cut and covered in abrasions and had peeled in places, in contrast with the tight, leathered complexion of the skin that remained. The lower jawbone was partly exposed. Casually, the Stragoy unsheathed a broadsword, casting a shadow over Korian.

The Stragoy raised the sword high over his head. Korian gulped in a large volume of air. The sword descended. Korian rolled to his left. The sword struck rock, spraying sparks. Korian reached for his weapon, but it was gone. He spotted it on the ground, but the Stragoy stood in his way. The creature lunged again. The tip of its sword carved through Korian's shirt, narrowly missing his abdomen.

Adrenaline is a powerful ally. Korian dodged another blow with nimble swiftness. He surprised himself, but then again, he'd never fought for his life before. He leaped to the side and clasped the Stragoy's arm. The creature's breath almost made him retch. Korian swiped his elbow, connecting with the Stragoy's head, knocking the creature off balance. Korian, too, slipped and fell. Ignoring the stabbing pain of the sharp rocks, he pressed forward.

The creature was unrelenting. Its shadow enveloped him again just as Korian's hand found his "V." He squeezed it tightly, ignoring the sharp edges that cut into his skin. He turned and swung, striking the Stragoy below the knee. The "V" sliced cleanly, severing its leg. The creature made no sound as it hobbled back and plunged over the edge.

Korian took another look over the cliff. This time he wasn't as stealthy. His chest heaved as he sucked in quick breaths. He found the man who had beaten the woman. They locked eyes. After years of wandering and avoiding exposure, he was no longer unseen. He gathered his things quickly and ran as fast as he could towards the only place that he thought could save him.

Herrick Mead was a rogue. In his thirties, he kept to himself, and he liked it that way. He had never been much of a talker, though he was expressive in other ways. He had always known there was something different about him. As a young adult, Herrick's thoughts had gravitated toward the bizarre. He had become consumed with thoughts of violence. At ten years of age, he had found a wounded orp in the field behind his parent's house and had satisfied a morbid curiosity by cutting off its head with a dull knife. He had been pleasantly surprised with how the act had elated him. It was the first time he had killed.

When Stragoy had raided his village four years ago, he had become caught up in the frenzy. While terror had raged outside his door, the remaining shred of his humanity had crumbled. He had picked up a knife from the table; the same table his mother had cleared, not an hour earlier, before the unspeakable horror had stormed into their village, and did what he had yearned to do for years: he slit his father's throat from ear to ear. Then, with his father's blood spreading across the cold surface, he murdered his mother.

Later, when two Stragoy had stormed into his home—hissing and spitting—they found Herrick standing over their bodies with blood dripping from his hands. Fearless, Herrick scowled at them with eyes colder than death. The Stragoy just stared at him for a long while and then, as if on cue, retreated, leaving him to his new reality.

Now, standing on the bank of a swiftly rushing stream at the base of the red cliff, surrounded by Stragoy and the bodies of those unfortunate enough to have stumbled on his path, Herrick, the barrel-chested man, was startled when a legless Stragoy plunged down the side of the cliff and splattered on the ground. It wasn't the Stragoy's demise that drew a reaction, rather it was the man who stood at the top of the cliff glaring down at him that did. It was a blatant act of defiance. The man stood there for a moment and then turned and disappeared from view.

"Find him!" Herrick shouted. "I want him alive."

Never before had anyone resisted and fought back. While disconcerting, it sparked a kind of excitement in Herrick. *I must let Aaron know*, the hulking savage thought.

Korian ran for hours. All he could see of his pursuers was dust rising into the air a good distance behind him, though he did not take any comfort in how far away the dust appeared. The distance could be deceiving. After all, he had not seen the Stragoy come up on him until it was too late.

Up ahead, the Linhar Desert loomed. Korian's chest felt like it was about to burst. He was panting and sweat painted his skin. The heat was unbearable. Each breath burned, but he carried on. He stopped and sniffed the air. There was no more odor of death.

His only exposure to this barren and foreboding place had been from the stories Finch had shared with him. He knew the Stragoy were closing the distance, but common sense said the creatures would not follow Korian into this desolate plain, into the most inhospitable terrain anyone could find themselves in. Then again, there wasn't anything common about these creatures.

There was no dividing line signaling the beginning of the desert. One moment he was contemplating his next move, the next he was surrounded by a vast sea of sand, with no roads or shelter. Korian's map did not offer any direction.

He tore a shirt he had in his sack and wrapped a section over his head. After assessing his water supply, he began his journey across the Linhar with naïve optimism.

The Azart cliffs changed in appearance depending on the time of day. In late afternoon, the rocks glowed yellow and orange, but in the light of the setting sun, they appeared streaked in shades of pinks and reds. At the base of the cliff, four men were buried in sand up to their heads. Stragoy formed a circle around them.

Herrick entered the ring of Stragoy and approached the spent men. He unsheathed his sword and circled them leisurely, with long, deliberate strides. He taunted them by swinging his sword towards the bases of their necks and stopping it inches away.

As the day grew old, the contrast between shadow and color blended into one another. One prisoner grimaced and retched. Tears streamed down his face.

"Why are we still alive?"

"We wait," Herrick answered. "Where were you going?"

He leaned forward clumsily until his thick, bearded face was inches from a prisoner's face, and he sniffed like a dog.

"I love the smell of fear," he said and howled with laughter.

Sunlight began to fade, and dark shadows grew in pockets between sunken rocks alongside the cliff.

A breeze picked up. From the shadow within a cavity at the base of the cliff came movement. A dark, cloaked figure materialized. In the murk, two bright flames stirred. Aaron stepped into the light of dusk.

He walked through the circle of Stragoy towards the prisoners until his own shadow engulfed the men.

"I was hoping I wouldn't find you like this," he exhaled, faking disappointment. "There's just too little time. Extreme situations call for extreme measures. I am going to ask you something. Please, think hard before you answer. Now, don't be foolish. I know what you want. I can give it to you if you answer correctly." He paused. "Where were you going?"

"Please," the oldest prisoner cried. "We were lost."

"I don't think you understand. You will tell me," Aaron said in a guttural whisper.

Terror gripped the prisoner. He looked into Aaron's eyes—fires of pure wickedness.

Aaron pointed to Herrick. The brute picked up a cloth sack, he opened it and poured a mass of insects from the flagon tree over his head. The insects tore across his face and into his ears, stinging and biting. His screams were stifled, as insects entered his mouth, working their way down his throat.

The other men looked away in horror. Aaron asked the man a second time, but he had already perished.

Then a Stragoy picked up another sack and walked towards the next man. Before the sack was opened, the man on his right shouted, "Natras Pass! We're going to Natras Pass."

"Now, that wasn't so hard."

Aaron raised his sword and plunged it into the ground.

"What are you doing? Kill me!" pleaded the man who had revealed where they were headed.

Aaron turned to the Stragoy, "Take this filth away. Feed them the leaf of the matchra tree."

Turning to Herrick, Aaron explained what he wanted him to do.

As evening approached, the temperature cooled to a deep chill. Korian walked deep into the night until he almost collapsed.

When he awoke several hours later, it was early dawn. There was a hint of auburn radiance in the eastern horizon. Once he had readied himself for the toils of the day ahead, he started out again.

He continued southeast as the sun rose overhead, and the day grew hotter. While he eventually acclimated to the heat somewhat, as the day lengthened, dehydration set in, and Korian's muscles cramped. Each evening, he felt nauseous, and it was becoming increasingly difficult to hold down water.

This went on for days. One night, before sleep came, he took a swig from his canteen. It was only a quarter full. Days blended together. Each morning, his joints throbbed from the cold of the previous night. Each day, hours passed before the pain subsided. As the days went on, the pain lingered longer. His lips were parched, and his face blistered. Soon, his canteen held only enough water for one more day.

He looked to the sky. "I'm going to die here."

That night, exhausted and hungry, he lay shivering beneath the starry sky. The idea of finding Sara and meeting up with the Manian had turned into just a fantastic notion, stripped of hope.

The next morning, he drank the last bit of water, ate what food remained and moved on. He found a section of the desert surrounded by large dunes on either side. The dry heat was sickening, his tongue and lips had begun to swell, and a hollow sound rang in his ears. Each step became more and more labored until finally he gave in to exhaustion, and he collapsed onto the sand.

He felt at peace. In that moment, there was no pain. He closed his eyes and waited for death.

The ground began to tremble. Korian thought he'd dreamt it, but a large section of the side of the hill buckled. The sand was being displaced. Something underneath was pressing it upwards. The movement stopped suddenly, but the trembling continued. Sand exploded into the air to his right. Particles came together and formed a shape, primal and terrifying but indistinguishable. It arced over Korian and crashed back, submerging beneath the surface.

Even in his weakened condition, Korian managed to get to his feet. The surface beneath his feet gave way as something crashed through the surface, emerging directly beneath him. The momentum sent Korian into the air. He sailed off to the side and onto a dune.

A creature of enormous size and width, its long body suspended between hundreds of legs, surfaced. Its legs moved in an unsynchronized fashion. Dust fell from its enormous form as it jetted across the surface, leaving three giant trenches in its wake. At one end of the body was a rounded head with a gaping, toothless, black hole of a mouth. It let out a bizarre sound unlike anything Korian had ever heard: hollow and cavernous, a series of sharp high-pitched shrieks in quick succession. It then disappeared back into the sand.

Korian struggled to his feet, but he stumbled numerous times as he tried to scamper up the hill. In his delirium, he reasoned that perhaps the other side of the dune may offer protection. Behind him, the ground shook, and the sand began to vibrate.

The effort proved too much. A lack of oxygen, malnutrition, dehydration and pure exhaustion got the best of him. The world began to fade. As Korian collapsed, he felt the sensation of flying again. The strange sand creature propelled him upwards toward the top of the hill. Before losing consciousness, Korian heard the creature's alien sound, as if rejoicing and then silence.

Korian dreamed. A guide came to him and gave him a painting of an old man surrounded by a crowd of smiling human and Ruid children in the courtyard of a majestic city. There was a woman standing beside the man, looking more than regal. He was told to look carefully at the painting and remember it as it represented his life's purpose. He could not make any sense of the dream.

Opening his eyes was painful, as was every other movement. There was no feeling at all in his left arm. He did not know how long he had been out. Above him, branches and leaves cast shade from the hot desert sun. One look around, and his excitement grew. He was staring at a small area of green in an otherwise dry, golden landscape. He saw a beautiful, lush spring with fresh water surrounded by vegetation. Painfully, he crawled with one arm and threw himself into the spring.

Water had never tasted as sweet. After a few minutes, he crawled onto the bank, and he sat with his feet submerged as feeling returned to his arm.

He remembered where he was. For the moment, he would take some time to recover and gain strength before continuing.

There were crudely swept tracks leading up the hill as if someone had done a very poor job of trying to conceal them. Climbing the hill, he looked over the crest. The desert continued beyond the other side of the valley for miles, eventually disappearing into the horizon. A thought crossed his mind. If it hadn't been for the sand creature, he would have missed this place.

He spent three days here, most of them sleeping. On the second day, he climbed a date tree to gather as many dates as he could carry. In the early morning of the fourth day, Korian, in better spirits, departed for the second leg of his journey.

The optimism Korian had when he began the second part of the journey had long since been replaced with anxiety. It was his twenty-eighth day in this deep, golden, rich landscape where light seemed to flow out from rocks and sand.

His supplies had held up reasonably well. Glancing up at the sky, he saw there was less than an hour of light left.

Before stopping for the night, Korian noticed the solid decks of clouds draped across the entire sky, with the exception of a narrow strip near the horizon. The hues of twilight were calming on this night. He lay back and slept soundly beneath the stars.

On the morning of the twenty-ninth day, he awoke before dawn. Mornings were always difficult, and his joints ached with the cold.

Late in the morning, he noticed the wind had picked up. Sand stung his skin. Far into the distance he noticed what appeared to be a rising wall of sand.

"Strihali?" Korian said out loud. He knew he had mere minutes before the vicious sand cloud would swallow him whole. *Where am I supposed to hide from that?*

The ground began to tremble. Korian braced himself as the tremors intensified. Large areas of sand began to buckle.

Not again!

Sand exploded into the air. The massive sand creature, which resembled a cross between a snake and a centipede, burst through, rising high into the air, curling at the apex and plunged straight down. Korian turned and ran the other way to avoid getting crushed. The creature surfaced and submerged again and again, each time diverting Korian's direction. It happened several more times.

Is it guiding me?

The growing roar of the wind was so loud Korian had to use his arms to cover his ears and shield his face. He skidded to a stop as the massive, angry wall of sand, resembling a giant tidal wave, approached from about a thousand feet away. He had seconds before it would reach him.

About twenty feet in front of him, the sand creature breached the surface again. Korian fell, squeezed into a ball, and he shut his eyes, expecting to be crushed by the weight of the creature. Instead, the rumble and its shrieks stopped suddenly and dissipated into the surging wind.

Korian opened his eyes. When the creature surfaced this last time, it brought something else up with it. A shiny, cylindrical object landed a short distance away. It was eight feet long and three feet wide and made of smooth, shining metal. It was bizarre and out of place, but he didn't care what it was as long as it could somehow serve as a refuge from the Strihali. There it lay, beckoning Korian in the same manner that it had beckoned Zoren.

The sun was now almost completely hidden as the approaching wall appeared to touch the clouds. He breathed in sand, and he gasped with the effort. A small hollow on the end of the object caught his eye. He held his breath, grasped it and tugged.

A sharp pain on each of his fingers made him recoil. It was as if the inanimate object had bitten him. Blood pooled on each finger from a series of tiny needle pricks. Suddenly, a black line appeared horizontally across the middle of the cylindrical object. It wasn't a line at all. The object opened. It hissed, as smoke escaped from the widening gap around its perimeter. The upper half opened, and without hesitating, Korian jumped in. He laid down the length of the object and the lid slammed shut, sealing him in.

Korian found himself in complete darkness, yet he felt safe. The surface beneath him was cold and solid—at first. After a few seconds, the composition of the surface began to change. It softened until his body began to sink into it. Half his body had pressed into the strange substance as if the pliable surface had quickly cast a mold of his body. His heart was pounding, and his temples throbbed. The walls inside the object were cool and smooth. He felt a sense of weightlessness. Cool air filled the object. A sweet smell like fresh flowers blasted his senses. It helped Korian relax, and the beating of his heart slowed.

His eyelids grew heavy, but then something strange happened. Light from a square screen above swathed him in a dim shade of gray. The light was captivating. He felt something cold against his face—the cool feel of solid metal clips. Each eye was pried and held open. He couldn't move his hands, nor did he want to. He felt safer and more comfortable than ever before in his life.

In the light coming from the square screen, he began to discern what he thought were two-dimensional shapes. He heard sounds resembling words talking over one vivid picture after another. The words and pictures passed by in quick succession too swiftly for him to see. He drifted to sleep. His conscious mind missed everything. He may as well have been staring at flashing colors. His subconscious was a different story. It was tuned in and absorbed everything.

The Strihali had reached him. Outside his refuge, the sandstorm raged. Then, with one swift swoop, the massive sand creature took the object into its gaping mouth and disappeared under the sand.

10

THE LIGHT THAT BINDS

THE WIND WAS cool and from the west, and in the sky, the sun hovered above the crimson clouds. It was late morning when Korian woke up, lying on his back on a patch of dried grass. He had no idea how he'd gotten there or where he was. Lying out in the open, alone and exposed, he felt as vulnerable as he did ten years ago when, foolishly, he had wandered into a pack of wolfen.

Korian's hair, disheveled and long, fell over his face. When he moved the long locks away, he winced when he inadvertently scratched his cheek. He looked at his hands in disbelief. His nails had grown an inch.

Sitting up was difficult. He managed to raise himself to rest on his elbow when a feeling of nausea and a dull ache in his belly overwhelmed him. He felt parched, weak and hungry.

How long have I been out?

There was no sign of the metal object. In the distance, about half a day's walk to the west, Korian saw the smooth crests of sand dunes folding over each other, rising above a series of verdant hills. A vision of the giant sand creature leaping over the highest crest played in his mind. Its horrible shriek made him shudder.

He assessed his supplies. The Lubics V was where it belonged in its sheath across his back.

Sara's ring was on a chain around his neck. The biscuits and bread in the sack he carried had become hard, the dates had dried and hardened, and little water remained. He drained what he could and painstakingly ate some dried bread.

When Korian attempted to stand, he was overcome by a feeling of vertigo, accompanied by an overwhelming sense of confusion. Strange thoughts and memories flooded his mind, each competing for attention. It was as if he was recalling details of a hundred vivid dreams at once.

He closed his eyes and placed his wrists against his head to keep his head from exploding. He relaxed and allowed thoughts to form. Suddenly, images rushed into his mind, images about rudimentary things about the language he speaks, the theory of language and writing techniques, new science he's never before seen, information about strange animals and their nature, a history he does not recognize of a world where structures and buildings were of such height, they seemed to touch the sky.

Korian opened his eyes. Slowly, he laid back down and focused on the clouds. A multitude of fresh images surfaced of an alternate history and of a different life in a different world. They surfaced in short bits, incomplete at times, leaving him to fill in the gaps with his own experiences. It was like he had awakened with two distinct sets of memories: his own and those of someone else.

Some sections of clouds had grayed. The sun, low in the horizon, sent beams through the clouds like fingers reaching out to lightly caress the desert. The sight made him recall something from a foreign memory from somewhere deep in his mind. Knowledge of mythological stories of heroes and strange creatures and gods that did not include Samjees. He had an uncanny knowledge of stellar constellations, but they were not of Endura's sky. His mind was filled with knowledge of sun gods and sea gods and gods of love and war. They were from a rich and storied history not belonging to Endura.

What's happening to me?

Numbers and shapes flooded his mind. He was acutely aware of mathematics and science and of medicine beyond what anyone on Endura could ever know or understand.

Suddenly, Korian recalled the moving images on the square screen inside the metal cylinder. He saw them only for a moment: quick flashes of unintelligible shapes and light before he fell into a kind of deep sleep. He could not recall the details of what they were but surmised they were some kind of message. He did not yet know how, but he was certain those messages had a part to play in the new thoughts and memories that invaded his head. There was one thing that he remembered vividly among all the flashes: a face, older and grizzled with wisdom, that spoke to him as a teacher speaks to a student. Although the face was burned into his memory, Korian was not able to recall the details of what he said.

He stared at his hands again, turning them to examine his palms. Streaks of dried blood remained from the punctures he got after grasping the strange metal object. Korian looked towards the desert.

I will find you again, he thought. "You hold far too many secrets," he said out loud into the desert. "But there is something I need to do first."

Arranging the multitude of thoughts and strange memories proved taxing, and the huge undertaking caught up to him. He was alone, his muscles ached, and his limbs felt stiff. He was far too exhausted to search for cover. "If you're out there, look out for me," he yelled into the wind, then added, "Don't abandon me now." *I hope you're right, Finch. I'm placing myself in his hands.* "I'll blame you if I don't wake up," he whispered.

A short while later, right there on the dried patch of grass, Korian fell into a deep sleep.

Next morning, Korian resumed his journey. The crisp, clean air felt rich and sharpened his senses. Moving helped him loosen up. It was tough at first, but as the hours passed, he began to feel more like his old self.

The terrain here was harsh. He was moving in a southwesterly direction that would eventually take him to the Shad Mountains. His plan was to follow the mountains east to Natras Pass. He wasn't yet sure what he would do when he found the Pass, he knew only that he had to get there.

Food was available but sparse. Occasionally, he would come across a small plant with smooth, fat leaves. However small, purslane was the most refreshing sour taste he'd ever had. He ate what he could until it soothed his hunger. Without finding water—no pools, rivers or streams on this leg of his journey—he managed his thirst by taking advantage of the cool nights, getting water by tying his shirt around his legs and walking through long, dew-soaked grass at night. He would wring out the water and drink.

As he neared the mountains, vegetation began to grow thicker on the vertical slopes. He entered Mindwood, an ancient forest. There he spent three days navigating his way through the close-growing trunks of tall trees. When he came out of the forest on the third day, he had to shield his eyes from the sun.

One day, on the third week after waking up on the dried patch of grass, Korian found something peculiar: an unnaturally high rim of dirt, sand and stone that stretched ahead a great distance. Curious, Korian climbed the mound to the upper ridge. When he reached the top, he found a magnificent giant hole in the ground greater than one thousand feet wide and over two hundred feet deep. The rim of rubble and rock surrounding the hole would have been round except on the opposite end, the side of the Shad Mountain had been ripped open. A massive hole was torn out of the mountain wall.

Impact crater, Korian thought. "Where did you come from?" he said out loud, imagining the giant rock or whatever it was that made this giant hole.

He looked to the sky. "When did you…?"

In another part of Endura, other events were in motion relevant to this tale. Five young men walked single file down a winding corridor in a narrow part of the Den. Nervous tension lingered in the air, but for the moment, the task assigned was out of mind.

"What's up with your sister?" Leith asked.

He was second in line behind Jannik. Leith towered over the bunch, thin with a black bush on his head. His voice was dry with no inflection. Behind him, Alrik snickered as the monotone echo of Leith's voice bounced through the tunnel.

"What do you mean?" Jannik responded.

Jannik's naturally raspy voice had an air of "where are you going with this?" in it. Jannik's was a dominating presence, even though he never tried to be controlling. He was a strapping young man, the kind that others look to, to lead. His impatient yet friendly gaze still made Leith slightly uneasy.

"I mean someone who looks like that," tilting his head to the side and raising his eyebrows, "shouldn't be alone," Leith said with a smile.

Leith was somewhat awkward socially, sometimes not knowing if what he said was appropriate, but it never stopped him from saying it nonetheless. He'd learned to deal with the consequences. Fortunately for him, his new friends tolerated this quirk.

"Don't you worry about my sister," said Jannik, growing tired of these kinds of remarks. It seemed his sister was always the subject of his friend's jokes. Truth was, he knew they had all secretly taken a shining to her.

"Maybe we got it all wrong," added Grayson. He was trailing the pack as he usually did.

Jannik stopped suddenly, and they walked into each other. After a few groans and innocent bantering, Grayson added, "Maybe she just doesn't have a thing for fellas." It was an earnest delivery. He was generally quick-witted and the loudest of the bunch, except when it came to Jannik's sister. And while he was rather awkward, his humor came usually on account of his awkwardness.

No acknowledgment came from the others. They collectively turned and resumed their travel. Heads shook as if to say, "Here we go again."

"Don't you see how friendly she is with Lilith?"

"So, what's wrong with that?" Jannik said, shaking his head.

"Ah, Grayson's heart's just a little wounded," added Lael, the oldest by two months at twenty-five. He expected, by default, to assume the authoritative role among his friends, but none of the others looked to him as such. None except Alrik, his younger brother.

"He's just trying to make sense of why she pays him no notice," he chuckled.

"Do you remember her birthday celebration at the Red Corner?" Lael continued without waiting for a reply.

"Grayson wasn't feeling well. Something about his stomach I recall, but he wasn't gonna let that get in the way of an opportunity," he chuckled again. "'I'm going for it,' Grayson said, then turned and set his sights on her. I remember the look in his eyes: a man on a mission. He knocked over a chair on his way to ask her to dance, and when he bent to pick it up, he shit himself."

All burst out laughing. Grayson smiled abashedly.

"Wait, wait, there's more. He was mortified, but there was no stopping him on that night. He decided to douse himself with wine to try and mask the smell," his voice quivered, fighting laughter.

"Everyone turned and covered their noses when he walked by. He grabbed her hand and pulled her on to the dance floor. As they danced, the look on her face was priceless. Got to hand it to her though, she gave it a try. She heaved three times over his shoulder, her face white as a ghost. Thankfully for him, nothing came out. She apologized gracefully, and then she raced out of the tavern without looking back."

They laughed until their bellies ached.

"All right, that's enough," Grayson said, trying to salvage some self-respect.

They neared the end of the corridor.

"Almost there!" Alrik said excitedly.

Lael's younger brother, Alrik, had energy to kill and the impatience of a child half his years. Yet at seventeen, he exuded confidence and had an air of authority that was real. As the youngest of the bunch, Alrik had been born in the Den. He had never been outside the subterranean city and was anxious to see the sunlight and feel the wind on his face.

They came upon a lanky, frail-looking man quietly perched

on a rock. He struggled to his feet. Even in the dimness, they could make out his pallid complexion and hollowed cheeks. He didn't speak. He just nodded.

Jannik turned to his friends. "All right, I need to say this before we go out there. I appreciate you wanting to do this, but you know this is dangerous. You don't need to do this, and I'd understand if any of you turn back now."

"You'd have done the same for any of us," Leith said. "Besides, it was only a matter of time until one of us was selected."

Jannik nodded and turned to the guard. "What do we say to get back in?"

With effort, the guard croaked, "*Dajra-kans, hamara.* Freedom's lost, the weary returning."

"Colorful," said Lael. "Very optimistic sounding," he added sarcastically.

"How are we supposed to remember that?" Alrik blurted out.

"Dajra-kans is Ruid for 'we enter' and hamara for 'our,'" answered Jannik.

The guard uncovered a small peephole and looked outside. He closed it, grabbed the latch with his boney hand, turned and pushed the heavy door outwards. With the door slightly ajar, damp cool air rushed in from outside to fill the corridor. Jannik and Leith helped the guard push it the rest of the way.

"Be alert, and may the gods guide your safe return," the guard managed dryly, as if programmed to say it repeatedly.

"We'll be back in a few hours," Jannik replied stepping through the door.

They were on a sunken ledge behind a great waterfall. Ahead of them, water cascaded down like a curtain, serving as the last barrier between them and the unknown.

This was the first time any of them had stepped outside the Den since their arrival. Friendships were forged inside. None knew of each other from their lives before the Den. Selected by a draw held sporadically when the need arose, as when something vital was needed from the surface, Jannik's name was randomly drawn to fulfill a task. Only names of men below the age of thirty were included in the draw.

Fine water droplets struck their faces as they avoided the cascading volume of water. They pressed against the wall, made their way out the side of the waterfall and started the trek down the path on the side of the bluff towards Natras Pass.

They navigated the path until they reached the bottom, and then they headed into the forest. It was early morning and the earthy smell and light shining through the trees into the fog painted the moss on the trunks of the trees a light gray. Water droplets were still dripping from large leaves. They were entirely engrossed with the righteous beauty and had forgotten what it was like outside.

Alrik was enthralled. He was in awe of the beauty and completely unprepared for the openness. He felt so small. The feel of the crisp air and breeze was alien to him, but he welcomed it, taking large, exaggerated breaths.

They came upon a path and stayed on it for an hour until they saw the east crest of the Shad Mountains looming between the trees. They followed the peaks east until they found the area they were looking for.

"There it is boys, just a little bit farther," Jannik said, breathing a little heavily.

They stood over a verdant valley about half a mile from their destination. At the foot of the mountains, they could see a basin filled with water on the left of the pass. Surrounding it were fallen trees and dead stumps and a colorful multitude of weeds and wildflowers. Just beyond the basin, at the base of the mountain and slightly up the side, was a thick forest. On the right was a rolling, lush, green hill. The pass in the middle ascended and curved around and behind the hill and out of sight.

Jannik looked up into the sky above and behind them. "Has anyone seen or heard anything out of the ordinary?"

"Just seems unnaturally quiet," said Lael.

Alrik was off to the side on his own looking restless.

"You okay?" Lael asked.

"We gonna do this?" Alrik answered, anxious to go.

"Hey, listen, you shouldn't even be here," said Lael.

With a smile Jannik added, "Well, maybe you should brush up on your chackra skills."

No one laughed. Their anxiety was now clearly obvious. Alrik had beaten his brother in a game and won the opportunity to accompany them.

Lael turned to Alrik and whispered, "What did you tell mother you were doing?" Alrik just stared across the valley at the pass. He didn't answer, and then he lowered his eyes sheepishly.

Lael clenched his fists, angry at his brother's selfishness.

"What were you thinking? You didn't tell her?"

"Guys? Listen up!" Jannik called out, saving Alrik from Lael's wrath.

They came together in a circle. Lael was still glaring at his brother. Alrik's eyes were down.

"All right, here we go. There's still no obligation," said Jannik. "If you want to stay here, we'll meet up with you in a while. If you're crazy enough to do this, we run all out and meet up on the other side. No one stops, no matter what."

He took a moment to examine their eyes. They looked ready.

"Okay, go!"

They bolted into the valley. Alrik reached the path at the foot of the mountain first. Except for the odd hole in the ground, or uneven surface concealed by long grass in parts, the sprint seemed somewhat uneventful. He turned to find the others. Lael arrived next, then Jannik and Leith. Grayson, slightly heavier and rounder than the others, struggled a bit and arrived last.

"Hey Grayson, maybe let up on some of that bread you love so much," Jannik joked. "You going to be alright?"

Grayson nodded. "I'm good."

They took a look back and around for any sign of the enemy. It was quiet and pristine except for five fresh rows of trampled grass. Off to the side, they noticed ditches scattered near the pool. There were human bones piled atop each other, serving as a reminder of the fate of their brothers and the horror of their new reality. No one said a word. They stared in silence for a moment with chests heaving. Alrik pulled himself away first. The others followed, and they moved out of the open and into the gap between the mountains where they felt safer.

Jannik took out a paper from inside his vest pocket. He studied the map for a moment while they all gathered themselves and caught their breath.

"It's about a half mile that way," he said pointing into the pass.

By now, it was mid-morning, and the sun had risen above the trees to their left. The pass was narrow: about twelve feet at its widest. It narrowed in some parts, and they had to manage in single file. There was a narrow section about three feet wide that covered a good five hundred feet just before arriving at their destination. The cave loomed in front of them, looking typically dark and rather foreboding.

"One of us has to stay here and keep watch. Any volunteers?" Jannik asked.

No response.

"Alrik will stay," offered Lael.

Alrik, caught off guard, was about to argue, but he refrained after seeing the look in his brother's eyes.

"You hear anything that doesn't seem right, you come get us," ordered Jannik.

Alrik reluctantly nodded. Lael reached over, and he took the sack off of his brother's shoulder. Each one of them carried an empty sack that was to be filled with the item they had been sent out to retrieve.

Alrik watched the four of them turn toward the opening of the cave and disappear into it.

There was just enough light to see in the cave but not enough to reveal all its secrets. A steady sound of dripping water and an ancient smell filled the space. The stalagmites and stalactites looked like huge teeth. In fact, stains on them looked like dried blood. It wasn't long before the darkness swallowed the boys up, and the path sloped down until the sunlight from the cave mouth faded. They descended cautiously, knowing instinctively that caves can be notoriously deceptive.

Up ahead, the darkness grew thick, but it did not last long. With each step, a hint of a glow became more and more discernible from what looked like a gateway up ahead. With each step, the light intensified. After fifty or so steps, they reached it. Standing in front of what looked like a stone archway, hewn from black granite, the four of them had to shield their eyes from the brightness of the light.

Jannik stepped through the gateway first. When the others crossed the threshold, they found the walls, floor and roof of the cave, from the gateway onward, covered in what appeared to be fine white sand, only each particle was aglow in a brilliant light.

Jannik spoke first. "Gentlemen, here it is. I give you madrascythe."

The others stared in awe.

"This amazing substance senses subtle changes in temperature, absorbs heat and begins to glow. Our body heat is all it needs," said Jannik.

Ahead, the ground divided into two paths leading to opposite sides of the chamber. In between was a bottomless abyss. The slanted walls tapered towards each other, but the ceiling disappeared into the darkness above. As they stepped forward, it was as if their bodies were casting a shadow of light on the walls. The substance they walked towards glowed brighter; the substance they moved away from, dimmed.

"This is amazing!" Grayson said and then added, "But how is filling these satchels going to make a difference?"

Sliding his hand on the wall, Jannik came away with a handful of what resembled wet sand.

"When mixed with water, it readily dissolves. We brush it on the cave floor and walls, and the madrascythe crystalizes upon drying to become part of the stone. When people are around, it glows. For centuries, it's connected dwelling places in dark zones of the Den, hence it's called the 'light that binds.'"

"This should be enough. I mean, this amount will certainly provide for that new chamber discovered under Riverside where the Ingal clan will reside."

"The old man will probably throw a party just for us," said Grayson.

This began a series of remarks from each of them describing what they were going to do, how drunk they were going to get, which girl they were going to pursue, etc. This continued for some time, then when their sacks were full and slung over their shoulders, they gathered near the gateway, took one last look back and headed back to meet up with Alrik.

The voices quickly faded after they disappeared into the cave. Alrik was alone with his thoughts, and the wind whistling through the narrow pass. Every sound in the narrow confines of the pass seemed amplified. Each step he took on the rough gravel surface reverberated off the solid walls.

What am I supposed to do now? thought Alrik, heart still pounding from the excitement of the day. He tried sitting and resting his back against the wall of the pass, but that didn't last. He paced outside the opening of the cave for a while, counting the echo of each footstep.

"Going to Riverside today," he had said. Funny thing is, it did not bother him to lie to his mother. "I promised to help the Ingals.'"

In fact, he had not bothered to tell anyone the truth. He paused and thought for a moment about where he was, what he was doing and why he was here.

"All this for a girl?" he said out loud. Old Ashford Ingals' daughter had caught his attention, or rather, she had stolen it. He'd seen her a few times but was too bashful to say hello. He was hoping that if she knew of his pending adventure, she'd notice him. It seemed to work because yesterday, the last time he'd seen her, she had smiled and waved at him. He felt good, and for a moment, he rationalized his decision to come along was a good one.

More than an hour had passed since the others had left, and he thought he'd try his luck at sitting down again.

"Come on guys, what's taking so long?" he whispered.

He ignored the sound at first, but a moment later he heard it again. It was a crunching sound, like footsteps on gravel. It was faint but still audible and growing louder.

He leaned forward to look into the narrow part of the Pass. He didn't see anything, but then he got a whiff of something dreadful. It was the smell of death and decay. It turned into a choking stench. He moved from worry, to concern and then to just plain fear.

He was supposed to just kill some time here, meet up with his brother and his brother's friends, get back to the Den and win the girl. Instead, here he stood, wondering what horror approached. His heartbeat began throbbing against his ribcage. His breath tasted like iron and hitched in his throat.

Do I hide inside the cave and hope they pass, or do I go in and tell them to find another way out?

The torture of the decision was unbearable. He had only minutes before what approached reached him. Crunch. The sound was loud. His face froze in a glassy stare when he thought he caught a glimpse of movement. Shadows on the mountain's wall grew larger. A sound, like metal on metal as if a sword had been unsheathed, echoed in the pass. First one, then another Stragoy came into view. They were a fair distance from him, but even behind the face shields, he saw the death-like eyes. Alrik had never seen a Stragoy before. Their appearance was terrifying.

He had to warn the others. Somehow, he managed to tear himself away, and he rushed into the cave.

"Wait." Leith stopped suddenly and motioned for the others to be quiet.

"What is it?" asked Grayson.

"Shhh!"

"Did you guys hear that?" Leith whispered.

They could no longer leverage the darkness to hide. The contents of the sacks killed that option. Footsteps approached from the corridor to the right. They braced themselves. A shadow emerged from the dimness. Lael saw Alrik running toward them in a mad rush.

"What are you doing here? I thought I told you to stay—"

"Stragoy…in the Pass."

The air and mood turned sour. Their faces turned pale in the light of the madrascythe.

"They're coming towards the cave," said Alrik, pointing towards the entrance.

"We have to get out of here. This way," Jannik said, already moving in the direction they just had come from. "There's got to be another way out."

"Well, if that's the plan, let's go," Grayson said wide-eyed. Fear was apparent in his eyes. "They're already inside," he said, as he ran past the others, fighting for breath.

A foul odour filled the room. They returned to the gateway hastily and onto the path on the right in single file, casting light on the madrascythe. They continued for some time in what seemed an endless chamber. Eventually, the path led downwards and to the right. It was a marginal slope, undetectable by the eye, but enough to feel they were pushing harder into the rock with each step.

Behind them, the Stragoy reached the gateway and passed into the chamber where the madrascythe filled the walls. No light radiated from the madrascythe they passed. Their decomposing bodies as cold as corpses failed to have a similar effect. Up ahead, light from the five friends flickered, calling to the Stragoy like beacons.

"Keep going. They're behind us," said Jannik.

Their throats burned from the lack of moisture. They had

taken no water with them. *It was only supposed to be a couple of hours*, Jannik thought. There was a pounding in his head, and his ears throbbed, strangely in tempo with his footsteps.

The path straightened and then ascended. Jannik began to jog, and the others followed. They reached a fork in the path and stopped. Footsteps neared from the darkness behind.

"This way." Jannik started to the right.

They came to a room with the familiar sound of dripping water and the rock structures that had looked like huge teeth when they first entered the cave. They had made it back to the entrance, only the ancient smell was gone. An odor of decay was in its place.

The five men approached the opening cautiously. In the Pass, one Stragoy stood with his back to them, and there were two more in the narrow part of the Pass to his right. Almost at the same time, heavy steps approached from behind. A hissing, snarling, unnerving sound grew louder.

"Guys, follow my lead," Jannik whispered.

"Run!" He didn't give them any time to think.

Jannik darted out, grabbed a firm hold of the Stragoy's belt, and pushed. Lael rushed to aid Jannik, and together they shoved the unsuspecting Stragoy into the wall. The Stragoy had no time to brace itself. First its chest, then its face, struck the wall. The impact crushed its withered nose, erasing it completely from its rotting face. The Stragoy dropped to one knee as Alrik, Grayson, and Leith sprinted out to join Jannik and Lael, who had already started down the Pass.

When the Stragoy came to its feet, the other two emerged from the narrow Pass. They jeered and hissed at each other, and then they started in pursuit.

Their breathing quickened more out of anxiety and fear than

from the run. The madrascythe weighted them down somewhat, but to a man, they were driven by something other than fortitude. Jannik for one wasn't afraid of death but rather of ending up undead like those who pursued them.

Grayson's chest felt squeezed, like he had been hit with a hammer, and the splitting pain in his side had spread to his shoulder and his neck. He'd fallen to the back of the group even though he was one of the first to emerge from the cave. Up ahead, the Pass tapered to a narrow crack. They had to slow and turn sideways to squeeze through in single file. It slowed them down significantly, so by the time Grayson reached this section, the Stragoy were a mere fifty feet away.

The group struggled through, ignoring scrapes and bumps for about a hundred feet, until the section opened to the widest part of the Pass. Grayson emerged and bent over in apparent distress. Behind him, the Stragoy hissed and sputtered as they pressed forward.

Alrik was well in front, but fatigue had crept in; his strides went from long and controlled to quick and labored. The sprint had become a jog. Lack of oxygen, dryness in his throat and a lack of water, had taken its toll.

"Keep going! Run!" Jannik shouted.

Alrik reached the crest of a downward sloping hill and saw the end of the Pass about fifty feet ahead.

The Stragoy stormed out from the narrow section. One was gaining on Grayson, who was wavering and beginning to stumble. He sucked in air and picked up his pace.

Alrik reached the end of the Pass. He had a queer look in his eyes. Lael, next to reach the end, got a sinking feeling after noticing that look on his brother's face. He'd seen that look before, just before Alrik made some foolish or rash decision.

Grayson's face had a pained grimace. With the Stragoy

almost upon Grayson, Alrik started without hesitation back into the Pass, darting by his brother and the others, who moved out of his way.

Lael's gait slowed as he feared the worst, but movement at the end of the Pass behind the wall drew his attention momentarily away from his brother.

A hulking man stepped out, holding a heavy bow with an arrow taut and ready. Surprised, Lael's footing gave way, and he tumbled, bounced and rolled, stopping three feet from the stalwart man. He was human, with a large, menacing frame and dark eyes that glared down at Lael.

"Get off the Pass if you want to live," Herrick ordered with a deep, husky voice. Then he raised his bow, drew it back a little more and took aim.

A Stragoy came up on Grayson swiftly. Its footsteps were heavy and loud, but the hissing was even louder. There was a grunt and then a vicious swipe of the sword. Grayson tilted slightly to the left. A gash appeared across his cloak from his right shoulder to below the middle of his back, but he felt no pain. He drew in a breath, held it and pressed on. The blow forced the Stragoy slightly off balance, buying Grayson some time. With a weary head, he looked up, noticing Alrik at the last moment bearing down on him. Instinctively, he leapt to the side as Alrik threw himself at the unsuspecting Stragoy's feet at full stride, swiping its feet from under him.

Down the Stragoy plunged. Its head hit the hard surface, knocking his face shield off. The side of his face scraped the ground; stones sliced and ripped what remained of the decaying flesh. Alrik slid and rolled in the opposite direction. His arms, side and legs, were scraped and bloodied. The friction ripped his clothes and the sack containing the madrascythe. Dust filled the air.

A second Stragoy approached, stepping out of the white

cloud of dust. Alrik lay squirming and grimacing. The Stragoy drew its sword over its head, but an arrow struck it in the middle of the chest. The force drove it backwards and onto his back.

Alrik worked his way onto his hands and knees but found bending his leg a challenge. A pair of hands grabbed him under his arms and heaved him up.

"Let's get out of here!" Grayson shouted.

The Stragoy Alrik had tripped then jumped to its feet. With half its face gone, it shrieked and roared and glowered back at them out of one eye. It was standing between them and the end of the Pass. An arrow struck it behind the ear and exited through its rotting cheek below the good eye. It fell.

Herrick was picking the Stragoy off one at a time. He drew another arrow from his quiver, he nocked it and took aim.

Jannik, fourth after Alrik, Lael and Leith to reach the end of the Pass, scurried past Herrick, who was too absorbed in his task to pay him notice. Lael, witnessing the events unfold, started back towards his brother, but a grip on his shoulder, like a vise, yanked him back.

"Get out of here!" Herrick roared.

Jannik looked on helplessly as Alrik, with Grayson's assistance, hobbled towards him. The third creature closed in on them.

"Move!" Jannik screamed, motioning with his arms. His friends were in the arrow's trajectory.

Herrick let an arrow fly, but it whisked by. He grabbed another and took aim.

Alrik, bleeding and in pain, stumbled and dragged Grayson down with him. The Stragoy caught up to them and dwarfed them with its bulk. Sensing their vulnerability, it slowed its attack. Cold steel touched Grayson's neck. The Stragoy's sword rested there for a moment as if marking the spot. The Stragoy brought its arm up, but its intent was foiled when an arrow struck it in the shoulder. It simply stumbled back, gathered itself and returned for a second strike. With blank eyes and an impassive stare, it raised its sword over its head again, the arrow still lodged in its shoulder. A second arrow buzzed by, ending its flight in the Stragoy's face. Its chest heaved, and it collapsed on top of Alrik.

Alrik and Grayson squirmed out from under the Stragoy and stumbled the rest of the way down the Pass. About twenty feet from the end, four more Stragoy emerged from the narrow crack.

"Go! Get into the forest, and don't look back," the stranger commanded.

Jannik and his friends did what they were told.

Thanks to the mysterious stranger, they had escaped the Stragoy, but now they were lost. They wandered till the sun was high in the sky. Few had been to this side of the Shad Mountains. In fact, Jannik's map did not have anything beyond the boundary of the highlands. Before them were only ridges sloping towards a forest filled with large trees. Sometime later, they were surrounded by trees.

An uncomfortable thought was growing inside Jannik. *How are we going to get back? I don't know of any other way in.*

Lael helped Alrik down onto a large branch of a fallen tree.

"We have to stop," he groaned. When they left the Pass in a hurry not two hours ago, Lael had relieved a tired Grayson from the burden of carrying his brother. No one had said a word until now.

"He can't go on without rest."

The others, too, sat heavily with their hands on their knees, except for Jannik, who stood staring ahead. He was doing his best to hide his growing feeling of anxiety and gloom.

Alrik was in pain. His clothes were torn, and blood had congealed in most places.

"You saved my life," Grayson placed a hand on Alrik's shoulder gingerly. Alrik winced. "I won't forget what you did," he added, managing a smile.

"What was that?" Leith asked scornfully, referring to the ordeal. It set off a series of questions.

"How'd they even know we were there?"

"That stranger just saved our lives," Leith piped in.

"Can't believe that just happened," said Lael. "Did anyone see if he was alone? I didn't see anyone else with him."

"What do we do now?" Alrik said, grimacing.

Eyes turned towards Jannik. Question after question was asked without an apparent need for an answer. They blurted them out, sometimes over each other.

"Guys," Jannik said. He turned towards them, and the badgering stopped for a moment. They looked a different bunch than the upbeat group full of optimism that started out a few hours earlier.

"We can't go back that way. Who knows how many more of those things are back there?" He paused, shaking his head and added, "We can't stay here either."

The group was spent and battered, but all agreed complacency would kill them.

"Fifteen minutes," he said, then turned to Lael, pulling him aside. "Take them east," he said, pointing into the forest.

"Why? What are you going to do?"

"I have to go back."

"You out of your mind?"

"We left him there, Lael. Granted, he was doing all right without our help, but he helped us, and we left him."

"What else were we supposed to do? None of us have ever fought anything before."

Outwardly, Lael may have expressed concern, but inside, he agreed with Jannik.

"If you're going to go back, I'm coming," Lael exclaimed.

There was a brief discourse, and then everyone, albeit with hesitation in some cases, agreed to go back.

A heated discussion about who was going to remain with Alrik and head east, came next. Alrik voiced his displeasure at the suggestion. Jannik convinced Grayson to stay behind. But then just as Grayson reluctantly agreed and bent to help Alrik to his feet, a branch snapped to their left.

The men stopped and listened. A large figure stepped between two tree trunks and over a fallen branch and approached. It was Herrick, who had a distressed look on his face. Dried blood mottled his beard and his black shoulder-length hair on one side. The bow was slung across his back, and a broadsword stained with blood was in his hand. A gash above his right bicep was visible beneath his gray shirt.

"What are you still doing here?" He bellowed with his low, sonorous voice. His eyebrows furrowed.

"Why are you helping us?" asked Jannik, ignoring Herrick's question.

The heaving of Herrick's chest slowed, and he relaxed his features. The deep furrows became thin lines.

"A blind man could have followed your tracks," he said, shaking his head in disgust while he grabbed a canteen from his shoulder and handed it to Alrik.

Secretly he was studying the young men. His plan was coming together better than he expected. "You're a brave one, lad," he said in a calm manner. It was the first time he had said anything that wasn't a command or spoken in an angry fashion.

Alrik smiled. He took a swig and passed it on.

"I'm Herrick Mead, and you are—"

"Alrik, Lael, Jannik, Leith and Grayson," Alrik said, pointing to the others.

Herrick smirked, and then he finished the sentence he'd started, "Lucky that I happened to be out hunting this morning," then added, "You're all right for now, but by nightfall, these woods will be swarming with those creatures. You shouldn't be here when that happens."

"Agreed, but we have a little problem. We don't know where we are," said Jannik. "What about you?"

"What about me?"

"You must have come from someplace."

"I've been on my own for years. No family, no friends. I've survived with these," he said pointing to his bloodied hands. "I've been wandering for the last ten years. I'm not sought and not missed. I prefer it that way."

"I stole this from my first kill," said Herrick, raising his sword admiringly. The furrows appeared again.

"I found the creature in my parent's home, standing over their bloodied bodies. I killed the repulsive thing, stole the sword, and took out as many of those rancid creatures as I could." He lied, finding it easy and natural. "I woke up sometime later in the woods, with no memory of how I got there and I've been alone ever since."

Sounding sincere in a lie was something he took pride in. His method was to believe his lie wholeheartedly and play it out in his mind. Then he could tell the story with a mixture of emotions—sadness and anger—and follow it up by assessing how believable he was by examining the expressions on the faces that stared back. He sensed skepticism.

"Where do you need to go?" Herrick asked. The response would let him know how much work he had ahead of him. An exact location meant little effort, a vague response meant some work ahead and a lack of trust. He was hoping for somewhere in the middle.

The five friends looked at each other and whispered amongst themselves. Jannik shook his head, and Grayson answered, "Towards Dema Falls."

Herrick saw disappointment in Jannik for the relative ease with which Grayson had offered this information. *Some work to do*, Herrick thought. He could tell Jannik was the leader of the bunch and the one to focus his attention on. He'd need some time to gain their trust. Perhaps a longer journey back to Dema Falls would give him the time he needed.

"I know of another way to get you there. It's around the highlands to the east, about a day and a half's journey towards the Syran Hills. I'll point you in the direction."

The friends huddled around Alrik. "What do you think?" Jannik asked. "Should we ask him to take us?"

"What choice do we have?" said Alrik.

"He's already saved our lives," said Grayson trying to sound convincing.

"Yes, but we don't know anything about him," Jannik said.

"Let's just ask him if he can take us there. We'll make a decision about what to do then," Lael reasoned. "After all, we can part ways when the waterfall is in our sights but not near enough to give the location away."

They huddled and discussed for another minute, and then Jannik turned to Herrick, who seemed indifferent to their apparent dilemma, wiping the blood off his sword with a large leaf.

"I know it is a fair distance for you, and we are already indebted to you for your courage, but we would be most grateful if you would consider helping us get back to Dema Falls. We promise that we will see you repaid with all the food, clothing, and supplies you can carry."

Herrick was pleased with the way the plan was playing out.

"Please, Herrick," Jannik pleaded.

Herrick was pleased with his treachery. He stared at Jannik for a while as if pondering the decision. "All right, I'll do it for the boy," he said walking over towards Alrik. He smiled and added, "He reminds me of myself."

They gathered their things and headed east.

11

JEWEL OF THE WILDERNESS

AFTER WEEKS OF wandering the verdant hills at the foot of the Shad Mountains, Korian came upon an ancient timbered forest, thick with brush and wild vegetation. It would have cost him more than a day to walk around it, and it wouldn't be the first primal forest Korian had passed through. So, he pressed on into the woods until he came to a slow-moving river meandering peacefully down from the mountains. There he sat and rested, after walking for more than eight straight hours.

Korian knelt, cupped his hands and savored the rich, cool, refreshing water. "Just a little farther," he said out loud.

After filling his canteen, he crossed the river and journeyed onward to the place, where many years ago, he had stumbled across the thing he cherished most.

Korian felt awake. After his desert ordeal, his mind was open to new stimuli and opportunities. Over the last few weeks, he'd become more and more accustomed to his new reality and better equipped to tolerate and control bouts of information overload.

When I get there, what then?

Finch had spoken often of the Den and the desire of many to find it. Most abandoned self-preservation for even just the hope of finding something that could perhaps serve as a sanctuary, and they paid dearly. The Den was supposed to be a hope for normalcy: a refuge where life was supposed to resemble a manner that had been forgotten. The Den was a yearning for freedom from terror and oppression...but was it truly freedom? Finch insisted the Den was a prison, worse even than the prison he and Korian lived in on the surface. His opinion was that the Den was devoid of the warmth and of the light from the sun and of compassion for people. How much comfort could people, whose lives have been destroyed, whose loved ones have been taken, find in strangers?

"That much despair has got to do something to a person."

Although Korian had no experience dealing with people directly, he did not agree with what Finch had preached. He never stopped or challenged Finch when he went on his rants, but for a reason Korian couldn't quite explain, he believed people could, in fact, find compassion in strangers. It was this belief that had driven him to find this place.

There were things from that day—the day Korian had met Sara—that he had not been able to reconcile. When he and Finch were inside the tunnel, before emerging and entering the abandoned outpost, he remembered hearing voices. Finch dismissed them as a boy's vivid imagination, but Korian thought differently and still did. Korian was certain there was more to that tunnel.

He was nearing the end of a forest. He came to a fairly steep hill and found a path that wound down between a number of widely spaced trees. On his march down the slope, the woods grew denser and his stomach grumbled, reminding him of how long it had been since he had last eaten.

When he reached the bottom of the hill, he stumbled onto another dirt path that ran between rows of taller trees. Something strange and out of place caught his eye as he walked at a leisurely pace. A shiny, egg-shaped shell with a long, narrow, slit-like opening was affixed to a tree. It looked ancient and worn and resembled a large eye. Normally, he'd stay and ponder it but satisfying his hunger took precedence.

He pressed on towards the outpost, but he stopped suddenly when an overwhelming premonition of danger swept over him. The hairs on his arms stood on end. He dashed behind the thick underbrush and waited, unaware of what exactly he was hiding from.

A minute later, there was a loud crack from the forest on the other side of the path. Korian froze. His body tensed. He felt vulnerable behind the underbrush, and he decided instead, to move behind the broad trunk of a large tree. It didn't offer any more protection, but it somehow made him feel safer.

It was early evening, and insects were buzzing around feasting on him. He was there for a half hour, ignoring the bothersome pests, when a pagyon strolled onto the path. The docile creature, covered in dark brown fur, bent forward and lowered its head and long, slender snout to feed on grass and forbs.

The pagyon resembled a deer except for the shorter neck and more slender body. It had two small horns on its head.

Lucky you, thought Korian. He relaxed somewhat at the rather tranquil sight, but less than a minute later, the pagyon raised its head and perked its ears. A piercing shriek broke the stillness. Something was coming from above. What it was he could not yet see. The screech was enough to freeze a man in his tracks. The pagyon froze. A sudden gust stirred leaves and dirt, and branches swayed in its wake. A large shadow descended between the trunks and swept the pagyon away.

Korian waited a moment, then he stepped from behind the tree and crept towards the path again. As quietly as he could, he crouched behind the underbrush and leaned forward. A large skine was hunched over with the pagyon clasped firmly in its powerful jaws.

From above the trees, two more skines soared into view and circled several times. Korian quietly returned to his hiding spot behind the tree. He peered around the trunk, and found he had a pretty good view of the path.

The skines descended, bared their teeth and snarled. Their growls were piercing. With its face and snout bloodied, the first skine raised its head and scowled at its smaller visitors. A vicious battle ensued. The larger skine's claws struck viciously. The violent assault and the ferocious shrieks were unnerving. Korian turned away. Branches cracked and enraged wails pierced the air. There was a loud roar, the sound of wings beating and then…calm.

Korian stole a glance as the large skine, with its prey clutched in one talon, disappeared into the forest. The other two skines were gone.

Korian waited. On the other side of the path, the primal sounds of the beast tearing flesh, growling and feeding on its prey, resumed.

When he first heard voices, he thought them in his head until he saw them: six men on the path. Five of them looked nervous, repeatedly glancing behind and into the forest on either side of the path. One of them, a rather staunch fellow, appeared to be leading. He carried a sword and a bow with arrows strapped to his back. He was considerably taller and had a sureness absent in the others. He looked rather ragged with blood on his clothes, beard and hair. Korian sensed something familiar about him.

They sauntered by, oblivious of the danger lurking almost immediately to their left.

Korian did not know them, owed them nothing, and he understood warning them risked his safety, yet he felt a compelling need to do something.

He stepped out from behind the tree to get their attention, but he was too late.

"We're almost there," whispered Herrick. "Up past those trees, the highlands will come into view. Just a little farther, and I'll get you where you need to go."

Jannik's and his friends' senses were heightened. Every snap of wood, whistle of the wind through leaves, warble of bizarre looking tree frog-like amphibians, as nightfall approached, had them on edge. They would nervously glance behind or into the forest, repeatedly.

"There's shelter up ahead," Herrick said, pointing towards the bend in the path. "We'll rest there until morning." His arm was still raised when a low, guttural growl came from off the path to the left. They froze in their tracks.

The bloodied carcass of a pagyon catapulted out of the shadow of the woods just off the path. It struck Lael and Alrik, driving them off their feet onto the other side of the path and into some spiny shrubs. The sack Lael carried tore apart, spreading madrascythe onto neighboring shrubs and trees. Immediately, parts of the ground, surfaces of plants and fine particles in the air, lit up.

Even before the carcass hit the ground, a large shape appearing to be more than any ordinary animal emerged from the forest.

Its shriek was chilling. The sound pierced their ears and numbed their senses. The skine swatted Grayson off to the side with a blow. It pounced on Jannik and pinned him to the ground with its powerful claws. Its talon held him down while the creature's weight pressed on Jannik's chest.

Startled, Leith, standing adjacent to Jannik, felt a powerful claw close around his throat before he even knew what happened. The skine leaned forward, spat and frothed while its head jerked left and right. Leith noticed a part of its left ear missing: a strange imperfection for such a perfect and deadly killing machine. The thought left him as soon as the skine pushed out its chest, spread its wings as wide as it was tall and let out a thunderous bellow.

Herrick looked on in surprise. *This is not part of the plan.* He was unprepared for this. He needed them alive. He charged, and with two hands on his sword, swung at the skine's head. The sword struck the leathery skin and thick bone of the skine's forearm and bounced off. With its weight still pressing on Jannik's chest, the skine flung Leith across the path towards Lael and Alrik. The sudden impact knocked them out.

Herrick swiped a second time. This time, the skine seized his arm and squeezed. The pressure was so intense Herrick felt his arm was about to be cleaved at the elbow. Into the eyes of primal rage Herrick stared as the skine clasped his head with the other claw and pulled it back to expose his neck.

Is this how fear feels? Herrick's thought, so irrational, swept through his mind and passed in an instant when the skine dug his teeth into Herrick's shoulder.

Jannik couldn't breathe. The weight of the skine was crushing. As soon as it had Herrick in his jaws, the creature began jerking its head from side to side, shaking Herrick like a ragdoll. Herrick's shrieks stopped, but the sharp jerks of the skine's head continued for a few more seconds and then…it abruptly stopped.

Its eyes opened wide, it released Herrick and wailed, deafeningly. Herrick crumbled in a heap.

A wide gash appeared on the back of the skine's leg below its tail. The enraged creature looked around, but there was no one there. The skine quickly dismissed the inconvenient interruption and focused on Jannik.

The skine clasped Jannik's neck, lifted him up and pinned him against a tree. Jannik gagged from the immense pressure on his throat. He clawed frantically at the creature, but it was like striking a wall of sharp, jagged rocks. The skine bared its teeth and leaned forward until its breath was warm on Jannik's face. It growled and exposed razor-sharp tines. Then its eyes opened wide for a second time, and it howled. This time, a large gash appeared on its upper back below the skull, spraying blood onto its wings. It released a battered and bruised Jannik, who crumbled to the ground. When the skine turned, Korian was on the path. He raised his leather clad hand and snared his "V" weapon out of the air.

The skine leaned forward and rested on its claws. It stood completely still for a moment, resembling a giant gargoyle. Suddenly it charged.

Using the deepening shadows of dusk, Korian darted into the forest for cover. He arced around several trees until he came back up behind Jannik, who was still writhing on the ground.

"Grab the others and get out of here. Pass the outpost and get to the tunnel on the left. You should find a way into the Den from in there," Korian shouted.

Korian was betting on instinct and on a strong feeling he had about that tunnel. They were out of options. If he was wrong, they'd meet their fate regardless. If his intuition was right, he had, at least, given them a chance.

As the last word rolled off his tongue, a large talon came down on the ground beside him. Primal rage was evident in the skine's red eyes when they glared down at Korian. Then, suddenly, intense pressure from a grip at the scruff of his neck paralyzed him. The next thing Korian saw was sky and trees passing by swiftly as he realized he was airborne.

He landed back on the path and used his momentum to roll back onto his feet. He grabbed Grayson's sack of madrascythe that lay to his right, and he darted into the forest on the opposite side of the path.

Jannik rolled onto his knees. Something sharp pinched the palm of his hand. It was a ring with a purple-shaped tear. He picked it up to examine it, but it burned into his palm. He winced and dropped it.

In the woods across from him, sounds of a struggle had moved deeper into the forest. Jannik picked the ring up by the chain, and he put it in his pocket. By this time, the others had also come to their feet, except for Herrick, who lay still, in a puddle of his own blood. Jannik and Leith, with Grayson's help, picked up Herrick. Alrik, with Lael dazed but able, along with the others, started towards the end of the path.

Darkness was almost upon the forest. They had to move fast. It was then that they heard a new flurry of activity and sounds of branches breaking from the forest. They hastened their pace.

"That's not skine!" screamed Jannik.

A swarm of Stragoy descended from the hills and from the path behind them. Their footsteps grew louder; the hissing, snarling and spluttering unnerved the young men.

They stumbled the rest of the way down the path towards the outpost and to the tunnel just as the stranger had said. In the distance, the skine's roars faded, but the Stragoy's frightening clatter grew louder as the five friends and Herrick converged at the mouth of the outpost and rushed towards the tunnel. By this time, darkness had fallen over the forest.

Inside the tunnel, light from the madrascythe illuminated their surroundings.

"*Dajra-kans, hamara!*" Jannik yelled, no longer worried about being heard. Nothing happened. The Stragoy had closed the distance by half.

"Come on! *Dajra-kans, hamara*," Jannik repeated.

When the first of the Stragoy entered the tunnel, the path was empty. They rushed in, came out the other side and pressed on, hissing and spitting. Soon, the last of them passed through the tunnel and disappeared into the darkness.

Korian weaved through the trees using light from the madrascythe as a guide. His mind calculated options and their probabilities of success. Behind him, the enraged skine, twice his size, cunning and vicious, was gaining.

Korian burst into a large clearing. "This will have to be the place," he said.

He opened the sack and ran into the open space, dispersing the madrascythe into the air. He counted his paces, and he remembered certain markers as he passed: a rotten stump at twenty paces, at forty-two a mound with a large rock. At a hundred paces, with the contents of the sack spent, he stopped and turned.

The clearing was alive with a plethora of blue and white hues and a multitude of vibrant shades. Tiny particles in the air danced in the breeze, swirling and looping and settling on rocks and other objects. The grass was alight where the madrascythe had fallen. Critters or other things that gave off even the most miniscule quantity of heat caused the intensity of the light to vary. Around Korian, the air seemed ablaze with what appeared to be millions of tiny fireflies.

The enchantment enveloping his surroundings vanished the moment the creature emerged into the clearing with a vicious growl. When it saw Korian on the other side of the clearing, it spread its wings, stooped and charged.

The air swirled and looped as the skine picked up momentum. At twenty paces, it spread its wings, and it left the ground. Korian grasped the Lubics V and assumed the throwing position. The skine soared about fifteen feet off the ground. Tracing the skine's path using his markers as reference, he calculated its speed and used the movement of the particles ablaze in the night to estimate wind direction. He let his weapon soar about three feet off the ground on a slight angle.

The "V" twirled and turned horizontal, and then at about twenty-five paces from where he stood, the weapon quickly arced upwards, meeting the skine just below the chest on its right side. Half of the object disappeared into its thick skin. The creature howled and crashed to the ground.

It lay motionless for a moment. Korian held his breath. The skine let out a grunt and slowly came to its feet with a snort. It pulled the weapon out of its side and tossed it on the ground. Blood gushed down its abdomen and leg.

The skine spread its wings, leaned back and roared. When it turned to a snarl, a strong gust of wind swept into the clearing from above. Faster than Korian thought possible, two skines descended. One struck Korian on the side of the head with its clawed hand, and everything went black.

When Korian woke up, the area was still illuminated with light from the madrascythe. It was still night. Three skines lay on the ground; two had their skulls crushed. The third lay still with cuts all over its body. Blood painted its thick skin an inky shade of burgundy in the dark.

Korian peered into the woods that were draped in darkness and listened. Just sounds of insects and critters. "Thank you," he said into the forest in a loud whisper. It looked like the work of his protector, reminiscent of the dead wolfen he had come across many years earlier.

A sound like a muffled grunt came from where the third skine lay. Korian approached it tentatively. It lay still. Its chest did not appear to move. *Must be the bump on my head*, he thought. Korian leaned in closer. "By the look of you," he whispered, "I'm pretty sure you didn't suffer."

The skine's eyes opened. A powerful claw clasped Korian behind the neck. With its long arm, the skine pulled Korian towards its snapping jaws. Its foul breath was warm on Korian's face. Korian resisted as best he could by pressing against the skine's chest. His arms were numb, and his bulging veins pulsed with his beating heart. The last of his strength and resistance began to wane. Korian took one last deep breath and held it. He looked into the skine's red eyes—open and fixed. Just before Korian gave in completely, the growling stopped, and the skine's grip slackened. It lowered its head, rested it on the ground, and closed its eyes.

Korian looked down at the helpless skine. He retrieved his weapon and did what he needed to do to end the skine's suffering.

The rain had ended. Everything was refreshed and invigorated. The world seemed saturated with the balanced energy of nature's renewal. Arching over the trees to the north was a great rainbow displaying its colors over the blue canvas sky.

A promise of new hope and change, or just a result of distorted reflection of sunlight in water droplets? Korian pondered. Perhaps as a boy he'd have believed the former. Today, he saw things with less ambiguity and more clarity.

It had been a week to the day since Korian had battled the skine. Since then, he'd converted a rundown building from the deserted outpost into a temporary shelter. A window at the front offered an unobstructed view to the tunnel. No one had come or gone since he had arrived.

What do I do now? He asked himself for the first couple of days, but as days passed, the desire for an answer waned. The ring that bound him to Sara, his inspiration and beacon of hope, was lost. Abandoning his hope had driven him to a loneliness he couldn't bear. It was a loneliness as natural as blinking his eyes, a loneliness that grew on him, a loneliness where no one wondered where he was when he was coming home. He felt isolated and lost in a dark place, as if loneliness was tied to him like a ball and chain, crushing and constricting him every day as if he were in prison.

He gathered himself from his slumber. Waking up was becoming harder as each day passed, but he pushed on, driven by some fortitude he did not understand.

He left his dwelling for food, but on this day, made a choice to head towards the woods on the eastern end. After walking this particular path through the woods for a while, he came across a shell fixed on the trunk of a tree. It was the second such shell he'd seen in a week.

This is odd, he thought.

Suddenly, a thought entered his mind. Korian wasn't sure of the source—from books he'd read or stories he'd been told perhaps—but he recalled the legend of Bebin and of the pilgrimage to Illian or Garden of the Gods. According to legend, in the year AZ 940, Bebin, a hermit, had a vision of a bright star surrounded by a ring of smaller ones shining over a deserted spot in the hills. This led to the discovery, after much searching, of Illian, also known as the Jewel of the Wilderness, a place that was said could have only been created by divine hands. A monastery had been built at this place where it was believed the gods sculpted the place where Prian, the Ruid father's spirit, endures.

The *Cerulean Book of Scribes* contains the account where, according to legend, within the Portal realm, Zoren adorned Prian's body with gifts in preparation for burial. Atop his chest, he placed a cowry shell in between his hands. It was a symbol of power, vitality and vision in the afterlife. The shell's unique resemblance to a half-closed eye led to the belief that it served as an artificial eye in the spirit world.

After the discovery of Illian, accounts began of pilgrimages to this sacred place. It is said that people travelled from all over seeking enlightenment or adventure; just the sense of following in ancient footsteps was inspiration in itself. The shells were secured to the trees to serve as markers to aid travelers in finding the place.

Where Korian's path in the woods ended, a steep set of stairs made of stone curved into a narrow cleft through a hill. At the top, the path continued, zigzagging towards the sound of rushing water.

When he reached the end, he came to a large terrace facing seven weathered stone statues of the gods guarding a magnificent monastery with a domed roof. Six of the tall effigies formed a hexagon, and one—tallest and wisest looking—stood in the middle.

You must be Samjees.

They and the monastery stood quiescent yet regal. Korian

marveled at the detail of the extravagant carvings adorning the monastery's surface.

The door to the monastery was unlocked, and he entered. It was like walking into the past: an ancient smell lingered, and the furniture and decoration, most of it worn and rundown, was from another time. The ceiling was decorated with madrascythe and carvings and fresco in parts. It looked like a clear night sky on a summer's eve, full of flickering stars and constellations. Time and neglect had taken a toll. Parts of the ceilings had fallen away and now littered the floor.

Around the perimeter, lamps were positioned in front of seven smaller idols of the gods. At the back, instead of a wall, there was a balcony, and a railing made of stone, separating him from a steep drop and the majestic view. From this balcony, overlooking the splendor of the valley, Korian truly felt the closest he'd ever been to the gods.

Illian, coined the Jewel of the Wilderness, or "sacred garden" in Ruid, was located in the steep, hidden valley nestled in Gareth Sarilam or "Place of Great Water." It was at the place where two great rivers met. The south face of the valley contained giant walls, terraces and ramps. The once great city of Nahire was to the north and Strathmere to the northeast, beyond the moorland to the east of the valley.

The place was carved after the great quake of AZ 720. On the northern side, the Clandian River, flowing down from the Shad Mountains, rolled off cliffs into the Marzian River. There were more than two hundred cascades spreading over nearly two miles.

He stood in awe for a time, taking in the grandeur. Time seemed to stand still. It was midday, he figured, when he found himself back in the terrace looking up at the statue of Samjees.

"Why?" whispered Korian, while gazing up at Samjees' statue. "Have I not suffered and paid for my mistakes? And what of Endura? You have forsaken us. What world is this where you allow this wickedness and murder to occur?" His voice took on a hint of ire.

"Why Finch? Why take him from me, and why not send a sign—something, anything to let me know before I left for this place that I've nothing here? You've toyed with me."

His ranting turned to shouts for answers, and he cursed. His face reddened. When he hurt his hands and feet hitting and kicking the statue, he started pushing it from the front, then the side. When that failed, he grabbed anything he could find to throw at it: mud, branches, rocks, pieces of the collapsed ceiling. He even threw his "V" and his canteen, and then he raced after it when he realized what he'd done. When he turned to glare at the statue again, there was a woman on the terrace.

Korian froze. He was disheveled, and he was breathing heavily. He moved his hair away from his face without taking his eyes off her. The woman just stared, a hint of a smile on her lips.

"Who are you?" he asked as he cautiously stepped past her to peer down the path to see if there were others.

"Just someone out searching," she said in a soft, warm voice.

Korian's shock at seeing her quickly turned to admiration.

"Are you displeased with something?" she asked mockingly, a sweet smile fixed on her face.

The statue was now stained with mud, vines dangled off its hands, and debris was scattered all around.

"I was merely expressing myself with more than just words—to get their attention that is."

The corners of her lips curled upwards, and her eyes sparkled in the light. Her slenderness was apparent beneath the snug bodice and a pair of hosen. She was youthful, with a kind of look that demanded attention even if she wasn't looking for it.

"You alone?" asked Korian.

"I am for the moment."

"What are you doing here?"

"I heard shouting and followed the noise. Like I said, I was looking for someone."

"I mean, where are you from?" Korian asked.

Korian was captivated. Her wide, almond-shaped eyes followed his every move. He was conscious of what he said and how he must appear, struggling to remain coherent when his heart was beating like a drum, its tempo rising. All he could focus on was the radiance that her skin exuded. Her complexion was slightly lighter than ivory, and her faultless dark ginger hair fell loosely over her shoulders in skinny, slack curls.

"I'm from a secret place. It's dark there, with a lot of sadness. My brothers and sisters live there together. We make the best of it."

"I think I know of this place, though I've never seen it. But I know of despair too—yet, I for one, the eternal doubter, have today had my faith in hope restored."

"How so?"

"I can't explain it in words, but I can show you."

Casually, she strolled around the terrace, admiring the large artifacts and forcing him to step out of her way a few times as if he wasn't there. He didn't mind. He admired her grace.

"Show me what?"

As she spoke, she stumbled onto a shiny V-shaped silver object. She leaned forward to reach for it when something fell from her bodice, dangling from a necklace.

"Wait!" Korian shouted.

She stood up, wide-eyed. It was a ring: his ring on her necklace. His mind raced. Then he came back to himself as his vision cleared. Initially blinded by her radiance, he realized how foolish he'd been to have overlooked the obvious: the shape of her face, her hair, and more importantly, her eyes, all these years later. There was no mistake.

"Sorry, that's mine," Korian answered. "I just didn't want you to hurt yourself. It really is quite sharp." He bent and picked it up with his gloved hand and put it away.

"Sara?" Korian blurted out.

Her eyebrows raised, and she pursed her lips. He looked down at his arms. They were covered in goose bumps.

"We've met before," said Korian.

"This is why I know the gods have not abandoned us. If the world was truly lost to despair, how could this beauty exist?" said Korian.

They were inside the monastery on the balcony overlooking the hidden falls. Some of the larger falls sprayed large volumes of mist into the air. Numerous rainbows spanned the expanse. The infinite wonders of Illian could not be described in words.

"It's so beautiful," said Sara.

"Yes, so beautiful," he repeated. He was looking at her.

She noticed Korian from the corner of her eye and blushed.

"Earlier, you said we had met before?"

She was toying with him. She remembered every detail of that meeting: of his face and his touch. She could still see the boy in his eyes. When she saw the V-shaped object, she was certain she'd found who she was looking for.

"We were children then. Our paths crossed in the woods not too far from here," said Korian.

"Yes, I remember. You shoved me to the ground, then you took my ring."

"Not quite how I remember it."

"I was whisked away before I could thank you."

Korian bowed. "Yes, I recall—quite impressive I was?"

Sara shook her head and smiled coyly.

"What of the handkerchief?" added Korian.

"What handkerchief?"

"The white linen I…never mind," he said, letting the matter drop. It seemed such a small thing now. "How did the ring come to you now?"

She turned and moved slightly towards him. The tilt of her head, the inflection in her voice, made Korian cognizant of her subtle movements. He'd never been in a situation like this before, but he sensed she might be flirting with him.

"Three days ago, five men and one badly wounded by a skine, returned to our refuge. The wounded one had saved the others from a pack of those hideous Stragoy. His wounds have been tended to, and he's recovering. Besides a few nasty teeth marks and some pretty serious scars, he'll live. Now, he's got a pretty impressive story to tell. Not many have been in a skine's jaws and lived." Sara chuckled.

"One of the men brought the ring back—he is my brother. He told me of a man who wielded a weapon like that one," she said and pointed to the "V."

"He said he had drawn the skine from them and dropped the ring in his haste."

Korian put the pieces together. "Who exactly are you searching for?" His excitement grew.

Sara gazed out over the grandeur of the cascades. "It's late afternoon; I never told Jannik what I was doing. By now, I'm sure he's figured it out and is out there looking for me." She paused and looked at Korian knowingly, "What happened to your skine?" asked Sara as she headed out of the monastery with Korian behind her.

"Don't know."

As he passed by the statue of Samjees, he glanced up and quietly whispered, "Sorry, and thank you."

"What?" asked Sara.

"Just talking to myself."

When they reached the narrow path through the crevice towards the stone stairway, she turned.

"What's your name?"

"I'm Korian."

"Well then, my good sir, I was searching for a man named Korian."

There was no one else in the world, or so it seemed. For Korian, despite living in isolation up to this point, despite being devoid of contact, or even the sight of another living soul, he'd always been aware that there were others alive and in hiding. He'd spent his life on the outside looking in. Without the benefit of experience, he'd lived through others, through what he'd read in books and more perversely, through what he'd learned from the abandoned belongings of the dead. More recently, as if his burden of isolation wasn't enough, his mind had been packed with experiences and memories belonging to someone else. Today he felt different. He felt alive.

Korian and Sara spent the remainder of the afternoon in the woods engrossed in conversation. The sun was low in the west, and their shadows were long and distorted from the fragmented light passing through branches and leaves.

Korian's stomach rumbled, reminding him just how long it had been since he had last eaten. He should have been famished, but nerves, adrenaline, excitement, anxiety, or a combination of everything had stolen his hunger. As Sara told Korian of her ring's history, how it burned her brother's hand and everyone else it touched, a maret crossed their path.

Korian pulled out his "V" and turned to Sara to ask her to wait, but just as he darted after his prey, she chose instead to follow him. She expressed an interest in his weapon, and instead of the pursuit of the maret, the talk turned to how he came across it. When he demonstrated it, she was intrigued and asked to try it. Needless to say, Sara's interest in the weapon spared the maret on this day.

He positioned her arm and adjusted her stance. It was the first time in years he'd had physical contact with another soul. The feel of her skin gave him a sense of warmth and comfort that soothed his soul—but there was something else. He sensed a slight quiver in her arm when he touched her. The feeling was like fire: an intense heat between them in a physical way. He was acutely aware of the beating of her heart. The feeling thrilled him.

She relaxed into him. The scent of her hair, like vanilla, caught him by surprise. He took an exaggerated breath and held it as if he was inhaling a piece of her. Upon realizing how obvious this must have been to her, he pulled away, embarrassed.

She smiled.

"Watch this," she said.

She threw it, and it soared until a tree stopped its trajectory.

"Impressive," said Korian, nodding as he started towards it.

"Come to the Den," she said softly and unexpectedly.

He stopped in his tracks. Her smile had disappeared, and for the first time, Korian saw Sara, flawed and human: her emotion authentic and real. It shook him. Perhaps he wasn't ready to return to reality, but facing the truth with Sara was enough.

He approached her and looked deeply into her eyes. He saw his reflection in her eyes and felt an overwhelming sense of comfort and peace he'd never felt before.

Sara, I will never leave you again. He thought it but didn't say it. Before Korian could respond, a loud voice from the path called out her name.

"That's Jannik."

A shadow cast from something above moved rapidly across the ground. They caught a glimpse of something large disappearing beyond the tips of trees. From the path came muffled cries and then scurrying. Korian and Sara looked at each other and started towards the sound.

When they emerged onto the path, a cloud of dust was rising from the outpost. Deep growls and frightening screeching sounds came from within the cloud. They got closer and the dust cleared. Sara screamed.

Jannik was cornered between a derelict building, a dried-up well, and a large mound of rubble to his left. Directly in front of him, a skine stood humped, punching the ground repeatedly with both clawed hands. It let out a deep, chesty rumble while its head jerked left and right. Then, in its customary fashion, it pushed out its chest, spread its wings as wide as it was tall, and let out a thunderous roar.

"Stop!" Korian yelled.

The creature turned its head towards Korian. Korian sprinted towards it. Slowly, the skine retracted its wings and came to an upright position. Korian placed himself between Jannik and the creature.

The creature's chest relaxed, and its vacant eyes focused on Korian.

"No," Korian said softly.

He approached the giant beast, stopping directly in front of it and he strained his neck to look up into its eyes. There was a moment of silence. There were wounds all over the skine's body: some had healed, some were still healing, and in others, crushed watercress leaves moistened by Korian's saliva were still present. The creature calmly tilted its head to the side and turned back towards Jannik. It bared its teeth, roared and then it flew off. The gust from the skine's wings almost knocked them over.

Sara ran into her brother's arms.

"So, now you know what happened to my skine," said Korian.

They stared at him; amazement was all over their faces.

"What?" asked Korian addressing their curious stares.

He told them what had happened in the forest, how the skine had charged him, of the two skines who had crashed the party and what had happened after he woke up.

"I felt pity for it. It's vicious, yes, but just an animal, doing what vicious animals do. I've been tending to its wounds since that day and, I haven't been able to get rid of it."

Korian smiled. Sara and Jannik relaxed. Jannik turned towards Korian.

He bowed. "I don't know how you did that friend, but I'm indebted to you…twice."

He stared wonderingly at Korian.

"Sara told me about what you did to the hybrin when you were kids; it makes for an interesting pattern." Jannik pondered that for a moment and added, "One day, I'd like to hear more about how you do that. For now, I have a message from a man named Crogan. He's asked to meet you. Will you please come with us?"

Korian looked at Sara. A look of excitement was on her face. There were so many things that came to mind when he looked at her. She was so beautiful. But the one thing that screamed at him the loudest when he looked at her was "home" and all the things associated with it.

"What does this Crogan want with me?"

"He is Ishtan Mar, the last of the Manians, and he is excited to meet the man who scraps with skines."

12

BENEATH THE SURFACE

HERRICK OPENED HIS eyes. Light cast from a candle, placed on a table in the corner of a small chamber, lit up the room. His feet hung over the edge of a bed. The air smelled cool and musty. His body was covered by a sheet of dampness. Muffled voices came from beyond a narrow-arched opening that led into a separate passageway.

The deep throbbing in his shoulder reminded him of his encounter with the skine. In hindsight, he couldn't have asked for a better outcome. *Fools have no idea what's coming.*

He had no idea how long he had been in this place, or where he was for that matter, but it was clear he was being looked after. He was still wearing his blood-stained clothes, but there was a dressing on his shoulder that had been expertly applied. Surprisingly, he had good mobility in his arm. When the skine took him in its jaws, Herrick was certain he would not open his eyes again, let alone retain the use of his arm. He felt he had been spared for a great purpose.

A woman entered the room. She was heavyset with prematurely graying hair pulled back into a bun. Her eyes had been dulled with age, yet there was strength in them. She was not a person to be taken lightly.

"Would you look who's awake?" she remarked with a smile. "Eril!" she called out.

A large man, more in horizontal than vertical proportions, with a moustache and a prudish expression, entered the chamber.

Herrick greeted him with a stern look and a nod. "Where am I, and how long have I been out?"

"You've been in and out for almost a week," answered Eril. "No need to worry. You're in good hands. Mother's taken good care of you. Lael told us how pleasant you are," he added with a smile. "Wintermere, on the fringe of the Syran Hills, or at least four levels beneath it," he added. "That's where you are. Welcome to our home."

Herrick did not respond. "I have to get out of here." He stood up and almost hit his head on the ceiling. "Where are my things?"

"No need to get upset, Herrick. It's normal to get that 'too confined feeling' at first, but that'll wear off. Your weapons are safe, but you won't need them here. If you walk around with them, you'll frighten people."

Herrick took a few steps towards the man. He refrained from expressing how he truly felt. *I don't need any of you anymore,* he thought. He clenched his fist and imagined bashing Eril's head into the wall, his brains and blood splattered across the room. He could almost taste the sweet, metallic liquid. He looked at the woman and thought the same, but he liked something about her. *I'm just going to strangle you,* he thought. He relaxed his fist and managed a subtle smile.

"Where are the others?"

"Lael and Alrik are about to head out to meet up with Jannik and the others over at Navalline. You'll see them soon," replied Eril.

"Lay back down, Herrick," ordered the woman, and she pushed him back onto the bed.

Perhaps it was surprise at the woman's resolve, perhaps it was the fact he was still a little weak, nevertheless, Herrick obliged. He decided to be clever about this. *I'll devise a plan, tear myself away from these hapless souls, learn about their underground dwelling and then contact Aaron.*

When tunnel number 157 ended, a sign on the wall, 'Arkens Post,' overlooked a great, wide bend that stretched around a series of chambers all set in a row. They followed the bend and passed countless arched openings: some windows; some doors, each with different signs—the Hermit, the Fountain and many others—adorning the walls above the doors.

They had taken almost a thousand steps down this bend when Jannik stopped. "Here we are."

They were standing in front of a sign that read, 'Red Corner.'

After they had entered this section, they had walked down a tunnel that was essentially shaped in a wide circle. Many people were gathered in this particular tunnel, working their way in and out of each door.

"This area is known as the rest way. It's a place for those who travel through the Den to pause and maybe sleep off the effects of a little too much ale," said Sara.

Madrascythe lit up the area brilliantly. It wasn't hard to pick Korian out of the crowd. His complexion was dark amidst a sea of ashen faces that hadn't seen sunlight for years. Eyes followed his every move. Sara noticed how nervous Korian seemed. She grabbed his hand and squeezed.

A few hours ago, from inside the same tunnel Korian had passed with Finch—the same one he had been watching, for the last week—Jannik had uttered two words and a cleverly disguised section of the wall opened into a dark passageway. They'd navigated from one tunnel to another while Sara and Jannik enlightened Korian about this new world.

"Everyone calls it the Den, but it's much more than that," Jannik said. "It was built long ago, centuries in fact. After its discovery, the word was, there was no sign of anyone having ever lived here. It was like a house had been built and left for someone else to use. Regardless, we're indebted to whomever built this place. We owe them our lives.

"Dark tunnels lit up with madrascythe link the underground settlements together," Jannik said. "Some have wide, sloping passages, others are narrow so you have to travel in single file, but they all have low ceilings, I'm afraid."

Korian was in awe. Adrenaline rushed through his body. He squeezed Sara's hand a little tighter. The underground was a marvel of engineering. Beyond the wonders of what he saw and how so many had survived under these conditions, Korian marvelled at the effort it must have taken to build. And on top of all that, he had never been around this many living humans at once.

Sara let go of Korian's hand and ran across the threshold into the Red Corner. It was a large, dimly lit chamber. The walls were adorned with paintings, and the shelves were lined with barrels and bottles. Dark wooden beams crossed the ceiling. A wooden staircase at the back of the room led to several small compartments used as sleeping quarters. The chamber was filled with patrons sharing conversation and tankards of ale and cider.

Behind the counter, a man with salt and pepper hair smiled a knowing smile. His eyes were cornered by crow's feet, and deep furrows creased his brow. Korian recognized him immediately. Sara's father was older and much thinner compared to the man that had impressed him years earlier.

Sara's father sensed there was a different air around her: a jump in her step. She hugged him tighter than normal. While still in her embrace, he noticed a striking young man standing behind her with piercing eyes: they commanded attention and drew him in.

"Father, this is Korian," Sara said smiling from ear to ear, never taking her eyes off Korian.

Isaac Deeson knew his daughter. He had never seen her like this: the perpetual smile, the way she touched the young man's arm. After brief introductions, it seemed to him that for his daughter and this young man, there was no one else present.

An hour later, Leith and Grayson arrived. Lael and Alrik were expected the next day.

After introductions, they shared conversation about the skine and Illian, about the Den and talked briefly about the Portal at Navalline. Jannik mentioned that Crogan would be coming to meet them soon. They sat at a table near the back of the room. Food choices were thin but available. They shared bread and porridge from three pots shared between them, oblivious of a man who had been watching them since they had arrived.

Korian learned much about them. Alrik and Lael were not spared even though they were absent. Alrik was the stubborn, restless one, Grayson the hopeless romantic and joker, and Lael always wanted to do the right thing, whereas Leith just went along with the rest of them, and Jannik was the levelheaded, logical one.

Korian seized the opportunity. "What about Sara?"

There was a pause as all eyes turned towards the young lady who had a coy look on her face, daring anyone to answer. No one spoke. There was laughter, but it was interrupted when a man quietly approached the table. He was holding a staff in one hand, and only his gray beard was visible beneath the shadow of his hood.

Crogan had arrived to the *Red Corner* hours earlier. He sat near the back of the room where he could get a good view of the entrance. When Korian had entered, Crogan's first thought was, *could this be him? Is this who the gods have sent to be our liberator*? He was just a boy. Physically, his complexion was darker, and he was lean, but not unlike Jannik. Crogan sensed something unique about this young man. A radiance surrounded him when he walked into the room. Those nearby seemed to feed off of it. Crogan sensed it from across the room and was drawn to him. When the conversation switched to Sara, it was the perfect opportunity to make his presence known.

"It's in her eyes."

Initially, Crogan's concealed and dark appearance startled Korian. Korian gripped his chair tensely, but the smiles on the faces of his new friends helped him to relax.

"Her beauty is beyond what you could ever possibly see," added Crogan.

"Oh, here we go again," said Sara, shaking her head.

"It's in how she sees the world. After all, isn't beauty just an impression? We're strange creatures, you and I. We find a rugged, dry desert, or the Urlean Mountains at dusk to be beautiful, though hostile, but where is the goodness in that? Something beautiful is not always good, but what is good is always beautiful. Sara's beauty lies in the impression she leaves on others. For me," he paused, "the impression comes in the form of teeth marks on my arse where she bit me fifteen years ago."

There was a delayed response, and then all rolled with laughter. Korian looked on wide-eyed with a beaming smile. Sara stood up and greeted the Manian with a joyful and familial hug.

"Are you ever going to stop telling that story?" she said with a smile. "I was having a horrible nightmare. I just rolled over and bit the first thing I found. I was ten years old!"

"Good thing you were sleeping on your stomach!" Isaac shouted from across the room. This was followed by another bout of exuberant laughter. Korian joined them.

Crogan pulled back his hood and introduced himself to Korian for the first time.

As the hours passed, words became slurred and conversations absurd. Although the room had filled up nicely, and the volume of drunken conversations had escalated to the point of shouting, Grayson suddenly stood, cup in hand and climbed onto the table, swaying while he fought to stay upright.

"'Tention!" he screamed. "Listen up!" After a few moments, the buzzing subsided.

"Today, a man joined our company from the surface. Korian. Remember that name," he said, pointing and swaying. "To him, we owe our lives. This crazy bastard challenged a skine and—as you can see—he still lives. I have it on good authority that just today when the beast assaulted my friend, Jannik Deeson," he leaned over and kissed Jannik on the head to a rousing applause and cheer, "Korian approached the beast and looked into its eyes." There was a collective gasp. "That's right. He told the skine to back away, with his *mind* I tell you. Not a word was uttered, and yet, the beast obeyed."

He laughed. "Three cheers for the Skine Tamer!"

The room erupted with cheer. Strangers clapped Korian on the back. All this attention was alien for Korian. While flattering, it felt awkward. Sara's smile relaxed him somewhat.

Grayson suddenly jumped off the table, bumped his head on a wooden beam running across the ceiling, and he fell limply into Korian's arms.

Sometime later, Grayson opened his eyes. When he saw his friends gathered around the table he was lying on, he smiled abashedly.

"Come on, let's go," said Leith, helping Grayson to his feet.

"Wait. Before you leave, drink this," said Sara, placing a tray on top of the table filled with several cups containing what appeared to be boiled water with dried leaves. "This has always worked for us after an evening of one too many."

They gathered round, and each reached for a cup. As Korian's hand neared his cup something strange happened. The contents fizzed, frothed and hissed. The solution vaporized, the cup swayed right, then left and toppled over. Korian turned to look up at the others, who had stunned looks on their faces.

"What just happened?" asked Jannik.

Korian shook his head and shrugged.

"What's in the cup?" asked Crogan.

"Just boiled water with some leaves," answered Sara.

"What leaves?"

"Leaves from the matchra tree."

Collectively, they placed their cups back on the table and stepped away.

"Nice trick!" teased Leith.

Heads turned towards Crogan.

"That wasn't me," said Crogan with a blank expression. "Has that ever happened before?"

"No," replied Korian. He thought of Finch. "That's nonsense," Finch had said about those trees and the alleged ability of their leaves to heal. As a result, Korian had never been anywhere near them prior to this moment.

Crogan turned to Sara and raised a brow in the direction of the counter. Sara left and returned seconds later. She handed Crogan a small bundle of dried leaves.

"Korian, give me your hand."

Korian obliged, offering his hand with his palm open. In it, Crogan placed the dried heart-shaped matchra tree leaves. As soon as they touched Korian's skin, they burst into flames. Korian jerked his hand away reflexively, launching the burning leaves into the air. They watched with surprise as ashes and scorched remains of leaves floated down around them.

"It looks like the matchra tree doesn't like you," said Crogan, hiding his growing wonder.

He stared at this young man with a kind of awe, trying unsuccessfully to hide his admiration. *You're a mystery*, he thought. *I hope that tomorrow you may be able to solve another mystery.*

"Okay people, fun's over—for us at least," said Leith, taking Grayson by the arm and helping him towards the stairs and the chambers above.

"I bid you good night." They disappeared through the archway at the top of the stairs.

Soon, Jannik retired as well. Only Korian, Crogan and Sara remained.

"Goodnight," she said, giving Crogan a hug. She moved to Korian and kissed him on the lips. He felt a fire rise up in his chest.

They watched her walk away. Korian, was so taken aback, he didn't say a word. He sensed Crogan smiling.

"I have known her since she was a child. She's a special one. Many have tried to steal her heart, but it has not been theirs for the taking."

"What do you mean?"

"You really have been that disconnected, haven't you? Then again, I've been around far, far longer than you, and I still can't figure them out."

Crogan put his hand on Korian's shoulder.

"Come. Walk with me."

"How did you manage to find us?" asked Crogan. They had left the Red Corner and approached Tunnel 156.

"A friend gave me a map, longer ago than I care to remember. He instructed me to find the Manian," started Korian.

"What was your friend's name?"

"Finch, a crabby old man, crazy as a mreg but like a father to me."

"He wasn't your real father?"

Korian shook his head, "He told me he found me as a child. I know nothing of my real mother or father."

They entered a tunnel. The madrascythe lit the way.

"Tell me about your childhood," said Crogan.

"What do you want to know?" Korian responded. He was light in the head and wanted nothing more than to sleep, right here on the ground against the cold, hard wall if he could.

"You'll need to trust me. I think Finch was on to something."

Korian began to recount his journeys and experiences: the strange entity he had never seen who always seemed to be two steps behind—looking out for him—his last moments with Finch, meeting Sara with her ring, finding the Jewel of the Wilderness, the death and destruction, the unbearable solitude, his encounter with the Stragoy, the desert, the sand creature, the metal object in the sand, his foreign memories, the skine, his weapon and on and on.

They were deep within the tunnel when Crogan turned to face Korian.

"Destiny and fate are strange things," Crogan said. "They sweep you up like a giant wave, smothering you and choking the breath from you. Before you know it, you end up somewhere, not knowing how you got there. Your path has brought you here for a reason."

Looking into Korian's eyes, Crogan pondered the possibilities but noticed something strange. His reflection in the young man's eyes moved. He looked deeper into his pupils, and for a moment, was swallowed up and carried away by key moments of his own life. He saw righteousness. A sense of comfort and warmth filled his heart and spread throughout his body. It was a feeling Crogan knew he would never forget.

Crogan smiled and stepped to the side. Something equally out of place in this underground world caught Korian's eye.

A single vine was jutting out from a tiny hole at the base of the wall. It twisted and forked into several others growing out of cracks in the wall. It became a mass of vines concentrated in a small section of the wall. Halfway up the wall and attached to a vine, was a single white rose.

"Beautiful, isn't it?" said Crogan, following Korian's gaze. "I come by this place often and marvel at it. Think about this for a moment. You and I have witnessed horrible things. Yet we go on. Some say for what? Why not end it on our own terms and find peace?"

Korian did not know how to respond. He continued to stare at the magnificent white rose.

"The reason is that although life is beautiful in all its imperfections, it is a force. Life always finds a way to endure. How else can such a single, beautiful flower flourish in such a dark place? Our people, too, will find a way to endure. As you and I and this flower endure. All we need is a spark, either to lead our people out of the darkness or to teach them how to prosper in such a terrifying world. I think Finch knew you would have an important part to play in this."

"Me?" Korian laughed.

"I believe I can help you find your path. I can even lead you to the door." Crogan sensed Korian interpreted that last comment figuratively. Crogan had every intention of leading Korian to the Portal.

They returned to the Red Corner. On their journey back, Crogan told Korian of the prophecy of the Harwill and of the Azura. Korian was intrigued but thought Crogan's ideas too outlandish and induced by alcohol. *First Finch and now Crogan. I'm not who you think I am,* Korian thought.

When they finally reached Korian's room, they bid each other a good night. Before Crogan walked out the door, he turned. Korian was sitting on his bed.

"Oh, about the girl, my naïve boy…open your eyes. Her heart has not been available for the taking because it belongs to you. It has…ever since the day she first met you."

He smiled then shut the door. His footsteps faded down the stairs.

13

SEEK AND YOU SHALL FIND

WILL SHYLER, NOW thirty-six years of age, was a long way from the clumsy sixteen-year old teenager who had stumbled upon the mysterious cove. Over the last five years, Will had been living in the Northern Territories walking freely among firstlings.

The terrifying ordeal at the Bridge of Mies was a distant memory. After helping Crogan to locate the third and final rock used to assemble the Portal, and several close calls and quick exits from more dwellings than he cared to remember, Will had stumbled onto this place. He had not heard from Crogan in over ten years.

Will had created a curtain in his mind, separating memories from the day he had arrived to the Northern Territories, from everything prior to that date. His memory had become foggy, just the way he liked it.

Today, was an exceptionally bright day. Families had gathered outside for a union celebration of a firstling couple that looked happy and very much in love. There was music and dancing and tables piled with savory, festive foods and drink.

"Good morning," said Nessa, a middle-aged firstling woman that Will knew well. She was a small woman with small features, who sported a particular jump in her step this day. She smiled. Will returned the gesture.

Nessa reached back and grabbed the wrist of a young lady who was standing behind her. She pulled her close and turned back to Will. "Have you met my daughter?"

"Hello."

The young lady greeted Will with a courteous smile. Her delivery appeared confident, but her smile seemed rushed. Her body language—the way she stood; her shoulders turned slightly to the side; unable to look him in the eyes—screamed many things, but definitely not confidence. Then again, she may just not have had any time for him.

It didn't matter. Will was beaming. The attention, respect and feeling of belonging felt beyond welcoming. He had a mind to pick Nessa up and squeeze her. Instead, he took her hand and respectfully bowed.

"It's you!" shouted a man from an adjacent table. The outburst caught Will by surprise. Lorcan, a particularly nasty looking brute, was pointing directly at him. He started marching toward Will with his arm extended.

"Will Shyler!" he yelled. The music and dancing stopped.

"Because of you, my daughters are dead!" Lorcan shrieked.

Those who stood near Will began to slowly move away. An unnerving silence lingered momentarily until a woman's voice from somewhere within the mob shouted, "You failed us!"

"We're all dead because of you!" shouted another.

A large group of firstlings had gathered opposite him. Lorcan had joined them. Will stood with his back to the forest. He began to sweat. A chorus of obscenities rang out, eventually growing to an angry roar.

Something struck his chest. Pain exploded down Will's abdomen and legs. Another object narrowly missed his head. Every firstling he could see, including women and children, held palm-sized stones in their hands. Stones started to rain down in a steady stream. One struck him in the abdomen and he staggered back. The pain was torturous. Another struck his knee. He heard a snap and collapsed. As air returned to his lungs, his cries of pain were drowned out by the roar of the jeering crowd. A stone struck his face. His vision blurred in one eye and slowly faded to black.

The roar of the crowd began to fade away. Will knew it would be over soon. He was able to hear his own screams now, steady and pained, but they drew no mercy from the crowd. From his good eye, he watched as Lorcan approached him cradling a large boulder. He raised it over his head and brought it down with all its weight.

Will woke up suddenly, tearing himself from his nightmare. He swallowed his panic. Beneath the thick blanket, he was shivering.

He sat up and peered out of the opening of his cave onto the valley below. The day looked overcast and the morning air was crisp. The weather had cooled of late, and soon snow would follow. Getting in and out of the region would become nearly impossible.

Shaking off the cold, he ate what morsels he had left and cast scraps onto the ground. The floor of the cave was littered with empty nut shells and bones. "Welcome to my lair," he said, and he chuckled.

The clouds had cleared as the sun climbed over this region of emerald hills and cobalt mountains. It was early autumn. The cascading landscape was a canvas of reds, browns and various shades of green. Nestled in the Darmire Mountains was a bustling firstling community; a haven for the homeless who had managed to cheat death. In the valley below, by the border of Paramear Forest, a flurry of activity was already underway at this early hour. It seemed to Will Shyler that any firstling still alive in all of Endura was there.

By the time he reached the village, it was late morning. He was careful not to be seen. Over the last five years, he'd identified prime areas that served best for hiding when he ventured down from the cave. He kneeled behind a grove of trees and watched the villagers go about their daily, mundane tasks. He had become content being with his own kind—but only from a distance.

"Good morning, Hammish," he whispered when the husky, bushy-haired, heavily bearded firstling placed a chera—chicken-like animal, wingless, with a longer neck and hair-like feathers—in the coop. His legs were disproportionately large for his frame. They rubbed together when he walked, causing an awkward gait.

"Thank you in advance," Will said.

Will had gotten to know the firstlings by name and familiarized himself with their mannerisms. Hammish, for example, appeared the brute but was the kindest soul he'd ever known. Will often felt sorry for him because others took advantage of his kind nature.

He crawled a little closer to the coop.

His attention wandered when a stunning young lady with long brown hair, pulled back and tied in a ponytail, stepped out of the doorway of a barn on the other side of the dirt path. She was like art for Will, sparking intrigue and mystery every time he saw her. She was slim, but her physique was not to be mistaken for weakness. Her actions were far from feminine, but there was something alluring about her.

A moment later, Golin, a dangerous looking firstling, stepped out of the door behind her and took her hand. Will had watched Golin for some time and had become well acquainted with this one. Golin, Will felt, had a talent for hiding his emotions. A subtle movement with his mouth, something stealthy—not a smile—a smile. He had powerful shoulders and a fierce long face, and eyes that always seemed to shine with ruthless laughter. His face was one that dominated, definitely not one to be pitied. Even though he walked calmly, his movement seemed large. Will sensed there was more to Golin, but one thing he knew for certain, something about him made Will feel uneasy.

The girl gave the young man a flirtatious smile, then a hug, and off they went into the forest.

The sound of children's laughter made him feel content. Fish from the sparkling blue lake down the hill were hung on lines to dry, craftsmen expertly forged tools in huts, fresh bread and wheels of cheese were carted around and distributed amongst the community. Thatched roof houses were scattered on the hills. For others, homes were burrowed into the sides of the hills with branches, tied closely together, serving as doors. To the west of the valley, the tall trees of the Paramear Forest offered further camouflage from the outside world.

The coast was clear. Will stepped out of the woods, strolled towards the coop, took a chera and casually walked back down the path without drawing attention to himself. He stepped into the brush and out of sight, silencing the chera by snapping its neck before he reached the forest.

He spent the rest of the day observing the energy of the people as he moved east, parallel to the village. Then he made his way towards the hidden path on his way back to his cave.

After several hours, Will neared the thickest part of Paramear Forest. Something seemed off today. A rotten odor hung in the air. The stench became unbearable and Will gagged.

Bushes stirred to his left. He felt a cold shiver as if ice-water had been poured down his back. He sprung reflexively and quickened his pace. After a few steps, he started to run. There was a hidden path beyond the trees he meant to get to. He didn't see the dark shape step out from behind the thick trunks until it was too late. Will ran into it in full stride, and they both tumbled.

The dark shape came to its feet and unsheathed a sword. The Stragoy turned and scowled. It was grasping a horn that dangled from a rope around its neck. With its other hand, it raised its sword. A wave of panic swept over Will. *With just one blast from that horn, the village he had just left would be overrun by these creatures.*

The torment and isolation he had endured, the reason for his failure, was standing directly in front of him. *You will not sound that horn*!

Will reacted, instinctive without thought, and he charged with a liquid grace, surprising the Stragoy. He dove toward the decrepit creature; his shoulder collided with its chest. They crashed to the ground and the Stragoy dropped the sword. Will swung wildly, bashing his fists into the creature's skull until his knuckles bled. The Stragoy, unprepared for Will's fury, swung the horn blindly, connecting with Will's jaw.

For a second, Will did not know where he was. He rolled to

the side and managed to pull himself to his knees. Something hard and sharp dug into his shin.

A second Stragoy Will had not seen lurking in the woods, charged. Its sword was raised over its head. Before the sword descended, Will's hand closed around the hilt of the other Stragoy's sword that had pressed into his leg. He gripped it tightly and lunged, surprising the creature. The sword plunged deep into the Stragoy's abdomen.

"For you, Pads." Will tugged, withdrew the sword and swiped downwards with both hands, cleaving the front half of the Stragoy's face.

The first Stragoy came to its feet. It grabbed the horn and scowled at Will.

"I can't let you do that," said Will. He threw the sword but missed the mark.

The Stragoy brought the horn to its mouth.

"No!"

The creature closed its rotting lips around it, folds of gray skin dangling from exposed emaciated muscle and bone, but an arrow struck the creature in the hand and knocked the horn away. There was no reaction of surprise or pain. Its lifeless eyes looked past Will to the three men and a woman who were charging out from the woods.

The young woman he'd spotted earlier in the village was in an all-out sprint. She carried a bow. The Stragoy picked up the horn and darted towards the last row of trees. The woman, surprisingly agile, drew and released an arrow without breaking stride. It missed, but she pressed on. The Stragoy reached the last row of trees and burst through. When the woman reached the end of the tree line, she expected to find an army of Stragoy waiting. Instead, she found a long, arid plain that ended in a series of high, rolling hills in the distance. She stopped and calmly drew, aimed and released. This one hit its mark, and the Stragoy fell.

Immediately, she drew another arrow, nocked it and turned it towards Will's face; the tip was inches from his eye.

"Who are you?" she shouted.

Will froze, wide-eyed. "Wait!" he said with a quiver in his voice. "I am not the enemy."

"Who are you?" she repeated louder while her three male companions surrounded Will.

Looking directly into her eyes, he saw her clearer—a fighter robbed of her little girl long ago. The muscles in her shoulders were taut. Sweat painted her face, and her chest rose rapidly with each breath.

"I'm Will Shyler, son of Mellis Shyler from Essra," he said.

"We have followed you for weeks. Why are you here?"

He gave no answer. Her slightly arched eyebrows, above piercing eyes, moved up and down as she evaluated him. She repeated the question, louder this time. The arrow remained taut.

"Company," Will answered looking directly into her eyes. "Disgrace," he added. "It beats you down. I have lived too long in the gray."

Slowly, her eyes relaxed, and the tension in her face went away.

"Seems we share a common enemy. That's a good thing for you," she said.

She shouldered the bow. Her demeanor had changed. She stared at him for a moment as if reconsidering her decision to trust him.

She nodded and said, "That's Golin, Griff and Torin from Fessenden. I'm Tana from Brackens Town. You need to come with us."

East of the firstling settlement, a fair distance away, in a camp nestled on a hill concealed by the shadow of the nearby mountains, Lorne Maggis stood with monocular in hand. His face had grown long. His red bushy brows were arched as he strained to look and comprehend what he'd just observed. He passed his hand over his shaved head, a habit he'd adopted since he had changed his appearance years ago. He was convinced the shaved head made him come off more menacing.

A smile crossed his lips beneath a finely coiffured moustache and beard. He wasn't expecting to see this. Lorne had been scouring the wilderness for years looking for the Azura, for any signs of firstlings or humans. He'd made quite a name for himself because of the terror he'd spread. He felt invincible sitting on his partekii waiting for word from the Stragoy he'd sent as scouts to search the nearby hills. He waited in anticipation for the glorious sound of the horn—music to his ears—but instead got a different surprise.

Quite by chance, he had pointed his monocular west at precisely the moment the woman struck down his spy with her arrow. The smile was not because of the resolve of these insolent firstlings, but because after all these years, he recognized another firstling from Brackens Town.

As Tana had struck down the Stragoy that had invaded her village, Herrick was out wandering about the labyrinth of the subterranean settlement, alone.

He passed many blank faces; most took no notice of him, but some eyed the mountain of a man suspiciously and then would look away. He had wandered for hours, only to find himself back in the same place. The settlement was a maze, and Herrick grew impatient.

The people he passed only had one objective—to exist. He

imagined them as tiny insect coursing through a giant hill. When he first had this thought, he envisioned stomping on them and snuffing out their lives. In fact, over the last few days he'd started to feel nauseous. His hands had begun to shake, as his thirst to kill was beginning to smother him.

The first time he had heard about the man they called the Skine Tamer, he was in the lowest level of the city.

"I heard he just looked at the deadly skine and it trembled."

"He has strange powers. I heard he can talk to beasts without using words," said another. "They call him Korian. He wields a magical weapon that returns to him after he throws it."

This last comment caught Herrick's attention, and he turned towards the conversation. One man was holding a thick, faded paper. It was a map. Herrick's hand began to shake. It wasn't long before the map was in his possession, and the remains of the men were lying twisted and broken behind a nearby wall.

Herrick, armed with a map and a renewed excitement, headed towards the upper levels. He recalled seeing a man holding a shiny, blood-soaked, curved, metal object at the top of the Azart Cliff.

Korian…could this be the man? He had to find him.

Next morning, Korian entered the large room of Isaac's place and joined the others seated at a table. The room was free of patrons at this early hour.

"Sleep well?" Crogan asked.

Korian nodded. The others looked spent from an evening of overconsumption. Grayson's head rested on his folded arms, the bump on his head was visible through his disheveled hair.

"Sit," Sara instructed and set down a hot cup of tea and a bowl with porridge.

Korian reached for the cup and paused.

"Don't worry, it's only tea." Sara said with a smile.

"Today is shaping up to be a special day," said Crogan.

"How so?" asked Korian.

"Crogan thinks our fortunes are going to change today," replied Jannik. "He believes we're going to find and uncover a priceless treasure."

"Where?" asked Korian as he took a sip of tea.

"If you have other plans, you best cancel them. We're off to Navalline," added Jannik.

Sara's smile disappeared. "Why can't this wait a couple of days?" Her mood had visibly changed.

Crogan gave Sara a knowing look. "It's time, Sara. Just as we discussed."

A short while later, Isaac and the group headed off on a half day's journey through the tunnels of the Den towards Navalline. Few words were exchanged. Sara was not herself. She did not say a word. She was a deep contrast to the woman Korian had met the other day.

Several hours later, they came to the end of a tunnel blocked by a heavy door made of solid rock, its width as wide as Crogan was tall. Beside the door, a man, charged with the dull task of tending this side of the door, sat on an old stool, resting his head against the wall.

Crogan greeted him with a nod. The guard pulled a lever and the heavy door opened to expose the flurry of activity underway on the other side. Sara took Korian's hand, leaned towards Isaac, and whispered something in his ear. Isaac nodded, and immediately, Sara and Korian turned and quietly began walking back down the tunnel in the opposite direction.

Crogan led the rest of the group across the threshold into a larger chamber. He turned and saw Korian and Sara walking away.

"Where are they going?" he shouted. "Korian!"

Korian and Sara started to run. Crogan rushed back through the doorway, but Isaac grabbed his arm.

"Let them be, Crogan. They will meet us in Navalline. Trust me," he said, with a firm hold of Crogan's forearm.

Crogan pressed, but Isaac squeezed tighter. In Isaac's eyes, Crogan saw a father's love for his little girl: a desire to make her happy at any cost.

"This can wait another day," Isaac whispered. "It's waited this long…"

This time, Crogan relented. His shoulders drooped, and he relaxed a bit. The feeling didn't last. It was replaced by a sense of cool, icy fingers scratching the nape of his neck.

Herrick entered tunnel number 42. This area was filled with people: some were active performing tasks; others were just passing through. At the end of the corridor, there was a door and another tunnel running to the left. On the right, was a large cavern with more than sixty holes carved into the ground. People were placing copper ore, four inches in length, into holes filled with andesite. Here, heated andesite melted the ore, which was in turn shaped into bowls, cups, utensils and tools.

Herrick felt invisible here. People were too preoccupied to pay him any attention. He found a spot near the wall, and he sat for a short rest.

There has to be a way in and out without passing a gatekeeper, he thought. It was only a matter of time before the bodies of those he had just murdered would be discovered.

He stood and started heading down a tunnel on the left, stopping after just a few steps. The large, stone door opened.

Herrick was startled when Jannik and Grayson stood before him. Their attention, however, was on a gray-haired man who had just shouted the name, Korian.

Herrick was supposed to be in Alrik's bed, or so they believed. *I don't need you anymore*, thought Herrick. Jannik and Grayson stood in front of him, vulnerable and unaware. He could easily crush them, but he dismissed the thought, for now. He was exactly where he needed to be and was determined to carry out Aaron's orders.

He remembered hearing that 'Korian' name before. *I got to get through that door.*

Herrick quickly slid behind a stack of crates that were piled beside the door. The group crossed the threshold with their backs to Herrick. He heard Crogan's name. Aaron had warned him about Crogan. "Stay clear of him," Aaron had said. "His power is beyond you."

The door was open and inviting at the moment. Using his hood to conceal his eyes and upper half of his face, he stepped out from behind the crates and as casually as he could, he put his head down and walked by the group.

Herrick spotted a woman and a man running down the tunnel. They turned right and disappeared from view, but not before Herrick saw what he was looking for. Slung across the man's back was that shiny, curved weapon.

The stars are lining up for me. Herrick's heart raced. "So close," he whispered.

Herrick stepped across the threshold, lightly brushing past the man they called Crogan, but something happened Herrick had not intended.

Crogan's entire body tensed. He felt a chill and sensed

something dark: a presence, Herrick's energy: a darkness that poured out of him, like an invisible vapor coming out of his pores.

"You! Stop!" Crogan shouted, pointing at Herrick.

Herrick acted quickly. He overwhelmed the unsuspecting guard on the other side of the door and snapped his neck. Before Crogan could reach the doorway, Herrick shut the large door and locked them out.

With no guard, he had given himself some time. Muffled screams came from the other side. Herrick smiled. Quickly, he started down the corridor in the direction the woman and the Skine Tamer had gone.

Crogan lunged at the heavy door as it slammed shut. A feeling of helplessness swept over him like a thick fog. *The boy is in trouble.* The words repeated in his mind.

"Open the door!" he screamed frantically. "My staff! Where is it?"

"Here," Jannik said pointing to the ground.

The staff had become wedged between the bottom of the heavy door and the ground. Crogan pulled with all his strength. The staff bent, but it would not budge.

"We need to get this door open, now," Crogan shouted. The urgency in his voice was clear.

"Sara!" Isaac called. "What's going on?" He started pounding the door.

A crowd was gathering behind them.

"What happened? Who was that?" shouted Jannik.

One man emerged with a large tool: it had a long handle and a blunt head on one end and a pick with a point on the opposite end. Leith took it and began striking the door just above the spot where the staff had become wedged. Grayson, with both hands wrapped around the staff, tugged with all his strength. Each heavy blow sent a painful shock up Leith's arms. He ignored the sensation and remained steadfast in his efforts.

Precious minutes passed. Finally, the staff gave a little. Jannik took hold. He and Grayson both pulled, and the staff came free.

Crogan tapped the elaborate end of the staff against the door and pressed it firmly, causing the staff to bend. He whispered something inaudible and lifted the staff off the door. One crack, and then many appeared, spreading in all directions. Crogan gave one final thrust with the palm of his hand and the door imploded into a cloud of dust.

He turned to Jannik. "Take everyone to Navalline, now. We've been compromised!"

"I'm going with you," Jannik said.

"You can't!" Crogan said sternly. "I need you in Navalline. Go!" he shouted.

Crogan crossed the threshold. He marched quickly down the corridor and disappeared into the tunnel on the right.

14
AWAKENINGS

SARA LEAD KORIAN into a large chamber. A wide, circular wall, about twenty-feet high, marked the end of the passageway. There was a large opening on the right. It was pitch black at the moment, and it looked to be another tunnel leading out from this chamber.

"Follow me."

Sara rushed toward a section of the wall, about ten feet from the left side, and using small recesses and protruding rocks on its face, she began to climb.

She scaled it expertly, knowing exactly where to step and where to grasp as though she had done this numerous times. Korian followed, impressed with her agility and strength.

She reached a narrow five-foot ledge, about twelve feet above the ground, and she climbed onto it.

The contour of the ledge's facing, its position on the wall, the spectrum of light reflected from the madrascythe on the neighboring rock, and the depth of the shadows around it, all contributed to masking the ledge and making it virtually undetectable from the ground.

From her perch, she noticed a lambent glow flickering far down the tunnel they were just in.

"Here comes Crogan."

"Hurry." She grabbed Korian's hand, and they disappeared into a crevasse in the wall at the back of the ledge.

Herrick found himself in a narrow tunnel filled with many bends and turns. Beyond the range of the light cast from the madrascythe coating the walls, the tunnel was completely deserted and dark. Herrick didn't care. His excitement grew and his hand had started to shake again.

When the tunnel ended, Herrick emerged into the larger chamber with the circular wall at the end of the passage.

Light cast from the madrascythe illuminated this area as well, but there was no sign of them. He looked around and found another tunnel on the right.

Herrick entered it, wondering if the man and woman he was pursuing had ventured into it earlier. There was no madrascythe here. He listened. After taking a few steps, surrounded by an impenetrable darkness and nothing but the sound of intermittent drops of water falling onto a hard surface, he cursed and decided to return to the large room.

Herrick examined the wall and noticed the rocks, holes and protrusions over its facing. He put his hand in a crack, gained purchase on a small bulge, and he started to climb. He reached a dead end and climbed down. He tried again, scaling the adjacent area and found another dead end. He tried two more times in other areas; the last attempt was in a section adjacent to the one Sara had climbed.

He was onto his fifth attempt and had reached just two feet from the ledge Sara had scaled, when he heard a voice.

"Stop!" It was a man's voice, barely audible.

A light kept flickering off the walls inside the tunnel he had emerged. Someone else was coming.

"Stop!" It was closer, and it quivered in its delivery, indicating the owner was running.

Herrick quickly climbed down. As he leaped off the wall, he glanced up and noticed something peculiar. He moved a little to the right and got closer to the wall…and there it was. There was a ledge, clearly visible from this vantagepoint.

For a second, Herrick contemplated climbing up to it, but whoever approached would find him before he could reach it. He contemplated confronting the owner of the voice. He had no weapon but that had never stopped him before. Aaron had warned him to avoid the Manian. He had no idea who the voice belonged to, but there was far too much riding on this to jeopardize it now.

Herrick clenched his fists, grunted in frustration and started into the adjacent tunnel a second time.

He meant to kill the Skine Tamer. He wanted to do that just for fun, but alerting Aaron about this place was what he'd been tasked to do. He had to find a way to the surface to warn Aaron.

Deep inside the tunnel, besides more darkness, Herrick found a potent stench. The ground here was spongy. Occasionally, Herrick's feet would sink and get stuck. He had to use his outstretched arm for guidance. The deeper he went, the louder the sound of his steps became.

A sound, like that of beating wings, started from above. Suddenly, a roar filled the tunnel. The area around Herrick's head swarmed with hundreds of wrets—bat-like creatures, with a wider wingspan and longer bodies. They knocked him to the ground. From his hands and knees, buried in guano, Herrick caught a hint of something that looked like pale tones of gray on the wall as if it had been brushed with a dim light. He could see water running down the rock with clarity. The pale light suddenly vanished, as the wrets swarmed and disappeared into the wall just opposite the section that had been brushed with the light. As the roar lessened and the last of the wrets departed, the pail light and hue on the wall returned. Herrick looked closer, and he found a narrow opening.

Beyond the wall there was a narrow passage. It looked tight, but still wide enough for him to squeeze through. He entered and wiggled his way until he emerged on a ledge along the side of the mountain. It was night and the moon, full with a reddish hue, oversized and bright, was in the sky to the west.

He covered the opening in the wall with his cloak and headed down the path to the valley below. He called out to Aaron and waited. A few minutes later, Aaron emerged from the shadow.

Sara and Korian stepped from the narrow passageway onto a ledge overlooking the majestic waterfalls that made up the Jewel of the Wilderness.

"Forgive me, Korian," whispered Sara.

"For what?"

"Before the rest of Navalline claims you, I wanted this night."

She sat down on the ledge, and Korian sat beside her. The

expression on Korian's face gave him away. She looked up at the sky. It looked wondrous on this night—so full of promise.

She was still looking up when she said, "Your eyes have a power I can't explain, but for all their mystery, they can't hide what you're thinking."

She smiled and turned to look at him. "I can see you don't know what I'm talking about, but you will soon enough. Everyone is waiting for you in Navalline. I'll bet almost everyone that's in the Den will be there to see the Skine Tamer, but by tomorrow, everyone who has not yet heard of you, will know your real name."

She touched his cheek with the tips of her fingers. There was a mixture of worry and excitement in his eyes. His heart was pounding, but not for tomorrow and the unknown. It was because of her touch.

"Don't worry, Korian, I'll be there to protect you." Her lips curled upwards to reveal a slight smile that made her eyes gleam in the moonlight.

"Everyone hopes that it's you."

"Hopes for what?" asked Korian, only half listening to Sara. He was focused more on the light in Sara's eyes, not in the literal sense, but in a kind of energy that infused him, as if it fed an insatiable hunger by just gazing into them.

"I already know that it's you," she replied.

That got his attention, but Korian just shook his head and pulled away slightly. A puzzled look grew to a confused one.

"A few more hours are not going to hurt anyone, right?"

She did not realize their fates were entwined with this night and with this moment.

"After all, those of us here in the Den have waited a long time, and yet, we're still here…still alive," said Sara. "A few more hours are not going to hurt anyone," she repeated.

Korian didn't say a word. He raised his hand and tenderly moved a few strands of hair from her face. There was no way they could have known what Crogan and the others already knew, that their sanctuary was no longer a secret, that time had run out.

"I have something for you," said Sara, gently taking his hand. She held it as she spoke, unaware of just how tender she was caressing it. She was trembling. Her breathing was short. She opened her hand. He recognized the ring and chain that he had credited to keeping him alive all these years.

"This belongs to you. Always has." She leaned forward to place it over his head. Her cheek brushed his. He was entranced by the silken feel of her hair against his face.

"She was right all along. She said I would know," Sara whispered. "Truth is Korian, I never needed the ring. I knew it was you from the first time I saw you."

His breath on her skin shot through her body in burning lines. The sensation of his touch was overwhelming, prickling the skin all over her body. He moved slowly to find her lips. The first attempt was awkward. They laughed nervously. They kissed tenderly, losing themselves in each other, making up for years of longing.

That night, the stars alone bore witness to the moment Korian and Sara shared, what they had known since the first time their paths crossed: apart, they just existed living half-lives, but together, they felt whole.

While Herrick and Aaron discussed the fate of the Den, on the other side of the hill, Sara and Korian found absolute peace.

Doric awoke in a dark chamber within Hellas Mons. He was lying in his own waste, barefoot and frail. Sixteen years had passed since the last time he had seen Oren. He was now a broken and unrecognizable twenty-eight-year old man.

Behind him, the latch turned, and the heavy door groaned. Someone entered the room and hovered over him. Whoever it was stared down at him in silence.

"It's a wonder you're alive," a man finally said in a confident voice with an icy undertone. "It would be so easy to crush your skull and end your misery." Doric sensed a foot hovering above his head. "But that would be a way out for you."

The rusted iron chains and shackles around Doric's wrists clanged against the cold ground as he rolled onto his side. He winced when his hip touched the damp surface. His side, a purple, mushy sore from continual scraping against the ground, burned as he pulled himself out of the slop and towards the wall.

Over the years, he had been shuffled around from prison to prison. Now, only his wrists were shackled since he was no longer able to walk.

Doric's waste was smeared across the floor. The room smelled of impending death. Sitting in the corner, with his back against the wall, he was breathing as heavily as a wounded animal taking its final breaths. Calmly, the intruder paced the room, eyeing the mutilated man.

"Time has not been good to you."

Doric recognized him. He was older, but there was no mistaking his identity. He wore a beard and his bald head was large and oddly shaped, giving him an outlandish and bizarre appearance. His complexion was now dark, due to exposure to the sun.

He was tapping his hand with his glove: one-two-three-thud, one-two-thud and repeat. Lorne managed a smile. Dawn's light had not yet fully entered the chamber, but Doric could make out the callous eyes; the same eyes that had tormented his sleep for years.

"Do you know who I am?" Lorne inquired. Doric remained silent.

"I underestimated your will. After all these years, you still breathe. What are you protecting? Who's protecting you?" He stopped tapping.

"I bring news. Looks like we found the humans. They're living like vermin. We didn't expect anything less. And we know where their new Portal stands."

Lorne walked towards the opening of the cave and looked over the desolation. He swayed left and right. His fist clenched and relaxed rhythmically with each lean. There was something in his hand.

"Do you see that? Between the clouds," Lorne pointed. "A blood moon and that strange star in the sky. It appeared last night. The sky is of such a crimson hue. Looks like it's on fire, doesn't it?"

He turned again towards Doric. "The red moon and the new star, signs of doom, fitting on the eve of the humans' end.

"You see, Doric," Lorne spoke with an air of arrogance. He was mocking Doric. "Aaron summoned me back here tonight. I had other plans, but they will have to wait. Aaron thinks you know what the meaning of the red moon is. He said if you don't talk, I can end you. We don't need you anymore." His hand rested on the hilt of his sword.

"But I have a better idea."

Lorne crouched, staring into Doric's grotesque face.

"Call out to him, to your Manian. Ask him."

Doric didn't answer. Lorne sighed and began to pace.

"I have spent the last ten years in the south, leading Aaron's army through the badlands. I'm known by another name now: Mort Eyoma, Ruid for 'he who incites terror.' Not bad for a kid from Brackens Town," he said with that air of superiority again.

"I was in the north when Aaron summoned me back to you. Do you know what I was doing?" he asked with a grin. "I found a small band of firstlings. Resilient they are, but there's something they don't know. I am Mort Eyoma, and they have no idea what destruction I'm going to bring to them."

Lorne leaned forward and placed something on Doric's lap. "I saw someone," he said.

It was a soiled cloth, the piece of fabric from Tana's dress or what remained of it. Chains rattled as Doric searched his breast. It was gone. Through his one good eye he glared at Lorne.

"She's alive, so beautiful and strong," Lorne said with a smile. "It would be a shame if suddenly," Lorne brought his thumb to his neck and mimicked slitting her throat.

"If anything happens to her—" Doric's voice was almost indiscernible. Scar tissue kept his face and mouth frozen, making it difficult to speak.

"I'll ask again. Is there anything I should know?" Lorne said raising his voice.

"Damn you!"

Doric shouted a few more incoherent expletives. Squirming, he howled in pain and despair. His larynx felt as if it would explode with every burst.

"All right then." Lorne left, closing the door behind him.

A fluttering sound entered his chamber. A tiny, winged creature hovered by the opening; it moved left, right and then rushed into the cave. He recognized the chestnut crown. It had been sixteen years since he had seen the skifter. It hovered a few seconds near his face. Its eyes turned different colors, and then it turned white. Doric watched it fly down the long corridor, through the opening and back out into the great sky.

"I think you're too late," Doric mumbled, recalling Oren's

story about the forewarning of change marked with the sighting of the rare bird.

It was early morning in a large room high in Hellas Mons. There was no light from torches or lamps as they would steal away the shadows Aaron used as his means of teleporting. In the dimness of the light from early dawn, Herrick sat at a long table in the middle of the large room tapping the surface rhythmically with his thick fingers. He stopped and removed the dressing on his shoulder. He wouldn't be needing it any longer. The sight of blood and scar tissue would only feed his hunger for more of it.

Lorne stood by the large gap in the wall looking out into the barren wasteland below. Dark plumes of smoke merged with the sky.

The door into the chamber opened, and a third heavyset man with stooped shoulders, entered. It was Damon Kinsey, the man who ruled the mountain and its slaves. He stumbled into the room and plopped onto the chair, almost breaking it under his weight.

"What's this all about?" he gurgled and coughed.

No one spoke. Instead, the sound of iron spurs clanged beyond the door. Herrick's tapping stopped. A man stood on the threshold of the doorway; legs astride and face covered in shadow by a dark hood. He walked in—as if floating rather than walking into the room. Nearing the table, he pulled back his hood.

When Lorne saw the man's face, he knew who he was. His hair, reedy and long, fell on his shoulder along one side. One half of his scalp was scarred and burnt, with strands of hair, like cotton, hanging in patches. Half of his face was charred into a permanent and grotesque grimace. A black hole remained where his eye had been. He was wafer thin, and the smell of death was all around him. His right eye, open wide, stared down at Herrick, then Damon, then Lorne. He snickered, stepping towards Lorne, who squeezed his sword tighter.

"You're the one they call Mort Eyoma," he said in a deep, harsh drone, nodding and sneering. The muscles on the burnt half of his face were paralyzed, making his half-smile threatening and monstrous. "Why?" he added mockingly, casually pacing the room.

Lorne's breathing quickened as he faced the intruder. His fingers were numb with the pressure of his grip on his sword.

"Cyrus." A guttural, raspy voice came from the shadow. Behind them the door slammed shut on its own.

Aaron stepped out of the shadow in the corner of the room, materializing out of the darkness to join them. He was holding something in his hand.

"There's no time for that now." Aaron waved his hand. Two chairs slid out from under the table. "Sit down," he ordered.

Cyrus Zagan was a ruthless and callous monster. For the first time since his childhood, Lorne felt inferior to someone. The feeling angered him. He sat down nervously.

Aaron placed a large map on the table, leaned forward, and with his gloved finger, burned an X across it.

Cyrus stood again. "You're wondering why I am here," Cyrus responded, circling the table. "Aaron has summoned us together because the Master is not pleased. No matter how many lives we have claimed, the truth is we have all failed. The Master is still imprisoned in the shadow while the child of the prophecy still lives."

"Tonight, there is a blood moon and other ominous signs. We must be on alert this night," Aaron warned. "Expect the unexpected."

Aaron turned towards Herrick. "Tell them what you know."

"I found their sanctuary," Herrick answered, pointing to the X on the map. He told them of the great city beneath the surface.

The others listened, though Lorne's emotions were mixed. Now that they'd finally found the Den, thoughts of how he was going to kill Doric entered his mind. He was no longer needed. He had longed for the task, but at the same time, dreaded it.

"You know what we seek. The Azura could be among them… he just doesn't know it yet," said Aaron in a loud whisper. "If he were dead, Hades would be free. That's not the case. The Portal is there in that hole," said Aaron in his guttural drone.

The embers that were his eyes hissed incessantly. "We destroy the Portal, we find the Azura and kill him, or we kill them all. If the Azura is among them, it will be finished. Either way, we end this and free Hades, tonight."

The men sitting around the table stood. Even Damon managed to rise.

"There are five hundred slaves here," Aaron said, sliding his hand across the map to just northwest of the X. "They can be here in a matter of hours," he added and pointed at the X. "Five thousand more are on the way. They will arrive in two days."

"You will return to their hole," Aaron said, turning to Herrick, "Assume control. I cannot step in that place," Aaron was pacing now. "The Manian has cursed it. You will need to do it on your own."

"There is one to be wary of," Herrick added. "They call him the Skine Tamer. I don't trust that one."

"Kill him first," said Cyrus.

"He is evasive," answered Herrick.

"Find him," demanded Aaron raising his voice. "Do what you must. If that fails, destroy the Portal. You're giving them too much credit."

"And the Manian?" asked Herrick.

"Leave him for me," Aaron answered. He took Lorne's sword from his sheath and handed it to Herrick.

Lorne's face flushed red with anger, but he did not say a word.

"And the firstlings?" Lorne managed in the calmest voice he could muster. He was trying to hide his anger, but his red face and the quiver in his voice betrayed him.

Cyrus smiled. He was the most feared. No one else was going to assume that title. He took pleasure in Lorne's apparent agitation.

"They are on the other side of Paramear Forest," Lorne added.

"Leave them for now; they are unimportant," ordered Aaron.

"They were mine. What changed?" asked Lorne.

"If this Azura is among the humans, it won't matter. He'll die among them and end their hope. The firstlings will just be sport for Cyrus."

Aaron approached Lorne, towering over him. He placed a gloved hand on Lorne's shoulder and said, "You will stay here. Once Herrick has finished his task, kill the wretch you keep as a pet. You've waited a long time for that."

Aaron grabbed Herrick's cloak. He pulled him into the shadow. "Do not fail," Aaron said in his customary guttural whisper.

The wind picked up and Herrick and Aaron vanished.

15

PARADISE LOST

CROGAN GENTLY NUDGED Sara's arm. He found them in an embrace, lying on the ledge atop a bed of leaves. It was still dark outside. Sara's head rested on Korian's bare chest. Everything seemed perfect. There was an immense stillness, not to be confused with silence. All was in perfect balance, so much so, he considered leaving the young lovers at peace. It was what his heart desired, but the voice of reason won.

Despite Crogan's attempt to be gentle, Sara jumped. Startled, Korian sprang to his feet.

"What's happening?" he shouted.

"Shhh. Come." Crogan whispered calmly. "We need to leave. The Den's been compromised." The urgency in his voice was unsettling.

When they were back in the main chamber, Crogan

whispered into Sara's ear, "See that he gets to Navalline. We don't have much time. You must convince Korian to walk into the Portal. I'm certain it's him."

"What about you?"

"I will meet you there. There's something I need to do. If what I think will happen comes to pass, we need him, Sara...we need him now."

Crogan, half turned and stopped suddenly. He touched Sara's arm again. "Sara...regardless of what you have in your heart, you have to convince him to walk through." He gave her a stern and a compassionate look, and then he left.

Sara grabbed Korian's hand and together they rushed down the corridor.

Crogan watched them until they had disappeared around a bend and then turned towards the adjacent tunnel; the one Herrick had entered.

"I know you're in there," he said.

Once inside the dark corridor, Crogan whispered into the elaborate crown of his staff, and a flame sprung from it. A long passage, about twenty feet wide at its broadest, lay before him. The only sound in this musty smelling vacant passageway was the eerie echo of water dripping from the ceiling onto a puddle on the ground. Beyond the flame's luminance, the tunnel lead into suffocating darkness.

With each step, his feet sunk into a river of wret waste, making walking a challenge. He labored through and passed by the gap Herrick had covered with his cloak. After a while, he ran out of tunnel and found himself on the edge of a dark abyss. There were no forks or other passageways. He was puzzled. *Where did you go?*

The first Stragoy entered the tunnel through the hole Herrick had used to exit the Den. One by one, Stragoy entered like parasites entering an open wound. Their numbers spilled into the larger chamber adjacent to the tunnel, where they stood like drones awaiting orders

Herrick entered. He felt whole again, adorned with a new set of weapons, infused with a renewed purpose and something more: he had come through on his plan to find the underground city. His excitement to satisfy his craving had him bursting with energy.

He saw a light down the tunnel. *Aaron wants me to spare the Manian for him. I don't know who you are,* Herrick thought addressing the bearer of the light, *but I'm not going to take any chances.*

He gave the order, and Stragoy fired arrows down the tunnel. They angled the arrows upward in an arced trajectory, taking advantage of the high ceiling.

On the other end of the corridor, Crogan heard a series of dull thwacks. A chorus of high-pitched sounds whistled toward him in waves. He froze, listening with heightened senses. He focused on vibrations and subtle changes in the air. Just before he extinguished his flame, an arrow passed by his ear. He could sense more coming. With the light gone, he closed his eyes. He turned to his left, and an arrow struck the wall and crashed to the ground as he had anticipated.

Herrick ordered a second wave.

Crogan raised his staff and swiped right, striking something headed for his head. He altered its trajectory ever so slightly, and he forced an arrow to soar past into the abyss. More arrows struck the walls and floor around him, filling the space with bursts of competing taps and nocks—short, quick and sometimes repetitive. Others sailed into the chasm. He swiped two more away.

There was a moment of silence when no more arrows came. Instead, he heard footsteps. Crogan opened his eyes. His pupils had dilated. A potent stench of decay reached him, followed by large shapes out of the shadow. He fought off three Stragoy with his staff and drove them off the edge.

A second wave of Stragoy followed. He battled four before one struck him squarely in his chest. The force sent Crogan off the edge with a Stragoy draped over him.

Crogan abandoned his staff and freed both hands. Freefalling in the darkness, Crogan battled his hideous assailant blindly. He swiped and struck the creature's head. Something moist and soft, came off in Crogan's hands. Probably dead flesh, dangling from its rotting jowls. He brought his knee up and managed to push the Stragoy off him. There was a loud crunch in the penetrating darkness, and then, only the harsh sound of the wind.

This is not happening, was Crogan's last thought before impact.

Herrick turned his attention to Korian and Sara. He returned to the circular wall and found the cracks, rocks and lip-like protrusions he had used earlier to scale the wall. This time, he managed to reach the ledge and found the crevasse in the back wall. He pressed through and stepped out onto another slightly larger ledge, that overlooked the majestic waterfalls. It was empty, but the impression of their bodies was still there in the bed of leaves. Herrick smiled. A few minutes later he was back in the large chamber.

"They're over there," said Herrick as he pointed down the tunnel.

The Stragoy just stared at him with blank eyes. Their features were even more monstrous under the light emitted by the madrascythe, cast by Herrick's body heat.

"Find them! I want them alive!" Herrick shouted.

A sea of grotesque featureless creatures started down the tunnel after Korian and Sara.

"I've never seen it this deserted," said Sara, breathing heavily as they reached the end of a tunnel. Korian ran left; Sara right.

"It's this way," Sara said tugging his arm.

"Shh!"

The sound of countless footfalls and the echo of distant grunting and hissing noises swept in from the tunnel behind them. There was no light accompanying the sounds.

"I don't like this," said Korian between breaths. "If there's something down there; anything that is alive, we should be seeing something…even a slight glow."

They waited a few seconds. The alarming sounds grew louder. Then they noticed a faint glow, but it was far down the tunnel.

"Come on, we've got to go," Korian whispered.

Sara sprinted. Korian followed closely behind. They had never run faster, but despite their best effort, whatever approached was getting closer.

They reached the doorway where they had separated from the rest of the group. The madrascythe in the large room, where copper ore was placed in andesite, shone brightly. The heat from the pits acted as catalysts, and the room was filled with a constant radiance.

"Sara. You have to hide. We can't outrun them. I'll draw them away…and lead them towards the Red Corner. I remember the way. I'll lose them, and I'll come back for you. They're not going to find you in there. The light won't give you away."

"Wait…don't leave," Sara pleaded. "We should stay together."

Footsteps grew louder behind them.

"Please, Sara, I've done this before. I can buy us some time." He kissed her on the lips. "I'll come back," he said, "I promise."

Sara reluctantly started into the empty cavern. She turned and looked back. The look in her eyes, screamed, "I'm frightened," even though she was calm. There was something else Korian couldn't quite comprehend. He felt a weight on his chest, followed by heat, not like being exposed to a high temperature, but rather, like a surge from within, a genuine warmth through his body, spreading from his chest. She smiled in a sad sort of way, and then she turned and disappeared into the room. The odd feeling went away, and Korian started to run.

A loud burst came from around the bend, a kind of snort and pained groan followed by the clanging of metal.

The door was gone. A dread unlike anything Sara had ever felt spread through her. She almost called out for Korian, but then saw a shadow approaching from the outside corridor. She watched as another shadow passed, and another, all of them pursuing Korian.

Around her, tools lay abandoned as if waiting for someone to return from a short break. She surveyed the area quickly. Her clothes were pasted to her skin. There was nowhere to hide. Frantically, she darted from one spot to the next. Her eyes were locked on the open doorway.

She found a narrow crease in the wall towards the back of the room. She reached it just as the sound of heavy steps and ghastly grunting noises entered the room. She squeezed through, working her way against the sharp, jagged stones that lined the wall, scraping her arms and knees and drawing blood.

A shadow, just outside where she was hiding, not more than three feet away, wriggled on the ground in her narrow field of vision. The hissing and snorting sounds that accompanied it were unnerving.

Others entered the room. Sara guessed there were three, possibly four, of these creatures behind the wall. She did not know if Korian's plan had failed. *Have all of them entered this room, or are there more of them pursuing him right now?* And there was no way she could know how many creatures had infested their city.

She heard a man's voice, deep and sluggish. "What have you got there? Seems a little out of place, don't you think?"

She could hear crates being opened and shut and moved about.

"'K.R.' Who do you belong to?"

Her eyes opened wide in surprise. She forced her arm up inside her top. It was gone. The exquisite white linen was in the monster's grip. She must have dropped it when she squeezed into this spot.

Don't worry about that now, she told herself. Only it wasn't that easy to ignore. After all, it was more than a piece of cloth. It was a symbol of fate, hers and Korian's comingled; it was a gift from her beloved; it was hope; more importantly, it was hers.

More shadows entered the chamber. The hissing was extremely loud and horrifying. Sara moved deeper into the space. Tears began streaming down her face. She arrived at a dead end. For the first time, she felt claustrophobic and her breathing hastened. About ten feet up the wall, she saw an opening. Ignoring all the noise she was making, she climbed out using the narrow walls for leverage.

On the other side, she found a path leading away from the cavern. She had no idea where it went, but she didn't care.

Hesitantly, she started down the path. Her assurance grew the farther she got. A hint of a luminance became visible up ahead. The light was troubling, and Sara slowed her pace. Two steps later, a large Stragoy, hiding and waiting, swung a long, rotted piece of timber, striking Sara squarely across her chest.

Sara was on her back fighting for breath when Herrick approached and stood over her. He had an evil grin on his face.

Korian sprinted in and out of corridors. The rumble of many footsteps on the hard surface seemed to come from every angle. It appeared his plan was working.

The pursuit abruptly stopped. Even more confusing; his pursuers started retreating. Korian listened while the alarming noises faded into the distance.

"Sara!" he cried out, and he started back.

"Samjees! I am begging you. Watch over her!" he shouted.

His gut cramped; his chest throbbed when he swallowed. When he finally reached the cavern where he had left Sara, he collapsed into the room, exhausted.

The room was deserted and destroyed. Crates were overturned. The room had been torn apart. It was a mere shadow of the organized workshop he had seen only hours earlier.

"Sara!" he whispered. No response. He repeated it again and again, elevating his voice with every call, but there was still no response.

Korian fell to his knees, beaten.

Behind him, from deep within the shaft that ran adjacent to the open doorway, came a booming thud. The ground shook beneath him. A second, louder blow followed, and the wall on the left side of the tunnel exploded inward, leaving a large hole into the chamber beyond.

Korian sprang to his feet and sprinted towards the gap. He had no objective other than to find Sara. One truth was undeniable though: he did not know his way around.

"Who's there?" No reply.

"Sara?" Nothing still.

He approached the gap tentatively and peeked inside. It looked empty. By the look of the rock fragments and what remained of the wall, it was clear the hole had been punched from the inside.

"Who's there?" he called out again, but only his words echoed back. Below, a distant sound of rushing water beckoned him. As he stepped down onto the narrow path against the wall that coiled downwards, he noticed a bright light upstream. Even at this distance, he could make out the deep rumble of a great crowd.

He hurried to the bottom. The roar from the large gathering became louder.

Navalline?

He was halfway to the source of the light when something caught his eye: a long wooden stick with an elaborate design on one end, peacefully floating upstream.

Korian jumped into the water and retrieved it.

"Where are you, old man?" he whispered. It was Crogan's staff.

A splash upstream stole his attention. Korian jumped out of the water and hid. He raised Crogan's staff and readied.

A dark contrast to the water became discernible. A headless Stragoy floated by. Korian exhaled, but then came another splash upstream followed by a pained moan. Korian readied. As the object neared, Korian saw arms, flailing. It was a man.

"Crogan!" shouted a surprised Korian. He jumped in to grab him. Crogan was a little groggy but coherent. The first words out of his mouth were, "Where is Sara?"

Just then, they heard a loud collective gasp, followed by screams and bedlam from a large chamber downstream.

The Portal stood dormant and mysterious. The thick black pool within the monolith doorway rippled from the subtle vibrations caused by the gathering of such a large crowd. Word had spread about Korian's arrival to Navalline, raising the curiosity of many. Some had come hoping their prayers had been answered, others were simply happy to be among excited people and to feed off their energy. Regardless of the reason, nearly every person from this underground labyrinth had made their way to this place.

Balconies and paths were filled with row upon row of people. A steady buzz of optimism filled the room.

Jannik, Isaac, Grayson and Leith were gathered by the Portal: their assigned meeting place upon arrival. Not knowing the whereabouts of Sara, Korian and Crogan was weighing on them. Isaac was beside himself with worry.

"Jannik!" called Alrik.

He and Lael rushed to meet him. There was something odd in their demeanor. Their faces were grim.

"What's wrong?" Jannik managed.

"Dead. They're both dead. Herrick!" Alrik cried.

"What are you saying?" asked Jannik, with alarm in his voice.

Alrik sobbed. He turned, bent, put his hand on his knees and retched.

"Herrick murdered them…our mother and father," said Lael. "He's all wrong. We led him right to us."

Several women on the upper part of the cavern let out horrifying cries, drawing everyone's attention. People were rushing to get out of the way of something. Pandemonium ensued. Bodies were pushed off the paths and fell to the crowd below. Whatever approached travelled down the path, spreading terror. A mass of bodies parted, making way amidst cries of horror. Those who had no idea what was going on were riveted. Suddenly, the reality of the situation became evident. Stragoy were in their domain.

Stragoy spread out among the people. They numbered in the hundreds. Vastly outnumbered, people still cowered and scrambled away to avoid them. Stragoy took up strategic positions throughout Navalline and began herding people into groups.

Herrick calmly stepped onto the floor and sauntered over to the front of the large room. He found Jannik and the others and winked. He paced for a while, reveling in the fear and electricity he felt in the air. The room turned quiet. When Herrick had his fill, he spread his arms, turning his palms upwards.

"My good people," he began slowly and deliberately.

"Today is a special day." There was another long pause.

"I, Herrick Mead, with my friends," he said, motioning with his hands towards the armed Stragoy, "have come to free you from this cold existence. How many of you long to see the sun again? To bask in its radiance and warmth? You have forgotten about the world up there, a world of such beauty. Instead, you live here, like vermin." Another long pause. Herrick continued to pace.

"I am your liberator. I will end your suffering."

"Lies! Don't listen to him!" Jannik yelled.

Herrick motioned to three Stragoy. They pounced on Jannik and beat him. People gasped.

"Enough!" Herrick yelled. Jannik writhed on the ground, battered and dazed; blood poured from his mouth.

"Before I can do this, you will need to do something for me," Herrick continued. "Give me your Skine Tamer." There was a low murmuring from the crowd.

Herrick motioned with his eyes. Two Stragoy emerged from the crowd, carrying a woman. She was beaten and bloodied, her face barely recognizable. They dropped her in a heap in front of Herrick. The crowd gasped. Isaac felt as though he had been disemboweled. He watched his beloved daughter whimper at Herrick's feet. Instinctively, he charged forward, but several men held him back.

Sara crawled forward slowly. After a few painstaking feet, she clutched something lying on the ground with trembling fingers. It was her linen. She brought it to her face and used it to muffle her cries.

"I ask you again," Herrick continued.

"Give me the man you call the Skine Tamer." Again, there

was no answer. There was a thunderous silence in the room. Only Sara's sobbing could be heard.

"All right," said Herrick.

Herrick stooped and raised Sara up to her knees. She was tiny compared to Herrick, who towered over her. Her right eye was swollen shut. With the other, she found her father, who stared wide-eyed at the horror.

"Sara!" he cried.

Grayson jumped to his feet as Herrick unsheathed his sword. Holding the hilt as if gripping a knife—blade downward—Herrick stood behind her.

Grayson charged. Sara's unwavering focus was on Isaac. Grayson shoved one Stragoy to the side and evaded another as an arrow caught him in the upper chest. He grimaced but kept on.

"Herrick, stop!" he screamed, but his cry was cut short. His eyes opened wide, as a spear plunged into his back, emerging through his abdomen. Grayson fell. Sara's battered face was the last thing he saw.

Herrick took a deep breath, shut his eyes and swallowed in the terror that filled the room. His hand was shaking. When he finally exhaled and opened his eyes, women began screaming. Panic, spread like a wildfire throughout Navalline.

"You were never going to give him up!" shouted Herrick. He raised his sword. "But I already knew that," he said under his breath.

The tip of the blade entered the bottom part of Sara's neck just behind the collarbone. With vacant eyes and meticulous precision, Herrick plunged the sword downward, on a slight angle, into Sara's heart.

Korian, with Crogan at his side, entered the room from the lower left side. Immediately he felt something terrible had happened.

People were grimacing, and their gazes were transfixed on something at the front of the large room. Women were beyond weeping; they were lamenting something.

On the ledge above and to the right of him, Korian caught a glimpse of an armored Stragoy holding a sword. Crogan noticed him too. They saw another and another. Korian's heart was beating faster; his breath was being choked out of him. As they made their way through the crowd, people gave way. Strangely, many were touching his arms and shoulders as he walked by. Korian took a few more steps and pulled his V out of its sheath.

"What's going on?" he implored.

"Keep moving towards the left," Crogan said.

The commotion of the crowd started to draw attention. Stragoy had begun to notice him. When he emerged from the crowd, what he saw sickened him. He glanced at the Portal and beyond it. He saw his friends and their faces pained him. What he saw at the front of the room ripped him apart.

Korian fell to his knees, dropping his weapon. The large cavern filled with a multitude of bodies was eerily quiet as if someone had flipped a switch and turned off the cries of horror and shock.

The linen his beloved had held close for so many years lay crumpled in the dirt. Always in his thoughts, he had hoped it had found its way home. So fair and pure before this day, now sullied and soaked in blood.

This can't be happening. Her delicate arms, covered with scratches and dried blood, were tied at the wrists. Sara was hung by both arms, her back against the large wall at the front of Navalline for all to see.

Several Stragoy approached and began encircling him. Korian didn't care. A deep pain, so inexpressive and personal, took over his entire being once he fully realized Sara was absolutely and irretrievably lost. Her angelic body, although bloodied, was at peace.

Tears welled up in his eyes. His heart was crushed. A possibility of happiness forsaken.

The Stragoy took a step forward.

Korian raised the blood-soaked linen in his fist and raised it towards his chest. The K.R. initials were still visible in the sea of red. He looked at Sara.

Her chin rested on her chest. Her hair, which hours ago had so tenderly brushed his face, was now stained red. Tears streamed down his face. They fell onto the linen, mixing with Sara's blood.

The Stragoy crept closer.

He had accepted his fate and was prepared. Slowly, he came to his feet, still clutching the linen. Korian turned towards his friends. He saw Jannik holding the limp body of his dead friend, his face contorted in pain. Sara's father was on his knees, shoulders drooped in grief. Alrik, Leith and Lael were huddled together. Their postures expressed defeat. He looked around at all of the people. Men's heads were down; women clutched their chests and wept freely.

He caught the eyes of a young girl who was fixed on him. She was indeed sad, but there was something else. Her eyes expressed hope and a plea for help. *There's so much sorrow*. He spotted Crogan, whose face held another expression altogether.

Crogan's face was vacant as if his mind had gone elsewhere. He was staring into space. What Korian didn't know was where Crogan's mind had gone. For Crogan, the Harwill's words came to mind, or at least this much:

Through fate he will find a passion like no other.

A tormented soul it shall lead to find truest peace.

But, when tears of his beloved fall and mingle with those from his own eyes

And fall upon a sea of red atop his family's name,

The purest pain and sorrow shall follow.

For it will be at that moment of sorrow,

When the world seems damned and hope is lost,

That the gods will open the gate and invite this fellow in.

I see it now, Crogan thought. *His tears are to mix with Sara's and the initials atop the blood-soaked linen. The K makes sense, but the R?* The sudden realization made him jump. "K.R., Ro, Korian Ro," he muttered under his breath.

Korian stared at Herrick, who was standing on a rock beneath where Sara was hung. What he saw hardened his heart. Sara's blood dripped steadily onto Herrick's shoulder, and he was relishing in it. *Was that a smile*? The animal had a grin from ear to ear.

The Stragoy took another step forward.

Korian's fists clenched. His face was strained and taut. He started to tremble. Eyes full of loathing became red, blistering charcoals that smouldered with hatred as he glared at Herrick. Herrick's smile slowly faded. The Stragoy took yet one more step closer. Korian's eyes radiated intense hostility as though he could incinerate everything within his field of vision to cinders.

At that moment, Korian raised his hand and held the linen above his head. The Stragoy took one step closer. Another step and they would be within striking distance. He looked at his beloved one more time.

He put his head back and unleashed a roar that grew to an ear-splitting shriek. Some covered their ears; others fell to their knees. There was wrath and strength in the bellow, but there was also more: there was an undeniable rally cry.

The linen burst into flames. Korian opened his palm and the

flame grew larger. The Stragoy lunged. Korian swiped his raised arm around in a circle. The flame lashed out like a fiery whip, striking all the Stragoy that stood around him and engulfed each one of the twelve Stragoy in angry flames. Then, just like that, the linen's plight ended in a puff of smoke. His outstretched hand was empty, and smoke wafted in a large circle around him.

As the Stragoy fell and fire consumed what remained of them, another two lunged towards him from behind. Korian rolled to the side and charged in Herrick's direction, but his path was blocked by a row of onrushing Stragoy with outstretched swords. He evaded them by turning the opposite way: towards the Portal. A spear sailed towards Korian's back just as he leaped into the black pool of the Portal.

The Stragoy's spear passed through to the other side.

Korian did not.

16

RESURGENCE OF THREE

A STEADY DRONE BEGAN to overcome the stillness in the large room. Herrick gripped his sword tighter. Gone was the arrogance from earlier. Faces were frozen in terrorized stares: a sea of pallid faces with mouths agape. Stragoy gathered around the Portal with weapons ready.

Crogan's senses were heightened. His heart raced. Grief, anger and elation overwhelmed him in this moment of clarity. He was coming to terms with the reality of what had just happened, the reminder so brutally displayed on the wall for all to see. The Portal, dormant again now, was full of secrets yet to be revealed.

Jannik groaned. He was lying too close to the enemy. Crogan grabbed him under the arms and pulled him back, ignoring the Stragoy standing dangerously close.

"You!" Herrick bellowed at Crogan from across the large room. "Where is he hiding?" he shouted, red faced.

Crogan ignored Herrick and whispered words of comfort to those nearby. This angered Herrick even more. He sensed Herrick's growing confusion and something else. *Is that worry?*

With a great sense of urgency, Crogan ordered those around him to step back from the Portal.

"Take him!" Herrick shouted, pointing at Crogan.

Five Stragoy turned and approached Crogan. Their weapons were readied.

Beneath the upper slab of the Portal, a ripple began in the black, liquid-like matter. The ripple spread, increasing in intensity. A small rock sitting on top of the slab stirred ever so slightly, and then it began to shake vigorously, until the movement pushed it to the edge and over. Suddenly, the entire structure started to tremble, and the dark pool took on a variety of radiant colors.

A Stragoy approached the Portal and stared blankly into the vacillating pool as if in a trance. From the black fluid, a small, pale green humanoid creature, barefoot, wearing pants and a tattered shirt, burst through with incredible velocity. He struck the unprepared Stragoy in the chest and knocked it off its feet. It was a far different Oren than the patient and kind creature who had once befriended Doric. This Oren fed off of the wickedness that filled the room. He clawed at the unsuspecting Stragoy's face, burying his thumbs deep into its eyes until it stopped moving.

Oren leapt off, scurried to the side, and he scrunched into a ball. Other Stragoy rushed towards him.

They never reached him.

Flashes of light, like lightning, spread across the Portal. There was a blinding streak of sheet lightning. The air was sucked in as the Portal imploded. A powerful explosion rocked the cavern. A fist of black smoke punched its way out from the murk, sending hungry flames and thousands of rock fragments outwards. Those on the balconies and the ground farther away from the Portal covered their heads and dropped to the ground, evading deadly rock fragments. The Stragoy weren't as fortunate. The explosion incinerated all the Stragoy that had gathered nearby.

The mystical Portal was destroyed. Smoke rose, twisted and filled the cavern. The buzz of the crowd changed to groans and whimpers. There was a steady hum in the room. The blast was so loud everyone's ears began to ring.

"Kill them. *Kill them all!*" Herrick shouted, wiping debris off his shoulders as he came to his feet.

The drone turned to ear-splitting screams and cries, but something unexpected was happening where the Portal had once stood.

The residual smoke was sucked up into the ventilation chamber. As the air cleared, Stragoy bodies littered the ground, and a figure, a man holding a spear, became discernable where the Portal had stood. His head was down. When he raised his head slowly and opened his eyes, those closest to him gasped.

Korian appeared older with a few more lines on his brow. Hints of gray adorned his long hair. His face was expressionless, though the corners of his mouth tilted downwards in a slight frown. He was brawnier than he was moments ago. He looked at Sara, who was exactly where he had left her.

Korian was aware of his surroundings: the fear and apprehension that hung in the air, the proximity of Crogan, Jannik, and his friends—and most importantly—Herrick. Stragoy surrounded Korian and approached slowly. His breathing slowed, but his heart raced. His mind returned to that moment when he had first seen Sara's body. This time around, he was consumed only with extreme anger and the overwhelming need for revenge.

The stench of death and decay snapped him back to the present. He turned towards Herrick, who glared back, an unsettled look was in his eyes.

The Stragoy, armed with swords, spears and pikes, charged. Korian raised his spear, and he, too, charged.

The enemy's eyes were focused as they met the attack. Korian swung his spear from right to left. As the spear sliced through the air, the metal shaft became pliable. The tip flattened, taking the shape of an axe. The transition was instantaneous. The sharp blade caught three Stragoy, cutting them down. Even before the spear's momentum stopped, it again changed shape, this time into a broadsword. The blade at the end of a huge arc sliced through the air, biting through a Stragoy's helmet, taking with it the upper half of its head.

The Stragoy in the crowd began to strike people down. One man, however, did something a Stragoy did not expect. He caught the Stragoy's arm before its sword came down, and he clubbed its head with a clenched fist. People standing by pounced and began scratching and tearing. Years of oppression and torture had blinded them. The Stragoy was torn to pieces.

Korian's energy was contagious; men began to fight. More joined the uprising, and they swarmed the Stragoy within the crowd who were isolated from the others.

Crogan rushed forward, taking a sword from a dead Stragoy. He swung wildly as the grotesque creatures charged. A Stragoy standing behind Crogan raised its arm to strike, but a streak of gleaming steel interrupted its descent. The Stragoy's arm, severed above the elbow, fell limply to the ground. Standing over it, Alrik shook with rage. His eyes were bright and infuriated, flashing through disheveled, haphazard strands of hair. A bloodied sword was in his hand. The Stragoy gawked at its stump mechanically as Alrik buried the sword into its side.

Stragoy after Stragoy charged Korian. He struck down one after another. He threw the spear overhand; it changed into a chain with a long spike on the end. It ripped into and through a Stragoy's chest. He pulled, a broadsword reformed, and he swung at an advancing Stragoy. Every time he swung, a Stragoy fell.

Herrick rallied the remaining Stragoy by the wall beneath Sara. They set up several lines with the over three hundred that still remained. Korian plowed through those outside the Stragoy line with ease as he made his way towards Herrick.

The Stragoy released a volley of arrows at the advancing men. Several struck their mark. Crogan and others joined the charge as another hail of arrows came. This time, a score of men fell.

An arrow grazed Korian's cheek. Other arrows soared past. The enemy had assumed an effective formation.

From somewhere behind Herrick came a loud thud. It shook the ground and the walls. Sara's legs, hanging lifeless, quivered against the rock with the impact. There was a second, and then a third, thud. Stragoy ignored the blows. The onslaught continued, and men continued to fall.

Korian trembled with rage. He clenched his teeth and bolted to his feet. He let out a guttural battle cry and charged.

Suddenly, a muffled roar permeated the rock, followed immediately by another thud. This time the wall gave, and an enormous dark hole formed. Giant rock fragments exploded into the room crushing numerous Stragoy positioned closest to the wall.

A giant shape draped in shadow and holding a thick trunk of a tree like a giant club stormed inside the gap. The enormous beast, taller than two men standing atop one another, swung his club menacingly as he burst through the hole he had just carved into the cavern. His single eye, in the center of his broad forehead, was deep-set, enraged and determined.

He loomed over the chaos. The trunk, with roots still attached and dangling, swayed heavily when he swung. Four Stragoy were flung into the air and sailed into the crowd where the angry mob finished them. The beast lashed out again and again and laid waste to Herrick's Stragoy. The line of archers was swiftly severed.

With a giant stride, he stepped over the pile of dead Stragoy at his feet. Each time his massive foot—bare and calloused—fell, the ground trembled. His movement seemed deceptively slow and cumbersome, yet he reached Korian in two strides, turning his threatening gaze down towards him.

"This is not your fight," Korian said, and he readied for a strike from this lumbering beast. Instead, the large eye, visible behind strands of black, reedy hair, relaxed.

"You best finish what you started," the beast said in a deep, husky voice. He turned towards Herrick. With thick legs tensed and exposed beneath an animal skin frock slung over his shoulder, the giant swayed back and forth while eyeing the remaining Stragoy.

Korian glanced up at Sara again, then charged. The cavern was filled with a thunderous roar from the multitudes who witnessed the clash. The remaining Stragoy were destroyed.

Herrick was alone. Korian, with his chest heaving, his face and eyes drenched with Stragoy blood, glared at Herrick. He pounced.

Herrick, keen on striking the smaller man down, was not prepared for Korian. Korian averted each blow. He swiped, lunged, and leaped with extraordinary agility, slicing Herrick's shoulder and reopening the skine's wound. Herrick's blows slowed from fatigue and loss of blood. Korian pressed farther, delivering blow after blow until Herrick's defense waned, and Korian struck away his sword.

Korian looked to Sara, suspended over the gaping hole, blood still flowing from her slender neck. Then he turned to Herrick, remembering how he had relished in her death, and sliced through Herrick's belly, spilling his intestines. Herrick fell to his knees.

"You're all fools!" Herrick managed in a hoarse and distressed voice. He held on to his exposed bowels, delirious with pain; he picked them off the ground and stuffed them back into his belly.

"You have only delayed your death. Thousands more are coming." He laughed and cackled. "In the north, what remains of your four-fingered friends will die. Endura's lost."

Korian swung his sword through Herrick's throat. The large man's head tilted back until it hung loosely by a small piece of flesh at the back of his neck. He fell back, and his writhing stopped.

In Korian's hand, the sword changed back to the spear. He took a few steps and staggered. Sara still hung on the wall. None of this had brought her back. Korian collapsed.

In the mayhem, a sharp pain started suddenly at the back of Crogan's head. He brought his hand up to it expecting to feel the warmth of blood. There was no enemy behind him wielding a sword, no arrow or spear. The pain brought a heavy, throbbing haze of confusion. His eyes watered and glazed, and a strange dryness filled his mouth. Blood poured out of his nose. He collapsed to the ground. Two words entered his mind that could have only come from one source.

A strange sensation, like that of hundreds of tiny needles, suddenly engulfed Doric's body. His blood vessels dilated. Dark lines, like black ink, spread under his skin throughout his broken frame.

He became acutely aware of every nerve, tendon, organ, muscle and bone as if they were waking up after years of dormancy.

What's happening to me?

Breathing became difficult and labored. His vision blurred, and there was severe pressure behind his damaged eye. His sight became a black veil. When he reached out to part the darkness, his arm did not move. In fact, his entire body did not respond. He slumped to the side limply, and his head struck the ground. Blood seeped from a deep gash above his eye. Suddenly, his body tensed and convulsed.

He sucked in putrid air and gasped as if someone had flushed his lungs. Tiny needles became painful jabs as though from a serrated knife. Still unable to move or scream, words formed in his head.

"*It hurtsssss!*"

The thought was so powerful, Doric's back, arms and legs contorted. Bone snapped, cartilage crunched, tendons hissed, as they ripped and repaired. His muscles expanded and moaned, as his skin stretched and mended. Muscles regenerated spontaneously, growing strong and taut. Capillaries renewed. His weakened heart and withered organs were infused with life. Bruises vanished. His legs stretched, and bone and tendons repaired. The skin from the fresh cut on his head came together and the cut disappeared. Bones in his face disintegrated into a thousand fragments and moved beneath the surface as if malleable. His skin filled with color. Doric's eyesight returned. He focused on the ceiling while the remaining parts of his face, a prominent nose and strong jaw, reformed. He sat up with new eyes opened wide to the sudden realization of what was happening.

Footfalls outside his door grew louder. Someone approached. *Not much time*. Doric grabbed his right thumb with his left hand, clenched his teeth and snapped the bone. His hand easily slid out of the shackles.

Lorne Maggis cracked his knuckles as he approached the heavy iron door. He put on his gloves and drew his sword. He passed the Stragoy that stood guard, and when he entered Doric's chamber, the man lay curled on the floor with his back to him.

Something about Doric seemed off. Lorne couldn't quite make out the uneasy feeling he had. A shaft of light from outside illuminated Doric's wretched form. His hair, covered in grime, appeared thicker and had a strange luster. Doric's face was hidden by hair, so Lorne couldn't see his eyes. They were wide, piercing and ready.

He placed his foot on Doric's shoulder and tugged with his heel to force the man onto his back, but Doric had other plans. Doric moved swiftly, too swiftly for an unprepared Lorne, and he swiped at his leg. Lorne's feet were swept out from under him, and he fell onto his back. Air left his lungs, and, in a panic, he dropped his sword. Doric, free of shackles, reached for the knife on Lorne's belt and pounced. Blow after blow of the butt end of the knife connected with Lorne's head and face, sending blood spraying into the air.

Doric placed the blade against Lorne's cheek. The cruelest living being, who had tormented him for years, was now barely conscious and at his mercy.

"How does it feel?"

Doric placed the tip of the knife by Lorne's eye. He pressed hard and cut into Lorne's flesh at his temple. Doric dragged the knife down, slicing to just above the lip. Lorne exhaled as his body slackened.

A Stragoy, who had been standing outside the door, entered the chamber. Doric hurled the knife, striking the creature in the neck. There was no reaction. The Stragoy simply swayed for a moment, and then it fell.

Outside the entrance where Herrick and the Stragoy had entered the Den, Aaron paced. Hours had passed since Herrick had entered the tunnel. Aaron's eyes blazed, sending smoke wafting into the cool air. Back and forth he marched.

Earlier, he had wanted desperately to step into the Den and lead the carnage, but things had not gone according to plan. He could see through the eyes of his Stragoy. It was carnage all right but not as he expected.

His eyes were fixed on the small gap. He was raging inside. After a few more paces he'd had enough. He thrust his arm forward, palm open. Stone exploded into the dark tunnel, turning the small gap into a large cavity, big enough to serve as a doorway.

Aaron approached the opening. He stood in front of the hole he had made and stared into the tunnel. He was clearly aware of the Manian's curse, but the desire to enter was too powerful. *You can't hurt me,* he willed.

Slowly, he extended his arm past the threshold into the tunnel, but immediately the dark armor that covered his hand burst into flames. He recoiled and stepped back, cursing.

While he patted the flames with his other hand, a vision suddenly entered his mind. It was from a chamber in Hellas Mons. Doric was hovering over Lorne. A very different looking Doric calmly sliced up Lorne's face and then turned towards him and threw the knife at him. Doric's eyes were wide and very alive. Aaron was watching things unfold through the Stragoy's eyes. It lasted mere moments, and the vision faded to black.

Aaron found a dark area adjacent to the opening in a recessed section of the wall.

"I'll be back," he whispered into the dark, vacant tunnel.

He stepped into the shadow and vanished.

Lorne groaned under Doric's weight. When Doric reached for Lorne's sword, Lorne hacked and glared at Doric. He started coughing up blood. Helpless and in the unfamiliar position of vulnerability, Lorne managed, "They're dead. You're too late."

The wind picked up and a rumble grew from the corridor. A gust of wind swept into the room followed by a large, cloaked shadow. Aaron had to lean forward to pass through the door. His eyes, burning embers, bore into Doric. Smoke was still rising off his hand. His whip snapped against the hard surface. The flagellum-like tentacles flailed angrily.

Aaron's arrival infused Lorne with life. He shot to his feet and charged Doric. The scuffle was brief. Doric blindly swung Lorne's sword, severing Lorne's left hand. Lorne's howls were deafening. He fell to his knees, and he clasped his stump.

"What have you done?" he shrieked.

Advancing, Aaron cracked the whip, fully extended, but it missed, as Doric leapt and rolled to the side.

Adorned completely in his menacing dark armor, Aaron stood less than ten feet away. He glared at Doric with two fiery eyes.

Doric came to his feet, but Aaron struck again. This time, the tentacles near the end of the whip, latched onto Doric's thigh. The steel tip snapped back and plunged into his abdomen just below the sternum. Snared and impaled, the pain was nauseating. Though his abdomen was covered in blood and his breath came in quick spurts, Doric kept his wits.

Aaron began coiling the whip hand over hand. With the other end still impaled in Doric's abdomen, Aaron began to pull Doric toward him. Ignoring the pain of his new wounds and the burning in his legs, straining to resist Aaron's tugs, Doric swiped with Lorne's sword and severed the taut, leather, serpent-like whip.

He fell back. With great resolve, Doric rolled to his knees, and with two hands, flung the sword overhead.

Aaron was not prepared. This insignificant slave was irritating him. When the tip of the blade struck his chest and dug into his armor until half of the sword was buried, Aaron roared, shaking his heavy skull shield from side to side like a rabid beast. His eyes blazed bright orange. Then he paused for a moment, calmly pulling the sword out of his chest.

"You can't hurt me with this!" Aaron screeched with an inhuman roar and tossed Lorne's sword aside.

With a pained grimace, Doric pulled the spiked ends from his thigh, and he extracted the tip of the whip from his abdomen. Blood seeped down his legs from the open wound.

Aaron charged. Doric glanced left, then right: nowhere to run. He turned and sprinted towards the only option he had.

Aaron closed the gap. Doric's wounds had only just healed when Aaron reached forward, swiping his sword at Doric's back. The blade sliced his tattered shirt and carved a deep, diagonal gash across his back. Doric, with blood seeping from his fresh wound, leaped out of the chamber and into the air as Aaron stopped at the edge of the opening.

Doric turned to face the sky. For a brief moment, Doric was at peace. After so many years, he was free, unattached to anything. The wind was his only companion—powerful and exhilarating—drowning out the rest of the world. The sun and mountains whirled before his eyes. With arms extended and chest out, he soared downwards as the gash in his back mended.

The moment of bliss ended abruptly when he crashed into naked branches. Tossed from limb to limb, torn and broken, after what seemed an eternity of torture, the ground finally ended his suffering.

Navalline was unusually quiet. The Portal, once a wondrous spectacle, was gone. The lumbering giant—a spectacle himself—knelt beside Korian, cradling his head in his massive hand.

When Korian opened his eyes and found the giant's enlarged head, with its single glaring eye peering down at him through strands of his hair, Korian's eyes opened wide, he recoiled—momentarily forgetting where he was—and he swung wildly, connecting his fists with the giant's nose.

"It's okay, Korian," the giant said in as soft a voice as he could manage without reacting to Korian's blows. His voice had an echo, not delayed like the echo from a cave, but a subtle delay as if his voice was layered.

"It's me, Gred," he said as if Korian was supposed to know who he was.

Korian began to focus. He frowned, as a wave of clarity washed over him. Suddenly, it all made sense.

"It's…you? All this time…you're the—"

"Yes," said Gred, attempting a warm smile.

Korian had always wondered what he would say if he ever learned who it was: *the phantom who's watched over me all these years.* He was expecting someone small; someone stealthy; someone fearless; someone with boundless strength—essentially someone that did not exist—but this…?

Korian studied Gred for a long while, and then his eyes slowly wandered over Gred's broad shoulder to where Sara's lifeless body was still tied to the wall. Gred followed Korian's gaze. He gently lowered Korian's head, and he lumbered over to Sara and untied her.

Isaac stepped from the crowd and slowly approached Korian. His daughter lay lifeless in Korian's arms. Isaac knelt and gently caressed Sara's bloodied face. He looked up and met Korian's eyes for a brief moment, because almost immediately Korian shut his eyes and lowered his head. In that brief exchange, Isaac saw profound sadness, a kind of hollowness caused by lingering grief and fatigue engraved on Korian's face. Isaac placed his hand on Korian's forearm. Their eyes met again. With tears in his eyes, Isaac nodded, and in that simple gesture, Korian felt an overwhelming feeling of warmth, acceptance and forgiveness.

Opposite where the Portal had stood, Alrik helped Crogan to his feet.

"Are you all right?"

"He's alive," said Crogan.

"Who's alive?"

Crogan ignored the question. He embraced a surprised Alrik firmly, but his mood changed once his eyes looked upon the dead. The giant was on one knee beside Korian; his head was down. Korian wept with Sara in his arms. Jannik, with his father in an embrace, also wept. There was sadness, yes, but there was something else. Crogan looked around the room. There was a shared look on many faces. Many were looking at Korian with reverence.

Crogan went to find Oren. The odd little creature was on the ground, not far from the place where the Portal had stood. Oren groaned, and he sat up.

Crogan tilted his head forward ever so slightly. "Oren," Crogan said, greeting his old friend. "Been a long time."

Oren groaned. "It has, yes." He grimaced and licked his lips. "But the worst is still to come, old friend."

"How is it that you were in the Portal?" Crogan said, a look of confusion was on his face.

"Ah, yes. The Portal. I came down the shaft stealthily," Oren managed.

"That's not what I meant." Crogan had known Oren a long time and was well aware of his deadpan wit.

"Well, Crogan, everything is not always as it seems," replied Oren. "I exist when I shouldn't, don't I? I passed into the Portal, and the Harwill has not spoken of me, yet here I am. Some things I cannot explain. The gods have a plan, and I, like you, have a part to play. I'm sure there will come a day when all of this will make sense."

Crogan smirked. "All right, Oren. I'll leave it for today. There're more important things to deal with. But the next time I ask you…give me the truth. I think I've earned it." Crogan smiled wryly.

At Crogan's request, everyone worked tirelessly to prepare for an exodus. In the meantime, the wounded were tended to and the dead prepared for entry into the afterlife.

Using his gift of foresight, an exhaustive activity involving withdrawing into his subconscious and utilizing—through a virtual third eye—his limited insight into the immediate future, Crogan was able to verify a window of opportunity of when the surface would be free of the enemy.

He summoned the men. "Take the omara and gather wood. Aaron's army is more than half a day away," he said, as half a day was the limit of his foresight.

"Don't fear a sudden ambush. Be swift. We need as much of a head start as we can get."

Piles of wood were assembled in two rows. The fallen were carried and tearfully laid in a row upon the summit of the pyres. Each body was adorned with a cowry shell on their chest. Sara was laid at the end of the first row. Grayson was laid beside her. The wood was set ablaze, and the torch was passed down the line. As the fires roared, Korian leaned in to give Sara a final kiss.

"I never got to tell you that I loved you," he whispered into her ear. "I have...from the first time that I saw you. You died far too young."

Korian kissed Sara's lips.

"I know now why I was sent...I failed you, Sara. I've known grief, but never grief like this, and I never will again."

The crackling of wood grew louder, and the temperature in the room rose.

"You were right. I should have never left you. Forgive me, Sara...I only just found you, yet, I saw my life laid out before me with you in it. I wish you could have died in your bed, old and gray, whispering something I could treasure."

He kissed her cheek.

"They look to me for salvation," he cried. "What do I do?"

The torch came to Jannik who ignited the heap of wood below Grayson. He waited, holding the torch, until the flame had engulfed his friend.

Korian kissed Sara's forehead. He took the torch from Jannik, and he took a long, hard pause. He leaned forward again and whispered, "Wait for me, Sara. I'll find you again," and he set the last pyre ablaze.

Gred, stood off to the side as the fires blazed and smoke filled the room. He paced continuously without taking his eyes off Korian. Lines on his brow, like deep troughs, had surrounded his large eye, and a grave expression had etched on his face. He waited, impatiently, as everyone stood for what seemed an eternity just staring blankly at the flames.

The thumps of Gred's heavy footfalls permeated through the space when he came up behind Korian. Many turned their attention from the fires to gawk at the giant who towered over everyone. Although he was still intimidating, fear of the one-eyed giant had eased. His calm nature seemed a marked contrast from the beast who had crushed Herrick's army of Stragoy.

"They'll be back!" he bellowed. "You're all going to have to leave."

He waited, but his remark garnered a weak reaction. "You're all going to have to leave, like...*now*!" he shouted.

"Agreed, but where are we supposed to go?" Jannik replied, raising his voice to be heard. He said what everyone was thinking.

"We'll be massacred on the surface," said Lael with a dreadful stammer.

"Why can't we just stay here and fight?" blurted Alrik.

"Well, that may not be that smart, at least not in here. You may have a chance through there," said Gred as he pointed toward the dark tunnel on the other side of the blood-stained wall, beneath the area where Sara had been bound. "There's a refuge, about a three-days walk down that passage."

"Dosdava?"

Oren stepped out from between Gred's thick, tree trunk-like legs and surprised everyone with the power in his voice.

"Yes. Dosdava," Korian repeated without lifting his eyes from the fire. "That is where we will go. Tell them to gather their things and hurry. Take only what can be carried."

Just over an hour later, they were in a long tunnel lined row upon row: men, women and children were homeless again. A stream of people and beasts, clutching onto hope, marched towards another unknown. Only now, something was different; there was a radiant optimism.

Many still buzzed about what they had witnessed in Navalline. For the first time in a long time, there was a prospect of a new tomorrow.

At the helm, holding a torch for all to see, was Gred. His head, large and intimidating with hair that hung like weeds, swayed with every step. Perched on one of his wide shoulders was Oren.

Not a section of this tunnel was levelled. The passageway was not as efficiently laid out as the tunnels in the Den. They pressed upwards and downwards, and at times, they had to avoid rocks that jutted out from the walls or from imposing stalactites that hung from the ceiling.

Twelve hours later, they reached a reasonably flat, large chamber where Korian stopped the group for a brief rest. Up ahead was a fork: two paths leading into distinct unknowns. He found a ledge and sat, reliving the recent events in his mind.

Aaron's army is approaching, a force beyond our world, guided by a wickedness that is unbound, yet why do some smile?

Korian found Crogan sitting with his back against a wall. He was in a trance. A thin stream of blood flowed from his nose. After a while, Crogan opened his eyes, and Korian waved him over.

Crogan staggered toward Korian's ledge. He was still fatigued: the effects of tapping into his foresight hours earlier.

"You alright?"

"I'll live," replied Crogan.

For the first time since Korian had emerged from the Portal, he saw Korian's eyes up close. They had aged, and now they carried a perpetual sadness. Although they had lost their innocence, they were even more piercing and determined.

Crogan sighed. "So, I think this is where I'm supposed to draw upon my prolonged years…leverage my extensive experience and my astute observations of human nature, consider the dark side that pervades some, and give insight into what could possibly explain the wickedness we have seen. I'd say something insightful that would help you make sense of this. You'd look at me and believe, because of the many lines and wrinkles that adorn my face, that my words are brimming with wisdom. You would miraculously feel better. You would take a breath and we'd move on, ready to take on whatever is next."

Crogan leaned against the wall to support his weary legs.

"But I have no words, Korian. There is no sense to this. Some like Herrick; like Aaron, are just born dark. They're wicked and without a conscience. They didn't become like that; they were born evil. This is *our* reality now. . . our fight to abolish this darkness. And now, you have the means, Korian. The gods have given it to you. You've just proven it.

"What happened back there wasn't your fault," added Crogan. "The gods have a plan and a mysterious way of—"

"Crogan, stop…you have no idea. You were doing pretty good up until that point. Curse the gods and their plan," Korian sneered.

"Alright, there's obviously something more behind those hard words," said Crogan. "I do hope you reconcile with them soon; with the gods, I mean. Hmmm—because I think it's important you realize…*that you still need them*!"

Crogan hiked his shoulders.

"Maybe you're right. Maybe I don't have any idea, but what I do know is this: we are in the darkest of times; the darkest period Endura has ever seen, yet, look at them. Do you see their eyes?"

Korian nodded.

"They have hope. They want more than to just survive…they want to live. You are the light, Korian. The gods sent you and you are the spark…you are the single magnificent white rose in the darkness."

Crogan's words made Korian think of the child who he had spotted in Navalline, before he had entered the Portal: so innocent and deserving of life, not oppressed but free; a symbol reflective of his people.

Then by coincidence or perhaps influenced by some unseen power, maybe even the gods had a hand in it, he found her in the crowd again. She was perched on another small ledge. Her face was expressionless, but her eyes were full of unspoken words. She was surrounded by a warm aura that captivated Korian. In its warmth, he felt Sara's presence. It made Korian want to help her—to help all of them. She smiled at him.

Crogan put his hand on Korian's forearm, taking his attention away from her.

"Speaking of a light in the darkness…" Crogan leaned forward and said, "Doric Devinrese."

"Who?"

"Doric, a huntsman who never really got the chance to be one," Crogan said.

"Hmmm, I only know of Will Shyler."

"Yes, there's Will and then there's Doric. I thought Doric was dead, and I was responsible. I've carried the weight of that failure. Instead, his story is an inspiration. Like you, he's a light in the midst of all this darkness. One day, I'll tell—better yet, he can tell you his own story…because he's *alive*. He has escaped from Hellas Mons, thanks to you," Crogan said.

"That's great, Crogan. But really, I don't know what I did. Whatever it is…if I did have a hand in it, I'm thankful."

Crogan enlightened Korian of their gifts: communicating telepathically and their ability to spontaneously heal, and how they had been restored when Korian emerged from the Portal.

"And now, Doric is heading to Jayens Fjord as we speak," said Crogan.

"Ah, Jayens Fjord? Warn him not to waver and to stay alert. Tell him not to stop moving and to keep his head up. He's heading into very dangerous territory."

"Of course," said Crogan, and then he smiled.

"What?"

"Why do you care about a man you've never met?"

"I—"

"Guess I was right about you. You have a good heart. You see, Korian, you were born a leader."

Korian scoffed.

Crogan squeezed Korian's arm. "I know who you are?"

"What did you say?"

Korian and Crogan locked eyes. Crogan's did not waver.

"I know who you are," Crogan repeated.

"What are you talking about?"

Crogan took a quick look around. They were beyond the earshot of others. Crogan leaned forward and whispered, "Ro, Korian Ro."

Korian exhaled slowly, "No, Crogan. You're mistaken."

"That's what I figured you'd say. How could you be so sure that you're not his heir?"

Korian just stared blankly.

"Alright, there are other things that need attention right now. We'll leave it, but…you *are* his heir," repeated Crogan.

As Korian pondered what Crogan had just said, Crogan suddenly blurted, "I've dreamt of the day the three of you—the Azura, Will and Doric—stand together for the first time. That will be a glorious day. The three of you would be a force that Aaron and Hades have not considered."

"Well then, I look forward to meeting them."

"And I look forward to seeing them again…as free men."

"Well, maybe we should pray to the gods to watch over them," Korian said sardonically, "or maybe we'll guide them, and they'll just have to rely on their wits, and their unique abilities…the same things that got them here."

This time, it was Crogan's turn to shake his head. "Samjees, please, just watch over them."

Crogan's eyes started to look brighter. He started standing without leaning and his voice had more vigor again.

"Just before you waved me over, I was speaking with Will. I relayed Doric's warning: that the firstling's sanctuary in the north has been compromised."

Korian gathered his thoughts.

"Next time you speak to Will, tell him to lead the firstlings to the Azart Cliffs. Find the Flagon Tree." Korian then told him what to do when he gets there.

"All right, and you," declared Korian, "You're going to lead our people through the tunnel on the right."

Korian gave Crogan directions detailing what to do when they arrive at the fortress. His time within the Portal was many things, and included in those things was an enlightenment and a greater awareness about Endura; things like knowledge of this fortress was part of it.

"Do what I ask and we may survive the horror that awaits us there. Should Aaron return, and I have not yet arrived—fight. Do whatever you must to survive. Hold them until I get back. Our biggest test is waiting for us at Dosdava. Do you understand? Promise me you will not let them give up, no matter the cost!"

Thousands of ashen faces looked back at the two of them. Hope and determination had replaced fear and anxiety.

"Something tells me I won't need to make them do anything."

"Good," said Korian.

"What about you? What are you going to do?"

"I need to get some answers."

"I'm going with you," said Gred, coming up behind them. The sound of his baritone voice startled Korian.

"Suit yourself," said Korian with a pause. "Just don't slow me down."

A look of bewilderment crossed Gred's face. He smiled.

"Bring him back safely," said Crogan.

"Promise me," Korian demanded.

Crogan was more than a little concerned with the intensity in Korian's words.

Crogan shook his head and sighed. "Whatever horror awaits us, I promise, we will not give up."

They bid farewell, and Korian, with Gred at his side, quietly slid down the corridor on the left.

17

A WISH

AT THE SAME time that Korian and the surviving humans walked down the hidden tunnel outside Naval-line, Will Shyler, with his new friends, strolled down the main road of the settlement.

Firstlings went about their daily routines, oblivious to the Stragoy that had stumbled onto their rural paradise without warning. Occasionally someone would look up, taking a quick glance at a new face but nothing more. New faces were not uncommon in these parts. Refugees from towns and villages destroyed by Aaron's army would steadily arrive.

Will's stomach was sick with unease from walking among firstlings, but he felt exhilarated. More powerful, however, was the overwhelming premonition of doom that seemed to be following him like a dark cloud.

This entire experience was surreal. He passed people he felt he knew. Hammin, who had just stepped out of the coop Will had robbed earlier, nodded a hello. Will nodded back and looked away guiltily.

Turning onto a path that appeared less travelled, Will stopped as a strange sensation washed over him. He placed his hand on Tana's shoulder for support. It was brief, but for a moment, he couldn't breathe. Every nerve fired at once, his muscles tensed and his legs cramped. When the feeling passed, he felt an uncharacteristic sense of calm.

"What's wrong?" Tana asked.

Will took a moment to regroup. "Strange feeling," he said, still breathing heavily. "The excitement must be getting to me."

"What kind of feeling?"

"Difficult to explain. It's like heat all over my body."

They continued at a much slower pace until Tana stopped in front of a lonely looking cabin. Bathed in the light of a vivid setting sun, the cottage, absent of shielding trees, was faded and brittle.

"Go on then," she said.

"Go where?"

Tana pointed towards the door, motioning with both hands.

The door swung open. A stout, aged man with a wise face and white beard stood in the doorway. His nose was scrunched. A look of confusion spread across his face. He ambled forward, stopping directly in front of Will. Something was familiar about this man. His eyes were deep set and piercing, with a compassionate quality. He had a stately look as though he had once held a position of authority. He grinned, extended his arms and embraced Will tightly. When the man finally released Will, tears were running down his face.

"He said you would return." He was smiling. "Do you remember me? I am Raif Merrin Auslant, from Essra."

Will's mind raced with memories of another time. He recalled Merrin, though he looked much different then. *I used to bounce on your plump belly as a boy*. This Merrin looked to be a mere shadow of his former self. He was well respected by the people of Essra, and by the looks of things, was well regarded by those here too.

After a brief exchange, they went inside and sat around a square table in the center of the room. Torin and Griff stood quietly by the door. They talked for hours about a different time when life was somewhat normal in Essra.

"I have to tell you," Will said abruptly.

Everyone in the room paused and looked at him.

"I've never known Stragoy to wander. I've not seen rogues before. There has got to be more of them out there," he said emphatically.

Tana and Merrin's faces expressed a similar concern. Golin on the other hand, was in denial.

"We've lived here for years. There's no cover from above, but we are well hidden by the mountains. The winters are bitterly cold. Access into these parts is restricted. I am sure there is an explanation, likely stragglers lost and wandering but no cause for alarm," Golin said.

"The one you killed," Will said, looking at Tana, "he had a horn. Do you know what that's for?"

"Yes, but he never signaled," Golin answered.

"It means there are more out there."

Golin still had an irritated look on his face.

"They are not going to return to their camp. We made sure of that. That's going to sound alarms, don't you think?"

The exchange carried on for an hour, but they could not agree on next steps.

Merrin interjected. "Why did you not return?" he asked. The

question caught Will off guard. It managed to lessen the tension growing in the room.

"Your father would wait by Rossland's Gate each day. He never lost hope that you would return."

"What happened to my parents?"

Merrin lowered his head.

Will did not pursue this further. Instead he said, "I couldn't face them. I didn't have the courage to face anyone. I ran and have been hiding ever since. But then I found your settlement, and even from the outside, I felt I belonged. I know…it sounds crazy."

Merrin poured a cup of tea. "That's not crazy. It's probably the sanest thing you've said," said Merrin while handing Will the cup. "You're welcome to stay here."

Initially, Tana thought Will was expressing gratitude when she noticed him close his eyes and lower his head. Suddenly, Will leaned back in his chair, dropped the cup and fell backwards. Lying face up on the ground, his eyes rolled back. Blood oozed out of his nose, and his face held a look of torture.

"Will! Are you all right?" Merrin fell to his knees and raised his arms, waving them about, unaware of what to do.

After a minute, Will gasped, opened his eyes and sat up.

"Crogan," he said with a smile. "That was Crogan," he repeated, ecstatic that his telepathic ability had returned.

"He said a man entered the Portal and emerged with the Manian's spear."

"The what?"

Will ignored Merrin's question, but his expression turned somber. "He warned me of something I already knew…death is at your boundary."

"Death is at *your* boundary?" Golin repeated, mocking Will.

"You have to leave before nightfall," said Will.

"What?" shouted Golin. "That's suicide."

"You stay here, everyone will be dead by morning. A group of Aaron's Stragoy are coming for us. The two from earlier are not alone."

"Are you certain?" asked Tana.

Will nodded, and he stood to address the group. "I'm sorry. You're going to have to trust me." His voice had calmed.

"Why would we trust you?" Golin shouted.

"That's fair," said Will. "Unfortunately, waiting to learn if I'm wrong is not an option. You'll have no second chance. They bring death, without reason or mercy."

"If you're right, where are we supposed to go?" Golin asked, his tone less contentious but still argumentative.

There was an awkward silence that lasted far too long, and then Will blurted, "I haven't figured that part out yet. I just know we need to get away from here."

"This is madness!" cried Golin.

"Perhaps, but doing nothing is certain death."

"How are we supposed to convince them to leave?" asked Tana. "This is our home. Even if you're right, they will not want to leave. They have a semblance of a life here even if it's not of their choice. Out there is certain death."

"I have an idea, but I'm going to need your help." Will related his plan. When he was done, Tana and Golin shrugged.

"Alright," Tana said.

Will started for the door. He stopped before crossing the threshold.

"Crogan said one more thing. He said I'm not alone. Another huntsman, Doric Devinrese, is still alive."

Tana stumbled back, falling onto a chair. Her right hand covered her chest. Her breath came in quick bursts.

No one seemed to notice. No one except Golin. He did not ask if she was all right. Instead, after a disappointed glance, he turned awkwardly and stumbled to the door. From the pit of his stomach, a dull pain spread through his body. The feeling was alien. He felt a loathing towards Will he could not explain and an even greater one at the mention of the name, Doric.

"He's alive?" Tana managed beneath her breath. After so many years, the wondering ended too abruptly. She was not prepared. What if she believed Will, and he was mistaken? It would be too painful to lose him again. New hope had entered into her heart, and she wouldn't be able to get rid of it anytime soon.

"We best get started," said Will as he reached for the door. "We don't have much time." He stepped outside, and in the sky above them, hundreds of black maledhen swarmed.

The maledhen had long since departed. It was evening, and there was a chill in the indigo darkness. The waxy moon and the stars were radiant, lending harmony to the night sky. The icy fingers of the wind pressed into the skin of thousands of firstlings gathered in the large field, the same field from Will's dream. They huddled in groups, drawing warmth from each other.

Word had quickly spread about important news that a new arrival to their settlement was going to share. The interest drew firstlings from the comfort of their homes. Merrin was growing concerned with the tension hanging in the crisp night air.

"What is this all about?" a man shouted.

"Please, be patient," Merrin pleaded, trying to appear calm.

"I hope you're right about this huntsman," he whispered under his breath.

A few more minutes passed. A torch flickered in the darkness behind a line of trees. Will, accompanied by Golin and Torin, stepped out from the line of trees into the open field and made their way through the crowd of firstlings. Golin and Torin dragged a large sack filled with something heavy and rigid, like a weighty plank. A stale and decrepit stench filled the air.

They reached elevated ground where a large boulder sat. Will climbed atop the boulder and looked over the sea of curious faces.

He froze. *What am I doing?* He was trembling, but not from the cool night. His stomach was in knots and his heart beat rapidly. *Hold it together,* he thought. *After all, all I'm going to do is tell them to pack their things and follow me, the firstling they most probably blame for their repression, and head out blindly into the wilderness.*

He started speaking and tried to hide the quiver in his voice.

"I know you are tired, cold and judging from your faces…a little impatient. You are wondering who this stranger is before you that has taken you from your homes." Thousands of penetrating eyes watched him with interest.

"I am Will Sh—" he began, but then decided to refrain from saying his full name.

"I'm Will. Because we're short on time, I'm going to get straight to it. The truth is," he paused, "you're all in danger. Death is coming and we must leave immediately."

A murmur started among the crowd.

"Is this a joke?" said a burly firstling.

"Who do you think you are? Why should we believe you?" shouted another.

He nodded to Golin and Torin. The two hauled the sack they

had dragged out of the woods up onto the boulder and raised it until the contents stood upright. They pulled back the cloth to expose the corpse of the Stragoy Will had killed earlier. The disgusting features with most of its face cleaved off were exposed for all to see. The crowd gasped. Sickened from the stench, Torin turned away and released his grip. The dead Stragoy slipped from Golin's grip and fell onto the ground.

Got your attention now!

"This thing..." continued Will, "was in your forest. It was looking for you. Others are on the way to finish what it started... to destroy you all."

"You brought death here!" screamed a woman.

"Unless you act quickly, you and your loved ones will die. It is only a matter of time!" Will bellowed back, not responding to the comment.

"What would you have us do?" a gray-haired woman shouted.

They were angry at the thought of having to leave this paradise, but they'd always known this haven was temporary. He was, after all, the bearer of the news. They needed a leader—fearless and sure—certainly not Will Shyler, a firstling who had been hiding for most of his life. *So many looking to be saved*, thought Will.

Will walked to the edge of the boulder and stared into the crowd. He took a deep breath, and then, with a power and conviction from a voice not his own, he addressed them a second time.

"I am Will Shyler of Essra, born to the Fraternity of Huntsmen, finder of the legendary cove and the Manian's spear." Will's heart was pounding. "But more importantly," he shouted, "I am a Ruid!" He found a stout middle-aged male standing near the front of the crowd. He pointed at him and added, "and I share your fear. It's a fear that chokes and smothers and because of it, we hide," he said. He moved on to another firstling before adding, "And together, surrounded by mountains, we feel safe… but we are not safe!"

He paused again. Several torches flickered in the wind.

"You have all known this day would come. So yes…go ahead and be angry. But know this…it is not this place that keeps you safe and protected…it is each other. You have a relentless will to survive. It's a force. You share hope; an inspiring hope that is contagious. And there is more . . . you have a powerful bond between you. I've seen it. You would give your lives for one another."

Will's eyes were piercing and unwavering as they met the eyes of firstling after firstling.

"Look to your left…look to your right. That is all you need," said Will, with as expressive an emotion in his voice as he could muster. It was genuine and the firstlings knew it. "You do not need this place. There is no future here beyond tomorrow."

Heads turned. Some firstlings cried. Most expressed fear. Will gave them a moment.

"I say again, if you stay here…you will die! There's a reason why—after wandering in the wilderness for more than twenty years—Samjees has brought me here. There's a reason why—on this same day—Stragoy have found you. There's a reason why—after more than two thousand years—the Gatekeeper, your Azura, has just today, emerged from the Portal as prophesied."

Firstling eyes remained glued on Will. He took another breath and said, "Are these not signs?" No one answered. "I know they are! Don't ignore them!"

Only the sound of a cooing child from somewhere among the crowd, mixed with the sound of sputtering torches in the wind, could be heard.

"I tell you this…I mean to follow the Azura to the ends of Endura," continued Will. "Follow me and I will lead you to him and to sanctuary. It is the will of the gods. But now, two choices you have. If you choose wisely, I will be at that path in one hour," he shouted, pointing up the hill towards the mountain. "Pack light. I leave you to your choice."

He stepped off the rock. There was a thunderous hush. He made his way towards the hill, and the crowd parted to let him pass. After a few moments, firstlings quietly disappeared into their homes—Merrin, Golin, Tana, Griff and Torin among them—until Will was alone.

The hour passed and the stillness rang in his ears. He feared he had pushed them all away to certain death. It was while he waited in the dark, with concern escalating to worry and then to fear, that he had heard from Crogan again. He now knew where he needed to go.

The field was still empty, silent and dark, and there was no sign of Tana, Merrin, or the others. He waited longer. Then, from the darkness, he heard footsteps in the cool night. A moment later, a woman labored up the path towards him. She was hunched over and her thin gray hair fell loosely over her face. She had two young boys by her side. Each leaned forward as they walked. A sack was slung over her shoulder, and the boys each lugged another on their backs.

"My dear boy," she said out of breath. She put her hand on the younger boy's shoulder. "Neelam says we need to follow you." The boy's eyes sparkled in the moonlight as they looked up at Will admiringly. "So, we will."

"I guess we're coming too," Tana said. Golin, Griff, Torin and Merrin all walked up beside her.

Behind them, orange and yellow flames from numerous

torches flickered in the wind. Streams upon streams of people began walking up the path until they filled the field and the adjacent forest. An exceptionally large firstling pressed through the crowd towards him. He placed his heavy hand on Will's shoulder. Will recognized him as the firstling who had shouted at him earlier.

"You best know what you're doing," he said grimly.

Will stared back. *I don't know what I'm doing.* Instead of saying it, he nodded in silence.

Merrin came up beside him and said, "All right, Will from Essra, lead the way."

Will led the more than three thousand firstlings out of the valley, through the forest and onto a winding path up the mountain. When they finally reached his cave, Will had a premonition he would never see his home again. They trekked through a series of tunnels until they exited the other side, angling onto a path rarely travelled along the top of a ridge. They stayed on this path until they arrived at a stand of rocks near the end of the ridge. They stopped here, ate, and after setting up a watch schedule, they rested until the sun began to rise.

At dawn, they made their way down the ridge and came to other outcroppings. They travelled south from there for almost a full day until they reached a place where the ground ascended into a forest of firs. Eventually, trees became sparse, signaling the end of the forest. Here they stopped again and prepared for the next night.

Will, Tana and Golin went on ahead. They found a steep path up a hill beyond the forest and slowly crept their way up the arduous slope. When they reached a section where the trail leveled before it ascended to a broad ridge, the view opened up.

"There," Will pointed towards the characteristic red rock. "The Azart Cliffs. We should be there by nightfall."

When they returned to the camp, Will found a tree and sat with an exhausted grunt. Tana and Golin found a place nearby. Silence permeated the area for a while until Tana said, "Will, what really happened to you after the Bridge of Mies?"

Although Will was exhausted, anxiety—the enemy of sleep—had him counting stars to get his mind off the burden he had taken on. There was no sleeping on this night. He pondered Tana's question before answering, but Tana wasn't finished.

"Nobody really seemed to know," she added, "but everyone seemed to have a story. Word was, that you went mad; or that you jumped to your death; or that you were turned into a Stragoy. I even heard that Samjees was so angry that he turned you into a phantom, reduced to haunting forests for eternity. You became the spook who would watch us from the woods and snatch up those of us who acted mean or malicious." Tana smirked. "I never believed any of it, anyway. Then there was Merrin, he would mention your name and ask Samjees to watch out for you. He's always believed in you. And then, when I spotted you a few weeks ago, I have to admit, at first, I thought you were a ghost, but then ghosts don't steal chera."

Will smiled. "You know something…I've never been asked that before…about what happened to me. Then again, I've never been around anyone long enough. Ah, and this…sitting here; sitting among you and everyone else, is surreal. Up until recently, I had avoided everyone. After that day on the bridge, I had not told a single soul who I was. Now…I just told thousands at once." Will scoffed. "I've gone from the most hated to the one everyone is depending on for survival, just like that. How did that happen?"

Will laughed, shaking his head in the dark. They sat in silence for a while.

"I just went into hiding," said Will. "I learned to live off the land; to steal," he said and laughed again. "Tana, the truth is…I'm a coward."

"You're wrong about that. You're no coward."

"Perhaps you're right. Perhaps I've been a fool, living that day over and over again. Hey, if enough time goes by, and if you let the past rule you, you tend to forget how you got here. I feel that I blinked and twenty years went by. The only reason I'm here, is because I didn't have the courage to kill myself." Will chuckled at that. "And just recently, I learned about a boy who has suffered many times what I've endured."

"Doric Devinrese?" asked Tana in a small voice.

It was dark, but Tana was still able to see the surprised look on Will's face.

"I was there when he was taken. It was Sammas Day in Brackens Town," said Tana. "I was just a child, as was he. I can still see the look in his eyes when Aaron took him." Her face wore a haunted expression. "All these years I thought he was dead."

"We all thought that. He's definitely not dead. He's been in Hellas Mons for over twenty years and endured more torture than anyone could possibly bear. He survived. He even found a way to escape…from Aaron."

"Can you reach him?" Tana asked, trying not to betray her feelings.

"No, only Crogan can."

"Next time you speak to Crogan, could you ask him to tell Doric something for me?" Water welled in her eyes. "Please tell him 'Tana is safe.'"

"If you go to sleep, I will send him the message right now."
He lay back down. "I thought you and Golin were—"

"Friends," she said. Lowering her voice, she added, "I love Golin but not in that way." She looked to where Golin was resting. Thankfully, Golin was fast asleep.

They sat in silence for a while.

"Will?" She repeated his name a few more times. Will was in a deep trance, similar to the one he had been in earlier in Merrin's home.

"Goodnight, Will."

Golin, leaning against the tree, opened his eyes. In the growing dark, he clenched his teeth. A flurry of emotions washed over him, none of which were good.

The next morning, the firstlings started out early. This next part of the trek was especially dangerous, partly because of the precarious climb but mostly because of the exposure. A significant part of their remaining journey was in the open.

Halfway across the flat terrain, a few maledhens began to appear in the sky. Others began to swoop in to form a murmuration above their heads. Soon the sky was filled with piercing squawks. The large black-winged creatures, circled and swooped. Their synchronous movement was as dazzling a display as it was mysterious. An hour later, they were gone.

It was late afternoon when they reached the edge of the Azart Cliff. Will gazed over the expanse and searched the wall on the opposite side until he found what he was looking for.

"Golin!" he called out. "Follow the edge eastward until you find a path. It'll be narrow, so be careful. Lead them down and across the river. Do you see that?" Will said, pointing to what appeared to be an opening at the base of the cliff. "Take them through there. It will lead to the top."

While Will's arm was still elevated, outbursts erupted from throngs of firstlings who were still on the lowland. Will climbed onto a rock, and he peered past the terrified multitude. As they scampered towards him, in the distance beyond them, Stragoy stormed out from a forest at the base of the bluff.

"Hurry!" shouted Will. "Follow Golin!"

The group hastened their pace but were still only as quick as the person in front of them. Golin found the path Will had told him about.

"Over here!" Golin shouted. "Follow me!"

From his higher ground, Will could see the row of Stragoy had spread across the plain. They were closing fast.

"Move!" he shouted. He leapt off the rock and into the distressed mass of firstlings, and he started his own trek down.

When Will reached the bottom of the cliff, some firstlings had already reached the top. The more daring and able ones had climbed the crag. Many were still scaling the wall on their ascent. Hundreds of firstlings were still streaming into the gap at the base of the cliff. Will needed to get to the top, quickly. He leapt onto the wall and began to climb.

He reached the top of the cliff, drenched in sweat and drained of energy. He rolled onto the rough surface, staggered to his feet, and he stumbled towards the Flagon Tree: the same tree Korian had passed many years ago.

The Stragoy reached the ridge across the canyon. Firstlings were still packed in at the bottom of the gorge; many were crossing the river; hundreds were still scaling the wall. A number of Stragoy sent a volley of arrows across the gap, but they fell harmlessly into the water—too far still to be effective. Stragoy began disappearing down the path after them.

Will reached the tree and examined it for a moment. It was exactly as Crogan had described. He found the hard-shelled jade fruit sitting thirty feet up. He searched the swollen trunk for proper footing. He stole a few breaths in anticipation of what was about to happen…and he began to climb.

Even before Will's hand touched the rough surface of the tree, large, ant-like insects swarmed from the creases in the trunk. They began covering his hands and feet, working their way up his wrists, forearms and ankles. The pain was excruciating as if being jabbed by hundreds of burning needles. At first, each sting was discernible, but after a few seconds, the pain became a dull, permanent throbbing. He tried desperately not to scream, but his shrieks drew the attention of every firstling. Fighting the numbing in his limbs, he pressed on until he reached the top of the bulb. Swarms of insects found their way under his clothes. His neck was covered. Numbness blanketed his entire body. He swatted at the insects and pressed up against the branch. Struggling for air, he realized he couldn't move. The poison had caused paralysis. His throat burned. He could not swallow. Then, his body began to spasm.

Golin and Merrin made it up the hill and approached the tree. The sight of Will was horrifying. He had turned into a black mound of pulsing insects, ticking, snapping and crawling over each other. They crawled onto his face. Will opened his eyes wide, gulped a breath of air, and then his face was completely covered.

"What's happening?" Tana yelled. "Where's Will?" Golin pointed and then pounced to restrain her.

Will's lungs were about to burst. He couldn't hold his breath any longer. The sound of insects clicking in his ears was driving him mad. He exhaled a steady stream of air, knowing his next breath would draw insects into his mouth.

Suddenly, insects retreated in droves out of his ears, off his head, face, neck, body and limbs. In a matter of seconds, what remained of Will was a swollen, misshapen, repulsive living corpse. He was a bloated mound of sores and blisters.

At the base of the cliff, the first Stragoy emerged from the path. The last of the firstlings entered the opening in the cliff and began making their way into the tunnel. A few stragglers were still making the climb.

Will began to convulse. A moment later, he sucked air into his lungs, and he sat up, shaking his arms. After a long minute, his body recovered. There was no visible sign of trauma on his skin.

"Are you okay, Will?" Tana shouted with relief.

Will nodded, taking a quick glimpse down the cliff. Stragoy had started emerging from the path.

Will hurried the rest of the way up the tree and reached the elusive fruit. He tore it off the branch, plunged the blade of his dagger into one end, and he twisted it. The fruit opened, revealing a bright, warm white light. There was movement inside. A long, slender, winged stick insect crawled out of the fruit and floated up out of the light to hover by his face. It observed him inquisitively. Will felt a weight on his mind as if it was being squeezed.

"What is your wish?" He could not tell if the words had been spoken aloud, or if they were just in his head, but the words were vivid. Before he could answer, the insect flew off into the gorge, and it soared down the cliff with such velocity that it became a streak of light.

The temperature over the Azart Cliffs suddenly turned cool. Thunderhead clouds appeared above as a cool breeze arrived from the west. The air became heavy.

Stragoy were now making their way through the river, towards the crag. Will knew he and his people were out of options. They had only the desert to the south. Hampered by the old and young, they were unable to make haste and had no way of outrunning the dreaded creatures that were about to swarm them.

"Come on. You can't abandon us," Will whispered in desperation.

"What did you wish?" asked Tana.

"The first thing that popped into my mind. End this nightmare, make the Stragoy go away, and get us out of here."

"That's three things. In what order did you say it?"

"What does it matter?" said Will, creeping towards the edge.

"It matters because nothing is happening," said Tana worriedly.

Stragoy were beginning to climb the cliff. "We have to get out of here!" Will cried out.

"Where do we go?" Golin shouted back.

"Look at us! We can't just sit here awaiting slaughter!" Merrin bellowed.

Golin turned and yelled, "Let's go! Now!"

A large leaf from the flagon tree brushed by Will's head as it fell into the gorge. Then another and another tumbled. Leaves from the ancient tree wilted and turned brown as if time had accelerated. The trunk quickly dried up, branches cracked, leaves continued to fall and the tree withered and died before their eyes. When the leaves had all fallen, the deadly insects followed on the ground, in a long procession, moving away from the tree.

At the base of the gorge, the water began to swell and overflow the banks until the base was flooded. The Stragoy found it increasingly more difficult to press through it. The flow of the river had dramatically increased, creating rapids-type pressure. Then, from the west, where the gorge curved out of view, the high crest of a giant wave appeared above the surface. It was racing past them on the way toward the gorge. Heart-stopping in its enormity, it came like a giant blue and white dorsal fin above the surface of the cliff.

There was a collective gasp from the firstlings, and they rushed back from the edge. The roar of the wind was deafening. When the giant wall of water reached the bend and turned towards them, frothing and splashing, the wall of rolling foam crashed into the opposite face of the cliff with such force, a large section of the wall broke and washed away. A tidal wave raced towards the Stragoy, carving into the sides of the gorge. The waters churned like an enraged beast, swallowing up the Stragoy and carried them away. As it passed, the swell pressed forward, like a massive tsunami, towards the east, rising all the while until it almost reached the top of the cliff. As the water's fury abated, firstlings cheered.

On the other side of the gorge, a single man stared. His features were not clear from this distance, but he was tall and fierce. The firstlings ignored him; they were busy rejoicing. Some even kissed the ground while they thanked Samjees.

Tana immediately dashed towards Will and wrapped her arms around him. He had never felt such a feeling of acceptance. He closed his eyes and welcomed it.

A rumble from behind, somewhere in the pulsating river, robbed him of the moment.

"What now?"

Beyond the edge of the cliff, the water, now level with the edge, began to effervesce. Large bubbles surfaced and the water frothed across a wide area. Something began to rise out of the water.

At first glance, it appeared to be a large square wooden house with a flat roof. It had openings on all sides large enough to be windows. As the object rose, a platform appeared in front of it. The house structure and platform sat on a large flat surface, rectangular in shape, with evenly spaced railings that spanned its length. In all, it must have been at least three hundred feet long and over a hundred feet wide. As the object continued to rise, a giant, flat wall-like surface began to dwarf the firstlings. Enormous volumes of water began to cascade down off the deck through the railings. The wall was the enormous hull of a giant ship. The rising wall, dark and smooth, eventually blocked out the sun. When it surfaced completely, the immense ship swayed like a restless giant.

A loud knock came from inside the hull. Will's eyes swept the hull as a crack appeared across the smooth, dark surface. It formed the shape of a hatch. The enormous hatch began to open, exposing a dark cavity. A large ramp eventually lowered, coming to rest on the edge of the cliff.

The silence was deafening. From the darkness inside the ship, an imposing man strolled out onto the ramp to peer over thousands of faces. The warmth in his eyes, shaped by lines and crow's feet, gave the impression of a smile. All present stared at him, looking awed, shocked and excited.

The man tilted his head to the side, allowing his ear to drain water. He raised a tankard and took a swig. Water dripped from his white hair and his clothing. His heavily wrinkled skin fell in loose folds. Strangely, his feet seemed fused to the ship. It was like he was part of the ship: his feet were wooden, up to just below the knees, and then blended into the part that seemed flesh and bone. The change wasn't sudden—like a hard line below the knee, wood then flesh—rather, the wood seemed to fold into the creases of his pants, which were of the same dark brown color.

"Who is your leader?" he called out to the group.

The crowd rustled. Tana and Golin stood near Will. Slowly

heads turned. Firstlings began standing aside to carve out a path. Everyone's eyes looked in the same direction. It took a minute for Will to realize all eyes were on him.

When Will reached the ramp, he was greeted with a warm smile.

"So, you are the one I have to thank for setting me free," the strange man on the ship said as he bowed.

"Will?"

"Yes?" Will replied, surprised at hearing his name.

"Well," he took another swig, "I am Captain Orpheus. Welcome aboard the *Winds of Freedom*."

Will's heart was racing. This strange feeling—vindication—was intoxicating. He was in awe. The gods had listened to him. He fixed his gaze over his people and the ship, silently expressing his thanks and gratitude.

Tana took Will's hand. "We are all safe because of you."

Will's face appeared calm but inside he was bursting with excitement. Firstlings patted his back. The large firstling who had first been so apprehensive before they had started on their journey, walked up to Will. He had a somber look on his face. He embraced Will, lifted him up, and he burst into exuberant laughter.

Several hours later when they were all aboard, Will, Tana, Golin and the others had gathered near the bow of the ship. They watched Orpheus walk up a steep ramp to a platform. His feet and hands, and each part of his body that touched the ship, fused to the wood on contact. It was so bizarre to watch him move about the ship. He looked out over the firstlings.

Will, though, turned to stare at the threatening, dark figure on the edge of the opposite cliff. He could feel the evil emanating and pulsing from him, even from a distance. Cyrus's sunken eye fixed on Will. It was hypnotizing. Will had to look away.

"Hold on!" yelled Orpheus, gripping the rail in front of him. After several minutes, cries came from the stern. A giant swell of water squeezed between the cliffs and headed towards them. Enormous waves splashed onto the surface of the cliff, spreading outwards. Cyrus moved back far enough to avoid the rushing water, every ounce of his grotesque features dripping with hatred.

When the swell finally reached them, the stern began to rise, and the ship moved forward. Mammoth waves swallowed up what remained of the flagon tree as the ship was propelled forward.

In the distance, Cyrus became smaller and smaller until he disappeared behind a hill. Soon, the Azart Cliffs faded from view.

18

THE IN-BETWEEN

IT WAS LATE afternoon. A day had passed since the firstlings had boarded the *Winds of Freedom.* Korian and Gred had been travelling in a northwesterly direction for about a day and a half since emerging from the underground city. The awkward pair had crossed the vacant countryside, with its lush, verdant hills; lonely forests; and narrow streams, in search of a place Korian had seen only in his dreams; a place where he was told he would find answers.

They were in a forest of tall trees when Korian stopped to examine his map. He had a puzzled look on his face.

"This place is not on the map," Korian said.

"Well then, let's eat while we figure out where we are," growled Gred. "I've not been to these parts either."

They'd barely spoken during their trek, so it still felt odd hearing Gred's voice. Gred reached into his bag, fidgeting anxiously.

"What was it like?" he blurted out. It was clear from the unsure look on his face and trepidation in his imploring eye, that he had been mulling this over for some time and had finally gotten the courage to ask.

Korian stared blankly, awed once again by the enormity of Gred. Gred's one round eye, blinked inquiringly beneath his thick bush of a brow, and it arched sharply in an upside-down "V."

"What was what like?"

"Inside the Portal."

Korian, surprised, asked, "What do you want to know?" managing a smile.

Gred smirked. "I thought for more years than I care to remember that I'd tasted loneliness, but this last day and a half with you…I've never felt more alone. You haven't said a word."

Korian raised a brow. They stared at each other a moment without speaking. Gred smiled first.

"All right, Korian," said Gred, coming to his feet and dwarfing Korian. "Tell me about the Portal. Then, I'll tell you something that only I know about you. It may help you with what you seek and maybe help you see things clearer."

Korian considered, staring at Gred wide-eyed for a moment. *Gred, you're the only person who knows me better than I know myself.*

"All right," Korian replied.

They resumed their trek. Over the next few hours, Korian talked and Gred listened like an oversized child beaming with excitement.

"When I entered the Portal, I was swallowed up by a cold, black pool," Korian started. "Beneath the water, my heart raced. I was cold, weightless and disoriented. I wanted to scream and escape the unbearable pain in my chest. Remember, Gred, I had just seen Sara pinned to a wall. It's a wonder I didn't give up right then, now that I think about it."

He paused, reliving the moment.

"Anyway, I found a transition: a section beneath the surface where the water changed from dark to light. Intuition told me to swim towards it."

The more Korian spoke, the more vivid the details of his account became. He withheld parts that he wanted to keep his own, though. His giant friend would never know the difference.

"Sara's face, her body sliced and bloodied, was still in front of me. In my delirium, I actually believed she was in the water with me, and that I could save her. I remember cramping up, and then nothing, just blackness.

"I woke up, lying on damp soil. A small fire was burning low. Though I knew I did not start it, I welcomed its heat. I felt for a string around my neck; Sara's ring was safe where it belonged.

"When I looked around, the pool of water wasn't so much a pool as it was a murky swamp. I was in a forest of threatening, gnarled trees. Their roots, above ground, coiled around each other as if lying in a dangerous embrace. The sky was cloudless with no sign of a sun or stars. The sky was just a vast, gray plain.

"That's when I saw him—Oren. I was frightened at first. Imagine seeing that skeletal little creature in that dark place. Oren sensed my alarm because he told me not to be afraid and added, 'You're welcome for saving you from the swamp,' with a chuckle. I couldn't help but stare at him in disbelief.

"I was a mess. My reality was shattered. Oren just kept muttering things I couldn't hear while he tended the fire. He left but returned a short while later holding a dead animal by the scruff of the neck. 'Swamp mreg,' he said, throwing it at my feet. He licked his lips a lot. He told me to eat and went about his business. I did not reply or speak to him, and there was no way I was going to eat that thing.

"'Suit yourself,' he said. He advised me that if I wanted to get back, I wasn't going to find my way through the swamp but rather through the forest. Then he disappeared into the woods. I just sat there stubbornly; it must have been hours before I realized nothing was going to change on its own. So, I stood and followed."

Korian took a swig of water. They were moving at a good pace.

"The forest was thick. I carved my way through it and fought to stay on the trail. I was lost in more ways than one, and I called out to Oren, unafraid of disturbing nearby predators. I simply didn't care. Hours passed. It should have been night, but the sky hadn't changed its gloomy disposition. Several hours later, I stumbled into a clearing where I found a swamp with the remains of a fire. I was back where I started.

"I heard his voice again. Smug that Oren is. 'Out for a walk?' he said, perched on a rock with his little legs crossed. I told him my name and asked what this place was.

"'Welcome, Korian, to the realm of Menzia,' he said, like I was supposed to be impressed. He told me Menzia is many things: a place for the lost or neglected, a paradise for fools, the fringe of things, or the in-between.

"'In-between what?'" I asked.

"'That is the question,' Oren said. Then he said there was someone who might be able to explain. I followed him into the forest, only this time when we emerged, we came into a large room with an open ceiling. The floor was covered in white sand and enclosed by tall, etched and eroded slate walls. Off to one side was an opening that led into a tunnel that, at that moment, was dark and foreboding. In the middle of the room stood a marble table. The Manian's spear lay on top of it, glistening vibrantly."

Korian paused to glance up at Gred's single large eye.

"Go on," begged Gred. His cheeks had reddened with excitement.

Korian smiled. "You could imagine my amazement. I started for the spear, while replaying over and over in my mind how I was going to bury it into Sara's murderer's heart. The image was so powerful I could taste it. After two steps, I stopped because a section of the black wall beyond the slab stirred.

"The wall was about the size of the side of a small shack, smooth and flat, resembling a big square mirror. A continuous thin film of water flowed downwards over its surface and disappeared into the sand. That surface then pressed outwards until a dark impression of a man formed. The wall swelled, as the shape bulged from the rock and the impression burst like a bubble, showering the room with tiny specks of light. I shielded my eyes. When the light dissipated, I uncovered my eyes, and a glowing image of a man stood in front of me. Behind him, the wall had become smooth and whole again, and the steady flow of water and mirror-like surface returned.

"The image was an aged man, intimidating, with piercing eyes. It was clear from his leathered skin that time had ravaged the man with meticulous precision.

"The apparition took a few steps. The spear slowly rose to hover above the marble slab. The specter opened his palms, the spear floated into them, and he closed his gnarled fingers around it.

"'Welcome, Korian,' he said. His voice held such strength and wisdom.

"I was confused and awed at the same time. Somehow, light passed directly through him, yet his features—the cloudy eyes, arched brows and chapters of his unnaturally long life etched into the lines on his face—remained crystal clear.

"'Who are you?' I asked him.

"'A weary spirit who has waited a long time for you,' he answered.

"'Where am I?' I asked.

"The specter softened his voice. 'Menzia is a sacred place,' he said. 'It is a place of dreams and illusions. A place where time stands still, where new truths and knowledge become a reality and where this new reality can change worlds. Menzia is where the Eilasor was forged. Right here, in this hallowed place.'"

"You stood where the gods forged the Eilasor?" Gred shouted in amazement.

"The apparition raised the spear and held it out to me. 'You have been graced by the gods, Korian. You were chosen and gifted with the power to restore the life and balance of a forgotten time. We can help you realize this power,' he said.

Gred stopped. "Wait…restore life?" repeated the giant, incredulously. "You could bring Sara back to life?"

"No, Gred, 'Restore the life of a forgotten time,'" corrected Korian. He pressed on, and Gred keenly followed.

"Oh," Gred said, visibly disappointed.

"But…the Eilasor, I learned, still *did* have the power to restore life."

"'Where is it? The Eilasor?' I asked the shimmering image.

"'Be patient,' the image said. 'The Eilasor is not here. It's in a safe place. One day you will again hold Sara in your arms.' Then he cautioned, 'To find Sara, you must still endure much suffering.'"

"It didn't matter," Korian told Gred. "I would suffer without question. I needed the Eilasor. Sara needed it. Or, perhaps it was I who needed it more."

"Anyway, I was overwhelmed. I asked the apparition if I was dead.

"I was told the contrary. That I was about to be reborn.

"I was impatient. Angry. I wanted to get back, but they told me I wasn't ready. I was not expecting what happened next. The specter handed the spear to me and said, 'Go on then. Leave.'

"I asked him to point me in the right direction. He pointed to the wall behind him. The same wall the apparition had stepped out from.

"As I started towards it, the apparition turned his palm to the sky. To his left, the surface of the sand stirred, and sand crystals rose to hover above the ground. Particles swirled and merged, fashioning themselves into a shape with an uncanny likeness to a Stragoy. The sand creature stood between me and the gateway to Navalline.

"I took a step, and the sand Stragoy moved. It was quite remarkable, in a frightening way. I froze. The sand shape's features turned dark, angry and even more repulsive. It charged, and I was no match for it. There I was, defeated and on my knees, the spear gone from my hands. The sand Stragoy, too, was gone, but the shimmering image of the man returned.

"'Do you think you're ready?' he said.

"You would think I would have listened after that. But I was too stubborn, too impatient.

"'Have you not heard anything?' Oren asked me, clearly irritated. 'In Menzia, time moves forward but beyond that wall, time stands still. Be patient and learn. When you're ready, and only when you're really ready, then you will return.'

"That was just over a year ago, Gred. Only a moment in time for the people of Endura."

"Are you saying you were in the Portal for a year?" asked Gred, his big brow arched.

"Crazy, isn't it? But yes. Finally, I again found the nerve to ask the apparition who he was."

"'I am Lucius Murough, Ishtan Mar, the first Manian and Manian to King Zoren Ro,' he answered."

Korian and Gred entered a secondary path to the one they had travelled for several hours. The ground here was levelled, and they were able to maintain a good pace.

"What happened to Lucius? Why was he there? Did he die?" Gred asked, firing off one question after another.

Korian smiled. He couldn't help but compare this brooding giant to a curious child. The image was humorous.

"I asked Lucius many times. Usually Lucius ignored the question, but sometimes he would answer by saying 'it's still not finished,' or 'sacrifice has a price,' but he would never elaborate, and I didn't pry. I knew he would tell me when he was ready."

"What happened then?" pressed Gred.

"I did as they instructed," Korian answered.

"'Walk down the dark tunnel, and find your way back. Do not turn back.' Each day, they said, 'Follow the path. Do not waiver from it. Beware of pitfalls and what might lurk in dark places or around corners. Remember, your mind is a powerful ally. Do not ignore it. Learn to improvise, adapt and overcome.' I was expected to make the journey down the dark tunnel alone every day.

"That was all Oren said. So, I took the path cautiously. There was nothing special about the tunnel. It was dim, long and narrow. When I emerged from it, the sky was still a dark gray, and the temperature was cool. Ahead of me, a path was laid over an emerald landscape.

"I moved at a steady pace. After a gradual ascent, I ignored a disorienting mist and small lumps of hail that stung. It was so cold my chest ached. Eventually, I knew I had to stop. When I looked back for the first time since I'd left the tunnel, in place of the mouth of the tunnel in the distance, a thick forest loomed. I thought this strange but ignored it and kept on at a slower pace.

"An hour later, I looked back again. The same forest was at my back. In fact, it was closer. Trees with branches like spiny tentacles, reached down over the path as if they'd been torn and stretched. It seemed the forest was following me. Strange, beastly sounds came from deep inside. The darkness beckoned me to enter. Forcing myself to stay focused, I tore myself away and pressed on.

"The path veered from one side to the other, but never did it turn back towards the tunnel. I followed the trail until I came to another narrow path six feet below the crest of a high hill. I was in great pain by then as I trudged into the wind. By that point, the hail had turned to sheets of rain that fell sideways. It threatened to knock me off the path. I stopped again to rest. I looked back, and there it was, the same menacing forest. The knotted trees seemed even closer.

"Still, I continued on. The pain became a dull throbbing. At some point, hours after I emerged from the tunnel, I stumbled into a thick fog. I travelled through, beyond exhaustion. Then, somehow, I blindly stumbled back into the large room. Oren was waiting at the edge of the slab with a huge smile on his face."

Korian and Gred made their way off the trail onto longer grass and softer ground. They were walking on a gradual slope towards a high hill. Smatterings of evergreens were scattered along the way.

"This became my life," Korian continued. "The next day, and each day after that, the cycle repeated itself. Each time I emerged from the tunnel I found a different path with new challenges. The only constant was the gray sky and the forest filled with ominous, gnarled trees that kept on my heels, pushing me forward.

I followed paths through streams and boggy ground, through grass, cold winds and one dark tunnel after another. I fought tremendous muscle weakness and numbness from the cold. I met winds that stole my breath, and still, each time, I made it back to the large room. With each day, I found myself a little stronger.

"As months passed, the paths became increasingly more challenging. I had to scale walls, cross gaps with steep drops by using shoots, or by using the limbs of trees. Each time, I pressed on in fear of those haunting, splintered branches nipping at my heels.

"At some point, months after I had entered the Portal, I started training with weapons. Each day, Oren would provide a new weapon, and I would take to it relentlessly. All this time, the spear remained untouched, sitting idle where Lucius had placed it on the table months before.

"As I got stronger, my mind got sharper. My body began to reflect the effects of my effort." Korian took a moment to admire his arms. His muscles were primed, taut and ready for unconscious reflex reactions. He smiled abashedly when he saw just how small they were in comparison to Gred's.

"Then one day, quite unexpectedly, Lucius appeared and told me to pick up the spear. I had been waiting a long time for that day.

"'The gods are not bound by natural law. There is no beginning or end to their power,' he said. He told me that I, too, have boundless power, that I was graced with it but my eyes deceive me. He ordered me to separate my senses from my reality.

"He then told me to pick up the spear, so I took it up with both hands.

"'It is part of you,' he said. 'Don't try to feel it. Don't just look at it. Will it.' Lucius then told me to bend the spear. I was confused. Naturally, I failed. Lucius told me the spear was a gift, and that I and the spear are one. He reminded me not to think about it, to treat it as part of me, an extension of my arm. Then, just as strangely as he had come, his image dissolved into millions of illuminated particles. A moment later, reminiscent of my first day in Menzia, a Stragoy formed from the sand, and it waved its sword at me.

"It charged, but this time I was prepared. I was balanced, poised and calm. I surprised myself, and from the corner of my eye, I could see Oren beaming.

"'Concentrate, Korian. Slow your breathing. The spear is part of you. Observe, anticipate, and be the aggressor,' Oren said.

"Several sharp bursts came from different parts of the room. Sand swirled and stung my face. When the sand settled, there were six more sand Stragoy before me.

"I slowed my breathing. I could feel the tempo of my heart, hear sand particles stir with each step, feel vibrations in the air. I cleared my mind. Anticipating the charge, I leaned to the left. I thrust the spear, impaling the first Stragoy in the chest. Three more attacked from my left. I envisioned the cutting edge of an axe slicing through them. The vision was so lucid I felt the weight shift in my hand. The tip of the spear widened to form a flat, broad head, thick on one side, sharp on the other. The spear transformed into what I had willed. Suddenly, an axe was in my hand. The change was instantaneous."

Korian stopped walking, and he looked up at Gred. "I cut the Stragoy down one by one," he said as he raised the spear and examined it in admiration.

They found a wooded area and paused to rest. Korian leaned against a tree, took a swig of water and turned to his big friend in contemplation, "You know something?" Korian asked, wide-eyed. "No matter how hard I tried, I could not find peace. They knew of my past, and I kept imploring them for answers to my questions, but Oren and Lucius never offered anything. Each day ended the same way. I would stand in front of the wall, and I'd stare at the dark sheen of the surface, envisioning the scene beyond it. Each time, Oren would startle me out of my trance. Each night I would dream of Sara, but my sleep was never deep. Each morning I'd wake, clutching her ring. It was always the same."

Except what he neglected to share with Gred, was that one night, Korian did ask Oren something different. This part he kept to himself.

"Why are you here, Oren?" Korian asked.

From his first day in Menzia, Korian had a pressing desire to understand certain things that didn't quite line up, logically. Finally, he found the courage to confront Oren.

The question surprised the small, wiry creature. "What do you mean?" Oren asked, licking his lips nervously.

"You know exactly what I mean," answered Korian calmly. Korian sat on the ground stirring the sand with a small stick he held in his hand. His head was down, his eyes were concealed by his hair.

"I can understand why Lucius is here," Korian pressed. "But you…?"

Korian tapped the stick on the sand, giving it one final tap as an exclamation then raised his head.

"Only King Zoren had entered the Portal before me," Korian said and considered it for a minute. "That was foretold. So why are you here?" he asked again, tossing the stick into the fire. "Why am I here?"

Oren followed Korian's movements closely. Now it was Oren's turn to sit down. He, too, began making a circle in the sand. Korian waited.

"Well, Korian, everything is not always as it seems. I exist, don't I? I passed into the Portal, and the Harwill has not spoken of me, yet here I am. Some things I cannot explain. The gods have a plan, and I, like you, have a part to play—" Oren's rambling was cut short by the appearance of Lucius's shimmering image beside him.

"Are you going to tell that lie again?" Lucius said. "The truth. It's time, Oren. Tell the truth."

Oren slouched forward and lowered his head. He exhaled. After a long pause, he began to tell his tale.

"I was ten years old when I stumbled upon the object in the Linhar. I believed—like you did—that it was the sand creature that led me to it. I'm certain of that. You know something…? Only you and I have ever laid eyes on that creature. And that metal object…it didn't open for me as it did for you—"

"That's because it was occupied," Lucius interrupted.

"Wait. I read about this in the old scrolls. So, you were the ten-year-old boy? That means…you are…Zoren?" Korian stood, looking for confirmation. "Are you, Zoren?"

Oren lowered his head.

Korian took a step back. Suddenly, he saw Oren in a new light. One moment, a strange, quick-witted little creature, full of wisdom and secrets, the next, with a kind of awe.

There was a long pause as Korian came to terms with what he had just learned. This tiny and frail creature, with his head down, had, over his long life, spoken to the gods, touched so many lives and had seen and experienced so much suffering. Korian gathered his thoughts. He had so many questions, but something else said, in all this, had piqued his interest. He would come back to Oren.

Korian turned to Lucius, "What do you mean it was occupied?"

"I mean there was someone that had not yet finished using it when Zoren found it." Lucius replied.

"You remember that giant hole in the ground you found south of the Linhar?" Lucius said. "You referred to it as…an impact crater from a meteor. That's what you said, right? But that's not what made it. It was an artificial craft—a giant, flying vessel that crashed on Endura a long time ago. When I say a long time, I mean tens of thousands of years ago. Almost incomprehensible when you think of it. The metal object you found in the desert arrived here in that thing."

Korian's eyebrows perked. "How could you know this?"

Lucius leaned on the marble slab. "After the desert storm in the Linhar, I awoke at the base of a strange tree, with no idea how I got there. This odd tree, alone in the middle of the desert, bent in a precarious position as if it had been shaped by the power of the wind, served me well as a canopy. It was just as strange as the mysterious child I found sitting beside me when I awoke. He was malnourished and dressed in tattered clothing. Finding another soul out there in that barren place seemed bizarre enough, but what was even stranger, was that he looked familiar. I looked closer and realized he looked like me, when I was four years of age.

"'Hello, Lucius,' the child said. 'Your obligation has begun.' He then told me about the gift that had been given to me: the power and control over conjuring and magic. He taught me how to use it and what I was to use it for. He told me I was to protect Zoren, as there would be several times when he would need my help. He also told me of the many tasks I was to perform."

Lucius's shimmering image added, "You see, Korian, inside the metal cylindrical object that came in that craft was a man. He came to us from somewhere beyond the stars. Inside he lay, dormant, waiting. He waited for tens of thousands of years. But something else waited too—the forces of darkness. Adam Hades inhabited that object until he was awakened when Zoren found the object.

"Tens of thousands of years is unfathomable," Lucius said. "I, for one, cannot understand how that would be possible, but this mysterious child told me you—the Azura—would."

Lucius looked at Korian and Korian looked back blankly. "He said the Azura would have the perception and insight to understand. You would know of the world Adam Hades came from," Lucius said.

Korian recalled the strange images, memories and knowledge that flooded his head after his own experience within the metal object. *That time I lost inside that thing has to mean something.*

"The Gods graced me with the gift of unnaturally long life," Lucius said. "Several times in my life, a mysterious entity appeared to me. Each time he would appear as an older version of myself, and each time he would advise me on what I needed to do."

"What kind of things?"

"Take that horrible night in the garden," Oren interjected. "Evil's influence reached out from the murk and started Endura on its ill-fated destiny. Adam had sprung a trap. He wanted the crown, that part was clear, but there was something deeper, something more wicked and primal going on behind his eyes. I've never been able to put my finger on it. Regardless, I stood in his way in more ways than one. When he ambushed me, I fought him—if you could even call it that—but during the struggle, he became impaled on the pointed stump of a fractured branch on the trunk of the matchra tree.

"Contrary to what's recorded in the *Cerulean Book of Scribes*, I have never killed anyone…at least not anyone living," said Oren. "I survived, yes, but surviving that night proved costly.

Dark forces had consumed him by then, and through him, those dark forces took his words, gave them power and…" Oren looked down and brought his hands to his chest. "This was the result."

"And here's where the mysterious entity enters the tale again," began Lucius. "It was the year AZ 41. The evening seemed colder than usual and reflected my disposition at the time: detached and angry. I always knew that day would come. I was just unprepared for that kind of treachery. My mysterious messenger appeared to me earlier that day. He looked slightly younger than I was at that time of my life. His message was somber: 'Queen Nuri is in danger.'

"Adam sent two men to murder the queen. It was a just a ploy, a distraction, to get Zoren alone. Adam made it so I had to choose: protect Zoren or save Nuri. I looked to Samjees to watch out for you. I chose Nuri.

"How could Nuri have known that day would have been her last in Nahire?" Lucius continued. "That night, when I entered her chamber, I found her bound to the bedpost, her nightdress torn to her waist, her face battered. Two men were in there with her," Lucius said.

Oren's eyes were closed, but his fists clenched as Lucius recounted the story.

"Nuri was not conscious. Her breathing was shallow, and blood covered her face and breasts. 'You're too late,' one of the men said. Their eyes were vacant. The voice of the one who spoke was flat, with no inflection. They were so strange, like marionettes controlled by a malicious puppeteer.

"In a kind of drone-like state, the man told me that before morning, Nahire would have a new king. I still can't explain what happened to me next. Seeing Nuri like that, realizing my inability to protect her, to protect Zoren…" Lucius raised his hand and looked at it. It was trembling. He made a fist and said, "A feeling beyond anything I had ever felt blinded me, and I summoned the power of the Manian I was cursed to bear. I destroyed those men. It was the first time I took a life.

"I took an unconscious Nuri and rode hastily from the palace. I don't remember how long I rode: weeks maybe. I arrived at this quaint, obscure little cove nestled in a valley, hidden from the rest of the world. That mysterious messenger was already there waiting for me. He told me the place was safe.

"I dreaded what I was about to do. Nuri was unconscious. 'Don't worry,' I whispered in her ear to reassure her. She had a big part to play in the fate of all citizens of Nahire and all of Endura for that matter. It was just not the right time. 'Your time will come,' I said. I just didn't realize that it would be two thousand years later.

"I was captivated by the place," Lucius added. "Every sound seemed magnified in the hollowness of the space. The air hummed around me as I carried Nuri toward the water while whispering words of conjuring into the crisp morning air. The air suddenly changed and grew thick. I extended a foot and held it over the water. When I lowered my foot and touched the surface, it supported my weight. It had turned solid, like a glossy black marble floor. I stepped forward onto the shiny, growing black slab and walked towards the center of the cove. I looked back at the bank, and there the messenger stood watching me, nodding and urging me on. I looked into the sky and told Samjees I was placing her into his hands. I kissed her cheek and laid her on the dark, solid surface. Slowly she submerged into the black slab until she disappeared beneath it."

Lucius looked at Oren. "I had to protect her."

Oren nodded.

"Adam's spies would have never stopped hunting her…once they knew. Forgive me, my friend."

"Once they knew what?" asked Oren.

Korian was thinking the same thing.

"I'll get to that later."

"Okay. So, were you supposed to bring her back?" blurted Korian. "If that was the plan, how do the huntsmen fit into this story?"

Lucius sighed. "To answer that, I need to jump forward seven hundred years."

Lucius began to pace. Oren sat with his head down, poking the sand with a stick.

"I stood by and provided guidance to each of Nahire's Kings for generations. Nahire prospered, even after Zoren had long since disappeared. Then came AZ 712. I had grown old and tired. I mean...what would you expect? I was, after all, over seven hundred years old.

"The Queen to King Edric IX gave birth to the future king. He was called Prad. But not two months after his birth, the prince mysteriously died. Nahire was plunged into despair. The queen became withdrawn, and her sanity became fragile. Madness replaced the hole in her heart.

"She began to speak to an imaginary child. She said the child was pale, with cracked lips that bled from the corners. In fact, she carried a handkerchief she'd use to dab his blood.

"Several months after Prad's death, the queen began to look for a woman, this invisible child of hers had told her dwelled in the Syran Hills. She was supposed to have the power to help bring her dead child back to life. Many passed it off as the banter of a mad woman, but then one day she disappeared. She was found weeks later, wandering, barefoot atop the Ridge of the Kings.

"We learned much later that she was with child. The queen

gave birth to a new son. Sadly, she died during childbirth. What I remember most from that time was how Nahire was shrouded in a thunderous gloom of wind, rain and darkness that lingered for days. There was no joy in the arrival of this second child into the world. He was called Aaron."

"Aaron?" inquired Korian.

"Yes, the same murderous creature that is hunting you down as we speak," replied Lucius.

"No one knows for sure what happened to the queen. She was blessed I suppose, or cursed. The thing is, I always knew there was something odd about Aaron. The citizens knew it too. Aaron behaved strangely. 'His eyes are not normal,' some of the elder women would say. Many felt uncomfortable around Aaron, but no one could explain these curious feelings.

"Aaron grew into a man, and then two days before his nineteenth birthday, I was awakened again by the messenger. This messenger was old and weary. He carried a regal looking spear that he used as a staff. When I looked closer, it was as if I had looked in a mirror.

"He told me to be strong, and that my obligation would end on the evening of Aaron's birthday. He told me that I would not be here to bring Nuri back, and that I had to find another way. I had lived for over seven hundred years and watched everyone die around me, so I was lonely, yes, but I was still terrified of death. I had so much unfinished business. Regardless, I returned to the cove to begin preparations.

"I found a secret chamber in one of the mountains surrounding the cove, and there I set the talisman, the sack containing the enchanted powder to serve as the catalyst for the resurgence of the new Portal, and the spear the messenger had given me. Before I left, I wanted to make sure only those pure of heart and intention would set hands on my gifts. Their blood would tell.

I set it up so that anyone not meant to set hands on these gifts would die trying.

"I had every intention of sharing the location of this place with someone I trusted. His name was, Crogan," Lucius said.

Of course, Korian thought, not surprised that Lucius and Crogan were connected. He nodded acknowledgment and Lucius continued.

"Crogan was a young student of magic and a good friend. I planned to tell him that when the darkness began to manifest itself among the living, it would be time to bring Nuri back. I never got the chance to tell him because on the night of Aaron's birthday, Aaron brutally murdered King Edric in the King's chamber.

"Aaron's actions were most unexpected, and I was unprepared. I returned from the cove and found Aaron atop the Ridge of the Kings, the highest point of Nahire, where all of Nahire's past kings were entombed. Zoren's tomb was among them, absent Zoren's body of course." He looked at his old friend fondly. "Aaron was waiting for me. He was ready to assume his reign over Nahire. I couldn't let that happen.

"Aaron had already begun his transformation. Darkness had stolen any humanity he may have had. Aaron's eyes were dark and piercing, but he was still human then. His strength was that of ten men, and he had his own power of sorcery. It was a dark magic.

"Aaron told me his father was not King Edric but Adam Hades. If Aaron was king, the world you came from, Korian, would have already been doomed. Hades' hatred would have poured through Aaron. Aaron knew that only I had the power to stop him and he meant to destroy me.

"We fought fiercely. I used the power the gods had graced me with, but it was not enough. Flashes of light, thunderbolts, fire, any object laying nearby became projectiles. We must have battled for an hour. In the end, I was exhausted and spent, beaten and dying. Broken stone, rubble and debris that had once been headstones, monuments and offerings to the past kings lay scattered. Aaron was about to prevail.

"He stood over me as I lay on the shattered remains of King Zoren's tomb. He raised a sword to end my suffering, but something strange happened. Aaron's eyes opened and glazed over. He dropped the sword and fell to his knees. A courageous firstling stood behind him holding the scythe he had used to plunge into Aaron's back. Aaron's shrieks were unnerving and horrid, but he didn't perish. He burst into flames. The blaze intensified, as did his pained shrieks, and he vanished. Like Hades, Aaron's spirit has endured.

"It was a firstling by the name of Tolimin Blane, the groundskeeper and a close friend of the king, who had saved me from dying at the end of Aaron's sword.

"The shrill wind was deafening. I was on my back when Tolimin knelt beside me. I was weak, unable to speak and out of time. I saw goodness and strength in his eyes and with the last bit of my strength, I reached my hand, placed it weakly on Tolimin's neck and transferred to him a piece of myself. A mark appeared where I held his neck: a circle the size of a man's thumbprint surrounded by five evenly spaced, small triangular peaks. I embedded a series of words, the Passage of the Cove, into his subconscious. With that done, I left the world of the living.

My body died, but its life force—perhaps the energy that gave me my power—transformed my body into a brilliant white light. The next thing I knew, I found myself here, in this place, where I've been ever since. But as I left the world of the living, the brilliant light settled into the broken pieces of King Zoren's tomb and vanished. The pieces absorbed some of that energy. Those are the stones that glow in a huntsman's hand.

"Will and Doric and all huntsmen before them are descendants of Tolimin Blane. Ever since that night, humans have held Tolimin Blane responsible for the king's death. It is the reason why humans and firstlings despise each other. Since that night, I have been tormented with my part in the separation of the races and of Nahire's demise."

Lucius looked to Korian. "Huntsmen have searched for the cove for over five hundred years; when the darkness began to manifest itself among the living...about the same time people started to disappear. Descendants of Blane have searched for Nuri for centuries, but it wasn't until Will Shyler...that she was found and then lost beneath the Bridge of Mies."

"Bridge of Mies?"

Lucius enlightened Korian about the finding of the cove and of Will's ordeal at the bridge.

"And the Eilasor?" Korian asked. "I mean, it disappeared from the monument you had built." Korian directed the question to Lucius, but Oren answered instead.

"After I went into hiding, Lucius gave me a *vasara*: a square-shaped flacon made of dull silver. Not long after Aaron's nineteenth birthday, I quietly took the Eilasor, or what remained of it, from the monument and placed it in the vasara."

"Of course," said Korian. "Only the king...could penetrate the surface."

"Where's the vasara now?"

"Safe. It's not as it once was anymore. Its power has waned. It served its purpose well. The Azura," Oren paused and corrected himself, "You, have taken its place. One day, I will take you to it."

"And what of the Den?" Korian asked, "Who built it?"

"I did," said Lucius. "and a secret society of masons. We

started centuries ago: it was one of the tasks given to me by the mysterious child. For over four hundred years, generation after generation worked in secret to build it so it would serve those who lived long after those who built it."

Korian leaned against a tree, took a swig of water, turned to his big friend and resumed his story. Gred's large eye sparked with interest. Suddenly, something stole Korian's attention.

For the first time since they had arrived at this place, he noticed something strange about the forest. The tops of the trees swayed, but there was no wind. It was as if the trees were moving, almost swaying with sounds of the forest that blended into each other like a haunting ballad. The forest was alive. There was more to Korian's story, but what he saw before him forced him to cut it short.

"Look for the living forest," Lucius had said. Korian had thought it was just a saying, but now he wondered.

"And so, Gred, I trained and prepared until I felt ready. Then the moment I had waited for arrived. I started for the wall. Oren beat me to it…you know the rest."

Korian ended his tale there. As he spoke the words, his focus had already turned to his environment. Gred mumbled something, but Korian was not paying attention.

"I'm sure this is it," he managed, cutting Gred short.

"What's wrong?"

"I think the Harwill must be close," said Korian, a little uncertain.

"Don't fret," said Gred. "As the legend goes, he finds you—he is not sought. I am sure you'll find your answers."

Korian's shoulders drooped. "I don't know if I can do this."

"Do what? What are you hoping to find?"

"What it is I am supposed to do. Can I even fight this evil? I mean, Herrick is one thing. Aaron is entirely different. And Hades…"

"Yes."

"Yes…what?"

"You can fight, Korian. And I believe you can win because you'll find a way. You always do."

Korian thought back to his time in the Portal. He had not left in the manner he had told Gred. Korian had faced Stragoy after Stragoy in many obscure places. They would materialize whenever Lucius felt the need for a test. Each time, Korian passed his test. Each time, Stragoy fell. One day, Korian awoke from a nightmare to find Lucius standing over him.

"It's just a dream, Korian," said Lucius. "Today, I need you to do something different for me. When you emerge from the tunnel, do not avoid the forest. Enter it."

Hours later, Korian stumbled back into the room and collapsed onto the sand. The spear was gone; lost in the forest.

When Korian awoke, a hot fire snapped nearby; the remains of a swamp mreg roasted above it.

"What happened in there?" asked Lucius. His image cast a bright radiance, lighting up the room.

Korian shuddered. "Sara's murderer was there, though I know it wasn't really him. I wanted to tear him apart, and then I froze."

"Hmmm. Fear!" Lucius said. "That's what you felt. It blinds you, distorts your thinking, your focus; it affects time and depth perception, but without it, there can be no courage. You must feel it to understand it. Better to face it in Menzia."

A flicker of light caught Korian's attention. The flame reflected off a long, metallic object atop the slab. He looked closer, and to his relief, he found the spear lying peacefully.

"Menzia is real and at the same time unreal. Remember?" said Lucius. "It is a place of dreams and illusions. Fear can destroy you if you let it. You have to learn to control it; after all, it is just a feeling like sadness or joy.

"What is the most powerful feeling you have ever felt?" Lucius asked.

Korian didn't need to think long. "Love."

"You have been blessed to have experienced it in your life, Korian. Remember that and…draw from it," Lucius said. "Let it smother you and protect you. The next time you feel fear, or any other threatening feeling, drown it with the rapture that love brings. Feed off it; channel it, and if need be, die for it."

"Korian!" Gred shouted, pulling Korian out of his trance.

"Sorry, Gred. I need to sit down."

Korian found a fallen log. Gred sat beside him as gingerly as a giant could. The moment of quiet was welcomed. Blissful in fact. Neither spoke for several minutes. Korian's mind drifted back to the Portal again. He recalled his final exchange with Lucius, the one that really drove him out of the Portal.

"Why are you imprisoned here?" Korian asked Lucius yet again.

"I am not a prisoner." His reply startled Korian. *Finally, an acknowledgment.*

Lucius' image sat on the slab and began tapping his hands on his knees. "The short answer is I've been fulfilling my final obligation."

"What is it with this obligation? I've heard it my whole life."

"It's complicated," said Lucius.

Lucius turned to Korian, his eyes were piercing and bright. "It was I who forged the ring you wear around your neck," he said. "Destiny and fate brought you and Sara together. The ring was to help you find each other in a world that would not offer you the time you deserved to cultivate your love."

Lucius's features turned grave. "There's something else. What I'm about to tell you will not be easy to hear."

Korian nodded. "Go on."

"Everything that has come to pass, as horrible as it has been, was supposed to happen. It was all part of a grand plan, thousands of years old, orchestrated by Samjees and executed by the Guardians. Everything…from me, to the Portal, to Gred, to Finch, to the Den…to Sara, we're all a part of it."

Korian slowly came to his feet. Lucius's shimmering image took a step back as an involuntary reaction to the intensity apparent in Korian's eyes.

"Your connection with Sara is not unique, Korian. Many of those you left behind in Navalline have felt the same pain and sorrow. Yours and Sara's passion is special but not unique. If it were, that would be woeful, and all of Endura would already be lost. There would be nothing to fight for. No matter how much firstlings and humans have suffered and lost, they would never raise their hand against the oppressors."

Korian's face flushed.

"But you…you had to go through this, Korian, because you are unique among humans. You are the catalyst. One day, you will learn why it had to be you. One day, you'll understand what sets you apart from everyone else. I can't tell you…because…I don't know. You'll have to find that one out on your own.

"Aaron was close. Herrick had you in his grasp. If not for the Portal, you'd be dead, and Hades would have won. Evil would have poured onto Endura through Hades—"

"And then Sara was…*murdered!*" Korian cried out. His face

had turned a deep shade of red. "She was sacrificed to draw… what…*wrath*?"

The enemy wanted him dead. Sara had become a pawn made to suffer. Korian felt alone, exposed to betrayal in all its fury. An unbearable pain and a different kind of feeling—alien and all consuming—started to weigh on him.

"I did not kill Sara, Korian. Remember that," Lucius reasoned. "I'm not the enemy."

"You…the Guardians…all of you might as well have slit her throat!" Korian slowly turned toward the table. He felt his muscles swell with blood. Veins bulged in his arms and neck as he slowly walked in the direction of the table.

Oren entered the room just then. He saw the look on their faces. "Korian, what are you doing?"

Korian picked up the spear.

"Tell me, Lucius. Was your obligation to turn me into your own version of Adam Hades? Of Aaron…a merchant of death?"

Korian took a step backward. "A hardened heart, consumed by revenge? A trained killer?"

He turned and swiped the spear at Lucius in a blind rage. The spear sliced through Lucius's shimmering image.

Lucius glanced at Oren and nodded. It was as if there was an understanding between them; like an acknowledgement that it had all worked, and the time had come. The look was an unspoken, *you know what to do*!

Oren darted for the Portal.

"Seek out the Harwill and learn the truth!" Lucius said as Korian turned toward the wall.

Korian paused. He grasped Sara's ring and kissed it.

"Remember, Korian! Draw from it. Channel it."

Korian stepped into the wall and vanished.

Lucius shut his eyes and dissolved out of the empty room.

After sitting for some time in silence, Korian turned to Gred. "Your turn."

"Hmmm…my turn?"

"You were going to tell me something."

"Ah, right," Gred bobbed his heavy head.

"You and I, have been alone most of our lives. We've both had a purpose. Yours is to bear this burden. Mine was another kind. For more than two thousand years, I've been despised and condemned. No companion, no compassion. I was not always like this. One day, I looked at the sun through human eyes, I went to sleep and awoke like this. I cursed the gods and tried many times to end my suffering, but as it turns out, my life was not mine to take.

"It was about three hundred years ago when I came upon a place away from the world of men and firstlings; a dark cave that I made my home. I had a good supply of food and shelter. It was a pathetic existence, but I adopted it and found peace. I merely existed.

"Then one day, I heard loud voices and commotion outside my cave. The fog was especially thick that day. White mist hung in sheets above the sky, obscuring the bridge above. I heard a woman scream. Then an incredible explosion vaporized the mist. Bodies rained down alongside burning pieces of the bridge. Some fell onto my ledge. Then, a woman landed on top of the straw and smothered the flames. Her eyes were closed, and she lay still. I thought she was dead. I scooped up her body, but as I raised her up, she opened her eyes."

"She was alive?"

"Yes. Somehow, she had survived the fall. Drifting in and out of consciousness, she awoke on the fifth day," he said recalling a memory. "She was ranting madly about a handkerchief. 'I had it in my hand and now it's gone,' she'd repeat and weep.

"A few days later, when she had calmed some, I spoke to her from the shadows. I was terrified of the same rejection that had plagued me all my life. She would have probably died of fright at the sight of me."

Gred's smile faded. "But she was in far worse shape than I originally thought. She had lost her sight and the use of her legs in the ordeal. I felt a compelling need to watch over her, to take care of her and protect her. Later, after she had learned of my physical features, she still accepted me as I was."

Gred cleared his throat.

"She mentioned the linen again, this time speaking of it fondly. It was to be a gift. She made it from silk of the blind, flightless moth that lived in the white mulberry tree in the Garden of Usea. She said she had worked on it meticulously day after day. She added that the silk she'd used had been given to her by Lucius well before she knew and well before the idea of making the handkerchief had ever entered her mind."

"Knew about what?"

"Before she knew she was with child," answered Gred.

Korian's eyes widened.

"She grew more frail as the weeks and then months passed. 'Tell my son about me,' she said. 'Tell him he was born for great things. His father doesn't yet know of him. I was taken before I could tell him, snatched up by Lucius one night, and years later, reborn in a far darker world. Tell him he is special.'"

Gred cleared his throat again.

"I lived a long, wretched life but never have I felt more sadness than when I promised her something terrible." He paused here to collect himself. "Before she drew her last breath, I reluctantly, and with my heart in pieces, did what I promised: I cut out her child from her womb so she could hold him in her arms."

Gred continued. "It was the most difficult thing I have ever had to do. It was a boy. As she held her son, I vowed to protect him." He looked then at Korian.

"And protect you I did."

"What are you saying?" asked Korian.

"You were torn out before you were ready to enter this world."

"She was my mother?"

Gred nodded.

"Where was that bridge? Did it have a name?"

"Bridge of Mies."

"Did she tell you who my father was?"

Gred shook his head. "No. Come to think of it, she never even told me what her name was."

After everything that had happened, the linen did, in fact, manage to find its way home. The linen and fate; fate and the linen; one and the same. It all made sense.

Korian thought of Lucius. The Manian had known that Nuri was carrying a child. It is why he believed Aaron's spies would have kept searching for her. It also meant that Crogan had been right after all. Korian played his time in Menzia over in his head. He kept coming back to the same conclusion. *He doesn't know. Oren doesn't know that he's my—*

A branch snapped. The two came to their feet. There was a burst of song. A beautiful melody drew their attention.

"Over here," said Korian.

"No, it's coming from over here!" Gred bellowed.

From behind a large, old, isolated tree with a wide trunk, Korian caught a glimpse of what looked like a fragment of a fine gray-white dress blowing in the wind. He expected someone to walk out from the opposite side of the trunk. Images filled his mind of an aged man with sagging skin that fell loosely in folds, that it wasn't fabric at all that he saw but skin that had weathered and stretched like sap; a skeleton covered in spotted skin, fine and fragile. But that couldn't be. Someone that grotesque was not capable of such song. He shook the frightening image off and waited. No one emerged.

He sprinted to the tree and peered behind it. There was no one there. The melody became a gentle, soothing coo, calming and enticing. Korian felt a tap on his shoulder and turned. No one was there. Yet a fair distance away, a woman strolled on the damp grass, ignoring Korian and his giant companion. She was wearing a gray-white dress. Her eyes were closed, and her head swayed slowly from side to side in time with the melody.

"Are you lost?" shouted Korian.

She gave no answer. She turned and walked deeper into the woods.

"We'll finish this later," said Korian as they followed the mysterious woman deep into the forest.

19

JAYEN'S FJORD

THE MYSTERIOUS WOMAN stopped walking, and the melody abruptly ended. She stood with her back to Korian and Gred. Up until this moment, both had been under the spell of the melody, and neither had paid attention to how they had worked their way up to the top of a high hill. The ground here was a flat section of rock, square shaped, with cracks running on the surface like a web.

With grace, as if she floated on air, she led them towards the middle of the square. She turned and faced the two, but her eyes were closed. She raised both feet off the ground, and a three-legged, wooden stool magically appeared beneath her.

Korian and Gred were spellbound. She was thin with pale skin. Her long black hair blew in the wind; strands gently caressed her ashen face. Her arms were long and slender and down to her knees. She wrapped them across her chest and back, until her hands rested on her shoulders. She was graceful and beautiful, not in a sensual way but almost as if she belonged in a painting.

Leaning her head to one side, she said "Yesss, I am, and I'm sorry you're disappointed." Her voice was startlingly deep.

"I didn't say anything," said Korian.

"You didn't need to," she replied.

Korian looked at Gred. "I was just thinking it."

"Thinking what?"

"I was thinking, 'Are you the Harwill?' I thought the Harwill was a man."

"Yes, and you are the Azura," she continued. "Gatekeeper," she added. She placed her hand on Korian's chest. "You have a good heart," she added. "Yesss…spirit is strong, as is your will."

Her head remained tilted, and her eyes closed. Her perfect complexion was relaxed and blank. "Yes," she said again slowly as if she just found the proof she sought.

"The blue crystal still has the power to restore life." She paused, then added, "As do you."

"Can I bring Sara back?" Korian asked, wide-eyed.

"No," she answered. "There will come a day when you will touch her again. Not in a dream or a memory but as real as your protector standing beside you. You will hold her again."

"How do I make this happen?"

"Shhh." She did not move her arms or hands.

"You carry much responsibility, and…you know this. What you do not know is your life is bound to Hades. As long as you live, he remains imprisoned in the shadow."

She writhed like a snake, and her head swayed as if receiving thoughts and visions.

"You will have to decide. Choose selfishly, and you die alone sometime long in the future; everyone suffers. Choose selflessly, and you die young; everyone suffers not, and Endura will proclaim your name."

"Yessss," she continued, "I see you have made your decision.

"Many come looking for answers, starved for knowledge or guidance. Most never find what they seek. Most look for the truth. If that is what you seek, I cannot help you," she said.

Korian was perplexed. This seemed contrary to what he'd heard of the Harwill.

"They say your power is never doubted. You are infallible and of ethereal authority and intelligence. Why then can you not help me with the truth?" asked Korian.

"Because you already know it. You just need to convince yourself. Except…" she paused, her eyes still closed, and she tilted her head to the opposite side.

"You have been deceived. You have all been deceived. But you already know this too. The matchra tree destroys wills. It poisons under the guise of beneficence. The matchra's alive and bound to Hades' spirit in life and in death. It will continue to poison and summon slaves to serve Aaron. Destroy Hellas Mons. Destroy the tree."

"I'm just supposed to walk in and destroy it?"

"No, use your new insight. Powerful that knowledge is."

"What insight?"

"Insight that comes from a long sleep."

"Are you talking about the time I spent inside the object in the desert?" Korian presumed that's what she meant. After all, his nails had grown an inch. That must have taken months.

The Harwill opened her eyes. She had no pupils. The whites of her eyes glistened in the moonlight. A hissing started from the ground. Smoke rose from the cracks. A sweet smell filled the air. The mist covered the ground, and a glow rose from it.

"Look into the mist," said the Harwill.

"I don't see anything," said Gred. A moment later, he was fast asleep on the ground.

Korian looked closely until finally he was consumed by the mist. After a blinding flash, he was somewhere else. It felt so real. Suddenly, he was on a plain, a fortress in the distance, a vicious battle in progress. The fortress was in ruins. Bodies were strewn about; dark Stragoy shapes were destroying and murdering his people. He saw a ghastly image of Crogan cut down by Aaron, a look of complete disbelief on his dying face.

"How do I stop this from happening?"

"Your spear, end it must in a monolith of rock, just as it was found. Only then will the pieces of death abound and wreak havoc on those dead who walk the ground."

"Riddles? That's all I get?" asked Korian in frustration.

"You will know what to do."

The nightmare engulfed him entirely. Korian reached up to shield his face as the vision changed.

Endura was a wasteland. Forests were destroyed, and the conditions around Hellas Mons spread throughout the land.

"This is what will happen if you fail," said the Harwill.

"I see there is another thing you seek to understand. Look deep into the mist. Lose yourself in time, for back in it you must go."

Korian's body involuntarily twitched. He was locked in a trance, standing upright and as still as a post for an hour. Then he jerked awake.

"I saw it with my own eyes. I saw what happened to our world." He spoke slowly with despair in his voice. The truth was so terrifying and disturbing he stooped and used his knees to support himself. "How can I explain this?" Korian asked the Harwill. "I don't know what words I could even use."

"Perhaps your protector can help," she said.

A glance at Gred quickly affirmed his doubt. Gred lay asleep, drooling onto the ground from his open mouth.

"Do not expect him to tell you anything beyond what you already know. Perhaps, he may lead you to a certain metal object?

From it you may find what you seek."

Korian turned towards the Harwill. Her eyes were closed again, and her expression had turned somber. The memory of what he had just seen was still heavy on his mind when another vision caused Korian to clasp his chest suddenly. He was in a dark chamber. His lifeless body was pale, cold and abandoned. He was seeing his death, and he reeled.

"Is this the future?" Korian said aloud.

"No one can know for sure." The deep voice of the Harwill echoed into the mist.

"I saw my death."

"That is inevitable. It is what has to pass for you to fulfill your destiny."

"What do you mean?"

"You ask if this evil can be destroyed. The answer is yes. To destroy Hades, he must be freed from the darkness, but Hades can only be freed upon your death. That is the paradox that you will need to solve. When you solve that paradox—and you will—rely on your eyes. They are powerful allies and will serve you well." She said.

"Find Hades, and you'll find your truth," she added.

"That's *it*?" asked Korian vehemently. He looked to where Gred was strewn on the ground snoring. He stooped and nudged him. Gred barely moved.

"You best hurry. Your people need your help. Remember, you will not succeed in your quest alone. Unite the races, or the wasteland you saw will come to pass."

Korian turned towards the Harwill. "How do we get back?"

he asked. She was gone and so was the stool she had sat on. Korian heard her voice one more time.

"Seek the huntsman whose heart mirrors yours. The one called Doric. You will need his help in the darkness."

Korian woke up his large friend. They were lost, with no memory of how they got to where they were. For several hours they took one path after another only to find they had come back to the same place.

"What do we do now?" asked Gred in his deep, yet child-like, voice.

Korian started to run. Gred kept pace using his enormous legs and exceptionally long strides.

"What did you do with the object?" Korian said between breaths.

"What object?"

Korian stopped running. He looked at Gred. His stare was direct and demanding.

"It is in a safe place," Gred answered.

"When we get out of here, take me to it."

"I will take you to it."

Korian grew impatient. "Help us!" he shouted, hoping the Harwill would hear him.

Instead of the Harwill's low, soothing voice, the squawk of a giant predator, and the sound of quick, powerful bursts of wind came from above. Its shadow smothered them as it came at them from over the trees. Korian and Gred shielded their faces from the dust and debris that the powerful wings kicked up. A giant skine, slightly taller than Gred, landed in front of them.

Several hours after Korian and Gred parted ways, Crogan and the survivors of Navalline reached the Fortress of Dosdava. Crogan emerged into a vast courtyard. As each survivor entered this new environment, they spread out to explore the massive structure that loomed before them.

Surrounding the courtyard was an inner stone curtain with a large iron gate on the left. Lined up along the widest section of the inner wall were blocks upon blocks of square, straw bales. The gate, ajar at the moment, opened to a transition section, where a second, larger, ancient stone wall stood beyond. Parts of the timeworn wall lay in pieces on the ground, though the massive rampart still had the power to impress.

It was a purpose-built structure with evenly spaced, thin vertical openings along the rampart that gave a narrow perspective to the vacant world on the other side. The openings, in recessed sections of the wall, were a foot thick, each tall enough for a man to stand and move freely. The rest of the wall surrounding these recesses was four feet thick.

"This is amazing!" Alrik's voice echoed from four stories up.

Crogan, Oren and the others caught up with Alrik. The young man had been eagerly exploring the topmost level of the fortress since they had arrived. When they finally assembled, peering over the battlements, with the sun to their backs and the wind on their faces, they were all captivated by the view.

A large mountain range on the left formed a barrier separating the empty lowland from the city of Strathmere. Above them, the ceiling of the mountainous canopy was only fifteen feet over their heads. Another mountain range was on the right, and between the ranges, was the flat plain. Where the plain ended, there was a steep vertical drop down to the angry Azif Lora Sea, and far in the distance loomed Hellas Mons.

The enormous rampart was nestled inside mountains that curved like a giant horseshoe. The wall was built with no gates or doors to keep those on the inside in and the boundless horrors roaming Endura, out.

Beyond the wall, there was no sign or evidence of life, making it feel peculiar, when from above the crest of the mountain, a dark speck became visible in the sky. It soared out towards the sea, and then it abruptly turned and started towards them.

"What is it?" asked Alrik.

"Maledhen," said Oren.

The creature gave a horrible squawk and grew progressively larger as it neared. The onyx-colored creature, the size of an owl, soared above them between the rock canopy and the battlements, eventually flying into the chamber. There, it circled three times and came to rest on top of the inner wall. It stayed for several minutes, and when it had seen enough, it circled once and flew off the way it came.

"Aaron's spy," said Oren.

"Does Aaron know we're here?" asked Alrik.

"He will soon enough," replied Crogan.

Crogan paced, and the others waited, anticipating instructions. Instead, Crogan surveyed the interior and the barren, flat land, the perfect location of this place nestled within the mountain, its accessibility from only one direction, and its breathless beauty.

"Fortress of Dosdava," said Crogan. "This is a good place," he said, turning to the others. "We will face them here."

"What?" shouted Isaac.

"We don't stand a chance," said Jannik, glancing back at the people sprawled in the large courtyard. "Do they even know what's coming?"

"I'm certain they do. There is fear in their eyes, but there is also hope and optimism, both powerful allies."

"Yes, but can hope and optimism fight back? We are outmatched," Jannik replied.

"If we send our men alone, we will be," answered Crogan, his message clear but unfathomable.

It was Isaac who said, "Are you saying we should send the women too?"

"I'm saying we do what we must to survive. The alternative is not an option."

"You're mad," said Jannik.

"If stating the truth is madness, then yes, I'm mad. Sooner than you care to believe, you're going to come face to face with an evil beyond what any of you can imagine. It relishes death and suffering. It is a force from beyond our world that will destroy anything in its wake. Don't think for one second the women and children will be shown mercy. When the men fail, and they will if they stand alone, anyone unfortunate to survive the initial assault will beg for death."

"What are we waiting for?" said Alrik breaking the silence with a wry smile. "We have work to do."

Lael shook his head. *A boy's foolish optimism and naivety at its finest*, he thought. The faces of the others around them displayed the gravity of what was in store. Unfortunately, they all knew they were out of options.

"What do you think they're going to say?" asked Jannik.

"We're going to find out soon enough," answered Crogan. "I think you'll be surprised."

"Did Korian say anything else before he left?" asked Jannik.

"He said we are going to defend this fortress until he returns." Crogan turned and headed down. He paused, turned around and said, "And that's what we're going to do."

When he reached the ground floor, he turned to Alrik and said, "Young man, I think you are going to get your wish after all."

It was just as Korian had instructed: find the long corridor a level below the surface that appears to end at a wall; when you reach it, keep going.

Strange instructions, Crogan had thought when he first heard them, but when they reached the end of a long, narrow tunnel with a low ceiling, he understood. Crogan reached towards the wall, and instead of finding a cold, hard surface, his hand melted into it. He stepped into it and vanished.

Jannik and the others remained outside.

"Get in here!" came a muffled voice from the other side of the wall.

They entered and found row upon row of weapons and armor neatly stacked on shelves and carts, coated with dust and webs. Without prodding, thousands of men took up arms.

"Remember, what approaches is no longer human. Feel no remorse. You are doing them a favor!" Crogan shouted, seeing the trepidation in their eyes.

Women, boys and girls swept in too, picking up unclaimed weapons without being asked.

Almost as soon as weapons were in hands, the teaching started. Oren showed one group how to work the bows. They kept on until they couldn't hold up their arms any longer. Crogan demonstrated how to hold and wield swords and spears; the process was tedious and frustrating. People were lined up in rows that stretched to the boundary of the cavern. With time fleeting, expectations were low. Much of the preparation was psychological.

"Remember, what approaches does not reason, does not display compassion, and will not fear the thought of losing a loved one. They serve one purpose and one master and are coming to take your lives."

The day had grown long and had given way to the luminance of the waxy moon: its light entering the chamber, reflecting off Oren's wide eyes, giving him a childlike appearance.

"They don't want to sleep," Oren said.

Crogan sat on the ground, tapping his head against the wall. He watched with admiration as men, women and children practiced sparring through the night, stopping only briefly for a gentle caress or embrace. Swordplay echoed in the large room. The mood was somber. Many slept despite the noise.

"Korian has shown them they can fight this evil," said Oren, "Now they won't go down without a fight."

"They don't have any idea of the kind of evil Aaron will bring," Crogan said. "None have faced him and lived…" He reconsidered. "Wait, I am mistaken. There is one who did."

Oren bared his stained teeth behind a beaming smile.

"Why the smile?"

"I told Doric this day would come," Oren said. "You see, Manian, there is always hope."

Doric entered a clearing in the middle of the woods; a slow-moving stream flowed through it. He splashed water onto his sweat-drenched face.

Just days ago, he had craved a swift death at the hands of Lorne Maggis, but now, today, even after years of abuse and depression, futility, pain, fear and rejection, he felt content. *I just had a long sleep through a cold, lingering, dark night, and now, I'm awake again,* he thought.

Several times over the last couple of days, Crogan had burrowed into his mind and sent a flood of information. He spoke of lives lost, of hope renewed, the emergence of Korian and of the difficult trials yet to come. The news was both uplifting and disheartening. But Doric feared he had been disconnected from his people for so long, he had lost touch and forgotten how to feel compassion, or that he could no longer relate emotionally to what Crogan had expressed. There was one thing however, that Doric's mind kept coming back to: "Tana is safe."

When he awoke on the floor of the dead forest, after leaping from his prison in Hellas Mons, Doric maintained a relentless pace. Without a destination at first, he ran through the night, through rough terrain and abandoned towns. He crossed the Lassit River and the Town of Woodston and outran Stragoy and Aaron's spies. He picked up abandoned clothes and other items from rotted corpses along the way.

Crogan's news had set him on a course toward the Jayen's Fjord. He felt filled with vigor. After his escape, he thought he'd be prepared for just about anything.

The air around him smelled devoid of malice. It made him feel alive. But there was something else in the air: another odor, not foul like the Stragoy, but more like raw acrid air with a heavy metallic tang.

He tilted his head slightly and listened. A slight rustling and scratching came from somewhere behind him. He turned and found, on the other side of the clearing, a rope tied to the branch of an umbrella-like tree. Tied to its other end, about ten feet off the ground, was a large chunk of meat. It looked like the hind quarter of a large animal. It swayed back and forth; the rope creaked eerily against the branch.

A rumble startled him from the woods on the other side of the stream. Something was coming towards him. A hybrin burst from the forest, forcing Doric back into a collection of thick bushes. He tripped as he came out the other side, and he fell into the remnants of a puddle that had pooled at the base of a deep ditch.

The hybrin heaved its enormous bulk over the stream and leaped over the ditch Doric had fallen into. The animal went straight toward the blood-soaked bait suspended on the rope without breaking stride. It opened its jaws, but the ground disappeared from under it. Into a giant pit the beast fell with a loud thud. The stillness from earlier was quickly replaced by sharp grunts and loud bursts from the trapped animal.

The hybrin's squeals became pained. Doric gathered himself, and he came to his feet as a heavy thump came from deep within the forest beyond the umbrella tree. The tops of trees swayed and shivered. Doric slid back into the ditch and pressed against the side to hide.

The ground trembled again. It was a far bigger tremor than the one the hybrin had made. A giant of prodigious size emerged from behind a tall slope. It was humanoid, exaggerated in proportion and at least sixty feet tall. A leg of tremendous girth, adorned with thick, dark hair-like iron spikes, skimmed over the trees and onto the field. The other leg followed, making a booming thud as it struck the ground. It's green frock, made of thick moss-like patches, crudely linked together by vines, hung loosely over its shoulder.

"What in the gods?" whispered Doric. Oren had told him about the Jayen. As promised, they were beyond anything Doric could have ever imagined.

The giant walked towards the umbrella-tree, reaching it in three strides. It stooped, stretched its long thick arm covered with the same thick, spiny hair and raised the hybrin out of the hole. It brought it to its mouth; the hybrin's shrieks stopped.

When the giant had finished feeding, it raised its huge head and sniffed in slow, exaggerated gasps. The giant turned its head towards the pit where Doric was hiding and glared in his direction, google-eyed. The bristles on its head, rods of iron, flailed and fell upon its broad shoulders like hissing adders. The enormity of the giant was terrifying, and its expression was grim. Its cheeks looked like a couple of large pieces of raw meat stained with hybrin blood.

Doric sprung out of the ditch and darted to the left. Behind him, the giant pushed out its chest and let out a tremendous bellow. It leaned forward and swung its arm in a large arc, striking the ground in front of Doric with its fist.

Doric, thrust onto his back with the force, rolled to his feet and darted through the stream and into the forest on the other side. He ran until sunlight faded and only slivers of light filtered in. Behind him, he could hear the thunderous roar of trees snapping and crashing onto the ground as the lumbering giant pressed through.

Doric sprinted between hundreds of rope-like shoots that sprouted up from the ground, climbing and clasping onto tree limbs to the forest's canopy. Debris, leaves and severed tree limbs continued to rain down behind him with a steady boom.

"So close to freedom," he muttered between breaths; his voice trembled with the effort.

So, this is the danger you were talking about? This isn't dangerous…this is deadly.

No sooner had he had this thought; he noticed the sun's radiance beckoning him up ahead. The line of trees marked the end of the forest. Several more strides and Doric realized the ground was about to end. Beyond the trees, the edge of a cliff loomed.

Doric blindly leaped at full stride. As he fell, he clasped a shoot as high up as he could reach. Its surface was barbed and spiny, and it tore the skin from his hands. The shoot bowed with his weight as he hung from it. It went taut and stopped Doric's descent. He hung, suspended for a moment, when from above, a tree sailed over the edge. The giant reached the edge of the cliff and peered down just as the shoot sprung free and Doric dropped again.

Doric's descent ended about twenty feet above another

semi-flat area that looked like a large ledge. It was actually a flat plateau about a hundred feet wide with another sharp ledge.

Doric slid to the end of the shoot. His hands were on fire—blistered and bleeding. As he looked down, the surface suddenly started moving farther away. The giant was using the shoot to pull him back up. Doric let go. When he struck the ground, his ankle turned awkwardly, and he heard the sickening sound of bone snapping.

The giant's enormous feet fell onto the plateau, not far from where Doric lay. The loud boom of its calloused feet on the surface, jarred Doric out of his fog. Doric rolled towards the wall and noticed a fissure at its base; he frantically crawled towards it. The giant reached down just as Doric squeezed into the opening.

In a fit, the giant struck the wall with its fist, like a spoiled child deprived of a toy. The wall trembled. Rubble fell onto its head and onto the ledge. The giant paid the debris no attention and then…something stole the giant's attention a thousand feet below.

The great ship, the *Winds of Freedom*, neared a narrow stretch of water separating two steep crags: remnants from a land bridge destroyed in the great quake from centuries ago.

Hours earlier, when the ship had approached Werun Falls, it wasn't a wall of thundering water cascading down more than three hundred feet that faced them. Instead, water on the west side of the falls had risen to the same level as the crest of the cascade. As the ship approached, firstlings on the ship's deck looked down onto the surface of what once was the crest of the falls. The ancient rope bridge snapped like a dried twig when the bow of the ship struck it.

The steep crags had widened. The distance, from wall to wall, was nearly half a mile. Between them were countless landforms rising out of the water like hundreds of small islands. The *Winds of Freedom* navigated carefully between the islands, passing great stone ruins jutting out of the water. Fascinated passengers looked over the sides of the ship and held their breath. Only the deep boom of waves crashing over the remains of an exposed, enormous, half-face stone carving could be heard.

"What is this place?" asked Tana.

"These lands were once home to the Jayen: a race of master stone carvers, giants of extraordinary skill and size, instrumental in the artistry of ancient Nahire," answered Orpheus from atop his platform adding, "Behold the fruit of their artistry."

The ship drifted deeper into the channel. They came upon a breathtaking view of sheer cliffs on both sides and a variety of underwater valleys and humps that created the illusion of a deep, dark abyss squeezed by wild slopes.

"What happened to them?" asked Tana, "The Jayen."

Orpheus didn't respond. His gaze was fixed straight ahead, eyes squinting with the wind in his face, his hands fused with the rails. The colossal ship's direction changed, slightly swerving around an island of rock the shape of a fir tree that had bent in the wind and was now frozen in that posture for all eternity.

On the steep walls of the islands were giant carvings of the kings of Nahire adorned with extravagantly carved wings. There were several carvings of King Zoren. One carving depicted Zoren holding the Eilasor. It was cleaved in half. The other half, a part of the face, half the upper torso, and the intact lower half, from the waist down, was on the wall of another island. The great quake had ripped the land apart and scattered it in pieces.

Some carvings were detailed and inspiring. Other carvings

depicted the Portal, the finding of the crystal and other events in Nahire's storied history.

"I'm not sure," said Orpheus, replying to Tana's question from earlier. With the emergency now averted, he was able to respond. "Some say many Jayen perished during the quake, but many of these carvings were added after the channel was formed."

On the left was a massive carving of a firstling. The large digit on the hands was overly exaggerated, and the rest of its features were grotesque. Above its head was carved the word "Karineen," meaning traitor. *That one must be Tolimin Blane,* Will thought.

"The Jayen once lived in harmony with the citizens of Endura. King Zoren had forged a synergy amongst the races. Together, the Jayen helped build the great city using their mastery of stone manipulation and their unique ability to climb steep rock faces. They had spiny hair on their arms and legs like iron spikes, which helped them cling to rock. In return, King Zoren offered the Jayen *cintra*, a seemingly magical spice for that race. It was said the spice curbed their excessive appetite, controlled an unquenchable thirst and avoided another bothersome habit… those giants pissed all the time."

Orpheus chuckled. "In King Zoren's day, the Jayen were accepted and respected by all citizens. However, this synergy ended when Nahire fell. Generations later, the Jayen have become detached from the rest of Endura. They now come across as a crass race. And like the rest of Endura, the Jayen hold firstlings responsible for their isolation."

The sun had settled over the edge of the cliff. Most of the firstlings were still on deck, catching the last bit of the breathtaking views and listening to the story, but some had since retired for much-needed rest. In spite of all that had happened, there was a wave of tranquility on the ship.

It didn't last.

A great shadow fell over the bow of the ship. Something struck the water on the starboard side. A large volume of water splashed onto the deck like a giant wave, knocking firstlings down and rocking the ship.

"What was that?" yelled Tana.

"I forgot to mention one other thing," said Orpheus.

Another large object fell from the sky and struck the water about twenty feet from the stern. This time, they saw it disappear below the surface. Massive volumes of water climbed into the air and soaked those closest. The ship swayed.

"The Jayen are stone hurlers. It is said they destroy ships that trespass in their realm."

Another boulder landed to their left.

"That was far too close!" shouted Merrin.

Another crashed. Then another. The ship continued to sway.

"Up there." Will pointed high up on the right side of the cliff.

A large, silhouetted figure stepped back from the edge and swung its arm in a throwing motion. When the massive boulder struck the surface, it gave perspective as to the sheer enormity of the figure.

Orpheus, in a trance again, ignored the firstlings' cries as water sprayed his face. He maneuvered the ship away from the dangerous boulders as they continued to rain down.

The attack stopped when what appeared to be a large black veil fell over the giant's head.

Doric slid down a narrow tunnel into a high-ceilinged chamber. His ankle had healed before he had reached the bottom. Outside, the giant's rants were replaced by frenzied scurrying sounds accompanied by loud grunts. Doric took a moment and looked around. It was dark, but some light managed to trickle in from outside. Stalagmites rose from the ground, and high above, the jagged ceiling seemed alive. It was covered in wrets.

Doric had an idea.

He worked his way back up to the gap and peered out of the narrow opening. He found the giant lurching from one side of the flat plateau to the other. Each time it made its way to the edge, it brought a massive boulder and hurled it down the side with a grunt.

When the giant turned the next time, Doric snatched a fist-sized rock near the entrance. He stepped out of safety and started screaming obscenities at the behemoth. The giant turned and charged at Doric, but Doric had already disappeared back into the hole, leaving the incensed giant crouched, pounding its fist onto the ground.

Inside the chamber, the giant's rants seemed to disturb some wrets; several began to fly in circles about the ceiling. Doric shouted to startle them some more. He then hurled his stone into the ceiling, and thousands of wrets scattered. Their collective screech was deafening. Doric covered his ears and crouched. Wrets swirled over his head. The cyclone of wrets stormed out of the tunnel towards the entrance and emerged from the cave in a rushing torrent.

They surprised the giant, who stumbled back, swatting blindly. The wrets completely swarmed its head until the space around its head, neck and shoulders turned black with the mass of the bat-like creatures as if a thick black sheet had been draped over the giant's head.

The giant staggered towards the edge. Doric raced out from the opening. With its arms still swatting wildly, and its back to the water, the giant stepped off the edge and disappeared. The wrets continued to swirl for a moment, and then they departed over the top of the plateau into the woods.

Doric slowly walked to the edge of the cliff and looked down. He expected to see the giant splattered on the rocks. Instead, the giant was suspended against the wall, several hundred feet below. Water frothed and crashed over a bed of jagged rocks beneath it.

You're not going to regenerate if you're in pieces, thought Doric, referring to the likelihood of success of a leap off this cliff.

The giant had used its iron-like hair to gain purchase and was holding on. It began to slam its forearms into the wall. Each time they struck the wall, the ground shook. With amphibian-like thrusts, and using its legs to propel its large bulk upward, the giant started ascending toward the plateau.

Doric had to think of something. On the surface of the water between the cliffs, he spotted a ship drifting by peacefully; it was still intact.

The giant had almost reached the surface. Doric stepped back from the edge. An enormous hand fell onto the plateau beside him, driving its thick fingers deep into the ground. Each thick, iron-like hair on the underside of its arm, pierced the surface, sending dust and rubble into the air. A second later, its other massive hand came down.

From the forest above came a rumble. *Hurry, not much time,* Doric thought. Trees plummeted over the edge. Doric glanced up, and four giants, each more menacing than the other, had reached the edge he had leaped from.

Doric pulled out a dagger and swiftly climbed onto the giant's hand—warm and thick like rubber—just as the giant's head appeared over the edge. It glared at Doric; teeth exposed, and its features, still grim. Its eyebrows, resembling large, bristly bushes, arched when the giant saw Doric.

Before the giant could react, Doric plunged the dagger into the tough skin of its hand. The goliath recoiled reflexively, swatting its hand out over the rocks. Doric found himself soaring out towards the middle of the channel. He managed to avoid the rocks at the base of the wall. When he finally reached the surface, the impact was like striking a brick wall.

The water quickly swallowed him up.

When Doric surfaced, the massive wall of the ship's hull loomed close. He grabbed a firm hold of a thick rope and he was hauled up. After what seemed an hour, he reached the rail, and he fell heavily onto the deck.

Lying on his side, drenched in water on the slick deck, Doric stared up at his rescuers. A crowd of firstlings had gathered around him.

"Doric? Are you all right?" asked Will.

Doric nodded acknowledgment, then slowly came to his feet, only to be faced with searching eyes.

There was a pale naturalness about Doric. Will could not help but stare in awe at the sight of him when he considered all the man had endured. Doric brushed the wet hair away from his face. It was the first time Will noticed the extraordinary length of Doric's digits, arched and pointed, like long, calloused claws.

Doric glanced up at the crag from where he had plunged. Atop the plateau were now five silhouettes. They stood motionless like tall trees, watching as the ship floated by. The last stone they had hurled had fallen out of harm's way. No more boulders had struck the water.

Tana had worked her way through the crowd to find Doric crouched in front of a young boy and girl; dirt was pasted on their young faces. Exhaustion had taken its toll, though their bright eyes stared at him in amazement.

"Hey, little ones." The young boy took the girl's hand and squeezed it tightly. The little girl simply stared at Doric. "That's right," Doric said. He smiled and ruffled the boy's hair, "Don't ever let her go."

Tana couldn't take her eyes off this devastatingly striking young man. Doric continued combing over the firstlings, looking for her. Even after being pulled from the water, dirt and filth still covered his body and made his unkempt long, honey-colored hair look dark brown. He was tall and lean, and although not apparent in his physical appearance, his eyes expressed the truth. His warm and genial smile simply masked his tormented heart. Tana saw right through him and longed to save him.

"Welcome aboard, young man!" Orpheus yelled from the platform, peering down at Doric with a smile. "Looks like you had a falling out with your new friends."

The firstlings laughed at that. They touched his hands and patted his back in a welcoming fashion.

Tana's palms were sweaty. Her heart thumped. *Make eye contact, Doric,* she willed him as he made his way towards her.

When his eyes finally found hers, neither looked away. Doric walked directly toward her; his heart was racing. She was the most beautiful creature he had ever seen. He remembered the way her coal-black hair shaped her diamond-shaped face. She still had the same eyes, only stronger. He gently took her hand. It was clammy and trembling.

Darkness had fallen quite suddenly and stifled the light. He could not see the tear streaming down her face.

"Welcome home," she whispered.

"Here we go!" yelled Orpheus. The tip of the auburn moon

peeked over the cliff to the north, providing a little light. It proved just enough for Orpheus to see in the dark.

"Get some rest," he called out to everyone aboard. "You will need your strength tomorrow."

The ship continued on its tranquil drift down the channel. The carvings on the cliff walls faded into the night. The Azif Lora Sea was waiting for them several hours ahead.

Doric and Tana sat together with their backs against the rail. In the dark, they appeared to be a single silhouette. Golin, not impressed, glared at them from a distance. No one noticed the dark look in his eyes. No one noticed him storm away to join the mass of spent firstlings sleeping below deck. Will, on the other hand, smiled. They were together again. He shook his head, amazed at how fate had brought them here. He turned to the sea. *What horrors await us?* He thought of Crogan. *What horrors await you, my friend?*

He clasped the rail tightly and sent Crogan a message.

20

FORTRESS OF DOSDAVA

DARKNESS FELL ON Dosdava. Oren kept watch, perched on a ledge at the top of the fortress. The moonlight cast a silver veil over the land. Normally at home with silence, Oren found the silence eerily unfamiliar this night. Only the distant sounds of waves crashing on rocks seeped in through the darkness.

This fortress, although a godsend, could only serve them for a short time. Their food supply was limited. Oren estimated it would run out in just a few weeks. If Aaron was strategic, he need only wait to complete his objective, but that's not how he operated. Oren knew this. After all, there would be no pleasure in that.

Oren's thoughts turned to Korian. *Where are you?*

When Korian and Gred had departed hours earlier, a sweeping premonition of doom had come over Oren. A numbing pain had started in his chest and climbed to his throat. He coughed as if that would help him shake this feeling.

A sound from the right side of the lowland choked his cough. Oren held his breath as a large silhouette emerged from the shadow. The black figure with a billowing cape looked haunting in the moonlight. It sauntered smoothly into the middle of the lowland before it stopped.

Oren's heart beat faster as icy fingers scratched the nape of his neck. The vast space between him and the figure offered no safety. Oren crouched behind a wall, but he was too late. Aaron calmly marched up to the base of the wall below where Oren hid.

A chilling voice came from the darkness, "Do not take solace in the fact that I cannot set foot in your fortress, Oren." Aaron's guttural voice was clear as if he stood right in front of Oren. "Before tomorrow ends, you will stand before me. When you look into my eyes next, you will be at the end of my sword."

A series of heavy footsteps, scratching sounds and heavy breathing followed. The raucous scratching got closer. Oren covered his ears, expecting to see Aaron's fiery eyes peer over the wall through the slits in his skull shield. Oren stood, took a deep breath and prepared to call out and warn the others when the noise abruptly stopped. Only the earlier sounds of waves crashing on rocks hung in the air. When Oren finally got the nerve, he approached the edge of the wall and peered down.

Aaron was gone.

The next morning, Jannik awoke to a bright blue sky. He heard his name above the morning sounds of people who were out and about nervously working to complete last-minute preparations. Leith called to him again from the uppermost level of the fortress.

As Jannik walked across the courtyard, no one greeted him.

Only fear was apparent in the eyes looking back at him. After all, these were not the faces of phlegmatic and fearless soldiers. They were the eyes of farmers, bakers, masons, spinners, blacksmiths, stable boys, mothers, fathers, children.

Jannik spotted a young boy alone on a bench, his head was down, and a sword was at his feet.

"What's your name?" asked Jannik.

"Moira," answered the boy sulkily.

"Why do you brood? You should be with friends."

"I heard some of the men say we are all going to die today."

"It's okay to be afraid. We're all afraid. A wise man once told me that at times like these, we need to depend on each other. It is more dangerous to lose than to win. The danger is not in dying. We are all going to die at some point. The true danger is what could happen if we let them win," said Jannik, pointing beyond the wall to the lowlands. "That's what we need to remember in the face of battle. That, and hope. We always have hope to hold on to." Jannik stood. "Besides, I watched you practice yesterday, and you know what I think? Anyone who crosses paths with Moira should be afraid." He ruffled the boy's hair, and a smile crossed Moira's lips.

Jannik had always thought of dawn as a fresh start to a new day. Today was different. The profound reality of looming death poisoned the air. It was a memory all too familiar for those old enough to recall life beyond The Den.

He spotted Alrik talking to Ashford Ingals' daughter. Even clad with armor she looked alluring. Jannik had always thought her spirited and strong. Seeing her dressed for battle somehow didn't seem surprising.

"Go on, Alrik. Do it. Come on," whispered Jannik. "Kiss her." A few minutes later, Alrik stooped, picked up her bow, handed it to her and turned to leave.

Jannik shook his head. It was as if Alrik heard Jannik's thoughts because Alrik suddenly stopped, turned, walked back to her with an unfamiliar confidence, wrapped his arms around her and squeezed tightly. He pulled away for a moment and then kissed her. She arched her back and touched his face tenderly. Each time he tried to pull away, she pulled him back.

"Finally!" Jannik whispered, managing a smile. "Watch over them, Samjees."

Morning gave way to afternoon. Duties and positions were assigned. Large cauldrons were strategically placed and readied. Preparations continued until long shadows began to appear on the inner wall, signifying the arrival of dusk. Men, women and children donned armor. *They almost look like soldiers,* thought Jannik. When he saw their eyes through the slits in their helmets filled with trepidation and fear, he remembered how far from being soldiers they actually were. Jannik got Moira's attention and winked.

Everyone took their posts and waited. An uneasy silence filled the fortress.

Just over an hour later, a man standing at the farthest battlement on the left side of the wall cried out, "There!"

Countless eyes looked his way. He pointed beyond the mountain range to the left. "They're coming!" he shouted.

A flurry of organized chaos ensued. Tensions were thick. The first line of Stragoy came into view. They spanned the width of the massive plain. From the battlements, the Stragoy, all clad in dark armor, appeared to be an unending parade of giant insects. They pulled many large, crudely built contraptions on wheels between their perfectly spaced rows.

I'm sure we'll find out what those are soon enough, Crogan thought. The marching grew louder.

"They have skines!" yelled Alrik.

Dozens of skines descended and landed among the approaching Stragoy. In the sky, hundreds of maledhens circled. The loud squawks, the steady march of the Stragoy on the rocky plain, and the angry roars from the skines were unnerving. For those who stood on this side of the wall, the moment seemed surreal. Fear gripped some to the point of retching. Isaac grabbed his son's forearm and squeezed it tightly. Oren gripped his small sword and felt for the object in his pocket. *Still there.* Alrik gripped his axe tightly, his eyes scowling. He was ready.

"Alrik?" Lael called out to his brother. "For mother and father!" Alrik nodded understanding without taking his eyes off the approaching army.

Aaron's tall, imposing figure stepped forward from among the Stragoy. He raised his arm. The march stopped.

The wheels of the wooden contraptions were hammered off by Stragoy wielding large hammers.

Crogan abandoned his post and spoke, his voice carrying easily inside the space.

"My brothers and sisters!" he yelled. "None of you were alive when this evil was born. None of you are to blame for it, though you have all paid dearly. This evil cannot be reasoned with. We will die today, unless we kill every enemy, be it Stragoy or skine, that comes at us. Know this. The gods have not abandoned us. I trust in each one of you. I also trust in Korian and in his return. We must trust in each other, for never has there been a resistance against this evil. Never, that is, until today. Let it be known that Dosdava is the place men, women and even our children clashed with Aaron's army for the first time. Let it be known that Dosdava is the place where Hades first trembled in the shadows. No longer will we wait for death. We will stop Aaron and his army here, and after today, Hades too will know fear."

Beyond the wall, the noise abruptly stopped.

The plain went eerily silent. The sea of Stragoy looked devastating. Their stillness was overwhelmingly menacing.

"What are you waiting for?" Crogan whispered.

A series of long, rapid clicks and knocks broke the silence. Boulders, some the size of large wagons, were hurled into the sky and soared towards them.

"Catapults! Take cover!" Crogan yelled.

The first boulder struck the rock canopy above them and exploded into pieces. The Stragoy roared from the valley below. The rock above the fortress wall absorbed the impact. It remained intact, but debris rained down onto those crouched beneath it. The thunderous crash, amplified by the size of the cavern, reverberated through the fortress.

Air in the fortress filled with dust and debris. The next boulder struck the top of the wall and shattered. Large pieces exploded into the gap like deadly shrapnel. Two men behind the wall were beheaded, another's face was sliced in half. Another boulder's momentum ended at the inner wall where it exploded into smaller fragments. Pieces tore through armor, shredding those in its path. Another struck the one-foot thick section of wall where archers were stationed. The wall ruptured, killing scores of men and women. A large crack appeared and ran down the outer wall in a jagged line.

A sarsen stone struck the rock canopy above. A section of the mountain, the size of a small house, broke free, and it plunged onto men and women, crushing them. Screams of horror and chaos competed with the rumble and thunderous boom of the boulders repeatedly crashing into the fortress wall. Pure chaos ensued.

The assault went on for hours. The wall itself, slick with blood, was weakened. Suddenly, the bombardment stopped. When the dust settled, bodies lay everywhere. Crogan feared the worst. He called out, urging his people to stand. Seconds passed. No one moved. He called out again. Some stirred. There was a series of groans and then one, then five more, then twenty, then hundreds came to their feet. Jannik and Isaac stumbled towards him. Crogan found Jannik's friends among the crowd. They were shaken but otherwise, they were alive. Sadly, many did not rise. Corpses and body parts were scattered throughout the rampart.

From the lowland, a rumble grew until it reached a thunderous battle yell. The Stragoy charged.

The weary survivors took their positions.

"Ready! Hold your positions!" yelled Crogan, stealing a look at the wall. *That's not going to hold for long.*

The survivors of the initial onslaught had no time to prepare, to tend to wounds, or to gather themselves. Their minds had switched off. Only a primal instinct to survive remained.

"Hold!" repeated Crogan. The Stragoy were now a hundred feet from the wall.

"Now!" Crogan shouted.

Archers sprayed arrows. Stragoy fell, but their vast number was barely affected by this first wave. A group of Stragoy carrying a large battering ram emerged from the mass. Arrows continued to rain down on them. Stragoy amassed at the base of the outer wall, so many in fact, the archers couldn't miss. The battering ram struck the wall where the crack had appeared. When one Stragoy fell, others took up their position.

Iron hooks fastened to thick, coiled ropes were hurled over

the wall. More and more Stragoy climbed on until the ropes swarmed with them. Those in the fortress managed to cut some of the ropes, sending Stragoy tumbling, but as one rope was severed, two more would replace it. It wasn't long before Stragoy began reaching the top.

On the west side of the wall, Leith swung blindly with a vertical slash as a Stragoy lunged at him. He parted a Stragoy's helmet and what remained of its skull. Other Stragoy charged and leaped onto the crowd. Leith and his fellow armor-clad, makeshift soldiers advanced and met the brutal assault.

Skines swarmed the battlements. They carried the Stragoy and released them into the crowd. Skines also settled on the bloodied surface and slashed like rabid beasts with powerful talons. The humans were no match for them.

Jannik swung his sword with both hands, but a giant skine swiped it aside with the bone and thick, leathery skin on its arms. It pressed forward. Jannik raised his sword again, but instead of the skine, a Stragoy stepped in front of him and charged. They fought wildly. Jannik managed to knock the creature to the ground; the impact jarred its helmet off. The grotesque remains of what was once a woman's face hissed and spat. Jannik pulled a dagger and thrust it into the Stragoy's head and buried it to the hilt.

A skine to Jannik's left roared. It was the skine he had confronted moments earlier. It slashed viciously, slicing through armor. Bodies piled up around it. It turned to Jannik and charged. It knocked him to the ground. Standing over him, the skine spread its arms, bent forward and roared. Saliva spewed over Jannik. But then, instead of the skine's claw ripping through his torso and exposing his entrails, a long axe connected with the beast's neck and severed its head. Moira stood above Jannik, covered in blood, wide-eyed and with his chest heaving. He dropped the weapon and helped a grateful Jannik to his feet.

Alrik and several others surrounded the skines. The men carved and sliced with swords in tandem. Archers turned their arrows on the skines, and others stuck them with spears, a strategy that worked because the remaining skines took to flight. All except for one.

An exceptionally large beast, bleeding and enraged, attacked viciously and swiped with its sharp claws, mauling everyone that came near. The carnage was too much for Oren, who up until now, had stood to the side. Oren leaped onto the surface of the cave, scaled it until he was directly over the creature's head and leaped onto the skine's back. Clutching the skine's spine firmly, with his other hand he plunged a dagger into the beast's neck repeatedly. The skine flailed wildly, but Oren held on. The skine stumbled towards the edge of the inner wall, and Oren leaped off its back. The skine roared furiously. Blood pulsed from its neck into the air. Eventually its roars lessened, and the blood stopped pulsing. It looked at Oren wide-eyed and tumbled off the edge.

The battlement was stained red. It was slick and walking was a challenge.

"Alrik, do it now!" Crogan ordered.

At Alrik's direction, people tipped cauldrons over the wall. Hot oil fell, draping the Stragoy on the ropes and all those tightly amassed at the base.

Archers fired arrows with tips ablaze. Fire spread rapidly. Hundreds of Stragoy on the ground were incinerated. Crogan waved his arm. The remaining archers reassembled and fired, slaughtering more Stragoy. The Stragoy did not react to the fire, or show any sign of pain, but their movement was hampered by the dissolving bodies. The horrible stench of burnt and decaying flesh entered the fortress.

Other Stragoy took up the battering ram, ignoring the flames. The barrage ensued.

"Do not let them through!" yelled Crogan.

Oren began scaling the wall back up to the top. Below him, men and women continued firing volleys of arrows through apertures, but the apertures weren't narrow any longer. Alrik, Lael and a crowd of men and women gathered by the gaping crack. Each time the battering ram struck the gap widened.

Oren found Crogan among the crowd fighting madly to hold the wall. Crogan looked up at him and shouted, "We can't hold them much longer!"

Isaac rushed to aid Crogan. The old man's face was locked in a grimace, and he was struggling to suck in air. A Stragoy surprised Isaac from behind, stabbing him in the shoulder. He winced in pain and disbelief. A second Stragoy reached the top of the wall and plunged his sword up into Isaac's abdomen. Isaac froze. He fell to his knees. Crogan watched helplessly as a Stragoy shoved Isaac's limp body over the ledge. Crogan struck the Stragoy down.

Below them, the stone around the growing gap crumbled. A dozen Stragoy stormed in with spears. Lael pounced, sword gleaming, slashing Stragoy high in the head and neck. As they fell, others rushed in. Alrik, Lael, and others lunged and stabbed. Some of the Stragoy fell to their knees. A volley of arrows followed immediately from archers lined behind them. Bodies of Stragoy began to pile up at the opening.

The humans fought valiantly. Expressions on faces no longer held the anxiety of earlier. Fear was replaced with sheer determination and purpose. Though their wills were boundless, it was apparent they were tiring.

The end is inevitable. Do something, thought Oren.

On the ground outside the fortress, Stragoy were storming, like beasts in a feeding frenzy. Oren felt for the object in his pocket. He withdrew the gift given to him by the gods centuries ago in Menzia. An unnatural energy surged from the stone into his hand and up his arm.

"Trust in it when all else fails in the face of the purest evil. It shall be a beacon of hope and serve to that end." Words from Samjees himself.

Lael, Alrik and the others on the front line were relentless. They cut down wave after wave of Stragoy. Suddenly, the line of Stragoy retreated, acting on some unspoken order. They moved like drones as if following a predefined program.

Oren turned away, leaped onto the ceiling of the cave and climbed onto the outside of the rocky canopy. It was almost dark now, and the orange moon peered over the horizon to the north.

Aaron stood in the distance. With the giant moon looming behind him, he watched with grudging admiration the resolve of these insignificant creatures who were surprisingly, fighting back. After several hours of non-action, Aaron grew impatient. He started forward, taking a few steps at first. He began to run. Oren watched as the dark shape in the growing darkness seemed to glide on air; his black cape flailed behind him. The Stragoy parted a path for him as he approached the battered wall.

Oren took the stone from his pocket, glanced at its shiny surface one more time and placed it in the pocket of the sling.

"Hear me, Samjees, and grant me this wish," he called out.

He started twirling his wrist. The velocity increased until the twirling chord and pocket appeared a solid circular line; its diameter almost as wide as Oren was tall. Then, putting as much of his small body behind it as he could, he released it. The stone sailed over Aaron's head into the sea of Stragoy.

It started with a slight vibration, but the tremor worsened. Stragoy tumbled from the wall. Large sections of the outer layer of the wall crumbled, crushing hundreds of Stragoy below.

In the middle of the lowland, towards the end of the swarm of frenzied creatures, a cavity appeared on the surface. The ground moved rhythmically up and down as if it was breathing.

Suddenly, the wall by the battlement section, which had earlier absorbed the shock of the rock falling from the canopy, surrendered to the tremor. The top portion of the wall and battlement dissolved under scores of men, women and Stragoy.

Leith slashed, sending two Stragoy over the edge. "Run!" he yelled, as the section adjacent to where he stood crumbled.

Stragoy closest to the edge, fell. Leith, raced to get off this doomed section, but felt a sharp pain in his left leg below his knee. He went to plant his foot, and he collapsed onto his face, shattering his shoulder and striking his head on the hard surface. The left side of his face was battered and bloodied. He couldn't see out of his left eye. He managed a look at the dissolving wall through his other eye as the Stragoy who had severed his leg turned towards him.

Leith crawled forward blindly. It proved too difficult and agonizing. He turned onto his back and faced the sky. The Stragoy raised his arm and swiped, but before the sword reached him, the remaining section of the upper wall and battlement, with Leith, the Stragoy and others, collapsed.

On the lowland, the cavity widened and deepened. The tremor changed from rhythmic to continuous and then became more intense, until the cavity turned into a yawning pit. Aaron stepped back from the pit, angry at the effect this was having on his assault.

A massive spire began to rise from the center of the pit. Its gray surface—rough and jagged—displaced mountains of sand and debris from the ground as it ascended, knocking Stragoy aside. The noise was thunderous as it rose into the sky. It looked like a massive slab of rock growing out of the ground. Then, with the moon hanging in the backdrop, the spire stopped rising, and the roar and tremor stopped.

"Is that it?" Oren screamed into the night.

The battle resumed with a renewed frenzy. Skines, sensing the weakened resistance of their enemy, returned with a vengeance. The humans braced for one last defense.

Oren fell to his knees. He began cursing the gods for forsaking his people. When the wind picked up, he felt they had acknowledged him. He still believed the gods were reaching out to him, when suddenly, a loud burst from above and behind startled him. It wasn't the gods. It was a large shadow that swooped down sharply, pushing the wind ahead of it. The pressure was so great, it nearly knocked Oren from the mountain. He realized at the last moment that an enormous skine was diving towards him. Oren braced himself. Just before the large beast struck, he noticed something strange. The skine flew past, just ten feet over his head. His heart raced. It was only for a brief moment, but he was certain of what he saw. There was a man on the skine's back.

The giant skine soared over the battlefield and past the spire, towards the moon, which had also climbed higher in the sky. The skine turned sharply and dove. When it reached the ground, a man dismounted, and the skine took flight.

The spire loomed before Korian, as did devastation and death. Suddenly, he knew what he had to do. The words of the Harwill made sense now.

"Your spear, end it must in the place it was found."

He could not tell from where he stood, but his arrival had sparked renewed vivacity and hope as his skine landed in the midst of the mayhem and began shredding Stragoy alongside his people.

The large brute of a skine, like a granite statue, broad and sharply angular, turned its gaze and attention to the other skines. It attacked them ferociously. One would have initially thought from the many scars on the skine's body, it would be weak and deserving of pity, but watching it dispose of others of its kind easily proved the opposite. The creature was regal in its movement and strength. The remaining skines flew off. Korian's skine charged after them and disappeared over the top of the canopy.

Hundreds of yards away, alone in the open plain, guilt overwhelmed Korian. He felt he had betrayed his people for not arriving sooner. In the distance, however, he heard not cries of loss and defeat but rather cheers representing resilience and hope.

From the other side of the giant monolith, the Stragoy turned their attention to Korian. With a wave of his hand, Aaron sent hundreds charging past the spire toward him.

Korian closed his eyes and slowed his breathing. When he opened them again, the world looked different: everything had slowed. Korian gave in to his senses, ignoring the fact that he was vastly outnumbered. He played out his plan in his mind, and when he felt ready, he waded into the attacking Stragoy.

Two of the beasts raced forward to collide with him. He feinted with his left hand, then a battle axe appeared in his right. He swept it forward, gutting the first Stragoy. Sprinting, he slammed the axe into the second, striking it on the collarbone and slicing down to the sternum.

He had reached a state of consciousness that was pure, reactive instinct. He had become, for all intents and purposes, devoid of emotion, like his enemy, only far more skilled.

He leaned right to evade a blow to the head and swung. The axe transformed into a sword, cutting the nearest Stragoy's legs off. Korian leaped into the air. The sword took the form of a pickaxe. He struck another Stragoy on the back of the head and somersaulted over it. Landing on his feet, Korian averted a blow and disemboweled the attacker. The line of Stragoy seemed longer than it was wide. Korian carved through them. Each time he swung a spear, sword, axe, hammer, or any weapon his mind envisioned, another Stragoy fell.

He stole a look to the left. Aaron was closing in. The spire was now within range, though too many Stragoy stood between him and it.

I have one chance to do this, he thought.

His weapon changed to a spear. He released it as hard as he could. It whistled through the air, sailing over Stragoy who were just beginning to surround him. Korian fell to his knees, and he braced himself.

The spear struck the spire and buried into it until it disappeared entirely. Immediately, a spidery web of cracks appeared at the point of entry. They spread rapidly like blood coursing through thousands of vessels as if infusing the spire with life. The sound was deafening. Then without warning, it collapsed from the bottom out in countless pieces. Small fragments of stone burst from the object in a spherically expanding shockwave of incredible pressure, striking all the Stragoy nearest the collapsing spire. Their bodies were shredded, disintegrating on impact and sprayed blood in explosive bursts. A deadly dust storm emerged out of the shockwave.

The wind was so powerful, Korian couldn't exhale air from his lungs. He was pushed back, sliding on his knees with his arms shielding his face. The expanding cloud of dust and rubble hid the fate of his enemies. As for Korian, he was untouched by the propelled debris; an invisible energy cloaked him in a protective bubble.

Aaron saw the approaching dust cloud. To his left, the collapsing spire cast a shadow. As the wall of rubble and shards reached the swarm of Stragoy gathered beyond the base of the battered wall, Aaron stepped into the shadow cast by the spire and vanished. The remaining Stragoy were consumed by the storm.

Bodies disintegrated en masse. When the storm's debris reached the fortress walls, the sound was a thousand times louder than a torrential downpour. The fragments and shards of the collapsing monolith exploded on impact. Stones, rubble and Stragoy body parts and blood splashed high into the air, covering everyone at the top of the wall. When the pounding stopped, the massive spire was gone.

The plain fell silent. All eyes were focused on the settling cloud of dust. Crogan wiped the cool, rancid liquid from his face. He could not believe what had just happened. A roar erupted from the surviving men and women, who then quickly disposed of the Stragoy who had made it to the top of the wall.

"There!" A woman shouted.

On the lowland, the silhouette of a man staggered towards the edge of the giant pit where the monolithic object had stood moments ago. He lowered his head as he reached the crater and jumped into it. He stooped, picked something up and cradled it in both hands.

Korian, still processing what he'd just done, with his ears ringing from the powerful wind, battered and worn, took up the Manian's spear with both hands, and he raised it over his head. With his chest heaving, and with the subtle glow of dawn signaled a new day behind him, Korian let out a victory cry.

The survivors burst into their own cheer; the volume so great it shook what remained of the rampart.

21
REAPER OF DEATH

THE CREST OF the sun had just broken the surface on the horizon, but remnants of the night had not yet dissipated. Survivors, lining the withered battlements, were still cheering long after Korian had lowered his arms.

Behind Korian, the rustling sound of small rocks and pebbles tumbling down the side of the steep bluff, disturbed an otherwise eerie calm that had settled onto the lowland. The cheering on the rampart suddenly changed to gasps. Korian's shoulders jerked back as if someone had poured ice water on his back.

About a hundred feet above him, on the slate wall of the cliff, a shadow stirred within a dark, recessed section of the wall. Two tiny, yellow sparks began to glow from within the dim. A tall figure stepped out into the ashen morning haze. Korian knew who it was, even before he saw him. The menacing figure stepped out of the yawning darkness, spilling hatred and malice so thick he could taste it in the air.

Aaron glared down from above; his eyes blazed behind the dark skull shield. Korian imagined the vilest expression on the other side of it, the contorted features of a beast, teeth bared, mouth quivering and drooling. The Harwill had told him this would happen. He had already seen the outcome and his own end. An army of soldiers who would die for him were powerless, reduced to being mere spectators behind a shattered wall. No help would arrive. There was no place to hide.

"You are not alone." The voice startled him. It was warm and flowing and familiar. He looked around but saw no one.

"They believe in you," it added.

He recognized its soft, endearing quality immediately. Sara's voice, so comforting, a sharp contrast to the beating of his own heart and its throbbing in his ears.

"I believe in you. We will be together, my dearest Korian… but not on this day." There was a brief pause, and then came one more word; a single word—penetrating and powerful—which gave Korian strength and conviction: *"Fight!"*

Aaron leapt off the edge, landing with a thud. He stood motionless. The loss of his army and the humans' victory was simply collateral damage. No true loss. Ultimately, he had what he wanted: the Azura within his grasp and the end of the resistance just feet away. He envisioned Korian's body at his feet and his decapitated head—lifeless eyes and ruddy flesh dangling from the neck—clutched in his hand, an example for all. Aaron marched towards Korian.

At the top of the remains of the battlement, Oren scampered down beside Crogan, a look of angst was on his jade face. "He's not prepared for Aaron," he said nervously. "We have to do something."

"We need riggings. All you can find. Hurry!" yelled Crogan. "Clear the rubble and rock from below. We need to get out there."

"It'll take hours!" yelled Alrik from below.

"We have minutes! Let's go!" Crogan yelled as he rushed down to assist.

Korian took a few deep breaths. His heart rate slowed. An unnatural silence fell across the lowland.

Korian and Aaron paced, studying each other, until Aaron spoke first.

"The Azura at last." His eyes were bright and fiery.

Korian didn't flinch at the maddening screech of Aaron's voice. This creature was beyond anything his imagination could have conjured.

"Behold your reaper of death," Aaron hissed, placing his hand on his sheathed sword. "When I'm through, you will walk the afterlife headless."

"Perhaps," said Korian sounding as resolute as he could. "If it's the will of the gods, I'm prepared." He paced, matching Aaron's every step.

Aaron let out a roar.

"There isn't anything you can do to me," added Korian. "I'm not afraid."

Korian turned to the people on the wall. "Behold! The mighty Aaron!" he cried out, brazenly turning his back to the deadly specter. "The ghost who believes he is a god. A god who hides in the shadows."

"Fool!" Aaron snapped. "Perhaps this was all part of a plan, a sacrifice for a prize? After all, do I not have you all to myself?"

Aaron shook his head and finger mockingly. "You're just like the others, a slave who looks to the gods for guidance, too foolish to realize their limitations."

"Perhaps, but you're too foolish to believe that you, a mortal, can become a god."

Korian raised his spear. A shaft of light from the rising sun gleamed off the sharp head of his weapon. The head flattened as the other end contracted. When the transformation was complete, a broadsword was in his hand. Aaron drew his sword. They charged.

Swords clashed and sparks flew. The speed of the exchange was extraordinary. Almost as soon as the clash began, Korian let his muscles settle into a rhythm. He countered every one of Aaron's swings, normally death blows. Aaron towered over Korian, but Korian's prowess was hypnotic. All of his training had led to this moment. Steel flashed, and the sound of singing blades rang in the air.

Korian's eyes fixed on Aaron's hands and shoulders, watching for predictive signs of direction. Aaron turned and swung. His blade hissed as it split the air. Korian thrust his sword vertically, catching it before it cut him in half.

Crogan, Oren and Jannik worked among exhausted men and women watching between gaps in the wall as they worked to clear a path. They were spellbound and absolutely terrified. Anything but a victory by Korian would spell an end to them all.

Korian lunged, narrowly missing Aaron's side as Aaron clamped Korian's arm against his chest plate. Korian tugged frantically, but the pressure—like a vise—pinched his arm at the bicep. The pain was numbing. Aaron swiped upwards with his sword, but Korian leaned back. Any more bow in his back would have snapped his spine. Aaron's blade sliced by, narrowly missing his face.

With strength that seemed boundless, Aaron jerked Korian back up forcefully. Suddenly, the butt end of Aaron's sword connected with the bridge of Korian's nose. Bone snapped and cartilage crunched. Blood splattered into Korian's mouth and down his chin. Korian realized, after the initial shock and delayed rush of pain, that he was airborne; it was only momentarily. He struck the ground and struggled onto his stomach. Winded, he cupped his nose and snapped it back into place. He swallowed blood and coughed.

Aaron was on him immediately. He swung while Korian rolled, thrust his legs up and returned to his feet. He saw an opening and slashed, gouging a long strip across Aaron's chest. Aaron ignored it and lunged. Even with the difficulty Korian had breathing, the stench of death and rot was stifling.

"You're beginning to tire?" said Aaron mockingly.

He feinted to the right, parried Korian's blow with an unnatural swiftness and clasped Korian under the arm. The cloaked specter effortlessly lifted Korian over his head and slammed him onto his back, again.

"Get up, Azura!" screeched Aaron.

Korian writhed on the ground while Aaron turned towards the wall, he raised his arms and shrieked, "Behold your Gatekeeper! Watch him die!"

When Aaron turned back, Korian stumbled to his feet. He spit out a thick glob of blood and readied for another assault.

Aaron paced in circles and swayed his head from side to side. He was enjoying every moment of this.

Korian charged with renewed rage, swinging with explosive fury, lunging and slicing, but Aaron met every blow, barely reacting to Korian's effort. For Korian, frustration was setting in, along with fatigue. He took another breath, spun and whirled his sword, exhaling loudly to intensify the force. Aaron caught the blade with his hand, right in front of his chest.

"You cannot defeat me," jeered Aaron. "No weapon, not even yours, can hurt me."

A wry smile suddenly crossed Korian's bloodied lips. The tip of his sword rapidly extended with the force of an arrow leaving a bow. It transformed into a spear and punctured Aaron's sternum, emerging his upper back. A beastly shriek rose from behind the face shield.

Korian withdrew his spear and stormed Aaron with a renewed determination. This time Aaron was not prepared. His defense was slower and less effective as he was driven back with Korian's blows. Korian switched tactics. The spear turned to a flail, then a sword, an axe, back to a spear and then several more weapons. He connected sparingly at first, and then when he had knocked the sword out of Aaron's hand, every blow would have easily struck down any Stragoy. He had become a machine, swinging with a deadly rhythm. Little by little, though, he tired. When he could no longer swing due to exhaustion, he stopped. His chest was heaving and his breathing was shallow. Fatigue became his enemy.

Aaron, quiet, except for the heavy breathing behind the skull shield, swayed, but he did not fall. Aaron's armor was battered and twisted. There were slashes and holes throughout, but there was no life-giving blood spilling from the wounds. A deep rumble came from behind the mask. The many punctures in his head, chest, shoulders, arms and side, sealed shut as the armor repaired itself. Aaron moved his head from side to side. There was no longer any sign of trauma. He extended his arm, and his sword sailed into his hand.

"Enough of this!" Aaron shrieked.

Korian raised his sword with two hands. Aaron attacked.

Behind Korian, a roar erupted from the wall, and a stream of armor-clad human survivors charged from the hole the Stragoy had made in the wall. Behind Aaron, the sun had almost completely risen above the horizon. Soon Aaron would not be able to use shadows for refuge.

Aware of the fleeting time, Aaron swung harder. He had

underestimated Korian's will. He swung again, with two hands this time. Korian countered, but the force of the blow was beyond Korian's strength.

Aaron swatted the sword out of Korian's hand.

On his knees, bloodied and spent, Korian looked beyond Aaron into the sun. A catastrophic feeling of failure swept over him. *I wasn't ready,* he thought, his shoulders drooped. Then, something strange happened. A shape emerged from the sunlight. Korian braced for the feeling of cold steel on his neck. But instead of Aaron's sword, he found Sara standing in front of him, bathed in a diamond haze and surrounded by a comforting light.

"Am I dead?" Korian asked.

Sara smiled and shook her head. Her power over his heart was boundless. "Embrace this. It's just the beginning."

He blinked, and she was gone, as was the light.

A shadow draped over him. Aaron approached and blocked out the sun. He raised his sword and swung. As the blade raced towards Korian's neck, an unforeseen gust of wind swept in and drove Aaron off balance, just enough, to disturb the swords momentum and downward angle. The tip of the blade grazed Korian's shoulder, slicing a shallow gash.

Strong gusts of wind came in pulses, followed by the enraged screech of a giant predator from above. A large skine swooped down, struck Aaron in the chest with its talons and came down directly in front of Korian.

Aaron steadied himself and turned again towards Korian, only to face an angry skine thrusting its claws into the ground ferociously. It stooped, roared and bared its teeth.

Alrik and several others finally reached Korian. They approached the skine cautiously and positioned themselves in front of Korian. The deadly skine paid them no attention.

"Very well," said Aaron.

More humans continued to arrive until a multitude stood before Aaron.

He pointed at them and said, "I will return with ten times your number to end this foolish resistance."

Crogan, mad with rage, lunged for Aaron, as did countless others. Before they could reach him, Aaron leapt up the side of the mountain. The skine followed.

On the ledge, in the murkiness deep within the recess of the wall, Aaron dissolved into the shadow. When the skine reached the ledge, swinging frantically in the dark space, he struck nothing but rock.

Aaron was gone.

Dawn had broken. The day was crisp, and dew had collected on the surface of what remained of the wall. A dense fog covered the sea as if a thick, white sheet had spread out below the mountain.

The once peaceful, yet desolate, lowland was now a mere shadow of itself. The great wall was in ruins, stained with blood. Abandoned weapons were scattered everywhere. The vast Stragoy army had essentially disintegrated. All that remained were fragments of body parts, mangled and indiscernible.

Bodies of their people who had perished were placed in the pit left by the spire. The remains of those lost were set ablaze amidst widespread lamentation and solemn words of respect for their sacrifice.

The wounded were many. Among the carnage, they could hear steady wails begging for water, which helped identify the living from the dead.

Exult over the victory, Korian thought, *and behold the price.*

Korian looked at the faces of those who had cheered not long ago, so full of hope, now wrought with misery. Jannik lost his father. Leith was gone. Countless others—fathers, mothers, brothers and sisters—had been lost. Anyone who had fallen on the Stragoy side of the wall and exposed to the collapsing spire was completely gone. The dead that could be found were now fuel for the raging fire.

Shouting rose above the snapping and crackling of the fire. "Korian?" Gred lumbered through the crowd, panting heavily. He had been running all night, following Korian and his skine for most of the journey and the smoke from the battle for the rest. Rushing to Korian's side, he dropped to one knee and bowed his head.

"I failed you," he whispered somberly.

Korian placed a hand on his shoulder, and Gred collapsed onto his stomach, exhausted. They exchanged not a single word more.

A fair distance away, Crogan stood looking down into the burning pit, ignoring the acrid smoke and ash. Jannik approached and placed a hand on his shoulder, the other over his mouth and nose.

"We have to take solace in this," Crogan said without averting his eyes from the fire. "There is no other recourse. This is our first but cannot be our last triumph. Otherwise, this sacrifice would be for nothing."

"Perhaps, but this is just the prelude," Jannik replied. "He will be back by nightfall, so we need to prepare."

Thick, gray smoke rose high into the sky, a clear beacon for the enemy. The smell was atrocious, creating heartbreak, as bodies continued to arrive from the battlement and were added to the blazing pit.

"We'll be gone by then," answered Crogan. Jannik turned, "The *Winds of Freedom* is on its way."

Jannik stared blankly. The smoke was, in fact, a beacon, but not just for the Stragoy.

Two hours later, rousing cries came from the mist over the sea. It was late morning, but the fog had not yet lifted. From the north side, the incredible ship broke through the wall of mist, gliding across the water with a sublime and stately passage. The deck of the *Winds of Freedom*, led by Captain Orpheus, was filled with firstling men, women and children, waving their arms wildly and shouting encouragement. Korian turned to Crogan to inquire, but the Manian was in one of his trances, staring blankly, a smile on his lips.

"My friend," began Korian addressing the skine, "I, and they, will always be grateful." He placed a fist against his chest. "It's because of you they still live."

The skine slowly lowered its head.

"It's because of you I still live," Korian added. Strangely, the skine now exuded a heavenly beauty. Gred, slightly shorter than the skine, exhibited an air of fear and respect for the majestic beast.

"Is he bowing?" asked Gred.

Slowly and deliberately, the skine stood upright, looking both frightening and regal.

"I guess we're even. If our paths should ever cross again, I can't very well go on calling you skine now can I? From this day forward, I will call you Horda."

The skine let out an uncharacteristic bray, bobbed its head twice and flew off. They watched it disappear over the mountain.

"Ruler of the sky. Fitting," said Gred.

"Yes, fitting indeed," Korian replied.

22

WINDS OF FREEDOM

THROUGH A DOORWAY hidden within the catacombs at the back of the fortress, the weary made their way down to the base of the cliff through a series of long, winding, timeworn stone steps. The ship loomed a safe distance from the threatening rocks. From a large opening in the ship's hull, a long, broad, wooden plank extended outwards and rested on the rocks.

On deck, firstlings lined the rails shouting welcoming remarks. Crogan walked up the ramp. He was the first to board. Other worn and wounded surviving humans, followed apprehensively. Soon, a steady stream of survivors flowed into the welcoming dimness of the ship's belly.

When Crogan reached the upper deck, Will was there to greet him. They embraced clumsily. While in the embrace, Crogan noticed Tana standing behind Will, wearing a beaming grin.

Beside her, a young man peered back at him with deep brown eyes. His thick hair, the color of sunrise, twisted over his brows and shoulders, providing a frame for a striking face. His hand, with a somewhat exaggerated firstling digit, clasped Tana's tightly.

Crogan's heart was beating so fervently, he thought it would burst. He pulled away from Will and embraced Doric tightly. There was regret, guilt, sorrow, pain and a longing for forgiveness in that embrace. His emotion was contagious.

"I forgave you long ago," Doric whispered.

Behind Crogan, Gred's large head and glaring eye came into view. When Gred finally boarded the ship, his hulking presence towered over everybody. Compared to the Jayen, Gred was small, but his appearance was more menacing. Doric and every firstling aboard the ship, goggled at the giant, who's curious eye kept blinking at them—opened and attentive. Gred smiled. Large furrows appeared on his cheeks like creases on dried leather.

Perched on his shoulder was a small greenish colored humanoid creature, licking his lips like a feline. Doric smiled. Gred lowered Oren onto the deck, and Doric fell to one knee to take in the sight of his old friend.

"Doric," Oren touched the man's cheek tenderly and studied him closely, amazed with his face, free of those horrid scars. The last time his big round eyes had seen Doric, he was a sad, tortured child. What stood before him now was a miracle.

"I knew this day would come," sighed Oren.

They embraced. "You saved my life," replied Doric.

At Gred's side was a lean, stately looking young man with a wisp of gray on one side of his long hair. He carried a regal-looking spear as he would a staff.

Korian locked eyes with Will. They gave each other a nod.

"Welcome," Will said.

"Thank you," said Korian.

"For what?"

Korian leaned forward and whispered, "For finding her."

Will simply nodded. He smiled and lowered his eyes as an odd feeling of lightness came over him. He didn't know why, but he felt as if an invisible hand had just lifted an immense weight off his shoulders.

Doric noticed Korian's eyes first; they were as hypnotic as they were piercing. In the dark pupils, he saw his reflection and could not bring himself to turn away. A strange feeling washed over him. He saw his life through the eyes of a bystander. Key moments, thoughts and events that had shaped him, the very essence of his being, love, compassion and tolerance. There was an absence of greed, jealousy or hate. Even after all Doric had been through, there was no hate. It was instantaneous, but in that moment, comfort and warmth filled his heart. He managed to tear himself away.

"You must be Korian," Doric said.

Korian nodded, a hint of a smile appeared on the hard line of his mouth. There was a hint of profound respect evident in Korian's eyes, and his heart held great admiration and awe for the spirit of the man standing before him.

"Hello, Doric."

Just then, Crogan put his hands on both their shoulders, "This, Doric, is the Azura."

Aaron materialized into a room with no entrance or exit: a dark space devoid of warmth. With each movement, loose stones shifted under his feet, and the sound echoed off the walls. He was alone. The scarce light cast from his fiery eyes showed the space to be an ovoid shape. The walls curved smoothly to the floor, arching a hundred feet above. The room was vacant, except for the spirit of evil that lurked.

Into the darkness, Aaron spoke. The confines gave his guttural voice a ghastly resonance.

"Father, I am here."

The room turned cold. The wails of a thousand doomed souls, carried on a brisk wind, encircled him. A low hum filled the room and drowned out the pained cries—steady and deep. Aaron sensed a presence.

"I found him: the Azura. We know who he is."

There was a hint of unease in the mighty Aaron's tone.

"The resistance is failing. They're trapped at Dosdava. The Manian is among them, as is Oren. By day's end, what remains of the resistance will be done, and you will have the Azura's head."

Aaron paused in the darkness. The low drone continued. A voice seeped out of the shadow, without pitch or color, cold as a winter's night. It spoke slowly, enunciating every word.

"I was spawned in darkness and born into light. I have been condemned to the shadows, suffering wretchedness. I thirsted for light once but now loathe it. I have an insatiable need to abolish it. The light tempts and lures. I yearn to snuff it, and all those who desire it, out."

The hum stopped, replaced with a dreadful sound that began to swell. The room quivered.

Adam Hades' voice burst from the shadow in a torrent. "You have stolen that from me!" Suddenly Aaron was airborne, thrust back into the wall, the crunch of armor reverberating into the space. He fell to one knee.

"You had him in your grasp!" The voice was sharp, shrill and piercing. Aaron's hands were clenched tightly.

"Where was that anger, that hatred? I gave you the power of a god, and you failed me."

Aaron came to his feet slowly. “I have prepared a force this world has never before seen. I will return and finish this!” Aaron shrieked.

The room quivered again. The darkness intensified. The fire in Aaron’s eyes had lost potency.

“It’s too late. You move through shadow. I dwell in it. Through it I see into the light. I see all. You’ll not find them.”

Aaron’s eyes blazed again. “I will end this! Leave it to me.”

The voice leached from the shadow once more.

“One day they will return. Make sure of that, and when they do, destroy them all. Do not fail me again.”

Aaron emerged from the shadow of the cave into the morning. He raged out of Hellas Mons in long strides, swinging his arms wide. He held his sword in his hand. The dark cape flowed behind him, rising and falling with each stride. Near the large rocks of the Tine Pass, men had gathered in disordered silence, anxiety apparent in their posture.

“There he is!” an obscene, ogre-like man shouted.

They scrambled quickly and formed a crude line. Aaron reached Lorne Maggis first. The firstling bowed his head. He was but a shadow of his once menacing self. His face was bloodied and covered in horrid scars, the largest spreading from his eye to his chin. Lorne’s stump, cauterized and wrapped, hung loosely at his side. He raised his head to look at Aaron through his swollen eyes. They were full of fear but could turn to anger in an instant. They met Aaron’s for only a second before turning away.

Aaron glared at him penetratingly. His scorching eyes invited and dared any one of them to look at him. He walked by each one. When he reached Damon Kinsey, the man’s hanging jowls quivered. Damon’s big, sloped shoulders drooped even more under the weight of Aaron's gaze. He raised his thick, fleshy arm and gestured towards the path with the abyss on either side that separated Hellas Mons and the lowland. Aaron did not turn his threatening gaze away.

Aaron reached Cyrus Zagan. His permanently grotesque grimace looked meek now. His single sharp eye moved wildly, though not towards Aaron. Nervously, he gripped his sword tightly until the chords of his wrist bulged.

"I have turned you into weapons; ministers of war," Aaron howled angrily, addressing them all. "I have given you power beyond what any of you deserve. Yet you've used it only to satisfy your sordid obsessions." He glared at Lorne.

He turned his back to them. "But you have forgotten who you serve. I serve Hades. You serve me. And from where I stand, you've failed.

"There are others out there who hide," Aaron continued. "You will find them and destroy them all. Until then, consider yourselves the lowest form of life. Less than them," he said pointing again beyond the Tine Pass and the narrow path between the chasms.

"The resistance is fleeing. The sea is going to hinder you. But I don't care if the sea rages with two-hundred-foot swells, or is infested with giant beasts. Find them and bring them to me. I want the Azura. Alive if possible, dead if you must. The horror that awaits them is one Endura has never seen before. Do this, and I will make you all kings."

Aaron turned and approached the sharp rocks of the Tine Pass that jutted up into the sky. He bent his knees and leaped. When he reached the top, what he saw inspired him. A lesser man would stare in awe, but Aaron was no man.

The ground where skines had not long ago dropped men to meet their doom had turned into a black, seething mass of row upon row of Stragoy. They stood listlessly, like drones waiting to be turned on. They held no regard for life. Above them, the sky crawled with maledhens and skines.

There was an eerie, unnatural stillness despite all the creatures grouped around Aaron. There was no need to address them, as they were connected by a telepathic link. They knew what to do.

Aaron had witnessed the first uprising and was consumed with rage. He wanted the Azura, but not for his father anymore. It was personal now.

The skies were clear and the water was calm. The only blemish in the sky was the smoke from the fire that had been prepared for the dead.

Soon, the fortress faded in the distance until it became a speck on the horizon. Passengers lined the railings on the stern and pressed up close to one another. They watched the land fade away, each in deep thought; it wasn't the land that faded away but their oppression and despair. Unfortunately, the nightmares and horrors stayed with them. Gone was all animosity or prejudice. There were no longer firstlings or humans, only races who shared a common enemy and a want to survive.

Aboard the great ship, fear hovered close. It would never go away. Their lives and futures had been shaped from the damage that had been done, and the trauma would be passed down for many generations to come.

Several hours later, they drifted into night.

The steady lapping of the water against the hull soothed Korian's mind. His head was heavy, his body worn. Korian looked around with weary eyes. All but a few slept.

Brilliant stars spread across the sky, offering a break from what would otherwise be an exceptional and lethal darkness.

Korian found Doric and Tana. She was leaning on Doric's chest, their hands clasped tightly.

Captain Orpheus' silhouette was visible on the platform, his hands fused into the rails, guiding the ship into the next unknown. Crogan was beside him standing still. Like statues, they scanned the darkness beyond the bow and directed the *Winds of Freedom* towards it.

A movement to his left averted Korian's attention. Oren scurried in the darkness, offering water to those still awake, and he placed blankets on those with the greatest need. Eventually, Oren lay near Doric and Tana and slept.

The hardened lines on Korian's face relaxed, and in the dark, he smiled. He had a quiet admiration for Oren. There was something striking in his unsightliness. What he lacked in appearance he made up for in other ways.

How could you love me? Thought Korian. *I am your son, yet you lie near Doric. You do not know who I am, it seems, or perhaps you know but have chosen to deny it. You fear me, because I remind you of everything you've lost. As a man, you are my birth father, only I do not know that man. I know only a hideous creature. But I see right through all that, Zoren. I see your strength; I see your kindness and I see your imperfections and pain. After all, despite your appearance, you are just an old and lonely man. It's probably better that you do not know that I am your son because I can never love again. Besides, my days are few in this world. Doric is more a son to you than I will ever be. Watch over him. Watch over them both.*

A short while later, Korian stood and made his way gingerly to the bow of the ship, careful not to disturb those who slept. The great ship pressed on against the current. He savored this moment of peace as he looked first into the darkness ahead and then to the stars.

A bright streak abruptly flashed across the sky. "Shooting

star," he whispered with a curious expression as if surprised he had uttered those words.

Thoughts surfaced; volumes of information compartmentalized from memories not his own. They rushed and flooded into his mind.

How did it come to this? He thought to ask the Harwill before the Harwill gave him a front row seat to the dawn of the Dark Age. In the mist conjured by the Harwill, Korian had travelled to another time, far back to a world that looked considerably different to Endura of today.

He was on a plain, basking in the shadow of a large mountain range to the west, just south of the desert. The vegetation seemed alien, unique, and it looked different from the foliage that now covered Endura. The smell was fresh and new. It was too real for it to be a dream. He recalled how the cool morning breeze stung his skin.

Roaming the plains around him but oblivious to his presence were firstlings going about their tranquil lives. They spoke a foreign, Ruid tongue and were slightly taller in stature than the Ruids of today. It was an ancient Endura, thousands of years in the past.

A loud boom destroyed the tranquility. It sounded like a mountain crashing to the ground. Firstlings scattered into the mountains. From the eastern sky, a giant fireball came hurtling towards them. The air ahead of it was compressed, the boom was deafening, and the ground trembled. It looked like a giant meteorite shooting across the sky at an astounding speed, eating clouds in its way.

When it neared the surface of the desert, still a good distance away from where Korian stood, its velocity decreased and a low, steady drone saturated the air. The fireball dissipated, and dark smoke wafted around the craft. The closer it got to the desert, the more it became apparent it was no meteor. It was far too symmetrical to be of natural origin. Guessing it to be about two hundred feet in width, it was wider than it was long and shaped like a stingray: flat on the underside and rounded on the top. It tapered towards the rear.

While it hovered, a hatch opened on its underside. An object emerged. It was silver and had a rectangular shape. It fell and crashed into the sand. A moment later, a second rectangular object emerged, and it also crashed into the sand. The first object made sense. The second was a surprise.

The craft came to rest at the base of the mountain. It hissed, and then several hundred compartments opened on its surface. Through each, a steady mist began to pour out in narrow lines, shooting high into the air until the air around him was filled with a haze. A pungent odor filled the air.

The craft continued to exhaust the mist from the compartments for twenty-one days until the emission abruptly ended. The craft let out a loud burst of air, like a long sigh and rested.

Time accelerated in the vision after that. Years later, how many he did not know, the craft exploded. Initially, the ground imploded into a fireball as air was sucked up to feed the massive explosion. A moment later, dust and debris were blasted up and outwards in a powerful shock wave while the fireball ascended.

He recalled the crater he had come across south of the Linhar, where the side of the mountain had been levelled. He had passed by the spot, and he had stood on the ridge where the craft had exploded.

I saw you arrive, he thought. *Who was in that second object? What was in that mist you brought?* He was certain that bright, metal object held answers to those and many more secrets. *That's going to have to wait for now.*

What followed after the craft's arrival was a lingering sickness that infested the land. It endured for thousands of years.

Its arrival spawned the Dark Age. During that dark period, the appearance of Ruids that survived began to change.

Their skin changed its texture. The hands of some began to transform. It started with slight deformities, and eventually, after many generations, the larger elongated digit became two smaller digits. Humans and Ruids were never two separate species. Humans evolved from Ruids.

Korian whispered into the sky. "You were the catalyst that started it all. All this death and suffering."

A word formed in his head, surfacing from some obscure memory buried in a region of his mind. He had no business knowing what it meant, but surprisingly, the word held meaning.

"Earth."

A world not unlike Endura, a place beyond the stars, the root of all of his new knowledge and foreign memories…all originating from there.

What kind of god or gods would make a world with this kind of evil and let it poison another? thought Korian.

"Are you okay?" Gred's voice startled him. "They are calling for you."

They had gathered on the platform near Orpheus: Crogan, Will, Golin, Merrin, Jannik, Lael and Alrik.

"Where are we headed?" Merrin asked.

"To the Trap!" shouted Orpheus.

"Please explain," said Alrik. Crogan smiled, impressed with the young man's confidence.

"In King Zoren's day," started Crogan, "During the Munus games, fighters used to retire to a place called the Trap to rest for the next challenge."

"All right," replied Alrik, "But what's out there?" The group turned to face the deep blue sea, and the unknown beyond the darkness.

"Does it matter?" Orpheus asked. There was a moment when none spoke as they all reflected.

"This is just the beginning," answered Crogan. He exhaled a long, drawn-out breath. "We're tired, wounded and weary. Time is what we need," he said, and looked to Orpheus, who had raised his tankard in agreement. They all turned to Korian. There was an uncomfortable pause. Korian's fatigued mind was slow to respond.

"Very well then, to the Trap we go."

A few hours later, the silver sea glimmered in the pale light of dawn. The atmosphere was comfortably peaceful. Into a new tomorrow the *Winds of Freedom* and its passengers steadily drifted.

At the bow, Korian stood with Gred at his side. In the vast unknown, he sensed a new dawn, a world that looked startlingly different than it did only two days earlier.

"I have not thanked you," Korian said, never taking his eyes away from the sea. "For looking out for me all these years." He turned towards Gred. "I would not be here if not for you."

The giant, menacing looking creature, towering over Korian, lowered his head bashfully until his long reedy hair covered his face. He fell to one knee, still looking down at Korian with his one eye opened wide. His expression was solemn, his thick brow arching into a sharp "V."

"I made two promises, Korian: one to your mother, the other to myself." Gred placed his giant hand on Korian's head clumsily and tapped with his palm. "You are my best friend," he said with a smile. "In fact, you've been. . . until recently…my only friend."

"Well, Gred, you know me better than anyone, better than I know myself." It was clear he wanted to say more, but he refrained. Then he added, "I just wanted you to know I'm glad you're here, Gred."

"What now?" asked Gred as he came to his feet. The two turned to face the sea.

"We, the survivors of a broken people," Korian started, "Will find another sanctuary."

"Will we find peace?" Gred asked.

"On the contrary, my big friend. I will never grow old and die peacefully in my bed. Whether I die today or in the future, unless I do something, all these lives lost, all the deaths of the innocent, will be for naught. Aaron and Hades will have won. In this darkness, Aaron and his servants and their thirst to abolish the light has blinded them. They will be unprepared for the storm I will bring in return for all that has been taken from us. They think we are retreating—we're not…I'm not."

Passengers began stirring. The deck began to come alive with many of the other survivors. Korian's new friends approached the bow where he stood.

Lucius had been right all along. He knew what it would take to force his hand. Beneath his breath he added, "For taking Sara from me!"

STORY OF RUID BEGINNINGS

The myth of the beginnings of this passionate people has been told for generations. To most, it's just that—a myth—even if it does manage to address one of the most pressing questions about the origin of life. Many believe that in lieu of any real evidence surrounding Ruid origin, the magical story of power and the creation that follows serves as a very appropriate substitute. Presently, much of the myth has lost its original truth and meaning. The biases of the storytellers have come to influence the essence of the tale. There is one account, however, captured in the Cerulean Book, that is believed to be authentic. What follows is an excerpt from the *Cerulean Book of Scribes.*

MYTH OF THE NIAKTZ

Long ago, the land was dark and arid and filled with emptiness and dead calm. They came, beckoned by a feeling of commonplace. Shapeless bolts of incredible energy with a power great enough to create, and at the same time, transform life. They were seven, who reigned over the spirit world. The land, though barren and calm, was alive and inviting and filled with an unbound promise.

Samjees, the leader, poured a part of himself into all things, forging a union between gods and the soul of this great land. The union unchained the power of the land's imprisoned spirit. Samjees had clasped the hand of a talented artist, unsure of his true potential and guided it onto the canvas so it could unleash its creation. Mountains sprung from plains, water flowed and channeled into seas, trees formed rich forests, and flat lands were transformed into rolling landscapes of emerald fields and verdant hills. The empty sea and land were filled with creatures of all shapes and sizes. The world was transformed and life flourished. The gods stared in awe at its beauty. What emerged was pure and magnificent.

Although bathed in unmatched grandeur, there was something amiss. And so, it happened, that from the spirit of the land came forth a majestic river. It flowed like a vessel twisting and turning out from the heart of the land. This river, which came to be called the Niaktz, was transformed by the land into a flowing bed of molten flame and fire. Each year, on the eve of the New Year, Samjees would gather up fire from the river and place it in the sky. Years passed, and one star became few and few became many until the night sky was filled. They gave light to the night, protecting the land from sinking into the darkness that was always present, always waiting.

The word Niaktz, you see, is Ruid, meaning "pieces of life." Samjees yearned to create a being to rule over this land and value its splendor. And so, Samjees molded a being from amarin. Samjees grasped the lifeless form by the two middle digits of each hand and slowly lowered him into the molten river. The middle digits fused and became one. It was there where the Niaktz breathed life into Prian, the first Ruid.

—Cerulean Book of Scribes

GLOSSARY OF TERMS ON ENDURA

There are several unfamiliar terms in the world of Endura, its history, myth and culture. Some terms have already been defined in the text. For others, the definitions and explanations below will assist in understanding:

Amarin – Dense clay-like soil lining the banks of the Lassit River. Infused with a naturally occurring oil-like substance, amarin cannot dry out, it is malleable and therefore perfect for molding. It cures in sunlight—depending on exposure—to shades ranging from white to dark tones of brown to almost black.

Azura – The Ruid word for Gatekeeper. The focal point of the Harwill's prophesy that foretells of a savior said to have the strength to fight those doomed to darkness and restore balance to the spirit world, and to the forces of good and evil.

Blue Book – See *Cerulean Book of Scribes.*

Bree – One of the Seven Guardians. The agent of beneficence and protector from evil of insatiable discontent.

Cerulean Book of Scribes – Another name for the *Blue Book,* is an ancient collection of scrolls first assembled by scholars in the great city of Nahire in the third century of the New Age.

Chackra – Popular two player game where each player takes turns placing pebbles on a square etched into the top of barrels or into stonework, aiming to align three in a row before their opponent.

Dark Age – A dark period in history spawned by a mysterious catastrophic event. It is the period when records of early humans were first noted.

Eilasor – A mystical blue crystal forged in Menzia by a union between the Seven Guardians and Zoren Ro. It was gifted to the Ruid and human races by the Guardians to protect the races against a dark insatiable evil.

Evaris – One of the Seven Guardians. The agent of contentment and protector against jealousy and the voracious want for power.

Firstling – Another name for Ruids. The term originated from the fact that Ruids were indigenous to Endura.

Guardians – Seven gods who reigned over the spirit world. Each Guardian served as an agent and protector against threats to the virtues of Ruids and to the balance of good and evil in nature.

Groll – One of the Seven Guardians. The agent of compassion and protector from wrath and malice.

Harwill – Oracle

Ira – One of the Seven Guardians. The agent of restraint and protector from violent impulses.

Ishtan Mar – Ancient Ruid word and another name for sorcerer.

Jayen – Giant race of humanoid stone carvers.

Lubics V – Sharp-edged boomerang-type weapon made of steel.

Madrascythe – Fine white sand particles found in the walls of a hidden chamber within Natrass Pass. It is sensitive to thermal changes and glows upon absorbing the slightest amount of heat.

Maledhens – large onyx colored bird-like winged creatures serving as Aaron's spies.

Manian – Sorcerer.

Matchra Tree – A mysterious large carnivorous tree that grows within the dark mountain of Hellas Mons.

Munus Games – Sporting event, popular in AZ 38 where men challenged each other to feats of strength and courage, including different forms of grappling.

Myth of the Niaktz – A magical story of firstling origin passed from one generation to the next for thousands of years.

Nahire – The last great city of Endura located on the banks of the Lassit River. It was once home to King Zoren Ro.

Natrass Pass – Narrow pass located south of Dema Falls, between two dizzying cliffs within the East Crest Mountains.

Navalline – Largest cavern within the Den.

New Age – The period when remarkable advancements in modern language, science and technology began. It started just shy of two thousand years before the start of this tale.

Niaktz – Ruid word meaning 'pieces of life.' It is a mythical river of flowing molten flame and fire, said to be the source of the stars in the sky and where Prian was born.

Orgo – One of the Seven Guardians. The agent of humility and protector against selfishness and the perverted love of self.

Partekii – Wild animals, domesticated during the New Age. They serve as the main mode of transportation for both humans and firstlings. Although anatomically different, they behave quite akin to horses on Earth.

Portal – Created by the gods. It was a gateway to Menzia where the Eilasor was forged.

Prian – The first Ruid molded from amarin by Samjees.

Raffa Diem – Ancient language, and the origin of the word "Ruid," meaning the number four, and the basis for the name of the race.

Ruid – Indigenous humanoid beings who inhabited Endura long before the appearance of humans.

Samjees – The oldest of the Guardians, and the supreme god.

Sammas Day – Harvest celebration named after Samjees, occurring annually on the first full moon of the ninth month.

Skine – Giant carnivorous winged predator of the sky.

Stragoy – Animated corpses of humans and firstlings in various stages of decay, transformed from the living into monstrous creatures that serve Aaron.

The Den – A complex multi-level and hidden underground city.

The Late Antiquity – Period before the Dark Age when Ruids ruled Endura. There were no records of humans in this age.

Thia – One of the Seven Guardians. The agent of reverence and protector against hate in all its manifestations.

Vasara – A square-shaped flacon, made of dull silver.

ABOUT THE AUTHOR

Giorgio Garofalo has always been a fan of fantasy and science fiction because of the freedom the genre gives authors to explore themes and present them in unique and unconventional ways. He was born in Toronto. Passionate about the arts, he explored music at a young age. He shelved his guitar when he entered college in pursuit of electronics but exited with a BSc in Chemistry. Currently and for most of his career, he's worked in the pharmaceutical industry as a senior leader in regulatory compliance and quality and now makes his home in a suburb just outside Toronto with his wife, Rita and his dog, Toby. In his spare time, he escapes to his corner of the couch to write, and when not working or writing, he plays his guitars and enjoys road trips to wherever his imagination and his bike take him.

Made in the USA
Middletown, DE
18 January 2021